A DARING FLIRTATION

"What are you thinking about?" Launceston whispered, leaning toward Alexandra.

"N-nothing," she replied. She felt his hand on her arm and her heart leaped at his touch.

"Tell me," he murmured, leaning closer to her, his breath just touching the temple of her forehead. "Were you thinking of yesterday or perhaps two summers past?"

"You shouldn't be reminding me of things that should never have been," Alexandra said, not daring to look at him. "Nor should you be prompting what ought not to be."

She felt the faint touch of his lips on her temple. "I am beginning to think you are just the sort of woman who enjoys being reminded of what ought not to be . . ."

Books by Valerie King

A DARING WAGER
A ROGUE'S MASQUERADE
RELUCTANT BRIDE
THE FANCIFUL HEIRESS
THE WILLFUL WIDOW
LOVE MATCH
CUPID'S TOUCH
A LADY'S GAMBIT
CAPTIVATED HEARTS
MY LADY VIXEN
THE ELUSIVE BRIDE
MERRY, MERRY MISCHIEF
VANQUISHED
BEWITCHING HEARTS

Published by Zebra Books

VALERIE KING

BEWITCHING HEARTS

ZEBRA BOOKS
KENSINGTON PUBLISHING CORP.

To Pat, with gratitude for many years of support

ZEBRA BOOKS are published by

Kensington Publishing Corp.
850 Third Avenue
New York, NY 10022

First Printing: October, 1995

Printed in the United States of America

Dear Reader:

Many times I have been asked where I get my ideas for my Regency novels, in particular the idea for *CAPTIVATED HEARTS* which involved characters from Greek and Roman mythology. My answer to that question lies in the fact that mythological references abound in the romantic poetry of the Regency era.

At some point, perhaps when I was reading Keats or Shelley or Lord Byron, I thought, wouldn't it be fun to write a story pulling Cupid and his wife, Psyche, from their quiet home in Olympus and involving them with my hero and heroine. What could be more delightful than having Cupid make use of his famous arrows in helping the hero and heroine tumble madly in love. Hence, *CAPTIVATED HEARTS*.

At the end of the story, Psyche bids a sad farewell to the heroine, Evanthea Swanbourne, who she has come to love. Cupid sees his wife's sadness at leaving her new friend and comforts her with the knowledge that she will one day return to England to help Evanthea's three daughters who, as young women, find themselves vying with one another for the affections of the roguish Lord Launceston. Hence, *BEWITCHING HEARTS*.

I hope you enjoy this second jaunt into the magical world of Olympus.

—Valerie King

Cupid is a knavish lad,
Thus to make poor females mad.
                    —*Shakespeare*

One

Cornwall, England
October, 1838

There is only one thing for it, Lady Alexandra thought as she stepped onto the sidewalks of Stithwell, *I am going mad. Utterly, completely, irrevocably mad.*

She had just emerged from the booksellers, having purchased a novel by Sir Walter Scott from the proprietor, Mr. Mawnan, and now stood looking across the ancient, cobbled High Street wondering if her sisters, Lady Julia and Lady Victoria, were still in the pastry shop.

She wanted to go home, to return to Roselands, before she became completely overwhelmed by the distress which continued to dog her heels no matter how much she tried to bring her mind to order.

She had originally believed a trip to the small market town would lighten her spirits, that purchasing a book or two, or greeting a familiar acquaintance who chanced along the street, or simply walking about in the cool, autumn air with her sisters, would divert her mind from her worries. But from the moment her family's town coach had passed by the five peculiar round houses situated near the Stagshead Inn, the weight on her chest had gotten worse. The history of the little houses was too reminiscent of madness for her to be comfortable since each had been built in the round, specifically without corners, in order to thwart the devil's doings since the architect of the houses believed that the devil couldn't hide in a house without corners.

If only her mind didn't have corners, she might yet be content. But her thoughts were shaded and nervous, leaping about, darting at her from darkened corners, only to disappear again. Was her mind indeed going down that vague, circuitous path to madness? Was she like her beloved great-great aunt, Lady Elle, who had held to her madness even on her deathbed? She didn't know what was real and what was not.

She was having the visions again, visions she had not had since she was a child of ten, visions of a man bearing enormous black wings. Lady Elle had had similar visions, and had told her that the handsome creature was an Olympian deity called Anteros, brother of the famous Cupid.

In the past sennight she had seen Anteros, if the black-winged man truly was this exalted being, no fewer than three times. Once he had even kissed her, awakening her from a troubled sleep in which she had been dreaming that a man was placing an oil, redolent of roses, on her lips. What was worse, the kiss had been extraordinary, mesmerizing in its effect on her heart—almost as troublesome and devastating as the kiss Lord Launceston, that vilest of rogues, had stolen from her two summers past. Well, not stolen, precisely, but taken nevertheless—and that without a whisper of propriety.

What torment, for now her thoughts were drawn most unfortunately to a man she wished she had never met, had never kissed, had never known—Newlyn St. Ives, eighth viscount Lord Launceston. That was the rub. For a reason she could not explain, whenever Anteros presented himself, her thoughts became full of Lord Launceston, a man she accounted unworthy of even a second's cogitation.

Anteros—Launceston.

What was happening to her? Why was this madness upon her?

She released a great sigh suddenly, grateful that the several townspeople walking about the High Street were not near enough to see or to speak with her. She knew her distress was apparent on her features and with only the greatest of efforts was she able to hold back her tears of fright and frustration which had been threatening to undo her the entire day.

Earlier that morning, when she had just completed her toilette, Anteros had appeared to her—if indeed he had appeared at all—and had actually spoken to her. His voice had disturbed her almost as much as his sudden presence in her bedchamber, for it was deep and resonant, not unlike Launceston's.

Launceston again.

Anteros's words, however, had been cryptic. *How beautiful you are, Alexandra, dressed in violet. The color of irises becomes you exceedingly. Mama will not like that you are so pretty, but then your ambition will not be to please my mother, but to please me. And you do please me. Very much so.*

She had nearly swooned with fright at being addressed by so grand a creature and wished that her corsets had not been laced up so tightly. Ordinarily, she was not a fainthearted young woman, but his sudden appearance had both surprised and startled her, as much by the portent of his speech as by the magnificence of his person—the gleaming silver of his hair, the fine black silk of his short tunic which revealed muscular thighs, the enormity of his black wings which she realized would have filled the chamber had he unfurled them, the black leather sandals strapped about lean, shapely calves, all of which combined to present a man, or a god, of great hypnotic beauty.

Anteros.

Alexandra drew her mind sharply back to the present and clutched her book more tightly beneath her arm, her drawn bag dangling from her wrist. Was she going mad as her dear, beloved Lady Elle had gone mad? Or was it the devil, come to play off his tricks—as the architect of the round houses would have certainly had her believe. After all, October was deeply upon the Cornish countryside and that gravest of days, All Hallow's Eve, was but ten days away.

Was she mad or was some ghost, bearing huge black wings,

merely trying to frighten her? She didn't know what to think and wished more than anything that Lady Elle had not finally succumbed to her years and passed on. Lady Elle would have known what to say to her to comfort her, but then Lady Elle had been a madwoman, or at least that was what she had been told.

Overhead, the sky was leaden and deepened minute by minute into a dark grayness. Rain would soon drench the town and the surrounding countryside. She felt utterly alone in her distress. Even her sisters had deserted her while she was at the booksellers, exclaiming they were bored of reading and wished to buy several pastries for their mama. Alexandra was not fooled, of course. Julia and Victoria, both of whom were younger than she, had a penchant for gossip and the pastry cook's wife was a notorious gabblemonger.

Alexandra had considered joining them, but the state of her spirits was disinclined toward society, so she remained behind instead, first to purchase her book, then to wait for her sisters on the sidewalk. She turned her face toward the freshening wind and again took a deep breath, trying to compose her thoughts, her mind, her heart.

She could smell the salt air borne on a stiff breeze, evidence that Stithwell was situated some five miles from the sea. The pungent currents of air tugged on her bonnet of violet silk and pushed at her matching silk skirts belled to a pretty fullness by five petticoats. She glanced down at her skirts and thought that in this Anteros had been right—violet suited her raven hair and fair complexion quite to perfection. She smiled thinking how in her mother's day as a young unmarried lady, a well-bred miss would only wear the palest of colors, a pale blue or pink or preferably white. But in these modern times, the darker colors were *de rigueur,* in fashion and in the decor of the home. Her gown of violet silk, nipped in at the waist, was as different from the quite odd-looking Empire gowns her mother once wore, as night was different from day.

Some things change, she mused, *like the fashions of the day, and some do not.*

She turned around and glanced at the thatched, coned roofs of the five round houses just visible over the rooftops of the shops along the High Street. Some superstitions remained century after century. Others disappeared. The memory of Lady Elle's visions of Mount Olympus had come forward to haunt her and remained unchanged, even after thirteen years. They were as vivid now as they had been when she was a child of ten.

Was she going mad?

She turned away from the coned roofs and looked down the street where the town green was shaded by several very old, unchanging beech trees. She saw children playing about the maypole and walking carefully across the low stocks. The sight of the children seemed to soothe the strange workings of her mind. Everything about the town was as it had been since she could remember. The beech trees were broad and sturdy, the shops were of a solid granite, unperturbable against even the harshest storm, and the familiar spire of the Church of St. Probus rose in stalwart majesty into the gray sky above. Stithwell in its foundation was unshakeable and in the present confusion of her mind she found that merely gazing upon the various aspects of the lively market town brought a measure of peace and comfort to her soul.

Stithwell was comprised of a great variety of dwellers and shops, of tin miners, granite quarriers, retired fishermen, two solicitors, a bank, an ancient almshouse, several mantua-makers and millinery shops, two bakeries, and a flour mill situated on the River Veryan which traversed the town at a lovely angle beneath a bridge connecting the King's Highway with the High Street. In addition, dozens of shops abounded, each specializing in wares which catered to the continual flow of traffic between the seaport of Falmouth and the River Port of Truro, as well as the attending gentry associated with the lands scattered between the two famous cities. She knew she was fortunate to have such a well-appointed town so near to Roselands and had Anteros not suddenly appeared visionlike to her, she would be inordinately content.

For one thing, her life was in excellent order for a young lady of three and twenty. She was the daughter of a wealthy nobleman, the Marquis of Brandreth, she was handsomely dowered and her prospects were superb. She enjoyed a London season each spring, a sojourn in Bath during the summer, and a celebration of the entire Christmastide season at Roselands in Cornwall. The remaining weeks of the year, the family lived at times at Staple Hall in Bedfordshire or at Roselands—whatever suited the estate interests or whims of either Lord or Lady Brandreth. In late October, Alexandra, her two sisters, her mother and father were nicely settled in. Nothing could be prettier or more cheerful than the fine, warm manor house of Roselands, except of course for its unsettling view of the partially ruined Castle Porth situated on a hill across a narrow valley from the manor. The castle had been recently acquired—according to the latest tittle-tattle—by a wealthy nobleman whose identity was still a mystery. Even the owner of the bookseller's shop, a portly, balding man by the name of Mr. Mawnan, had expressed dismay over his lack of knowledge of the man.

"I know everything and everyone in Stithwell and hereabouts for miles!" he had exclaimed indignantly, but not without a smile. "Yet I do not know the name of the gentleman who has bought Castle Porth. You may imagine that my reputation is all but ruined!"

"I imagine nothing of the sort!" Lady Alexandra had returned warmly. "It is because you read too much that you remain in ignorance. If you gossiped more, like the pastry cook's wife, I daresay you would even now be in possession of the gentleman's identity. But if you ask me, it cannot be to your discredit that you are still uninformed."

"Does the pastry cook know his name?" he had asked anxiously, not quite perceiving the intent of her conversation.

"I don't know, but his wife's propensity to gossip, rather than to *read,* has led me to believe she will always be the first to know the latest *on-dits.*"

"Ah," he cried, the worried frown on his brow relaxing as

his face broke into a smile. He lifted a finger and shook it at her, his cheeks reddening at her compliment. "I see what you are about! Indeed, I do!"

"Mr. Mawnan, are you blushing?" she had asked teasingly.

Mr. Mawnan chuckled, wrapped up her book and bid Alexandra to enjoy *Ivanhoe*.

As she stood now with her eyes closed, her face still turned into the wind, the faint blast of a trumpet sounded from the top of the High Street a full half mile distant. She turned toward the rise and opened her eyes. A cart, drawn by a single, plodding brown horse, made a slow progress up the grade leading her eye to a large, black vehicle, which crested the rise and began a swift descent toward the cart.

Alexandra's heart stopped for a brief moment as she watched the maneuverings of the reckless driver. In the end, he was able to swerve his team of four quite magnificent horses sufficiently in order to avoid a collision, but left in his wake the waving hat and indistinct curses of the cart driver whose own poor horse was presently rearing up and attempting to escape his harness. She lifted a brow in disgust. The coach driver was probably some sporting mad buck from London, anxious to prove his abilities by driving pell-mell through a quiet country town, all the while risking the lives of everyone present.

She would have supposed the driver would have slowed his horses after such a happenstance, but even at the distance of half a mile, she could see he had no intention of checking his four, powerful chestnuts.

How could such a man enter any village or town and not be aware of the risks he was taking in driving at such a breakneck pace? Didn't he know that there were always children about the streets, dashing impetuously where they ought not to be while engaged in a game of tag, hide and seek, or hitting and chasing a wooden hoop through the many winding lanes about the small market town? Evidently, he did not.

From across the street, the small tinkle of a bell caught her ear and she turned her attention to the pastry shop whose roof was being repaired by the hanging of several new gray granite slates. Her sisters were just leaving the shop, their arms laden with several packages.

As Alexandra watched her siblings slowly step onto the sidewalk and give a closing tug on the door behind them, she noted not without considerable pride that her sisters were quite lovely, beautiful in fact. Julia and Victoria shared the dark brown locks of their mother, unlike Alexandra whose hair was black like their father's now silvering hair. Ever since she could remember, it had always been pointed out to the family that while Julia and Victoria resembled their mother, Alexandra bore a nearer likeness to Lord Brandreth. Of course the truth was that each daughter had taken at random the various features of not only their parents but of their grandparents as well. In fact, the one common feature the sisters shared—and that by the oddest quirk of fate—was the large, blue eyes of a woman they had never known, Lady Brandreth's mother who had died when the marchioness was but a child.

Julia wore a forest green cape of fine Merino wool over a tight-waisted gown of red, green, and gold plaid wool. Victoria, the youngest, wore a navy blue knit shawl over a wool gown of scarlet. Even though Alexandra brangled with her sisters frequently, she still could not deny the rush of affection which flowed over her at the sight of petite, fiery Julia and the prettier yet more reserved Victoria.

How different they all were, she thought. Victoria was given to flights of fancy and tended to see all of life just as she wished it to be while Julia was mad for any lark and flew into the boughs at the least provocation. As for herself—oh, dear, just how would she describe Lady Alexandra Staple? She knew what Launceston and his friends called her, *the Frost Queen*. Only she wasn't so cold and unfeeling as their unkind appellation suggested, she wasn't! Or was she? Of the moment she wasn't sure. She had for so long been the eldest of three sisters, and to some extent responsible for their conduct in society, that she supposed anyone on less than intimate terms with her might construe her manners and demeanor as icily proprietous. Certainly Launceston did, but then his opinion was hardly worth noting, she concluded with some satisfaction.

Since her thoughts had been diverted she only now recognized the fact that her sisters were behaving oddly and not at all like themselves. Absently, Alexandra took a step forward trying to determine what, if anything was amiss. The sisters were facing one another, each sporting a fine display of dark brown ringlets to either side of each fair cheek, and gawking at one another in a most unladylike manner. Alexandra could only smile for they appeared like simpletons—Julia's heart-shaped face was turned up toward her sister and Victoria's firm jaw now fell agape even further as she let out a squeal which was quickly picked up and echoed by Julia. A hug ensued, as their numerous packages—one at least of which must have included a fresh pastry or two—fell to the granite sidewalk to scatter about plaid and scarlet skirts.

Alexandra could not imagine what was possessing them to behave so oddly on the streets of Stithwell unless perhaps they had just received some astonishing yet pleasing news from the pastry cook's wife. She blinked, unable to conceive of what was afflicting them. "Julia! Victoria!" she called across the street. The sounds of the approaching coach now reaching her ears— merciful heavens, how quickly the team and coach had covered the half mile! "What is it? What has happened?"

Her sisters turned toward her as one and gave a joyous shout. Each picked up their skirts in gloved fingers and forgetting their packages, turned to run into the street, oblivious to the presence of the oncoming coach.

"Wait!" Alexandra cried out, one of her hands outstretched and warning them to retreat.

"What the devil!" a man's voice thundered. "Whoa! Whoa!" he called to his team again and again. The girls stopped and stared and screamed, each racing at the very last moment out of harm's way like geese before a charging hound. The horses were lathered, their mouths foaming as they came to a halt several feet beyond Alexandra.

She ran behind the coach and found her sisters shaken but not in the least hurt. "Thank God you are all right!" she called to them. "Whatever made you run into the street in that foolish manner?"

"Oh, it was foolish, Alex," Victoria said, a hand pressed to her cheek. "But we had just received the most astonishing news. You won't credit it!"

"Never mind that," Alexandra said sharply. "You nearly got killed because of your impetuous conduct."

"But we weren't killed, Alex!" Julia retorted, a little indignant. "Oh, it is just like you to behave as though the world is tumbling about your ears when it is only raining. I certainly saw the coach in sufficient time to avoid getting hurt and so did Victoria."

"Sufficient time?" Alexandra returned, dumbfounded. "Julia, don't be a gudgeon. You were nearly run over by four horses and I don't need to tell you what would have happened had you not escaped their hooves. But I won't brangle with you here, for of the moment I have only one desire—to speak with the driver of this coach! Imagine risking his horses and the lives of anyone else who might have ventured into the street by driving so recklessly, so thoughtlessly! He must be an imbecile!"

She turned on her heel and approached the driver's side of the large vehicle which she now determined to be a sporting coach known as a private drag. The vehicle was as large as a mail coach in order to accommodate the owner's many sporting mad friends and acquaintances who wished either to accompany him to a race-meeting, where the coach formed an excellent grandstand, or to observe his skill as a master of four reins-in-hand. A crest, which she did not pay the least heed to, was emblazoned both on the boot and the door panel. At the rear of the coach, perched above the boot, were seated two grooms who eyed her askance and next to the driver was a thin man who sat very tall and seemed vaguely familiar to her.

As she approached the right side of the coach, and saw that

the driver was descending, her anger grew more powerful still for he had confirmed her opinion of his sporting pursuits since he was wearing a many-caped dark wool coat. His coat was a popular article worn exclusively by the man who fancied himself at home to a peg and who was a member of the Coaching Club, an organization which enjoyed a membership composed of that wretched group of individuals who were addicted to gaming and to the enjoyment of any number of vile pastimes such as the viewing of boxing matches.

With his back to her, the driver climbed, then leaped lightly down from his high seat atop his glossy, though in parts mud-stained, gentleman's drag. He wore a black beaver hat low about his ears and his blond hair was curled over the collar of his coat. Just as he turned around to face her, Alexandra drew in a breath preparing to ring a peal over his head.

But as she opened her mouth to speak, the only word that came forth was a disgusted, "You!"

An arched brow rose in response to her critical exclamation and a sardonic sneer overtook the distinctly handsome features of Newlyn St. Ives, eighth viscount, Lord Launceston.

"I should have known it was you," she cried. "Who else would have had such inconsideration, such complete disregard for public safety!"

"Those two females were your sisters?" he bellowed. "And who else but one of the Staple sisters would have attempted to cross a street in front of a swiftly moving coach and four."

Alexandra glared at the man before her. How much she despised Lord Launceston as she had from the first—well, not precisely from the first, but she always tried to forget about her initial encounter with Newlyn St. Ives. She hadn't known who he was then and he had kissed her, but she wouldn't permit herself to think about that, or to remember the depth of pleasure his scandalous embrace had once given her. No, she wouldn't dwell on it for a second.

"Forget about my sisters for the present, *my lord*—" how much she enjoyed saying *my lord* with just that cynical tone which always caused his eyes to narrow, "what about the children that are ever-present in any small town? What if one of them had darted into the street, in front of your plunging horses, what would you have done then? Going as fast as you were, I shall tell you—there wouldn't have been a thing you could have done except maul the child beneath the hooves of your beasts and the wheels of your coach."

He seemed slightly taken aback, a considering expression entering his hazel eyes. "I should hope that any good parent would have warned his child away from the dangers of playing on the High Street."

"Oh, yes, of course," she returned facetiously, tilting her head and glaring at the viscount, "I quite forgot how important it is that the world step aside for you. Do not let the children play, for Launceston is coming! How silly of me."

At that she watched his nostrils flare, and a red heat enter his famous hazel eyes. She felt him grab her arm just above the elbow as he led her none too politely out of the street, away from his coach, away from the ears of the man seated atop the coach, who she now recognized as the viscount's closest friend, the honorable Mr. George Trenear. "How dare you," he whispered. "How dare you speak to me in that perpetually haughty manner of yours, *Lady* Alexandra. Just once, I should like to see you come down off your high ropes—just once!—and be a real woman, with kindness on your tongue and in your heart, like the day I first met you! You take on quite a hawkish appearance, *miss*. And if you don't mind my giving you a hint, you shall end your days an ape-leader if you are not careful, for there is nothing pretty about the way your smug self-assurance sits on your face when you are coming the crab."

Alexandra looked into eyes that blazed with fire, heat, and rage. No man ever spoke to her as Launceston did. She tried to pull her arm out of his grasp but he held her firmly, his strength evident in the fact that she couldn't so much as slip her arm a quarter inch from his hold on her. She opened her mouth to speak, but no words followed. His criticism had struck her deeply and perhaps not without some justification. She had always despised those who were filled with conceit and self-satisfaction. Was she guilty of being such a person? In her confusion, she could only address the graver concern.

"Regardless of my flaws, if you will but take a moment to see the children on the green, there, behind you, perhaps you will then see the reason for my harsh words and appearance."

He did not avail himself of the opportunity to take up her suggestion, but continued to look into her eyes, his own still accusing and angry. She sensed that he had not completely heard what she had said and that his thoughts had drawn inward as he continued to hold her arm.

She felt peculiar suddenly as he watched her, her breath becoming trapped in her throat. Her attention shifted quite strangely from his anger and his accusations to the fact that she knew she would have been far more capable of handling this man had he not been quite so handsome. She felt missish and foolish as she let her gaze rove his features, yet at the same time she could not keep from doing so. His hair was blond, streaked almost white from years aboard sailing vessels. His eyes were almond-shaped and a brownish-hazel that could appear quite dark in a dim light, yet almost gray, with flecks of green when the sun was full in his face. His brows were a deeper version of the color of hair, thick and arched. Lines flared out from his eyes, a reflection of his thirty years and his life at sea and in India. His nose was straight, yet slightly aquiline. His jaw was both firm yet oval in appearance. His shirtpoints touched his cheeks very low, as was the fashion, and he wore a slim, burgundy silk cravat tied about his neck. His black greatcoat came up high at the back of his neck and framed very much to perfection his blond hair, his hazel eyes and his skin darkened from having roamed the world for years. With a start, she realized that had she not despised him so very much, he was physically just the sort of man who appealed most to her.

Her growing sense of panic at being held captive by both the strength of his hand and by her schoolgirl's attraction to him, prompted her to summon her courage. "Let me go," she whispered, wanting ever so much to be free of his hold on her.

He leaned toward her, menacingly. The light in his eye turned, shifted, became something more than anger. The hazel of his eyes grew quite dark. She wasn't sure what he was thinking but she suspected his sentiments had metamorphosed into something that both frightened yet excited her. She felt dizzy, like the other time, and wondered . . . was it possible he meant to . . . ?

He drew closer.

"No," she murmured. How strange she felt, like she was touching heaven and hell at the very same moment. "Let me go," she reiterated, again trying to twist from his grasp. "You're hurting me."

His eyes grew indistinct and misty. He drifted his gaze to her lips. He took another step toward her, pressing the bell of her violet skirts backward a little. "By God if we weren't here—if we were alone, I'd—"

"Launceston!" Julia cried, interrupting him and rounding Alexandra to peer into his face. "Do let Alex go. You must forgive her, you know, for she is the oldest and always feels that she must forever be instructing the entire *beau monde*. Only tell us, is it true?"

"Yes, tell us it's true!" Victoria added, coming up on Alexandra's other side to also address the viscount. "Oh, it must be true!"

Alexandra felt his grip on her arm slacken. He looked at her once more, giving her a sharp, penetrating glance which had the miserable effect of robbing her of breath. She stepped away from him and fortunately felt his odious spell on her begin to dissipate. Her sisters swarmed over him, pelting him with expressions of excitement, adoration, and hope.

"Oh, yes," Julia cried, batting her lashes up at him. "We can want for nothing more than your presence here in Stithwell this winter, my lord. If it is true, then you will have made us the happiest of ladies."

"Tell us it's true," Victoria gushed. Each had taken hold of one of his arms and they stared up into his face in acute love and desperation.

Alexandra did not know what to make of him, or of her sisters and their peculiar conduct toward him. If what was true? What did Julia mean by his presence in Stithwell for the winter?

"I apprehend," he began, turning and smiling down into each adoring face, his own expression as wretchedly condescending as ever, "you refer to my recent acquisition."

"Then it is true!" Julia cried, tears starting to her wide blue eyes, her heart-shaped face glowing with pleasure. "Now we shall never be bored again!"

Victoria left Launceston's side and drew Alexandra into their circle. "This was the reason we so foolishly dashed into the street, Alex. We had just learned that Launceston is the new owner of Castle Porth! Isn't it marvelous?"

"No," Alexandra breathed, feeling as though she had just been struck a stunning blow to the head. "It's not possible. Roselands will never be the same." Her mind and heart became quite empty as though for a very long time she had been in the midst of a great battle and without warning the enemy had inflicted a terrible, vicious blow. Now, the battle was lost and the war had come to an abrupt end. She didn't know what to think and the truth made only the barest sense to her.

Launceston, the new owner of Castle Porth.

When a raindrop struck her bonnet, then another and another, Alexandra met Launceston's victorious gaze. She said, "With weather to match my sentiments regarding your arrival in Stithwell. Unlike my sisters, I am not so sanguine about your new acquisition. In fact, it is my sincerest hope that you will dislike the rain, the town, the sea, and everything about Castle Porth so that within a few weeks you will be gone."

"Alexandra!" Julia and Victoria reprimanded her in unison, scowling up at her. She was taller than both her sisters, a Long Meg like her mother.

"How kind of you to offer up such a charming welcome,

Lady Alexandra," Launceston returned. "I am completely over-whelmed. But I must say that I don't believe your hopes have much chance of being fulfilled for already I find very much to like about Stithwell." Since at that moment her sisters were looking at her instead of Launceston, he let his gaze drift over first the twenty inches of her waist then most roguishly her lips and her face.

She was justifiably vexed. "Oh, you may go to the devil for all I care!" she cried, not caring in the least that the viscount had provoked her into uttering a complete vulgarism.

"Alexandra!" her sisters again cried in unison, their blue eyes wide with disbelief and shock. She ignored them and after drop-ping the viscount a sarcastic curtsy, she turned on her heel and recrossed the cobbled street. Launceston's deep laughter rolled over her back. She hated him, truly she did.

She still could not believe it was true—Launceston to reside so near to Roselands!

First she believed she was going mad and now Launceston had come to live at Castle Porth.

What a perfectly wretched day!

Two

When Launceston climbed to the top of the drag, he quickly took the reins in hand from his friend, Mr. Trenear, and with a shout and flick of his whip, set his fine, matched team of chestnut geldings in motion.

"The devil take that woman!" he cried, again flicking his whip in a hard movement over the ear of the leader. The sound slashed through the air, an accurate reflection of the state of his temper.

The cobbles of the High Street soon gave way to the loose, macadamized stone of the highway. The rain was light but steady and before long the horses' coats were wet and dripping.

Mr. Trenear, a sleepy-eyed man with a long face and a dry sense of humor, pulled his beaver hat low about his ears, secured the top button of his great coat, and responded to his friend's curse. "Perhaps *the devil* already has," he suggested lazily.

Launceston glanced sharply at Trenear, pondering his cryptic response. He knew his friend well enough to suppose that something other than a slur upon Lady Alexandra's temperament resided beneath his remark. George Trenear was a tall, thin man, with clear blue eyes, a pinched nose and thin lips which generally twitched before they smiled. He possessed not just a keen wit but an incisive understanding of his fellow creatures. He had an instinctive grasp of the nuances of humankind and rarely failed to provide a sort of blinding insight into even the most baffling and provoking of circumstances.

As his exquisitely sprung gentleman's drag whirled over the

crushed stones of the road, Launceston began to suspect that Trenear was even now attempting to convey one of those eye-straining truths.

"The devil, eh?" he queried. "You refer to me, I suppose."

Mr. Trenear's lips twitched.

Launceston uttered a crack of laughter. "I kissed her once—I admit it—but that was before I knew her. Damn and blast I've never known a woman to crawl so neatly beneath my skin before. I have but to look at her and every nerve in my body rises up and complains. She has a viper's tongue and a nest of vipers for a heart."

"Deuced fine-looking female, though," Trenear commented dryly.

"I'll give her that," Launceston returned with a sigh. As irritated as he was with her, he would not deny, even to himself, that he had never seen her equal. Her hair was an exquisite black which, since he had first chanced to see her locks unbonneted, dangling to her waist and gleaming in the full sunshine of a summer's day, he knew to be thick and lustrous. Her eyes, which she shared with her sisters, were wide, generously fringed with black lashes, and colored a deep, regal blue. Her skin was infinitely fair and delicate in appearance. Her nose was straight and patrician, her face oval, her lips neither full nor thin. And when cloaked with passion, the sum of her features was sensual almost beyond bearing. "She's more beauty than most," he added. "But her disposition makes up for the greater part of it."

"You're just on your mettle because you've met your match and you don't know what to do about it."

"My match!" he responded with a harsh laugh. "You're wrong there, Trenear. Dead wrong."

"Am I? Well, perhaps I put it to you badly. Let us say that Lady Alexandra is the one female whose heart you'll never conquer and well you know it."

"I can't conquer her heart because she hasn't got one."

"I don't know about that—*on dits* have it that she's been in love with Mylor Grampound for years. Supposed to make a match of it."

"Mylor Grampound!" he cried, dumbfounded. "You must be joking. He's of such a gentle disposition that she will have eaten him up before the wedding breakfast is over. Someone ought to warn the poor fellow."

"Perhaps you ought to," Mr. Trenear suggested with the faintest of yawns. "Pretty country hereabouts, isn't it? You can smell the sea."

Launceston grunted in response, his thoughts still fixed most heinously on Lady Alexandra Staple. He stared down the road, keeping his eyes centered straight ahead. He was still furious at his encounter with her and wondered if it was possible that such a woman could be his match as Trenear had suggested. This thought he dismissed with a snort—Lady Alexandra was not for him. Not for him to endure the coldness, the censure, the unkindnesses of a Frost Queen. When he married, his wife would be warm and passionate with honey perpetually on her tongue.

He gave the reins a slap and the horses picked up their pace. Why was it he had supposed that he could own Castle Porth without being affected by the nearness of Lord Brandreth's family? What a sapskull he had been to have dismissed the fact that Roselands was a favorite with Lady Brandreth. He had known as much, of course. Whenever he had had an opportunity to converse with the marchioness, invariably she would speak of Roselands and the renovations she was undertaking. He had not told her of his interest in the castle primarily because he had not wanted to raise the hopes of either Lady Julia or Lady Victoria. He knew that each of Alexandra's sisters was suffering from a *tendre* for him, *tendres* he had encouraged solely because the sight of one of her sisters on his arm would cause the Frost Queen to positively burn with rage. Her lips would grow pinched, her blue eyes deepen to a lovely violet, and her jaw would settle into a gentle gliding motion which he could only construe to be a gnashing of teeth.

He couldn't keep from smiling. She was devilishly easy to provoke which made the whole of their tempestuous relationship both endurable and at times positively pleasurable. In fact, earlier when she had told him to go to the devil, he had been gleeful in his enjoyment of the moment. She so rarely lost her stultified demeanor, that seeing her so beyond herself had been worth the whole of the otherwise infuriating conversation.

But was she his match?

He glanced up to the right and saw that the castle, *his* castle, was now within view and all his doubts about having purchased Castle Porth dissipated. The sight of the tall towers of granite, castellated and turreted, reached out to him as no other place ever had and gave him a strong sense that he was coming home.

Ever since he was a boy he had wanted to own the castle which had at one time belonged to a distant cousin, Kynance Redruth. He had visited the dilapidated and partially ruined structure as a boy of thirteen some seventeen years past, the same year the Marquis of Brandreth had purchased Roselands. At that time, his world had recently fallen apart for he had buried both parents six months earlier, each having succumbed to that dreaded disease known commonly as putrid sore throat and less commonly as diphtheria. His father, who had been a second son to the sixth viscount Launceston, had struggled to support his wife and children on a rector's living. Their deaths had seen the siblings—five in all—dispersed to distant relatives or as in his case, to Eton and by the time he was seventeen, to sea as a midshipman.

At the time that his uncle, the seventh viscount Launceston, sent him to Castle Porth to visit their cousin, the honorable Kynance Redruth, it was hoped that Mr. Redruth would take beneath his wing the unruly eldest son of the Rev. Justin St. Ives. But Mr. Redruth was a confirmed recluse and his dislike of having his castle invaded by a stripling had been evident from the outset. Their parting had been indifferent and precise— Mr. Redruth would pay for Newlyn St. Ives's education at Eton and Newlyn St. Ives would leave Mr. Redruth in peace.

Each had lived up to his bargain and thus began the cessation of all familial connection not only between Launceston and his patron, but between Launceston and the rest of his family until he had set sail from India for British shores some two and a half years prior. Though he made no effort to renew his acquaintance with Mr. Redruth, he had succeeded in reestablishing connections with each of his three sisters and his brother along with their spouses and offspring. All were married, all had spawned a progeny worthy of the good vicar and his wife, all had encouraged him to marry and to set up his nursery in short order.

He had wanted to. He had for a long time wished for a large family. He had returned from his adventures abroad both wealthy and ennobled, since the seventh viscount Launceston had not only failed to produce a male heir but had also failed to check his horses on a curved road in the Cotswolds and had suffered a broken neck. Between his wealth and nobility, he most certainly had no lack of attractions. Indeed, he understood by the current tittle-tattle, that he was considered by many matchmaking mamas, as the most eligible gentleman on the Marriage Mart. If a proper bride had eluded him, he was not precisely certain why. Yet, as he again glanced up at the dark castle, misty through the rain, he somehow sensed that his future had been bound long ago to the crumbling collection of stones.

As he kept his horses moving at a brisk pace, he recalled his visit of seventeen years prior. He had spent three weeks in Mr. Redruth's company, or rather lack of it. His cousin had been gone for most of the three weeks and had left Launceston to amuse himself, which he had by searching out every garreted corner of the ancient, sprawling castle. Treasures abounded— narrow winding stone stairwells leading to prisonlike rooms, attics filled with several suits of armor, swords, books, maps, and of course a variety of furniture from a variety of centuries. Perhaps this was the castle's greatest tug on his sensibilities, the presence of great continuity, of decades of living and dying, of the strength and solidity of a building made of tough, gray granite.

Built in a horseshoe and bearing a thick outer wall as an ancient fortification against invaders, only one portion of the castle had succumbed to the exigencies of time—the southwesterly walls which had seen the complete destruction of a turret and a bedchamber below. On the ground floor, beneath the bedchamber had been a beautiful chapel with three arched windows, each ten feet high and a full four feet from the ground. The oak pews and pulpit had long since been sold or burned or rotted, no one knew precisely which, and one corner where the west and south walls met was nothing but a gaping hole. The wall with the arched windows was all but gone except the most easterly portion which had been saved in order to protect the structure of the east wall and to keep the outline of one side of a window. The south wall was jagged and low, the wall having disintegrated no further than the original base of the windows four feet from the stone floor.

At thirteen, Launceston had spent hour upon hour in the chapel, during the day and frequently late into the night when the stars would form a sparkling curtain over the absent ceiling. He would sit on the low wall, contemplating his future, missing his family terribly, and staring up into the friendly night sky, endeavoring to set aside the crippling pain of the present.

One night, when the loneliness of his young years had overwhelmed him, he had hidden himself in the darkest corner and let his grief roll through him for the hundredth time. He had never been so alone and wondered if life could ever be sweet again as it once had when he had been safely nestled within the tenderness of his family.

It was in the midst of his greatest despair that the ghosts had first appeared in the chapel. He should have been frightened by them, but for some incomprehensible reason, he wasn't. Instead, their presence had managed to lift him from his gloom and force him into the future.

The woman and her son had been a lively, energetic pair, full of schemes and mischief and life. The passion with which they discussed a rather questionable plan—to rid their family of the woman's despised daughter-in-law—had struck a chord within him. Though he certainly found their motives suspect, at least they were in possession of the courage to address with zeal and imagination what seemed to be a plaguing difficulty.

The woman had been dressed as his mother had dressed before her demise, in garb reminiscent of ancient Greece and Rome. She had also been extraordinarily beautiful, with long, wavy hair that seemed to shift colors in the moonlight, with eyes that were a deep violet, or perhaps blue or green, he wasn't sure—they were simply large, lovely, and mesmerizing. But more than just her features, her entire countenance had been exquisite, the way she tossed her head, held her shoulders or swayed in delicate movements when she walked, not unlike Alexandra. In fact, now that he considered it, Alexandra's beauty was very much like this woman's which certainly accounted for why half of tonnish society fairly reclined at her feet.

Thoughts of Alexandra brought his attention suddenly back to the present. He realized his horses had slackened their pace considerably and gave them a quick snap of the reins. He might have remained in the present, but Mr. Trenear had fallen silent and seemed content to view the passing hills, shrubs, and trees as the coach whirled inexorably forward. The increasing rain, which thrummed on his beaver hat as well as the nearness of Castle Porth again dragged him back to his memories.

If the woman had been beautiful, her son had been quite handsome as well, with silver hair, features which clearly reflected his parentage, and a distinctive cleft chin. He also most strangely bore a pair of large black wings. Launceston did not know a great deal about ghost lore, but even so he could not recall ever having heard of a ghost bearing wings.

Who were these ghosts, he had wondered.

He had kept very still among the lichen-covered stones and fallen granite blocks. He had watched and listened intently to their conversation and how they intended to make use of the chapel in their schemes. He had been so awestruck by their appearance that very little of the conversation had actually reached his ears but he did recall that the woman's daughter-in-law, who they called Butterfly and both professed to hate, was clearly the object of their mischief. By the nature of their discussion it would seem they intended to banish her to live in the castle away from the man's brother, forever, if possible. He couldn't remember much more than that except that they were both quite aggravated by "Butterfly's" conduct, and wanted her separated from the woman's other son.

"But it will take decades," the woman had said, with a frown on her pretty brow.

At that, the winged man had thrown back his head and laughed. "What is one decade or two to us?" he had queried, a remark which had convinced Launceston that these two at least must be ghosts.

After half an hour, they both moved toward the east and simply vanished. Though he had continued to frequent the chapel ruins from that moment on, hoping to hear more of their schemes, he never saw either of them again.

As he considered the remarkable nature of what he had seen and heard, he began to wonder why it was that he had been so deeply affected by their appearance that night and why he had been drawn to purchase Castle Porth. It was as though some mystery was at work within him, something he could not explain. All he knew was that he had to return to live at the castle, if not for always then at least for the present time. And if Lady Alexandra was one of the prices he would have to pay for owning the place that had so oddly taken him from despair to hope, then so be it. Besides, he could manage Alexandra Staple.

He smiled with no small degree of satisfaction as he thought of her again. He knew something that Mr. Trenear did not—that the Frost Queen, for all her pretenses of being a model of decorous propriety, was not indifferent to being kissed. He recalled the look on her face when he had held her tightly by the arm just a few minutes ago. He had seen her cheeks become suffused with a blush that had nothing to do with embarrassment. He had watched her lips part by way of an invitation so sensual that even now as he thought of it, his blood flowed warm with anticipation. She had been begging for a kiss and by God the next time he saw her alone, he would give her that kiss and then he would see just how hypocritical she meant to be.

"So what do you say?"

Launceston glanced at his friend and frowned slightly. "Sorry, Trenear, my mind was elsewhere. To what are you referring?"

He gave the reins another slap and guided his horses easily around the next curve in the road.

"I was saying," Mr. Trenear drawled, "that I would be willing to wager you the ruby brooch against your team of chestnuts, if you think you could bear to part with them."

Launceston was shocked. "The brooch?" he queried, uncertain he had heard Mr. Trenear correctly.

"Yes," Mr. Trenear responded beneath lazy eyelids.

Launceston whistled long and low. George Trenear's ruby brooch was an infamous piece of jewelry which Mr. Trenear, a Nonpareil in the art of gaming, had for many years saved for wagers of a very specific nature—ones that appealed to his sense of avarice and which invariably were impossible for his opponents to refuse.

"For the past two years since I have come to know you, Trenear, you have refused to stake the brooch in any of a hundred wagers I have suggested to you. Now you offer it, against my chestnuts, and I am astonished. Unfortunately, I failed to hear the nature of this proposed wager, so review the essentials for me. Just what manner of wager has somehow captivated your fancy of a sudden?"

The lane leading to Castle Porth, which was now a visible silhouette in the darkening gray of the Cornish twilight, appeared to the right. With a careful guiding of the reins, he soon saw his bright, quick team pounding up the lane which led to both his home and to Roselands. The lane was bordered for a considerable distance by rhododendron shrubs on the south and a "stone hedge" on the north upon which walked two children and a dog, the former well-cloaked against the rain. The stone wall was wide enough to have formed a footpath to the base of the hill upon which Castle Porth was situated, a distance of two miles from the King's highway.

Mr. Trenear laid his wager before the viscount. "I will part with my brooch if within ten days you are able to seduce the heart of the Frost Queen, hint at marriage, and receive for your efforts an enthusiastic acquiescence."

Launceston could not help but ease into a satisfied smile. "Done," he responded without so much as a second thought. He had but to recall to mind the look on Alexandra's face when he held her arm gripped tightly in his to be convinced of the outcome of this wager.

"Eager are you?" Mr. Trenear queried. His laughter which followed brought a scowl to Launceston's fine, fair face. In all the years that George Trenear had been in the habit of wagering his brooch, he had not once come within an inch of losing it.

But not this time, my good man, Launceston thought. *Not this time.*

Three

"He has told me no less than three times," Julia cried fervently, her head lowered as though opposing a strong wind, "that he finds my fiery disposition much to his preference." She glared at Victoria as though daring her to refute her.

Victoria, so different from Julia, merely lifted her chin slightly and smiled in a superior manner in which Alexandra knew her youngest sister was destined to overset her elder. "And he has told me on more than three occasions that my poetic manner of viewing everything about me charms him exceedingly."

"Poetic!" Julia exclaimed. "More like theatrical!"

Victoria drew in a long, sharp breath her eyes taking on a Valkyrie appearance as she prepared to engage the enemy. "Theatrical—you who speak of *fiery dispositions,* words which I do not hesitate to tell you sound as though they have just emerged from one of your circulating library novels and haven't the barest amount of sensibility or . . ."

The words faded from Alexandra's ears. She was seated on the right side of her family's town chariot, Julia on the left and Victoria in the middle. The rain had become a steady thumping on the roof of the coach.

Alexandra turned away from the battle beginning to resound beside her. She had for so long listened to her sisters brangling about which of them Lord Launceston favored that she was now able, for quite long periods, to ignore them both. She had heard this particular argument a score of times since each of her sib-

lings, upon having made the acquaintance of his lordship this
past season, had fancied themselves in love with him.

At first, Alexandra had tried to point out Launceston's failings
to them, but to little avail. Both Julia and Victoria were badly
smitten with *tendres* for the arrogant viscount which, instead of
dimming and fading with time, had appeared to increase in violence. She had given up some months ago attempting to reorder
their minds or hearts and for that reason was able to close her
ears to their incessant squabbling on the subject.

Besides, she had far greater concerns underfoot than the mere
speculation as to which of her sisters Lord Launceston was
likely to cast his eye. The news that the viscount was the new
owner of Castle Porth certainly was never far from her thoughts,
but the closer the town chariot drew to Roselands, the more
consumed was she with whether or not Anteros would be awaiting her return. Two days ago, when she had returned from shopping in Stithwell, upon cresting the rise above Roselands, she
had found to her dismay that even at such a distance, she could
easily see Anteros, framed within the window of her bedchamber and waiting for her.

Would he be there today? she wondered. If she saw him in
the window again, would he be real or a mere fabrication of
her imagination, a sure sign that she was slowly but quite surely
going mad.

As the Roseland coach reached the end of the stone hedge
which parted the lane—the left taking the traveller to Castle
Porth and the right, to Roselands—Alexandra's heart began to
hammer against her ribs. Only a bend in the lane separated her
now from a view of Roselands.

The base of the hill around which the postillion was carefully
guiding her father's matched team of bays, was cloaked on the
right with a woodland of fine beech trees. Once the coach
passed out of the woodland, the lane would emerge to overlook
a wide grassy valley in which Roselands was situated on high
ground on the north side. A stream ran through the valley over

which a narrow, ancient granite bridge had been built four centuries previously.

Raindrops were streaming steadily down the postillion's hat, a criss-crossed network of rivulets matched by those on the front window glass. The view was somewhat obscured through the front glass, but not, unfortunately through Alexandra's side window which was only dotted with raindrops. There would be no mistaking Anteros if he was waiting in her bedchamber.

Each turn of the wheels set her heart to racing harder still. A few more feet and Roselands would come into view. She took a deep breath, leaned forward, and placed her hand on the side window glass. Raindrops continued to slant across the clear glass, but not sufficiently to mar the view. A few more turns of the wheel—the east chimneys came into view, then the east wing, she could see most of the house now and there—the west wing.

"Oh, my goodness," she breathed aloud, unaware she had done so. She could see him clearly, particularly since though rain still pelted the coach, across the valley a pink shaft of late afternoon sunlight had broken through the clouds and was spilling over Roselands, setting it aglow in the most glorious golden-pink light.

She heard her sisters gasp and for a moment she supposed that Julia and Victoria actually saw what she saw—for there, framed by the multi-paned glass of her bedchamber window was the distinct form of a man wearing a short black tunic and bearing enormous black wings.

"It is no wonder," Julia began in an awed whisper, "that Mama was able to persuade Papa to purchase Roselands when he already had a fine property in Bedfordshire."

"The light on the grass in the valley—!" Victoria exclaimed. "Would that I could paint as Mr. Constable. I have never seen Roselands appear to greater advantage."

Alexandra turned to look at her sisters, stunned. Why were they speaking of Roselands, sunlight, and Constable? "But don't you see that man in my bedchamber window?" she asked, unwilling any longer to keep her dark secret from her family.

Both her sisters leaned forward to scrutinize the window of Alexandra's bedchamber. She saw their frowns and their efforts to see what she saw, but at the same time she knew by the perplexity on each face that they did not see the black-winged man.

Alexandra leaned back against the squabs and felt tears of sheer frustration bite her eyes. When she turned back to look at the window in question, he was still there and now his arms were folded across his chest, almost defying her. She could all but hear his mocking laughter.

Then it was true, she thought despairingly. She was just like Lady Elle—she was going mad, just as her beloved great, great-aunt had gone mad. She was seeing the return of visions she had once shared in great companionship and communion with the old woman who had been beloved by her mother and her father.

"I don't see anyone," Victoria said. She was sitting next to Alexandra and because her nature was sweet, Alexandra felt her sister slip her hand into her own and give it a squeeze. "Whatever is the matter, Alex? Why do you have tears in your eyes? You are just overset because Launceston gave you a severe dressing down, but never mind. I'm sure once you apologize to him, all will be well."

Alexandra opened her mouth to speak, to dispel Victoria's belief that she was merely overset by her quarrel with Launceston, but she could not. More than anything, she wanted to tell her sisters all, to explain about her childhood and the many things she had seen by Lady Elle's side, all the shared visions of Olympus which the old woman had culled forth by simply requesting to see the latest events on Mt. Olympus. She wanted to tell Julia and Victoria about Anteros and how his wings were so beautiful and so exquisite that when he unfurled them fully, the feathered tips would touch one wall of her bedchamber and the scarlet draperies flanking the windows of the opposite wall.

But she couldn't. There was still part of her that hoped beyond hope he would simply go away, or at least her visions of him. Then none of it would be real, and she would not have to doubt her sanity any longer, and she could return to her life as it had always been.

She closed her eyes for a long moment as the coach swayed its way down the lane, heading toward the bridge. She wished him gone, over and over, she wished him away forever.

She opened her eyes, stared at the window of her bedchamber and he was gone! He was gone. Perhaps she had been imagining him after all. Perhaps all she had to do from now on was to simply wish him gone, to wish him away and he would be gone. She breathed a sigh of relief. He was gone and she could now return to her life as it was.

She could return to her life.

Her life as it was.

With these thoughts came an impression of emptiness and of hollowness so strong that while previous thoughts of Anteros had caused her heart to race forward in fright, her current thoughts seemed to cause her heart to simply stop beating.

A most profound and unsettling notion occurred to her—she no longer wanted her life to be *as it was.* Yet why she felt this way, she didn't know. For some reason, ever since the past London season, her life had become a trial to her instead of the joy it had for the most part always been.

Each morning for months she had been awakening to a sense of despair and *ennui* that defied explanation. She went to bed full of longings that made no sense to her, no sense at all. Her music, which had formerly been a source of great inspiration to her, lacked the ability to hold her interest. Her poetic scratchings had lost their savor, her efforts with the watercolors had begun to seem like so many disjointed, useless dots and splashes all thrown together to create nothing of beauty or of meaning.

She had tried to speak with her mother about her strange sense of restlessness and distress, but because her mama had recently hired a new architect to construct a few rather Gothic-

looking enhancements to Roselands, Lady Brandreth had not
seemed able to fully enter into a discussion of her unhappiness.
In the end, while showing Alexandra a picture of a Turkish
dome, her mother had brought the discussion to a close by stat-
ing rather firmly that if she searched her heart and the past very
carefully she would discover precisely why she was overset now.

"I could tell you what I see, Alex," she said with an understanding smile in her dark brown eyes, "but you would not
believe me. Search your heart, and look to this past season for
the answer, for I believe something extraordinary happened to
you then, or perhaps even earlier than that, but you will not
own to it."

Alexandra had not known, and still did not know, precisely
to what her mother had been referring. The season had been as
each season prior had been, full of a heady round of social
engagements which left her alternately exhilarated and fatigued.
She had collected numerous *beaux* in her court, and she had
been proclaimed the reigning Beauty by dozens of her friends
and admirers. She rarely sat out a set, she was seen at the opera,
she was invited everywhere. There had been in effect nothing
unusual or extraordinary at all about the season, except of
course for the fact that Launceston had been present to cast her
pleasures in the shadow of his sardonic brow and biting tongue.

Of course, she had not first met Launceston during the season, not by half. She had met him once, though never learned
his name at the time, the summer prior, in Bath, a chance meeting about which her family was entirely unaware.

As the horses' hooves could be heard striking the hard stone
of the bridge which echoed into the clear, rock-laden stream
below, Alexandra's thoughts turned more deeply into the past,
to a summer's day a little over a year prior, when she had been
walking with her maid for a considerable distance outside of
Bath along the grassy banks of the River Avon. Her maid, Lydia,
who was quite young, had begged permission to run into the
beechwoods in order to collect a bouquet of bluebells. Given
that no one was about, that the sun was shining and warm on

her skin, and that her heart was full of pleasant thoughts about life and her poetry and the serene society to be found in Bath, she easily gave her permission.

Once Lydia had disappeared into the woods, however, Alexandra had been startled by the sensation of freedom which suddenly overcame her as she realized she was alone and unprotected, that she was, in fact, free in that moment to do whatever she pleased.

Her first act had been to remove the constraining straw bonnet from her black locks and with a particularly wild impulse pulled her hair from the constricting braids coiled about her ears, a style she sometimes wore beneath her bonnets. She pulled off her gloves and threw them into the air. She began twirling about in circles, letting the tall grasses sweep about the pale blue silk of her wide skirts and five petticoats.

She felt quite young in that moment, unfettered by the increasingly strict modes of conduct being placed upon young ladies of her day. A new philosophy was rushing through England, of extreme politeness, of manners, of rigid self-control. For the most part, Alexandra was not opposed to the high expectations placed on young Ladies of Quality. At the same time, therefore, she could not precisely account for why it was she had felt so joyous twirling beneath the deep blue sky, unbonneted, ungloved, and entirely lacking in restraint and discretion.

She fell into the grass and shaded her eyes as she looked up into the deep blueness above. Her heart was beating quickly, her fingertips tingled, her ankles ached. She laughed and laughed then rose quickly to approach the river where she began to ease her way down the bank to the water's edge. Finding stones tucked between blades of grass, she dislodged several and using the flattest began skipping the stones into the swiftly flowing water. After several attempts, she finally achieved a skip of four and jumped up and down clapping. She was about to twirl around again when she was interrupted.

"And what manner of day is this," a man's deep, resonant

voice had called to her, startling her, "that I have been so blessed by the gods that I should find a water-nymph awaiting me?"

Alexandra remembered turning around and thinking she ought to feel horrified by his presence since she was alone and unprotected. But for some incomprehensible reason, she wasn't, not in the least even though while he sat so at ease on his fine black horse she could easily see he was quite possibly the handsomest man she had ever seen. He had blond hair, streaked by sunshine, which he wore just past his collar as was the style. He had short side whiskers, which was also *de rigueur.* His nose was straight and sharp but quite attractive, his cheeks were high and striking, the line of his jaw firm. His brows were arched over what was his best feature, hazel eyes which shifted color as the light shifted, sometimes brown, sometimes blue, sometimes green. Newlyn St. Ives, Lord Launceston, though she had not known as much at the time.

"Sir!" she cried, breathlessly. "You have given me a start."

"I should like to give you much more," he had said quite scandalously as his eyes first took in the long flow of her black curls which were now dangling in pretty ringlets across her shoulders and down her back, then drifted over her full bosom and remained fixed to the smallness of her waist. For the barest moment she felt naked beneath his gaze.

When his eyes travelled back to meet her gaze, a smile of amusement and appreciation lit up his face. "Faith, but you are quite beautiful," he continued, as he slid his leg easily over the haunches of his horse and jumped lightly to the ground. Catching the reins of his horse, he led the black gelding to a nearby rhododendron shrub and tied the reins loosely within its woody branches.

Alexandra recalled having watched him with much pleasure and not even a whisper of fear, even though given her careless hair and gloveless hands, he had taken her for the willing maiden she was not, at least not precisely. The man before her was a marvel to her, for even in the way he walked she could see that he was at ease in his body. He appeared strong and athletic, perhaps a man who was sporting mad. His shoulders were broad and tapered to a narrow waist, his legs were long and lean. She was a tall woman, but he was taller still and something in his eye, or the way he carried himself, or the passionate expression on his face told her she might be meeting her ideal.

There had also been nothing wavering about the man, for he had had but one purpose in interrupting his ride, to accost a water-nymph. And so it was, that when he approached her, he said not another word but simply caught her up in his arms and before she could protest, placed his lips firmly on hers.

She had struggled a little. She had tried to push him away. But he had held her more tightly still, releasing her only enough to catch her at the back of the head with one of his hands and to force her to look at him. With a frown he said, "Don't be nonsensical. You want this kiss, else you would have run away from me long before now."

Alexandra had opened her mouth to protest, but in a moment of insight she realized he was right, she had wanted him to kiss her and to refuse him would have been the height of hypocrisy. For that reason, she had responded by throwing herself at him, catching him with both arms about the neck, and letting her lips land squarely upon his.

Somehow, however, she caused him to lose his balance and he toppled over into the grassy bank behind him, taking her with him. Laughter resulted, rich, full, robust laughter which ended in a kiss which Alexandra thought she would never in her life forget, for in the tangle of the fall and the desire to fulfill his original intention, he had covered her with the length of his body, as a man loves his wife, and tasted deeply of her mouth in a way which left her breathless and dizzy.

"Who are you?" he had breathed across her lips, across her cheeks and into her ear. "I have never known such a sweet taste before. Tell me your name? Where do you reside? I must see you again. I must know you completely." She felt his hands suddenly on her thighs and a blinding awareness of the terrible predicament in which she had placed herself suddenly shot through her.

With a strength born of panic, she had pushed him off of her and scrambled away from him before he could so much as protest. His laughter had followed her, along with a pleading quality to his voice as he begged her to return to him if for no other reason than to help her brush the mud and dirt from her light blue silk skirts. But his laughter and the teasing sound of his words again forced her into an awareness that she had behaved wretchedly and had encouraged the stranger to believe she would give him something she most certainly would not.

She ran away from him. She had thought he might pursue her, but since Lydia had at that moment been returning from the beechwoods, her arms laden with bluebells and ferns, she suspected the maid's presence might have deterred him. When he did approach her, he was again astride his horse.

She had bid her maid quickly braid her hair. Poor Lydia had been deeply distressed by what she could see had happened to her mistress and had exclaimed her stupidity in having left her mistress alone. But Alexandra had forbidden her to shed tears, especially since the man was nearly upon them.

"What is your name?" he called down to Alexandra.

"None of your concern!" Lydia had shouted. "Go away you dreadful rogue!"

The man had broken into a wide grin. "What does that make your mistress then?" he queried, his question directed at Alexandra.

"Do you not know to whom you are speaking?" Lydia had objected. "When the Marquis of Brandreth discovers you have attacked his daughter, you shall soon forget your smiles and insults!"

"Brandreth?" he queried, his black horse sidling awkwardly, his brows drawn sharply together in a frown. "Do not tell me you are a gentlewoman and not some maid dressed up for a day's adventure in her mistress's clothes?"

"You are speaking to *Lady* Alexandra Staple," the maid responded, still struggling with Alexandra's braids.

"Indeed?" the man responded, lifting his brows. "Well, then," he added, bowing to Alexandra. "You give me hope, my lady, indeed you do! But I won't beg your pardon, because I don't believe it is necessary nor do I believe you would ask it of me." He had then doffed his hat and cantered away.

She remembered the whole of it as though it had been yesterday. She would never forget how she had for days afterward longed for the stranger to call, or to appear at the Pump Room some morning, or the assemblies on Tuesday and Friday nights, but he had not. The fact that he had failed to seek her out and to call upon her had been the beginning of the formation of her ill-opinion of his true character. Further investigation during the ensuing months prior to the start of the season only served to prove her unhappy opinion time and time again. The man, by description, had been confirmed to her as viscount Lord Launceston, a wild creature who had made his fortune in India and who had returned to England a few months prior to claim the estates, title, and lands as heir to his late uncle's viscountancy.

When she finally met him during the season, she was so full of disapprobation, that when they were introduced she met his warm smile with a frosty extension of two fingers and a haughty stare. His response had been quick and rather violent, for he had taken her fingers and rudely possessed himself of her entire hand. He had swept her hand behind her back and drawn her tightly against him. "You weren't so prudish last summer," he had whispered. "Are you to be like all the rest?" After which he had released her with a jerk and strolled away, the only witness having been his friend, Mr. Trenear.

War had ensued, a war of wits and of tempers. And now he was to be her neighbor.

Victoria's voice intruded. "What is wrong, Alex? You haven't answered any of Julia's questions and now you appear so sad that I vow I don't know you. Is it because you are always quarreling with Launceston?"

Alexandra knew she could no more explain the whole of her sentiments to her sisters than she could explain her unhappiness to herself. For that reason, she answered, "I believe so." When she turned and saw the concern on each of her sisters' faces, she added, "But for your sakes, I shall try to do better, I promise you. I don't know how it is that Launceston and I brangle so, and now that we are to be neighbors, I will make every effort not to set up his back so frequently as I do."

Her sisters expressed their joint belief that were she to make even the smallest push that Lord Launceston, who really did have a good heart and who could be the most amusing companion, would respond in kind.

Alexandra was not in the least convinced but perhaps as much for her own sake as for theirs, she made up her mind to lay aside her former grievances and do what she could to achieve a more amicable relationship with his lordship.

When the ladies were deposited at the front door of Roselands, Alexandra watched her sisters leave the fine entrance hall to go in search of their mother who the butler, Mr. Baddam, informed them was in her office with her architect, and turned to mount the square staircase. As she lifted her violet skirts, *Ivanhoe* tucked beneath her arm and her fringed reticule dangling from her wrist, she felt the strangest dizziness assail her as she began ascending the stairs.

"Oh, no," she murmured beneath her breath.

The faint smell of roses drifted before her and her heart again increased its pulse. She felt breathless as she reached the first landing and paused to regain her breath. After a moment, she continued. She had the most peculiar sensation that someone was near her and she felt unaccountably dizzy, a prickly feeling which resembled quite oddly the way she had felt when Launceston had kissed her two summers prior.

Alexandra.

Did she hear her name? She looked all about her, but no one

was near the staircase, either on the first floor above or the ground floor below.

Oh, no. Anteros is here, she thought. Then she hadn't imagined him and why was the fragrance of roses everywhere?

She continued to mount the steps. She heard the flutter of wings.

Anteros was here, with her. She knew it. But why? What did he want from her? Why was he pressing her?

She moved to her bedchamber and entered the room, her heart pounding frightfully in her throat. She was somehow not surprised, yet still unnerved, when the door closed by itself behind her. She spun around and nearly swooned again at the sight of the extraordinary black-winged man, with silver hair, standing in front of the door, so handsome, so proud, so intense.

"You are Anteros, aren't you?" she queried, trying to keep her voice from quivering as she tossed her novel and her reticule gently on the scarlet velvet counterpane of her bed.

He nodded to her. "I've come for you, Alexandra. I've come to take you back to Olympus with me. You are to be my wife."

Four

Psyche picked up one of the five English hunting puppies which were playing and tumbling within the confines of a large wicker basket, and held the little female pup on her lap. She was seated in her painting room and had just set aside her paintbrush, a little frustrated that she could not quite seem to capture the charm of the feisty, four-legged beasts on canvas. She ruffled the pup's ears and let it bite at her fingers, but not too hard because the puppy's teeth were horridly sharp.

She cooed the pup's name. "Naughty Aphrodite! Naughty girl! Now don't let my mama-in-law know that I have named you after her. She would instantly grow another head and mouth with which to double her berating of me night and day were she to know our little secret." The puppy flopped on her back and continued to chew on Psyche's finger.

Psyche smiled affectionately at the helpless creature, and again turned her gaze to her portrait of the white pups. Just as she was about to pick up her brush again, she was suddenly struck by a sensation of fear so great and so real—followed sharply by a premonition of some terrible mischief—that had she not been safely ensconced in her chamber, deep within her home, she would have believed herself in mortal danger. Even then, the feeling of danger was so profound that she instantly returned the puppy to its basket to rejoin its litter mates. Though she suspected she was not herself in danger, she still could not keep from rising from her stool and scrutinizing every corner of her chamber for even the smallest sign of wrongdoing.

But she found nothing.

She left her painting room as though in a trance, walking slowly into the adjoining hallway, through the grand dining hall and into the great receiving chamber with ceilings three stories high, and waited and listened. Still, nothing. She left the receiving room and entered the spacious entrance hall. The front door was open, as it always was during the day in every home in Olympus. She approached the doorway, and looked out, the vista of the beautiful Olympian valley below as peaceful and sedate as always.

Cupid's home was perched on a gentle hillside and from the front windows the glittering river Styx, which emerged in great beauty from the Underworld at quite a distance from Pluto's kingdom, could be seen nestled in a wide, verdant valley ever sloping toward the Mediterranean Sea. Two decades prior, Cupid had promised her a new home, far from Aphrodite's sphere of acquaintances, but neither she nor Eros could bring themselves to part with the spectacular view their home afforded of a land Psyche had truly come to love with all her heart.

Ordinarily, the sight of the valley below, and the glittering ribbonlike river, served to soothe any distress she might be experiencing. But as Psyche looked out over the valley, the feeling of dread failed to diminish. If anything, with each passing shift of the sun in the sky, the sensation increased.

After a few minutes when nothing untoward presented itself, Psyche decided to try easing her distress by returning to her painting chamber. But just as she passed back into the great receiving room, she heard several neighboring dogs set up a howl and a familiar swishing sound brush the air behind her.

"Oh, no," she murmured. The dogs always howled when the messenger god, Mercury, appeared. The wings on his sandals apparently created a whirring sound which seemed to give great discomfort to any nearby canine. When she heard the little pups also set up a high-pitched crying of their own, she was not surprised, when, upon turning about and facing the entrance hall, Mercury suddenly appeared in the open doorway, in full flight.

He passed through the entrance hall and as Psyche quickly moved out of the way, literally dove into the great receiving hall, pretending to trip upon entering her home, an antic which resulted in the practiced execution of three perfect somersaults. He landed finally on his feet, the wings of his sandals now calm as he stood on the beautiful amethyst and marble floor both smiling and frowning at her.

He was something of a clown, had a reputation for being a very clever thief, and prided himself on his inventions. Apollo's ability to please all of Olympus with his extraordinary music was due in part by Mercury's finely crafted instruments—he had in fact invented the flute some twenty centuries prior. Beyond his abilities however, his warmth of character and the silliness of his antics never failed to please Psyche.

"Oh, Merk!" she cried with a laugh. "Whatever are you doing here? And why do you appear so red-faced and out of breath, as though—oh, dear!" Instinctively she knew Mercury's sudden arrival had everything to do with her recent premonition that all was not well. "Then I was not misled by a strange prickling sensation all down my neck which foretold of some mishap. Don't spare me, my dearest Merk—tell me what is amiss. Is it Eros? Has he been injured—or, or, consigned by his mama to Hades for—"

Mercury, who was indeed out of breath, lifted a hand and gasped. "No! By Zeus, you always worry about that absurd husband of yours! Forget about him for a moment. You are right—I am—quite out of breath. Been travelling as though—a—centaur was after me. One moment—" He gasped in several ragged breaths and doubled over, supporting himself with a hand on his knee. After a moment, he continued, "There—much better! Prepare yourself, my little Butterfly. I've been sent by the oracle to fetch you. It is a matter of extreme urgency that you come with me, at once, or all will be lost!"

"Whatever do you mean!" she cried, taking a step forward,

her mind beginning to dart forward and backward all at once. "Oh, I knew something was wrong, that something dreadful had happened. Of course I'll come. Only let me get my shawl, and, and my reticule—"

"You must forget your shawl—you must not delay. I was given strict instructions. If I do not have you at the oracle in five minutes, the portal will close."

"The portal?" she exclaimed, moving quickly toward him. "To earth? Oh, Merk—is it time, already? Evanthea must have need of me, just as Cupid said—faith, how many years has it been? Oh, I can't believe it—I can't credit it! I have been so busy painting that, oh, my goodness, have two decades and more gone by? How I have missed Evanthea—but by now she will no longer be a maiden as she was when I knew her but a matron, with children fully grown—three daughters—" She placed her hand on his shoulder, preparing to depart with him. Her small, light figure had always made it possible for Psyche to travel easily with him.

"All of that is true—and more. Are you ready?"

"Yes," she nodded.

He slipped his arm about her waist and held her close to his side. Psyche felt the vibrations of a low whirr rumbling beneath her feet. Every once in a while, the tips of the wings on his sandals, fluttering madly like a humming bird, tickled her ankles. Slipping her arms tightly about his neck, she felt herself become quickly airborne, held securely by one of Mercury's powerful arms. When necessary, Mercury could move with lightning speed, as he did now.

"Which oracle?" Psyche asked, as they began moving over the softly rolling hills of the valley in a westerly direction. "Trophonious? Delphi?"

"Dodona," he returned loudly. The rush of the wind against their faces made hearing difficult.

"Jupiter's oracle?" Psyche returned, startled. "But then he is certain to know of my departure from Olympus which is strictly forbidden."

"He will know nothing," Mercury responded. "I alone received the message and unless you wish it revealed to Zeus, I am bound by the oaths of my office to keep such information restricted exclusively to the receiver. What is your will?"

Psyche chuckled. "You know very well what my answer must be," she responded still in a loud voice. "Tell his majesty nothing on pain of death!"

The sounds of Mercury's sympathetic laughter trailed behind her as they rose yet higher into the air.

The grove of oaks to the south of Olympus housed the famous oracle, one of many which in former times had served any mortal wishing to discover the future. Presently, the various oracles connected the future with the gods and goddesses of Olympus exclusively and were no longer available to mortals. In addition, Zeus discouraged any involvement with the mortal realm and had limited travel to earth for those who were not deities through designated portals at assigned times. The deities of course could do what they wished but since Zeus strongly disapproved of any attempt to alter the forward movement of time and history, and supported his disapprobation with the frequent use of lightning bolts, few bothered to leave Olympus.

As they began their descent into the grove of oaks, and the rush of air was less pronounced, Psyche queried, "But how has it come about that a portal has been granted without Zeus's knowledge or permission?"

At that Mercury seemed to draw inward and the ensuing silence again brought a prickling of gooseflesh traveling down Psyche's neck and back. She was nearly as frightened as she had been before his arrival but was now afraid even to hear his answer.

"I am not permitted to say," was his cryptic response.

Psyche wanted to press him, but her knowledge of Mercury's character and the seriousness with which he discharged his duties, forced her to restrain the questions which rose quickly to mind. Drifting over the tops of several ancient and magnificently gnarled oak trees, Psyche watched as a clearing came into view. "Is there nothing you can tell me?" she asked at last as he descended into the clearing and set her gently on a soft patch of grass. The rich, pungent smell of the oaks filled the air.

He released her and turned to look anxiously into her eyes. "I can tell you nothing but I believe the oracle will reveal to you all you need to know before your departure."

"I see," she said quietly. Above the treetops the sky was a deep blue. She turned about in a circle. She had expected to see a temple or an altar at the very least, but there was nothing. "I don't understand. Where is the oracle?"

"You've never been here then?" he queried.

She shook her head. The wind blew in a long gust through the grove. The leaves of the oaks rustled and for a moment Psyche was certain she could hearing singing. A moment later, a woman, known as a priestess, appeared some twenty feet distant, wearing an exquisite black silk gown, banded about her narrow waist with embroidered strips of black silk. Her sandals were black, she wore a black headpiece of onyx, her hair was black, her eyes were black. She held one hand aloft and seated prettily on her hand was a delicate black dove. Psyche remembered the legend of the origin of the oracle at Dodona, that a black dove had flown from Thebes in Egypt and had alighted here in a grove of oaks. Purportedly, the dove would speak. She wondered if this was true.

"You have brought her in time, Mercury, now you may go," the priestess said. So, the dove did not speak.

"As you wish," he responded.

Psyche was again frightened and clutched at Mercury's arm, preventing him for a moment from leaving. "Tell Cupid what has happened," she whispered.

Mercury glanced at the priestess who unfortunately shook her head in the negative. "Goodbye, Butterfly. Come back to us. Please."

She wanted to assure him she would, especially since a peculiar sadness had entered his eye, but he rose abruptly into the air and was gone before she could speak the words.

"You must pass through the portal now," the priestess said, gesturing with an elegant wave of her hand to her left.

Psyche watched in amazement as a swirling blue light appeared. "The portal," she breathed, her heart racing in her breast. "I've heard of it but I have never before seen it!"

She began walking toward the portal but addressed the priestess. "Will you not tell me what is going forward and why I have been summoned in this manner? Mercury has told me nothing."

The priestess closed her eyes in a mystical fashion. "Neither can I," she murmured. But at that moment a sharp wind blew through the grove and the leaves rustled wildly. "Wait!" she cried, appearing to listen to the sound of the wind in the leaves. "There is something you must know after all. Something exceedingly important. You are required to return within ten days, by the hour of midnight on the day known in Albion as All Hallow's Eve, to the chapel ruins at a place called Castle Porth."

"Castle Porth—but I don't—"

"Silence! If you do not return by midnight to this place and reenter the portal which will be waiting for you, then you will be consigned to earth to live out your natural life as a mortal, to die, to never return again to Olympus. These are the words spoken to me from the future."

The fright Psyche had previously experienced returned to her in great force. Tears strangled her throat and burned her eyes. "Never to return?"

"Precisely."

Psyche was now standing but five feet from the portal. "Only tell me, what is it I am meant to do at Castle Porth? Is something wrong with Evanthea and Brandreth?"

A pause ensued. "I know nothing of these of whom you speak, only of a young woman named Alexandra who Anteros means to bring back to Olympus. He must not be permitted to succeed. Should he bring her back, the future of the world will be altered so significantly that in years to come, a great power will rampage the island and in the ensuing conflicts the civilizations Zeus has worked so diligently to protect will come to an end. You must prevent Anteros from bringing Alexandra back. You must also see that Alexandra willingly gives her heart to a nobleman by the name of Launceston, for when they wed they will provide their country with great warriors. Now go, at once! You have but three seconds before the portal closes."

Psyche did not hesitate, but turned toward the blue light and ran into the center of the swirling mass. What she found within the portal was enormous pain which rent through every joint of her body and sent a thousand candles bursting into flame in her head. She opened her mouth to scream, but no sound came forth.

Alexandra knew that Anteros was holding her folded within his black wings, she could feel his lips on hers, she felt her heart responding with great love to the creature who was kissing her. Yet none of it seemed real, as though she was walking through a dream and that the moment she awakened, she would realize how silly the dream had been.

But how very safe she felt within the circle of his arms and his lips were sweet beyond description! At the same time, she sensed in his touch, a pervading loneliness that struck a similar chord within her own soul. She was as much surprised to discover that there was a part of her that was dissatisfied in her solitary state as she was to comprehend that such a sentiment existed so sadly within the heart of the man now kissing her.

Perhaps her thoughts reached him for he drew back slightly from her and looked down into her face, his own handsome features a mask of concern. "What were you thinking just now?" he asked, quietly yet sharply.

"I could feel your aloneness," she responded, lifting a hand to touch his cheek with the back of her fingers. "You are very handsome and warm and loving," she continued, speaking the honest musings of her heart. "Why is it you have not taken a wife before? Surely there must be a score who would have you and love you and bear you a nursery full of winged children?"

She looked deeply into his eyes which grew misted and distant. When he spoke, his voice had dropped to a bare whisper. "There is only one I've loved—" he began, then stopped. He closed his eyes and breathed deeply. He appeared as though he was forcing himself to concentrate. When he opened his eyes a determined smile accompanied an expression which had grown intense and purposeful. "I have been waiting for you, Alexandra," he said langourously.

Was he lying, telling a whisker? She couldn't know for certain, especially since his voice had a mesmerizing quality which increased the strangeness of the encounter along with her sense that he was both real, yet not real.

He continued, "I have found you, it is you I want, and you I mean to take back to Olympus with me. Come." His wings were still folded tightly about her and she felt her feet leave the floor of her bedchamber. She knew he was lifting her up and that he meant to steal her from Roselands. Why was it she didn't care that he was taking her from hearth and home?

She closed her eyes, ready and willing to go with him, but a moment later, something had changed. She felt his entire being quiver strangely.

She opened her eyes and saw that he was looking up at the ceiling. "Excellent," he murmured. "It has begun, just as Mama said it would."

He looked back at Alexandra and smiled with deep satisfaction. "We won't be able to leave just yet and if I know my mother's abilities, I shall have a full ten days with which to persuade you to wed me."

"But I will go with you now," she breathed, leaning into him. How was it she was being so brazen with the winged god?

"Eager, are you? Well, we shall see." With that, he placed a full kiss on her lips at the same time returning her to the floor.

When her feet touched the patterned Aubusson carpet she felt his wings release her and a moment later he simply vanished.

"Anteros!" she called after him, feeling inexplicably desolate that he had left her. But he was gone, and in his stead, a low, heavy vibration had begun to fill the chamber.

Fear bolted through her. She backed away from the center of the room, toward the corner of her bedchamber and slipped into the space between the wall and her wardrobe of carved oak. "Oh, dear God, what is happening?" she cried aloud. She pressed her hand to her mouth as the vibrations increased.

A blue light suddenly filled the room, turning the scarlet and golds of her bedchamber to an exquisite violet and green. The light became increasingly bright, brightest near the ceiling, so much so that she had to look away from it in order not to be blinded.

Just as suddenly as the light had appeared, a beautiful, young woman flowed quickly through the funnel of light. Her head was thrown back and her mouth was agape as though she was in terrible pain.

When she was six feet from the floor, the blue light disappeared, sounds of pain emerged from her mouth and she fell, landing on her right leg first to fall with a heavy thud to the floor, lying unconscious on her side.

For a long, long moment, Alexandra stared at the young woman who looked familiar to her. Slowly she emerged from the space by the wardrobe and approached the delicate being. After only a minute of scrutinizing her, Alexandra recognized the young wife of the god of love—Psyche.

Tears filled her eyes at the sight of the injured mortal, a woman who had become immortal because of her marriage to Cupid.

Wary of the area which had held the blue light, she gave a wide berth to the now-absent funnel which had appeared in nearly the center of the chamber. She dropped beside the pretty woman and took up her hand. "My dear Psyche," she murmured. "Poor Butterfly. Please don't die. I beg you will not die." She patted her hand and stroked her forearm. "Wake up, I pray you."

For several minutes she spoke softly to her, patting her hand, stroking her cheek and forehead, willing her to survive her painful journey from Olympus.

Finally, as though responding to Alexandra's commands, Psyche's eyes fluttered open and she drew in a deep breath, almost as though she was taking in life for the first time.

"Where am I?" she asked, lifting a hand to touch her left temple. "My head aches abominably. What has happened to me? Where am I?" She looked about her. "How strange this chamber appears. So many little objects everywhere!" Her eyes shifted to look into Alexandra's face. "Who are you?"

"Poor Butterfly," she responded quietly. "You are in my home and it would appear that your journey from Olympus was quite painful. I am Lady Alexandra Staple. And I know who you are—you are Psyche, aren't you, wife of Eros?"

"Yes," Psyche nodded, wincing, drawing her hand from Alexandra's gentle grasp and holding her head, still wincing. "I am remembering the journey. I have never known such torture. But I am feeling better and better." She remained lying quietly on the floor, breathing deeply. Alexandra did not want to disturb her by either speaking or moving so she remained where she was trusting that in a few minutes Psyche would be acclimated to her new location in Cornwall.

Alexandra did not have long to wait. "So you are Alexandra," she said, letting one of her hands drape over her side as she turned slightly to look up at her. "Am I correct in believing you have two sisters, Julia and Victoria?"

Alexandra nodded.

"Then Evanthea Swanbourne, who married the Marquis of Brandreth, is your mother and the marquis is your father?"

Again Alexandra nodded. Lady Elle had once told her that Psyche had taken a particular interest in her father's courtship of her mother but until this moment she had believed that her great-great aunt had fabricated the story as part and parcel of her insanity. Now she did not know what to think. After all, when she had mentioned the story to her mother, Lady Brandreth had laughed aloud, saying it was all nonsense and merely the strange workings of Lady Elle's addled mind.

Psyche continued. "How clever of the oracle to have known where you were. But dear Zeus, my whole body aches as though a thousand minotaurs have trampled over me."

She sat up, wincing in some pain, and grabbed at her right leg. "Oh, no," she whimpered. "Something is wrong with my leg, my ankle, I think."

Alexandra looked down at Psyche's legs. Her long white gown, fitted snugly to her small waist by thin, overlapping bands of gold, fell just to her ankles. She could see that Psyche's right ankle was already beginning to swell.

"When you entered my bedchamber, you fell very hard on your right leg before tumbling unconscious to the floor."

Psyche appeared as though she would start to cry at any moment. "What a disaster," she moaned. "I was supposed to be of help to you, to protect you, and now I've bungled it before I've even begun."

Alexandra wondered if Psyche was referring to Anteros's recent arrival at Roselands and his insistence that he meant to take her back to Olympus with him. Come to think of it, now that he was gone from her bedchamber she was shocked by the knowledge that had Psyche not arrived when she did she might even now be gone forever from Cornwall and residing with Anteros as he wished.

"You refer to Anteros, don't you?"

"Then he is here?"

"Yes, and—and he has kissed me and, and insisted he means to make me his wife."

"That is what I was told and that is why I am here to keep him from doing as much. He has some powers and certainly when he kisses and touches you I daresay you will feel compelled to oblige him, but you can't." She then groaned and began rocking forward.

"Oh, dear," Alexandra murmured. "We must make you more comfortable. I suffered a similar injury when I was but eleven. I fell from a horse and bruised my ankle. Unless it is broken—which I trust it is not—there is only one treatment for your injury. You must rest your leg."

"I haven't got time," Psyche wailed, tears now trickling down her cheeks unchecked. "Little more than a sennight and then I must return to Olympus or I will be trapped here forever. You see, Zeus made it quite impossible for any of us who were not deities to come to earth. He kicked up such a dust about my last adventure—when I was helping your mama—that only if a deity allows you to pay a visit to earth, are you permitted to come, and then the duration of the visit is limited severely. In my case, whoever it was that ordered my journey—though I am beginning to suspect it was my mama-in-law—has given me only ten days, after which time I must return to Olympus at a strictly appointed hour or I shall be consigned to live out the remainder of my days here."

"You were told to come here?" she asked.

At that, Psyche looked up at her and met her gaze squarely. She opened her mouth to speak then apparently thought the better of whatever it was she meant to say. "Not precisely—that is, the whole of my journey was so odd that I'm at sixes and sevens."

"You took a very bad fall. It is no wonder you are confused. Can you slip your arm about my neck? I'm very strong. I'm certain I could support you to my bed."

Psyche agreed and with a few minutes' effort, as Alexandra supported her about the shoulders, the young woman was reclining on Alexandra's half-tester bed.

Moving to the foot of the bed, Alexandra lifted the lid of the chest situated there. From within the chest she withdrew a pillow encased in white linen which was embroidered with golden autumn leaves. With great care, she placed the pillow beneath Psyche's knee and lower leg in support of her ankle. Psyche bore the discomfort well, emitting only a small gasp when she eased the ankle onto the pillow. Taking great care, she removed Psyche's pretty gold velvet sandals which were strapped in thin bands up to her knee. As she slipped the second sandal from her small delicate foot, she noted not without a smile that tiny seashells had been painted on each of Psyche's toenails.

"Did you do these?" she queried, leaning down to peer more closely at them. "They are quite beautiful and marvelously detailed."

"Yes," Psyche said. "Silly, aren't they? I spent an entire afternoon working laboriously on them and nearly breaking my back by being bent at the waist so awkwardly, but what do you think my husband said when I showed them to him?"

Alexandra held her sandals in one hand as she stood beside the bed and looked down at Psyche. Already smiling in amusement, she shook her head waiting to hear what Butterfly would tell her.

In mock seriousness, Psyche lowered her voice in evident imitation of her husband. "Very clever," she said, "but let me tell you of more important matters. Vulcan has a new method of forging my arrows. You see, he sends the Cyclops to the nearest volcano where they set up his workshop. Then with the heat of the volcano, he melts the gold, forms my arrows to perfection and there you have it—the finest arrows ever. Even Artemis was all agog when I showed her his latest efforts. She again begged me to give her one of them but I of course refused. She never could abide Vulcan, you see, so he will not forge even a single arrow for her! Hah!"

Alexandra laughed, feeling inordinately comfortable with her unexpected guest. "He sounds like every man I've ever known. But then, they never do really understand how it is we both try to please them and at the same time long for their approbation."

"We are slaves to our hearts," Psyche returned with a smile, mocking herself in the gentlest manner. She searched Alexandra's features, one by one, then said, "You don't look a great deal like your mother or like Brandreth."

"I have been told as much often and often. But tell me, you

are clearly acquainted with my parents and so I can only suppose that what Lady Elle told me was true—that you were indeed involved in bringing them together. Why is it then that neither of them have the least recollection of you?"

"How very odd! They should remember me—oh, of course, now I remember what happened. Zeus thought it best that they not be permitted to keep their memories of me and of my husband and of everything that happened some twenty or more years ago."

"But what of Lady Elle's memories?" Alexandra asked, looking down at Psyche with a frown. "It was she who told me of you and of all that happened."

Psyche pondered this question then shook her head. "I can't account for it, unless Zeus forgot about her. He is not without imperfections and an occasional lapse of memory, let me tell you!" She then looked away from Alexandra and smiled faintly. "He is like a father to me. I adore him. I only wonder what he will say when he learns I am here."

Alexandra crossed the room to the table beside her wardrobe upon which sat a pitcher of water and a gleaming white ceramic bowl. She poured the water into the bowl, then dipped a linen cloth into the water. Wringing it out carefully, she returned to the bed. "I was used to think I was going mad," she said, smiling shyly down at the young woman whose gentle spirit had somehow created an aura of friendship and warmth which both surprised and pleased Alexandra. "You see, when I was a little girl, I used to sit with Lady Elle and listen to her stories of Olympus." She laid the cloth on Psyche's swelling ankle and since the room was cold, increasingly so because the night was falling and the rain was still drenching the surrounding hills, she spread a knitted afghan of scarlet and royal blue wool, over her legs.

"Thank you," Psyche said. "I knew Lady Elle," she added, a reminiscent light in her blue eyes. "She had quite a spirit, as I recall, full of fire and great warmth. I would have doted on such a woman had she been my great-aunt or my grandmama. When did she pass away?"

Alexandra shook her head. "Some thirteen years ago, when I was but ten. She used to have many visions of you and Cupid, of his brother, of their mama, and many other residents of Olympus. I shared in some of them, which she bid me keep secret from Mama and Papa, only apparently her visions weren't so secret after all since about a year after she died, Mama was telling me that poor Lady Elle was as mad as Bedlam for she spoke of the gods and goddesses of ancient Rome and of Greece as though she could actually see them. I was so shocked to learn that mother's opinion was that dear Lady Elle was mad, that I began to doubt my own sanity. Since with her passing, however, I no longer saw the visions, I soon came to believe that I had been experiencing some sort of curious phenomenon attendant to my childhood. You see, I didn't want to believe I had Lady Elle's *illness,* so I convinced myself that I had been humoring her all that time, pretending to see what I had not seen. That is, until recently."

"Anteros?" Psyche queried, a soft frown between her brows.

"Yes," Alexandra breathed with a sigh of relief as she drew a chair forward and sat down beside the bed. "Oh, Psyche, I had indeed thought I was going mad! You cannot imagine how grateful I am to learn that I am not and that the visions were very real, that you are real and that *he* is real!"

"You can't leave England, Alexandra. It is most important that you remain here. Anteros simply cannot be permitted to take you back to Olympus. Only now that I am injured, I do not know how we can stop him from doing so."

"I don't understand," Alexandra said, shaking her head slowly and trying to comprehend all that was happening to her. "Why does he want *me* and though I certainly have no interest in going to Olympus since my life is here with my family, why do you insist that it is of the utmost importance that I remain in England?"

Psyche appeared to give great consideration to Alexandra's pressing questions. "I can only tell you that the oracle has indicated that your presence in history is most critical. The reasons given are vague, only that the future would be affected in so harsh a manner, that the complex, tapestried threads of your society would be unraveled."

"I am to have such an influence?" she asked, dumbfounded.

Psyche tilted her head and responded, "Do you know what I think? I am come to believe that every mortal has a unique place in history, a task to fulfill, a thread to contribute to the whole of life. For Anteros to try to steal you, or anyone, from earth when it has not been permitted by Zeus, is to court disaster. So, though I cannot give you anything larger than a firm belief you—or any other mortal—must remain and see to your own destiny, I hope with all my heart that you will strive with every ounce of the strength you possess, to keep from falling into Anteros's snare."

At the end of Psyche's impassioned plea, Alexandra experienced a sense of foreboding and of wonder so powerful that she knew in the deepest places of her heart that Psyche was speaking a great truth to her. So potent was the sensation that she felt herself changed, as though she had been awakened from a sleepy state to which she would never again return.

Alexandra recalled suddenly the mesmerizing kiss Anteros had placed on her lips, how he had borne her into the air. "I would have gone with him!" she cried aloud, blinking several times before addressing Psyche. "He was just about to transport me away, when you fell from the air. Oh, dear! It only now occurs to me that he must have put me under some sort of spell because I vow I would have gone with him like a lamb to the slaughter."

"Oh, dear," Psyche returned, biting her lip. "It would seem, as your mother was used to say, *we are in the basket.*"

"Indeed, so it would seem."

Five

Cupid heard the puppies crying from within Psyche's painting room and sensed that something was amiss. He had returned from Vulcan's workshop only a few minutes earlier bearing seven new arrows of finely cast gold, only to find his house dark and deserted.

Night had settled into the misty corners of Olympus. An owl hooted in the distance. Overhead the stars were gathered in a thick, milky band across the sky.

How empty his house felt, strangely so. Empty and forlorn, as though even the walls were grieving the absence of their mistress. He shifted the arrows in his hand, letting the sleek, round shafts ripple over the soft curves of his palm. Over and over he let the arrows slide, thinking, pondering, evaluating the meaning of the sensations which continued to flow over him.

Where was Psyche? Wherever she went, she must have left suddenly and sometime past because even her handmaids had retired to their separate living quarters at the far edge of his estate and she had left her puppies all alone. He walked into her painting room and stared at the portrait of the pups. He drew in a sharp breath. There was so much of life in her art. The puppies which stared back at him from the canvas were as real as the ones now yipping at him from their basket.

He crossed the chamber to pat each one on the head, looking down at them with a frown. "Where is your mama?" he queried softly. A pink tongue licked at his fingers. "Hungry, are you? Well, we'll have to see to you right away then." As he rose, he lifted the wheat-colored wicker basket by the handles on each end and carried the puppies toward the nether regions. Two of them tried to stand and were knocked over by the jostling movement of the basket as he moved toward the back stairs.

Over the past two thousand years he had frequently arrived at his home only to find Psyche gone for she had many acquaintances and was a devoted and loyal friend. The merest whisper of trouble was always enough to send his wife flying in support of those she loved. Her heart was as generous as any he had ever known which was why he loved her as he did. Neither the stars nor the sun held the smallest glimmer of beauty without her presence in his life. He might be the god of love, but he rather thought that Psyche more fully expressed love than any other being in Olympus. She was unselfish, sympathetic to a fault, and would perish rather than permit someone she loved to continue in pain and distress.

A sword of fear sliced through his chest. Without being able to explain to himself why, he suddenly sensed he was in great danger of losing that which he loved most.

Just as he began his descent into the kitchen to feed the puppies, he heard a sudden and profound fluttering of hundreds of small wings—the wings of doves, if he was not mistaken.

"Good," he said aloud which caused the pups ears to snap to attention. Perhaps his mother would know of his wife's whereabouts.

He quickly retraced the three steps he had descended and walked toward the terrace overlooking his vast estate.

When he stepped onto the pink-flagged terrace he found he was right. An exquisite chariot, drawn by a flock of doves, was resting on the wide terrace which overlooked the pride of Psyche's hand, her magnificent gardens, pools, stone walks, and orchards, all of which climbed the gentle hill behind his home. The smell of orange blossoms, which bloomed during every season in Olympus, was heavily in the air.

"Mother," he called to the woman descending her chariot in

full balldress. "I wasn't expecting you tonight! But how lovely you are! Is that a new gown?"

"Yes," she breathed, her voice a melodious refrain which echoed on the soft, warm breeze that surrounded her as she moved.

He tilted his head slightly as he surveyed both her countenance and the beauty of the diaphanous gown of a shimmering tullelike fabric carefully arranged in a series of folds over a clinging gown of silver and gold silk. In her hair were crystals which glowed with a light all their own and reflected the beauty of her eyes. He could not remember seeing her happier in literally centuries. Her complexion fairly glowed, her eyes shone with an excitement he wondered if he had ever before witnessed, and her deportment was as though she was floating instead of walking.

He set the basket of puppies down on the terrace and possessed himself of one of her hands. Giving it a squeeze, he teased her, "Have you recaptured Ares's fancy at last, Mama?"

She lifted surprised brows. "Whatever do you mean? You know very well I gave up chasing *that god* a long time ago."

"If you have not succeeded then, in some object of yours, to own the truth, I can't begin to account for the glow upon your fair features!" he returned, smiling fondly down on his parent.

She seemed a little taken aback. "I—well, that is—I can't begin to imagine to what you are referring, dearest one."

"I refer only to your great beauty and to the happiness I see evident on your lovely face. My heart is warmed at the sight of your contentment."

Venus pressed her son's hand. "You were always such a good boy, my darling Cupid."

"And you are a most excellent mother," he responded, exceedingly gratified that after so many years he could honestly offer her such a compliment.

In recent years, ever since Psyche's last adventure on earth when his wife had *borrowed* Venus's magical Cestus and two of her love potions, his mother had been both kinder to Psyche and a more devoted parent generally. She had even stopped trying to trick Psyche into visiting the Underworld from which place once she crossed into the land of the dead, she could never return. It would seem she had accepted his wife at last and had even given hints that were they to become parents in their own right, she would most happily accept the role as Grandmama.

Really, if he weren't concerned for Psyche's absence from his home, he would have every reason to be in this moment a very contented man.

"What do you have there?" she asked, releasing his hand and gesturing to the pups who had again set up a hungry whine.

He smiled fondly down on their white little heads. They were staring up at him and at his mother, yipping and whining, impatient to be fed. "Psyche has wanted them forever so I took a brief journey to England three weeks ago, with Zeus's permission of course, and found them for her. Needless to say, she was *aux anges* when I presented them to her."

"Yes, of course. Now that you mention it I do seem to recall her having mentioned them the last time I spoke with her which was nearly a fortnight ago, though at the time I did not believe she meant you had given her real little beasts. I thought perhaps some fine little china figurines from the Japannes. Remarkable!"

"No, real pups, I'm 'fraid."

Aphrodite's disapprobation was clear. She lifted her brows and shrugged her shoulders. "Well, you know I have no interest in dogs though I imagine Artemis will want to have a look at them, being a huntress of some merit. Eventually I daresay you'll want to get rid of them all."

"Why would I want to do that?" he asked, startled by the nature of her question. "These pups belong to Psyche, not to me. I wouldn't dream of giving them away."

"No, no, of course not," she said hastily. "I don't know what I was thinking. But as for why I've come this evening, I had hoped you might be able to tear yourself away from your little cottage and the attentions of your wife—just for one night—to escort me to Jupiter's palace? He is giving a ball in my honor—yes, Papa and I are no longer at war—and I had hoped—"

"Ordinarily, I would have happily agreed to your request, but something has come up and I'm not certain what I ought to do next. You see, Psyche is gone."

"Your wife is gone?" she queried, opening her eyes wide and batting her lashes in what struck him as a peculiarly false manner. "Whatever do you mean, gone?"

He frowned at her, wondering if she had something to do with his wife's odd absence from his home. But this seemed unlikely given her more recent peaceableness. "When I arrived home a few minutes ago, the house was dark, the pups were crying and Psyche was nowhere to be found. I can only assume she's been gone for some time, inexplicably so. You can see as much by the state of her pups."

Venus glanced at the basket again and flared her nostrils slightly. "I suppose you must be right. Well, what does that matter? She is probably gone to Mercury's palace or some such nonsense. Though why she dotes on that ridiculous fellow I shall never know. At any rate, I'm sure she'll return while you're dressing for the ball. Oh, do say you'll accompany me, my darling boy! Please, it would mean a great deal to me and I am certain you make too much of her absence. Indeed, I am fully persuaded of it!" She drew near him and lifted a hand to pat his cheek. "I've missed you dreadfully of late. You can ride in my chariot and we can reminisce about the past, when you were a child and Anteros used to chase you about the gardens trying to hit you with a stick."

Eros looked down into her beseeching eyes, beautiful eyes which changed color with her moods, or the angle of the sun, or the twinkling of the stars. He loved her very much, he always would. She was his mother.

"Besides," she pressed him, "it is very likely that someone at the ball will know of her present whereabouts."

Cupid realized this much at least would be true. Zeus's fetes were always well-attended and if enough of Bacchus's wine was imbibed and a sufficient number of tongues were loosened, and if some mischief was rife, he would undoubtedly learn what he needed to know by attending the ball. For that reason he agreed to go with her.

She clapped her hands and bid him hurry. He immediately took the pups to the nether regions. He fed them and saw them settled in a contented, jumbled heap in their basket. On a scroll by the large oven, he left word for Cook to care for them until either he or Psyche returned.

A half hour later, he was by his mother's side in her chariot of pearl and burgundy velvet, the doves rising higher and higher in the air. As he glanced at his mother, he again vowed he had never seen her happier. Could he have assigned a reason for her contentment he would have supposed her to have tumbled in love, or to have recaptured an old love which was why he had teasingly pressed her about Mars. However, he usually knew of such events long before they became generally known—such was the role he played on Olympus. But he had not received such a premonition, nor had he heard so much as a mite of gossip regarding his mother's amorous adventures.

Really, her glow of happiness was a complete mystery to him.

"So is there nothing I can do?" Alexandra asked, her hands clasped tightly on her lap. She was still seated in a chair beside her bed, her gaze fixed worriedly upon Psyche's troubled brow. For the past hour they had been attempting to solve the truly puzzling dilemma of how Alexandra was to avoid falling into Anteros's snare. "Do you think he will succeed in working his wiles on my heart?"

Psyche shook her head. "If only I could have brought with me a vial of my mama-in-law's potion—a sort of antidote for love—then we would have no concern for his tricks."

"A potion?" she queried.

"Yes, it is an oil steeped in a secret recipe of herbs and flowers. Aphrodite also has one that encourages the heart. I believe she makes that potion exclusively from the oil of roses."

Alexandra gasped and touched her lips. "Does it smell sweetly of roses?" she asked, her glance darting to Psyche's beautiful blue eyes.

"Why, yes, it does—oh, dear—do not tell me—"

Alexandra nodded.

Psyche pursed her lips together. "Then it is as I suspected. They are in league together and I believe I am coming at last to understand their true intent." She sighed deeply and for a moment Alexandra thought her new friend might begin to cry. "Occasionally, I remember thinking that it was too good to be true—all of Aphrodite's professions of appreciation and love over the past two decades—and Anteros's as well. The pair of them were being so kind to me—" Alexandra watched Psyche's lip quiver. "They have both hated me, you see—Venus and Anteros. I suppose they are jealous that Cupid loves me. Oh, how stupid I have been, to have thought that somehow I had won them over!"

Alexandra watched two tears trickle from Psyche's heavily fringed lashes and roll down her cheeks. She could not keep from leaning forward and patting Psyche's hand. "Don't cry, " she said.

"I—I won't. I mustn't," Psyche responded, wiping her cheeks with the back of her hand. "We have enough difficulties for the present without my unhappiness encumbering our efforts. We must find some way of protecting you from Anteros." She fell silent apace and after a moment continued, "I know that regardless of all the love potions Aphrodite or Anteros might employ, or even Cupid's arrows, should they fly awry, that the strongest antidote for a false love is a real love. Is there someone you love, Alexandra?"

Alexandra opened her mouth to speak, then closed it, her thoughts turning abruptly inward. She knew she had never truly been in love, ever, though she did have quite a strong fondness for Mylor Grampound who had been her friend since her first season some five years prior. "I won't pretend that I have known love, for I haven't, but there is someone who has held a special place in my life for a long time."

"Lord Launceston," Psyche announced firmly, a smile easing the trouble from her face. "You don't need to tell me for the oracle already has, that is—why, what is it? Why do you appear so horrified?"

"Because—because, for one thing I am surprised that the oracle would even know of my doings, or of Launceston, but beyond that, truly I don't love him at all. In fact, I rather despise him. He is a cretin of the meanest order!" She drew in a deep breath and shifted her gaze to stare at the smallest puff of dust which had crawled from beneath the bed and now sat at the base of her scarlet velvet bedskirt.

Imagine Psyche supposing she was in love with Lord Launceston! Of all the absurdities!

She could barely tolerate the thought of such a sentiment. Yet how quickly her mind ranged backward until she was once again in Stithwell, standing on the sidewalk with Launceston, his hand gripping her arm, as she looked into flaming hazel eyes.

The force of his thoughts, of his will, had surrounded her in that moment and her whole body had tingled with warmth and something akin to excitement. When he had held her arm so tightly, she had believed he had wanted to kiss her—a punishment perhaps—and for the barest moment she had wanted him to do so, but for the life of her she couldn't imagine why.

His cutting words came back to her, reminding her of why she despised him as she did, *Just once I would like to see you come down off your high ropes and be a woman with kindness on her tongue and in her heart.*

How completely wrong he was about her, for she was just such a woman. His error was in thinking he deserved her to be kind to him. In her opinion, he deserved no such tenderness for he was thoughtless and cruel and led the hearts of innocent ladies astray whenever it so pleased his vanity to misuse the fairer sex.

Why then did the mere mention of his name distress her so? Why did the memory of his kisses of last summer haunt her with the power of the most fiendish nightmare? Why had his presence during the past London season cut up her peace and robbed her of her tranquillity? And why had the oracle, *the oracle,* joined her name to his?

She could make no sense of it, all she knew was that she was not in love with him, nor would she ever be.

"I can see that I have overset you," Psyche interrupted gently. "I did not intend to and I also apprehend that you dislike Launceston beyond words—almost as much as your mother despised your father before she came to love him, but of course that was an entirely different situation."

"You can't possibly mean to compare the two!" Alexandra exclaimed indignantly.

"Of course not," Psyche assured her hastily. She then opened her mouth to speak, then closed it and shook her head.

"What is it?"

"I don't know—I'm not sure," she answered. "I think I am merely confused as to why the oracle would speak of you and Launceston as though you were destined—a circumstance which I now see is quite absurd given your distaste for the man—but I begin to wonder, would it be possible for you at least to make use of him, to pretend you are in love with him, in order to withstand Anteros's assaults? Do you think, in other words, that if you were able to set aside your disgust of this man, it would be possible for you to get up a flirtation with him?"

For some reason the notion which Psyche was presenting to Alexandra caused her cheeks to grow quite warm, not less so than because she rather suspected a flirtation with Launceston was precisely what such a man would want from her. "I believe so," she answered at last.

Psyche's entire face relaxed into a smile. "Excellent. Well, this is the most hopeful I have felt since I fell from your ceiling some few minutes ago, and invaded your life. Now, there is one other matter of extreme importance I feel I must put to you. Pray, can you tell me where I might find Castle Porth? You see, the oracle has dictated that on All Hallow's Eve, I must be at the chapel ruins, precisely at midnight, in order to travel back through the portal to Olympus."

Alexandra could only stare at her. She blinked several times. It was obvious to her that Psyche did not know that Launceston was the owner of the castle. "How very curious," she murmured.

"How is that, my dear?"

"Well, you have suggested to me that the oracle believes Launceston and I are somehow connected, do I have the right of it?"

"Most assuredly."

"And the oracle stated specifically that you were to find the portal in the chapel ruins of Castle Porth."

"Precisely."

"I find this most amazing—truly, I do. Launceston, only very recently, acquired Castle Porth."

"Indeed!" Psyche cried, her blue eyes widening. "But where is this castle? I sincerely hope that given my injury it is not too far distant."

Alexandra could only laugh. "Not by half. A mile only, at the top of the hill yonder. Had night not fallen and were it not still raining, you could see Launceston's home from my bedchamber window."

"Well, then!" Psyche cried. "It would seem that the Fates have been at work beforehand. And what is the name of your home?"

"Roselands."

Psyche broke into a trill of laughter. "The flower of love!" she exclaimed. "What a delightful joke, I only wish Mercury was here to enjoy it with us! He is forever funning and would think it a perfect irony that Anteros has been here, plying you with Venus's oil of roses. I am glad to see you are smiling, Alexandra. Indeed, try not to take any of this too seriously. Yes, yes, I know that many important things are at stake, but I have lived in Olympus, among warring, sometimes petty gods and goddesses for so long, that this one thing I have learned—sometimes it is best to get over rough ground lightly."

"We have a similar expression," Alexandra responded. "And I shall endeavor to avail myself of its wisdom. For now, however, you must rest your ankle as much as possible so that you will be able to travel to Castle Porth on All Hallow's Eve. For myself, I can see I must call upon Lord Launceston tomorrow morning and somehow inveigle myself into his home."

"What?" Cupid cried, dumbfounded.

"Oh, by the Vehemence of the Furies, I thought you knew?" Diana, the huntress, stared back at Cupid with eyes liquid and satiated. She was clearly drinking in his astonishment with as much pleasure as if she had tasted of Bacchus's most famous wines.

"But how? When? How did you find out?"

"Merk is in his cups again, of course. I daresay within the hour the whole of the assemblage will know of your wife's departure and of your mother's part in it."

"You are a wretched gossip, Artemis, but for once I am grateful you told me what was going forward before it was too late."

She took a step toward him. "You are indebted to me, then?" she queried, the veiled look in her eyes a hint. She was a tall woman and almost met his eyes at his level. Her blond hair was sun-streaked since she rarely passed her days within doors and faint lines fanned out from the corners of her dark brown eyes.

Diana, twin brother of Apollo, had only one true interest—the hunt—a fact visible in the curved strength of her arms, the lithe, athletic manner in which she moved, and the swell of her calves revealed by the short tunic she was wearing since she rarely donned the flowing gowns preferred by most of the goddesses.

Tonight was no exception. Her tunic of amber silk hung from unelaborate knots at her shoulders, was cinched at the waist by violet silk cording and the skirts of the tunic barely reached to her knees. As though having attempted to adorn herself in deference to her host and father, Zeus, she wore a narrow violet ribbon laced into her somewhat unruly chignon which was in turn held in place by a large, wooden comb. The comb, not surprisingly, was engraved with the head of a stag.

There was not an inch of feminine vanity in Artemis. If she had a fault it was her single-minded obsession with the hunt and ever since he could remember she had been trying to finagle one of his arrows from him. He lifted a brow and responded firmly to her original hint, "I owe no debt to a gabblemonger. You will have to do better than that to get an arrow from me."

Scowling at him, she stepped away and moved on.

His eyes quickly scanned the assemblage. To his right he saw his magnificent grandpapa and heard his roaring laughter as that deuced fellow, Mercury, told him some joke or other. The fête was a happy, successful one and as his gaze caught the glow of the crystals threaded through his mother's hair, his temper flared.

So it was all a sham, he thought angrily—her kindnesses toward Psyche all these years and more. Secretly she had been plotting to rid Olympus of his wife once and for all and by Pluto, this time she might just succeed.

As he began walking toward her, the crowd parted, giving way to him as he unfurled the breadth of his wings and divided the chamber in order to approach her without hindrance. With a small measure of satisfaction, he watched her pale beneath the fury of his gaze. If he had doubted Diana's gossipy morsel, he couldn't have any longer, not with the guilt he saw darkening her eyes. He remembered suddenly her cryptic words about how he would of course want to be rid of Psyche's pups and also that she seemed nervous when he begged her to account for her extreme happiness.

Dash-it-all! She was happy because his wife was gone!

Damn-and-blast!

When he reached her, he stood in front of her, his nostrils flaring, a filial reflection of the mother, as he glared at her. "How dare you harm my wife!" he accused her harshly, refusing to use even a modicum of restraint.

But Venus quickly recovered her guilt-laden countenance. She squared her shoulders and met him head on. "Your wife is no wife at all to you! Tell me, Cupid, why does she closet herself in that ridiculous chamber of hers, plying little brushes and pretending to create works of art when everyone is laughing at her behind her little back? To ignore you, of course. It is clear to everyone except you that Psyche does not and has never loved you. She is incapable of love or of any of the finer sentiments."

"Which you are?" he snorted sarcastically.

"I am," she stated with finality. "My love for you knows no bounds."

"You haven't got the smallest notion of what it is to love but I won't argue with you on that score, only tell me about the portal and my brother and tell me now."

She did not hesitate but spoke proudly of her schemes. "Anteros is in a little English hamlet called Stithwell, where Psyche now resides and where she has but ten days to see a mortal named Alexandra betrothed, if not married, to a nobleman by the name of Launceston."

"Up to your old tricks again I see, just like the time I brought my bride home and you gave her a dozen, impossible tasks to perform."

"Only three," Aphrodite countered smugly.

"Three or a hundred! You knew she could not succeed without help and you know as much now. Well, if you for one moment think I won't help her, you are grievously mistaken. I have an arrow or two that will see the job done to a nicety, or did you truly believe I would stand by and do nothing?"

"Do what you must," Venus returned impatiently. "But you are making a serious mistake. You are better off without her and if you will but search your heart you will know that I am

right. I will only add that she must return by means of the portal
in the chapel ruins of a castle called Porth, within the specified
ten days, or she will live out her life and die on earth as any
other mortal. You cannot bring her back yourself as you have
done in the past. As for the task she must accomplish, your
brother has vowed she will not succeed regardless of the help
she receives. He at least loves his Mama. Besides, Psyche will
herself fail to pass through the portal. In the end, she will permit
her love for her friends to take precedence over her avowed love
for you and then you will know precisely the true state of her
heart where you are concerned, oh foolish boy!"

Her expression was so triumphant that Eros saw her through
a darkening film of red and he understood familial murder in
that moment. About him, he felt the stunned press and silence
of Zeus's guests. He wanted to hurt her, to destroy her and by
Jupiter if anything happened to his beloved Psyche he wouldn't
be accountable for what he did to her.

For the present, however, his object was to find Psyche as
quickly as possible and for that reason he had only enough time
to enact a small piece of vengeance on his jealous mother. He
took her stiffly by the arm and with a veiled movement used
his free hand to withdraw a small dartlike arrow from a secret
pocket in his tunic. Without saying a word, he guided her toward
the entrance of Zeus's palace and led her to the guards—two
quite ferocious-looking and extraordinarily ugly centaurs who
were stonily standing watch, each hoof as still as a lake on a
windless day.

"What are you about, Cupid!" his mother cried. "I suppose
you mean to take this badly. But one day you'll thank me for
it. What you see in that female, I will never know. I have performed you a marvelous service—oh! What have you done?"

He had driven the arrow deeply into her side and once it
painlessly pierced her flesh, it simply vanished. At the same
time, he turned her to look at the uglier of the two guards. The
centaur barely shifted his gaze toward Cupid, his black eyes

questioning, the thick brown fur along the back of his coat bristling with anxiety. "Guard, may I present my mother to you?"

"Of course, my lord," the centaur responded respectfully, if nervously, as he inclined his head to the famous beauty.

Cupid then stepped away from his mother, gave a single, strong flap of his wings and flew into the air. One backward glance told him he had succeeded in his efforts, for Aphrodite was already sliding her hand along the length of the guard's back and leaning her head lovingly against his furry shoulder. His arrow had performed its function to a nicety. In addition, the curious citizens of Olympus had begun to pour from Zeus's palace and as he rose higher and higher in the air, the laughter of Jupiter's guests reached his ears.

His mother in love with a centaur. Well, that would bring her down a peg or two!

Cupid finally reached Stithwell long past midnight having taken the time to consult the oracle at Dodona before setting out on his search for Psyche. What he learned was the present whereabouts of his wife—she would be found in a large manor house called Roselands, sharing a bedchamber with Lady Alexandra. He had wanted to know more—for instance, the location of Roselands—but the oracle was not forthcoming. He therefore spent the better part of two hours upon his arrival at Stithwell searching for the manor house.

He had found a charming little house near the ocean which had been landscaped over several acres, with an astonishing rose garden. How his dear Psyche would have enjoyed the sight of such a garden! But once inside this dwelling, neither Psyche nor Alexandra were to be found, only a tall man who was dressed in a dark blue brocade dressing gown and who sat in a winged chair reading the romantic poetry of Lord Byron.

He moved on quickly, travelling eastward from the man's house and encountered a valley in which was situated a rather dilapidated castle on a hill which in turn had an impressive view of a beautiful manor house. Roselands. He was sure of it, especially since Stithwell was so nearby.

He went first to the castle and a brief examination of the ruined portion of the dwelling revealed to his satisfaction that the crumbled stones had at one time been a chapel and therefore must be the ruins to which his mother had referred.

A moment later, he was flying toward the manor house.

Cupid finally found his wife snuggled cozily in a large, half-tester bed, a mob cap over her pretty brown curls and warm covers tucked beneath her chin. She shared the wide bed with another female who he supposed was Lady Alexandra. He looked at Alexandra now, surprised that her beauty almost equaled his wife's, though he was quick to see that her expression was troubled as though she was attempting to solve a most pressing concern.

He again looked at his wife and was preparing to awaken her, when his common sense prevented him. Where would he take her? Not back to Olympus, she could only return through the portal. Better to let her sleep and to speak with her on the morrow about how she planned to help Alexandra.

How small and fragile she appeared as he watched her, his heart beginning to flow with love for her. He couldn't bear the thought that she might fail in her mission and miss passing through the portal at the appointed hour. He loved her so very much, more than his mother would ever comprehend. Faith, but he would do anything to ensure her safe return to Olympus. Anything.

She would need his help, of that he was convinced. The task before her was nearly as impossible as the first trials Aphrodite had ever placed on his wife's mortal shoulders—the separating of grains, the gathering of golden fleece from murderous rams, the errand to fetch a little of Persephone's beauty from the Underworld. These tasks had nearly separated him forever from Psyche even then. But he had helped her and others had helped her as well, for she was beloved in Olympus.

If he needed to, he would ask Mercury to help him, but for the present he felt confident he could manage whatever was required. For one thing he had his trusted and potent arrows with him. If Psyche's efforts failed in the coming ten days, he could simply transport Alexandra to Castle Porth, shoot both Launceston and Alexandra each with an arrow, and see that a clergyman married them before the spell of his arrows had a chance to weaken.

His gaze again drifted to Alexandra who he scrutinized carefully. He noted again the worry on her brow, and the way she clutched the bedcovers up to her chin. He dipped his mind into hers for a brief moment and learned of the nature of her distress, that she was a creature torn into two parts—one longing to be loved, the other unwilling to be loved.

In that moment of revelation, understanding filled him. He was not here to act hastily or with a conviction that the sole design for the current situation was to entrap Psyche to earth. For some reason, the heavens were concerned for this woman. She needed not just the firing off of one of his arrows, but the sympathetic encouragement of a loving heart—Psyche's heart.

In the long years he had lived as an immortal on Olympus, he had learned that sometimes the events which were instigated by a deity caught up in the throes of jealousy and vengeance, frequently carried beneath that act a necessary lesson for those involved. This much he had learned from Zeus which was why, he supposed, that his grandpapa had not involved himself in his quarrel with his mother earlier. On some level, Zeus must be aware of all that was going forward—and he had permitted events to unfold however they would.

Grateful at least that there was a sense of sublime purpose and meaning in his wife's presence at Roselands, he bent over her head, kissed her softly on her cheek then quickly disappeared in the direction of Castle Porth. He had only one present aim, to discover Anteros's whereabouts and to watch him closely.

Six

"They are all so pretty!" Psyche exclaimed. She was sitting up in bed, her lower leg and ankle still supported by a pillow. Together she and Alexandra were attempting to decide just how she ought to be gowned when she paid her morning call upon Lord Launceston.

"But I fear none of these will do," Alexandra sighed. "Summer is gone. Besides, not one of my gowns is sufficiently, er, provocative for a man of Launceston's stamp!"

Psyche shook her head and giggled. "Men are so predictable, aren't they?"

Alexandra met her friend's gaze and both ladies burst out laughing.

After having slept fitfully, Alexandra had awakened with a start as a scheme for settling her difficulties seemed to have presented itself in those last few moments before waking. She had been caught in a vivid dream in which she had been waltzing with Launceston and of course brangling with him. He had been telling her that her gown of forest green silk, fashioned in the Empire style, did not belong in his ballroom. She had argued that of course it did since his ball was a masquerade.

When she awoke, she knew precisely what she needed to do—to somehow persuade his lordship to give a masquerade ball on All Hallow's Eve. In doing so, she could offer to manage the details of the fête which would provide her with just the opportunity she needed to escape Anteros's advances. At the same time, the masquerade would provide a secretive cloak for

Psyche. She could come to the castle, without much hindrance in the face of so much activity, in order to effect her return to Olympus through the portal at midnight.

But how to persuade Launceston—that was the rub.

When she had explained her purpose to Psyche, the beautiful immortal had blinked her eyes once then exclaimed that such a masquerade would suit their requirements to perfection. "You will be so frequently in his company that Anteros will not be able to steal you away. But do you think Lord Launceston will agree to a ball?"

"I know him well," she had responded. "He delights in flirting with the ladies of his acquaintance, particularly if they are gowned to his liking."

It was at this point that Alexandra had drawn her best morning gowns from her wardrobe, all from the summer past, and laid them out on the bed for Psyche's inspection.

As she looked at them now, she shook her head as did Psyche. None of them would suffice, it seemed.

Out of doors, the day was cool, the heat of the summer long gone, the grass of the lawn pale green and shimmering from a morning frost. Late October was that curious time of year when the season seemed to change all at once, the cold air of an approaching winter seeped beneath the window sills, down through the chimneys, even through the small pores of the granite which formed the outer, Elizabethan shell of Roselands.

Alexandra therefore couldn't pay a call on Lord Launceston in any of her exquisite summery gowns—not her most charming, tight-waisted morning gown of cherry and white striped silk even though the little red coat particularly enhanced the deep shade of her lips and the richness of her black hair. Nor could she wear the light blue silk gown draped with fine Brussels lace. Nor the apricot muslin which moved over her five petticoats like the wind over a lake. No, summer was gone and autumn had entrenched itself in the countryside.

She also didn't think the acute modesty of these gowns would answer her purposes either. Each was made high to the neck as becoming a Young Lady of Quality in the reign of Queen Victoria. An increasing modesty was becoming the order of her day though it had not always been so.

Her gaze was drawn to her dressing table. Above the table was a scattering of etchings, daguerreotypes, watercolors, and one small portrait of her parents the first year they were married. Her father was tall and handsome, his quite athletic figure enhanced by the costume of the day which included a coat of blue superfine tapering to a narrow waist. He wore breeches of a soft buckskin tucked into snug-fitting top boots. In effect, there wasn't a line of his body which was not exposed by the dashing clothes he was wearing, so very much in contrast to the men of her day who wore loose trousers and coats not nearly so well-fitting as her father's.

But it was to her mother that she turned her attention, for the gown she wore was almost ethereal, a lovely white muslin cut low across the bosom, caught up high under the waist and clinging to her pretty feminine figure in quite Grecian lines. Launceston would certainly have delighted in such a costume. Her brown hair was dressed in a knot atop her head and cascaded behind in a loose flow of curls. The effect was both innocent yet sensual.

She tried to imagine Lord Launceston dressed as her father was and herself as her mother was. She realized his lordship would appear to quite serious advantage in buckskin breeches and she quickly set aside the image since it was having an effect on her ability to breathe. In turn, how would she look? Certainly the flowing, Grecian style suited her height and she did have a reasonably pretty bosom so that undoubtedly an Empire gown would have given cause for Launceston to have approved of her appearance.

If only she could have worn such a gown today, then his lordship would be very much inclined to enter into her schemes—of that she was convinced.

She turned back to her wardrobe in which hung the gowns made up with an eye to winter. She pulled them out one at a time, then put them back, until she came upon a velvet confection of royal blue. The rich, vivid color would certainly enhance her eyes and with the clever skill of Lydia's needlecraft, the high cut of the gown could be lowered intriguingly within a few hours.

When she showed the gown to Psyche and suggested the alteration, Psyche approved heartily and the decision was put into immediate effect. Summoning her maid, she told Lydia what it was she wanted, all the while struggling to keep her embarrassment from overtaking her. Lydia opened her eyes wide, dropped a quick, startled curtsy and said she would see to it at once.

Four hours later, at the stroke of one, Alexandra descended the stairs to the front door, the family coach awaiting her. She had been hoping beyond hope that she would be able to leave the house without her family learning of her intention until after she was gone. But as fortune would have it, just as she stepped onto the black and white tiled entrance hall floor, her mother emerged from the drawing room, an open letter in hand and her eyes glowing.

"There you are, Alexandra. You will not credit it, but Annabelle will be able to visit us at Christmastide after all. Isn't this—wonderful news?" The smile fell from her mother's dark brown eyes and was replaced by astonishment. "I did not know you were going out." Her bespectacled gaze swept for only the barest second to the low cut of Alexandra's gown, before returning to her eyes. She blinked several times, pushed her spectacles up to the bridge of her nose and swallowed quite visibly.

"Y-yes," Alexandra stammered, drawing her gloves of yellow kid over trembling fingers and avoiding her mother's dumbfounded gaze. "I—I, that is, yesterday I brangled horridly with our new neighbor, Lord Launceston—"

"Victoria and Julia said you were fairly at daggers drawn."

Alexandra nodded, struggling to pull on her gloves. In her nervousness she had put her thumb into the same hole as her index finger. "I truly feel I owe him an apology and so I intend to go to the castle in order to, to offer him one immediately."

"Just as you should," Lady Brandreth returned with a frown between her brows. "And though I don't mean to delay your departure, or to question your choice of apparel—after all, you are well past your majority—but are you very certain your gown is of an appropriate—oh! Oh, goodness gracious! I hear your father coming! Perhaps it would be best if you hurried along, then." Before Alexandra knew what was happening, she felt her mother's hand at the small of her back, pushing her toward the front door.

"Th-thank you, Mama," Alexandra murmured, as she slipped through the doorway.

Evanthea Swanbourne Staple, Marchioness of Brandreth, leaned her back against the closed door, her gaze fixed to the black and white tiles in front of her. So many startled thoughts scurried through her mind that she did not know how to order them—what was the real reason Alexandra was going to Castle Porth, why was she so nervous, why was she wearing a most unsuitable yet devastatingly attractive gown, what mischief was brewing beneath her roof?

She did not know whether to feel frightened out of her wits or euphoric with joy. Dare she permit her motherly hopes for her daughter to rise to the skies!

"Evan?" a masculine voice called to her. "Why will you not answer me? You appear as though you've seen a ghost."

She lifted her gaze and found that her husband was standing directly in front of her and looking down on her with a worried frown in his gray eyes.

"Oh, my dear," she said softly. "I heard you down the hall— but I didn't see you, that is not until now and then here you are!"

He took her chin in hand. "You sound perfectly birdwitted, my darling. Whatever is the matter?"

His gaze was too penetrating, his mind too clever for her to attempt to dissimulate, so she didn't even try. "I haven't the faintest notion," she responded. "But your daughter, Alex—"

"Is that who ordered the carriage brought round?"

"Indeed, yes. Alexandra has gone out to pay a morning visit on our new neighbor."

"Launceston?" he queried with a surprised lift of his brows. Alexandra's dislike of him was well-known in his house. "Alone?"

Lady Brandreth sighed, and slipped her arm through his. "Come and have a glass of sherry with me, my dear," she said, drawing him toward the crimson drawing room to the left of the entrance hall. "She gave me some humbug about needing to apologize to him. But that wouldn't fadge. She's never apologized before when she's brangled with him."

"And she's certainly had cause before now."

"Precisely so. Brandreth, is it possible she's tumbled in love with him?"

"I hope not," was his less than encouraging reply.

"Why do you say that?"

"Because he's the devil of a reputation and very little is known of the fellow because he's been in India these many years and more."

"If Alexandra has taken a fancy to his lordship, do you truly believe we have cause to be worried?"

"Yes," was his flat, pointed reply. "Well, well. This is certainly an astonishing turn and it would seem I must call upon Launceston myself sooner than I had anticipated. Do you care to accompany me?"

Lady Brandreth felt her cheeks grow warm. "What, now?" she asked, startled. She was entirely unwilling for him to see Alexandra in the gown she had worn for her visit.

"Why not and why are your cheeks suddenly suffused with an adorable blush? Don't tell me Launceston has captured your fancy as well."

Lady Brandreth breathed a sigh of relief at the direction of his thoughts. "Well, he is dreadfully handsome," she stated, releasing his arm but turning into him at the same time.

"I don't hesitate to say that I take strong exception to that observation. Ought I to call the fellow out and be done with it?"

She shook her head. "He's *considerably* younger than you, Brandreth. I would fear the worst."

He scowled down at her. "You are in love with him, aren't you? He's stronger, handsomer, and by some reports, wealthier."

She slipped her arms about his waist and gazed lovingly into his face. "But there is one respect in which he is nothing to you, my darling. I'm sure of it."

"And in what respect is that, my love?" he queried tenderly. His expression softened and he leaned down as if to kiss her. She could not mistake the nature of his thoughts.

Lady Brandreth felt her lips twitch in spite of her desire to keep her expression steady. "You've a higher rank," she announced bluntly.

He gasped, drew back slightly and narrowed his eyes. "And I thought you were making such pretty love to me," he cried. "Vixen!"

She pulled away from him in a quick backward step and with a smile she meant to be a dare, set off on a run through the crimson drawing room. She gave a shriek when she heard him follow immediately after her. Her heart began pounding as the chase commenced. Her skirts, billowing over six petticoats, were so wide that she had some difficulty maneuvering through each crowdedly furnished chamber—first the crimson drawing room then an antechamber with velvet wallpaper and furniture in mixed hues of blues, reds, and gold, then a long dining room decorated en suite in gold upon gold. Next she passed into a long gallery but just as she reached the door leading into the morning room, she felt his hand upon her arm.

She was caught!

He took her up roughly in his arms and his lips crashed down on hers with a passionate force which robbed of her both her breath and her will to escape him again. Nothing was quite as comfortable as the manner in which her husband of four and twenty years would attack her, she thought with delight. If only she hadn't developed such an odd condition—well, she wouldn't think of *that* just now.

After a long moment, he released her, but kept her embraced in the safe circle of his arms. "How is it your beautiful brown hair is scarcely touched by the years? My darling wife, you are as lovely to me as the day—well, as the day I lost the race to Shalford—you were wearing a green silk bonnet trimmed with red cherries and a green silk carriage dress. Did I ever tell you I lost the race because I vow I had never seen anything quite so pretty in the whole of my life?"

"A hundred times, my love," she whispered, her heart warming to the sweetness of his adoration for her. After so many years, he was still as handsome as ever, though lines now crinkled beside his eyes when he smiled and his thick black hair was touched at the temples with a regal display of silver. He was an excellent husband, she wanted for nothing. Her only concern for the present was that each of her daughters might be as happy in their choice of husbands as she had been in hers.

Her thoughts drifted to Launceston and Alexandra's peculiar gown.

"Why are you frowning?" he asked. "Are you worried about our daughter?"

She nodded. "What—what if he breaks her heart?" she asked.

"Then I shall see him flogged," he responded with a smile.

"Do be serious," she said. "I don't want my darling daughter—or any of them—to be wounded by the callous indifference of a man bent on pursuit and nothing more."

"As I said before," he responded, "I most certainly shall further my acquaintance with Launceston to ensure his motives toward Alexandra. But beyond that, Cupid does not always order our hearts where we will. And if memory serves me correctly, you and I did not precisely have an easy beginning ourselves."

"No," Lady Brandreth responded slowly. "No, we didn't, did we—and see how well our marriage has progressed."

"Speaking of progressing, how would you like to progress up the stairs?" He drew her more tightly to him and kissed her neck just below the ear.

"What, now?" she queried. She then swallowed hard and pulled herself out of his arms, disliking immensely that she needed to turn aside his present desires in the face of her unexplained physical ailments. She didn't know what was wrong with her—and every day her peculiar symptoms seemed to be worsening, but until she knew what was afflicting her she believed it best to keep her husband at arm's length. "Really, I am quite busy today. The architect shall be here at three o'clock." She lifted the letter she still held in her hands, "Oh, and you will never credit it, but Annabelle and Shalford are coming to us in December."

"I am delighted, truly," he responded quietly, his brows drawn together in a deep frown. "Evanthea, though I don't mean to dismiss your enthusiasm over Annabelle's forthcoming visit, will you not tell me why you've refused my hints these past two weeks and more? It is not like you. Now why are you crying? I did not mean to make you cry. Only—only it seemed for a moment you wished for my advances."

"I am not crying," Lady Brandreth responded, sniffling and biting back her tears. "Only—that is. You must give me a little time. Of late, I have not been—*entirely well.*" There, she had said it. She had spoken her worst fears aloud.

"My darling!" Brandreth cried, placing his hand under her chin and lifting her face so that he might look into her eyes. "Whatever is wrong? Tell me, you must tell me!"

She quickly placed a hand on his chest. "It is nothing—I'm sure of it, only, for the time being if you would be so kind as to oblige me, to be patient—"

"But have you consulted with a doctor?"

She shook her head.

"Evanthea," he said. "You must let a physician examine you. Indeed, you must!"

Evanthea let the tears fall and she collapsed against his chest, her spectacles falling askew. She hadn't known how distressed she was over her strange ailment until she saw the concern in his eyes. "You are right," she said through her sobs, pulling her spectacles away from her face.

"I insist on sending for a doctor immediately."

"I will only see Dr. Newquay, if you please," she said, barely speaking above a whisper. "He is quite knowledgeable besides being kind and understanding."

"Then Dr. Newquay it shall be," he responded holding her tightly against him.

Alexandra heard the noise—a strange scraping sound—and didn't know what to make of it. She was tempted to rise from her place on one of two beautiful red sofas and search out the origination of the noise, but she thought it likely Launceston was even now on his way to greet her. Twenty minutes had passed since Cuthbert, the butler, had shown her quite decorously, into the great hall of Castle Porth.

Earlier, just as her carriage had pulled into the castle's horse-shoe-shaped court, Launceston had cantered his fine black gelding across the newly laid gravel to meet her. Scarcely an inch of him was not touched by mud since rain of the day and night before had soaked the lanes all about Stithwell. Both he and his black horse had stains up to their shoulders and Launceston even had a few speckles in his cheeks.

She had thought that his recent exercise had given a warmth to his smile and a brilliance to his eye which the ballrooms of London had never been able to achieve. He had expressed an almost suspicious delight in her arrival, had begged her to make herself comfortable in his principal receiving room and as soon as he could rid himself of as much mud as possible he would join her in the great hall.

So here she sat, somewhat stiffly since the nature of her errand was full of self-interest, hearing strange noises in the hallway beyond the great hall, her hands folded tightly on her lap and her nerves thinning with every second that passed.

She took a deep breath and glanced about the lofty chamber. The north wall, forming a principal granite wall of the castle's shell, housed three tall arched windows, each flanked with what she could see were new crimson velvet draperies, hung on brass rings on heavy poles, and tied back with thick, gold, tasseled cords. The windows overlooked a fine view—which she had examined three times since her arrival—of the distant rooftops of Stithwell visible beyond the low hills which obscured Roseland's view of the small market town. On the wall adjacent to the windows, was a massive stone fireplace in front of which sat two identical sofas bearing beautifully carved mahogany frames and large claw-and-ball feet, each facing the other. The sofas were covered in a crimson velvet that matched the draperies. Several soft, down-filled pillows in a dark, almost blackish green velvet edged in gold acanthus leaves were scattered over the sofas.

The remainder of the long, spacious chamber was filled—quite modestly by modern standards—with two comfortable prie-dieu chairs made of mahogany in tapestried fabrics, low in the twirled leg and high at the back, three tête-à-tête chairs, heavily carved and upholstered in patterned silks of reds and greens, and several standing lamps each bearing three globes. A rosewood pianoforte, a gleaming harp, and various tables supporting ferns completed the room's principal arrangement.

Alexandra approved the chamber, noting particularly that Launceston's choices did not lean to the extreme as did so many of her acquaintance. For herself, she could not help but feel that filling every square inch of a chamber with busy patterns, overly carved furniture and an abundance of bric-a-brac kept the human spirit in an anxious state.

Glancing at an antique ormolu clock on the stone mantel, she saw that another five minutes had passed. She was still listening intently, wondering if she would again hear the strange scraping noise.

She held her breath.

There it was!

The sliding scrape, like a heavy portmanteau being dragged across stone, met her ears, only this time she thought it might be just outside the doors of the great hall! Was Launceston carrying something? Her curiosity began to blend with her impatience at having had to sit kicking her heels so long and on impulse she rose from the sofa and crossed the room to the carved oak door, situated across from the windows.

She stood before the doors, her heart sounding in her ears. What would she find if she opened the door? Anteros perhaps?

Summoning her courage, she laid her hand over the brass doorknob and pulled hard on the right door, jerking it open. She was greeted by the sight of the empty antechamber beyond, decorated in contrast to the great hall in gold velvet and a busy wallpaper of gold and red flowers.

Was she imagining the scraping sound or was it possible Anteros was up to his tricks again?

Again the sliding scrape called to her, but this time coming somewhere from the direction of the hallway to the right. She now felt compelled to follow the direction of the sound and after making two turns, she found herself in the deserted entrance hall. Gleaming wood stairs rose to the first floor at either side of the entrance hall and immediately to the right of the front door a long gallery travelled beyond the entrance hall to the west leading to a narrow staircase which she supposed must end in a tower situated several stories above the ground floor.

Alexandra moved to the center of the entrance hall and waited, wondering where the sound would next lead her—to the tower, to the first floor, or through the passageway directly in front of her on the ground floor. She listened intently. The castle was quiet except for the occasional faint laughter of the servants coming from the direction of the long gallery.

In front of her, two gleaming suits of armor stood facing one another on the short stairwell walls which flanked the arched hallway beyond. It was from this hallway that another scraping noise resounded.

In the many years that Alexandra had lived at Roselands she had not once been to Castle Porth. The previous owner, a Mr. Redruth, had been a recluse of no mean order and had snubbed her parents' few attempts to become acquainted with him. She was therefore completely unfamiliar with the passageways of the ancient structure and was beginning to feel very small within the tall granite walls.

She approached the two suits of armor and stared down the unlit hallway. Her heart began to beat strongly in her breast. She knew a sudden desire to return to the safety of the great hall but again the scraping sound beckoned her forward. What was it about her nature that urged her on, instead of pressing her to retreat? Was she being bold or just plain foolish?

Without pausing, in spite of her doubts, she passed into the dark hallway and saw a natural light at the end of the passageway.

The hall opened up into a small antechamber, decorated only with an ornate gladiatorial table upon which sat a tall oil lamp. To the left was another hallway which led where, she couldn't imagine and to the right was a long hall, lit with natural light in two places. One was a single arched window closest to the antechamber. The other was a multicolored light passing through a stained glass window. Directly across from the closer, arched window was another adjoining hallway and stairs which Alexandra suspected led to the nether regions below the ground floor. In keeping with the warrenlike design of the castle, at the end of the hallway was a short flight of stairs.

Now where did that lead to? she wondered.

She was unsure where to go next and took a deep breath, turning to look at the dark hallway to the left then back again to the lit hallway to the right. She gave a nervous tug on the short peplum at the waist of her royal blue velvet gown and decided that she had much rather not go down another darkened hallway and for that reason approached the hallway to the right.

She left the antechamber and began walking down the hallway, passing the arched window and the servants' stairs. When she reached the short stone steps, she looked up and saw that the stained glass window was of a medieval shield—amber lions in the upper left and lower right quarters, accented by white crosses surrounded by blue glass in the upper right and lower left quarters. It was quite beautiful, especially the lions which had been skillfully recreated with dozens of bits of glass surrounded by lead.

She climbed the steps and when she reached the landing she found that she could see through the stained glass window into the chapel below. There, much to her surprise, was Launceston, wearing striped wool trousers, a black wool coat, a white shirt and a narrow, black silk cravat. He stood with his back partially turned toward her, his blond hair curled just over the rise of his collar, his fists on each hip, his stance wide, his head turning from one side to the next as though he was trying to solve a puzzle. Perhaps he had heard the noises as well.

She watched him through the colored glass, her thoughts leaning toward him. She felt strangely mesmerized by the sight of him. The scraping sounds which had seemed to lead her here were now all but forgotten as her original purpose in coming to Castle Porth rose sharply to mind. Would she be able to persuade him to give a masquerade ball? Was a man of his stamp *persuadable?* She glanced down at the décolleté of her bodice and felt a blush creep up her cheeks. What manner of madness had come over her that she had worn such a gown? What was she doing? Did she mean to seduce him?

She looked back at Launceston and felt both silly and inadequate in her schemes. She knew so little of him after all. Only that he was a Nabob and that his parents had perished when he was quite young, perhaps fourteen, perhaps younger. He had attended Eton and instead of progressing to University took to the high seas. Upon his return to England, he had inherited his title and had recently purchased Castle Porth.

But who was he truly, she wondered. She found herself growing quite curious about him—in a mildly detached manner of course. For one thing, in the five years since she had come out, he was the first and only man to have kissed her as he did. How many times had she scrutinized the memory of that kiss? A dozen times, a hundred? Over and over she had examined its meanings and implications—with regard to his character, with regard to her own, with regard to the sort of man she hoped one day to wed.

When she considered her future, and the many different sorts of gentlemen who abounded in London, in Bath, and in Stithwell, she always found herself comparing them to Launceston. Would this man, or that, dare to take her in his arms as Launceston had? Could she be content with a man who was too afraid of her to even consider approaching her in the daring manner Launceston had two summers past? She wasn't certain why it was, but she knew that many quite suitable gentlemen were nervous in her presence. Was it possible she did indeed behave like a Frost Queen as Launceston had so unkindly informed her upon more than one occasion?

Whatever the case, whether her fault or no, the fact that Launceston had once assaulted her, had changed forever how she viewed the men of her acquaintance—and herself.

Feeling rather humbled, she decided to return immediately to the great hall.

But just as she turned around, she was met by the sight of Anteros leaning against the wall and staring at her with a mocking expression in his eye.

"Hallo, Alexandra," he said lazily. "Have you missed me? I have been searching everywhere for you."

Seven

She gave a gasp and backed away.

His laughter rippled over her as he folded his arms across his chest. "You must come with me," he said. "I have lived too long without a wife and you shall be mine."

She could scarcely breathe, her mouth as dry as powder as her heart thumped in breast. "I shan't go with you!" she cried. "I—I love another. My heart is already given."

He seemed surprised and lifted a lazy brow. "Indeed?" he queried.

"Yes—Lord Launceston, that is why I'm here. I am in love with him, but, but my parents do not approve of the match. I—I intend to elope with him if needs be." She heard faint footsteps on the stairs within the chapel and knew that Launceston was coming.

"You are breaking my heart, Alexandra," he whispered. He extended his arms to her and a mesmerizing dizziness swelled over her like an ocean wave. As before, she felt his loneliness as though it was a tangible thing and her heart went out to him. He needed her, she would go with him, she would be his wife.

"I will go with you," she whispered, suddenly and completely enamored of him. But when she began descending the short flight of steps, he glanced behind her and a scowl overtook his brow.

"Zeus take it!" he murmured. Just as she reached the bottom step, her own arms held out to him, he faded from view and drifted ghostlike through the walls in the direction of the lofty entrance hall beyond.

"Lady Alexandra?" Launceston queried from behind her.

She did not immediately turn around for the dizziness was still upon her. She lowered her arms, wishing Anteros had not left her so abruptly. She blinked several times, her mind reluctant to draw away from the image of the god of unrequited love slipping through the stones of the wall.

"Alexandra?" she heard Launceston ask again.

Still her mind would not respond. She eased off the bottom step onto the stone floor of the hallway and turned around to face him. She saw him through a mist. She pressed a hand to her eyes and tried to bring clarity to her thoughts.

"I'm sorry," she began. "I don't know precisely what is troubling me." How could she explain Anteros to Launceston? She took in a deep breath and continued, "I suppose I should have waited for you in the great hall, but I heard the most curious noise—"

"A scraping sound?" he queried as he began descending the stairs.

"Yes, precisely." She still felt unaccountably dizzy. Where was Anteros? Why did he leave her? Didn't he know she couldn't live without him?

"Are you all right?" Launceston asked.

She drew in a deep breath then another. The mist before her finally evaporated, she saw Launceston clearly and realized with a start that Anteros had worked his wiles on her again.

"Oh!" she said slowly. "Am I all right?" she reiterated. "No, that is yes, of course I am. It is just that—my curiosity bested me, I'm 'fraid. I felt *compelled* to follow after the noise. I beg you will forgive my ill manners." She felt strangely lethargic. When he reached the bottom step, she extended her hand to him. "I should never have ventured so far into your home."

As Launceston stepped before her, he took her gloved hand in his and looked into large, blue eyes. The light from the stained glass window illuminated her beautiful features in lovely shades of gold and blue light. He felt as he had the summer prior, when he had first come across her alongside the River Avon, bonnetless, gloveless, seemingly unencumbered by the increasingly cumbersome society in which they both lived. He remembered looking into her summery eyes, wide and innocent, fully alive, and had felt all of life rush over him in a stream of vitality and strength so powerful that his sole desire had been to take her in his arms and partake of her life. He had never experienced such a sensation before nor since. But now that she was before him and regarding him with such a soft almost sleepy quality, he wondered what it would be like to kiss her again. Would he feel as he had the first time?

Women had always been a confusing commodity to him. Give him affairs of business, of Trade, of the high seas, of tea and cloth, of tobacco, wines, brandy, and firearms and he was at home to a peg. But set him in a room of females and he was fairly loath to know what the devil to do with them. For some reason, perhaps that he was known to have acquired his wealth in the exotic land of India, he seemed to excite a strange sort of admiration in females. He was hounded by lonely ladies of rank and swooned over by young innocents who fancied themselves in love with him. Lady Julia and Lady Victoria had each hinted broadly that their hearts were given and a proposal of marriage would be welcome. Even Lady Alexandra had thrown her arms about his neck on their first meeting, but with her, unlike every other situation he could recall to mind, he had done no less than she!

What was it about her, then, that gave him pause as he lifted her fingers to his lips. He was remembering at the same time his wager with Trenear, but it was not the wager of which he was thinking which caused his heart to simply stop as he held her gaze and felt her fingers trembling beneath the touch of his lips.

Faith but she was beautiful, and more than beautiful, something beyond just pleasing to the eye. Light emanated from her reflected in the glow of her skin, the clearness of her blue eyes, the courage he had seen her display on more than one occasion. As though the same light suddenly illuminated his mind, he realized that regardless of the ways in which she treated him as contemptible he could no longer deny that what he held in his heart for her, besides admiration of her physical form, was a firm, unflappable respect.

"You have my permission to search through every corner of my home, if you wish for it," he said sincerely. "I have not known you this year and more without having understood a little of your character. As it happens, I should have joined you some few minutes past had I too, not been drawn away from my duty to you by the same noise."

"Like something heavy being drawn across the stone floor?" she asked.

"Yes—louder in some parts, then faint, then louder again?"

Alexandra was relieved to find someone else who had heard the same sounds. "When I entered this passageway, all was quiet until I saw you through the glass. A moment later the sound was behind me."

"And did you discover the source of that sound?"

Alexandra blanched. "Yes—that is, no. I mean—" How could she tell him about Anteros?

"A ghost perhaps?"

She swallowed hard and averted her gaze.

"Don't be frightened," he said and quickly took up her arm to guide her back down the hall in the direction of the great hall. "You saw a ghost, or perhaps an image of a man, is that it?"

"Y-yes," she responded uneasily. "I guess that is what I saw—a tall man with silver hair."

"And black wings?"

She gasped and stared up at him.

He patted her hand encouragingly. "You are not the first. The servants have been complaining of his presence since my arrival yesterday."

"Oh!" she cried, at once relieved and surprised. "Do tell me all. I vow I am overcome with all that has happened—the noises and finding the, the *spectre* in the hallway, almost as though he had been waiting for me. It was most unsettling."

"First a glass of sherry to calm your nerves—and mine. Then we shall sort out the whole of it."

A few minutes later, she was sitting forward on one of the crimson sofas, sipping her sherry. While the wine warmed her veins, she listened to Launceston regale her of his arrival at Castle Porth and the fact that his entire staff had reported seeing a man—a man with wings—in the hallways, in the kitchens, and in the chapel ruins on more than a score of occasions.

He sat beside her, one leg crossed negligently over the other, his arm resting on the back of the sofa. He spoke easily and in a relaxed manner which set her at ease. She soon found herself leaning back into the soft cushions of the sofa herself, an arm draped across her stomach, the other keeping her small glass near her lips. He was making her laugh.

"The scullery maid came squealing into the dining chamber and said she had been accosted by a ghost who tried to steal a kiss from her—and she an *innocent* maid, or so she claims! If she has never been kissed then I have never been to sea."

"What a wicked thing to say." She should have been scandalized by the nature of his anecdote but for some reason she was not.

"You have not seen the scullery maid," he responded with a laugh. "Ah, you are trying not to smile. What a delightful giggle you have, Lady Alexandra."

She felt herself blushing, not less so than when the smile already on his lips, reached to his eyes. How warm and appealing his hazel eyes were, his expression welcoming in the dimness of the great hall.

Feeling in danger of falling into the warmth of his eyes, she glanced about the chamber. It was quite ancient and undoubtedly had known the joys and sorrows of a score of generations. In times past, the large fireplace had probably been used to roast large haunches of venison to serve a bevy of knights and ladies. Was it her imagination, or could she hear from across the years the merriment of an age gone by in which men strode about in snug-fitting tights and tunics of mail and women laughed as they danced down the length of the hall in long, flowing gowns, coiffures beribboned, braided, and flowing with roses, pansies and bluebells. She thought Launceston would have made an exceptional knight.

"What are you thinking?" he queried.

Alexandra looked down at the remaining sherry in her glass and slowly took a sip.

She ought to ask him for her masquerade ball. But not just yet.

"Of knights and ladies," she responded. "They must have danced at Castle Porth at one time."

"Undoubtedly."

"Do you ever wish for yesteryear?" she asked, her gaze sliding back to his. She didn't know why she posed the question, but once it passed her lips she realized she wanted to know how his mind worked.

He lifted a brow and sipped his sherry before answering. "I don't dwell on the past overly much," he said. "I have read history a little, I have pondered—though not frequently—the identity of previous occupants of the castle, but have I wished for the past, or to dwell in the past? What a singular proposition. I suppose the past will always hold a certain charm and mystery, but I suspect I am far too fond of my curricle to be in a hurry to live in a time when the only mode of transportation was a horse, or a palanquin on top of a horse. And though I enjoy riding, I had far prefer to race from London to Bath in a chaise and four than to trot the same distance astride my best gelding."

"These modern times," Alexandra mused, smiling. "Who would have ever thought that such daring speeds would rule our century? The mail coaches travel at nearly ten miles an hour and the railway is entirely beyond belief!"

"Indeed, it is!"

"But tell me of India, for I know you lived there for some years."

"Yes, when I was not at sea."

Alexandra listened to him speak, her attention riveted as much to his words as to the expression in his eye and on his face. Not long into his history, she let her glass rest between her hands which were settled on her lap. She forgot entirely that she brangled nine minutes out of ten with the man before her. Instead she travelled aboard a ship with him, battled storms and the treacherous dead calms of the sea, she worked alongside him in India, smelled the bales of tea, drank in the vision of Indian princesses hidden behind exotic silk veils in every color imaginable, she rode on an elephant, heard the drums in the chase of a tiger, walked the streets of crowded, dusty cities and dined on strong yellow-colored rice.

An hour later, the chiming of the ormolu clock on the mantel ended the magical journey for her. "Oh, my goodness!" she cried. "Where has the afternoon gone? I had only meant to stay a quarter of an hour and now nearly two hours have passed. But I have so enjoyed listening to your stories. I have never known anyone who has lived as you have lived."

"I don't often have a willing audience—I have found since my return to England that very few have an interest in matters beyond the edges of our island."

Alexandra was about to assure him that she was quite different, but since at that moment she recalled why it was she had come to Castle Porth in the first place, she remained silent for a moment, a silence which began to weigh in the air between them.

"Have I offended you?" he finally asked.

"No, no, of course not!" she responded. "It is just that—well, it would seem I am about to risk ruining what has been the most peaceful discourse between us that I can ever recall."

"And how might you do that?"

She let out a quick sigh. Reluctantly, she answered him. "Because I fear I must now own that I have called upon you this afternoon to a purpose—a very specific purpose."

She saw the friendly light in his eye fade and a wary expression take its place. Chagrin now filled her and had the enormity of her need not pressed her, she would have simply bid him farewell and kept her request unspoken.

Instead, she fortified her will and prepared to do battle knowing she could accept nothing from him today but an acquiescence to her schemes.

"I shall be plain," she said quietly. "I wish for you to give a ball, in nine days, on All Hallow's Eve."

He was so taken aback that his mouth fell slightly agape and he stared at her for the longest time without blinking. "You wish me to do what?" he asked, astonished.

"To give a ball—a masquerade ball."

He laughed outright. "You have confounded me. Only yesterday you were coming the crab over me and complaining of my character. What has changed that you must come to me today—," here his gaze drifted purposefully over the décolleté of her gown and afterwards back to her face before he continued, "—to make such an outrageous request of me? I would think myself flattered, even pleased, were we on more amicable terms generally."

"Then you will not oblige me?" she asked, thinking she had been quite stupid in her approach.

"I did not say so—only, I am suddenly filled with the greatest curiosity. First, I wonder why you want me to give a ball but more to the point, just how did you mean to persuade me to it?" He leaned toward her in a provocative manner and placed a hand on her arm. Lowering his voice, he added, "Though I've little doubt you do have the ability to persuade me—I've known as much these two summers and more."

Alexandra found her temper flaring instantly. Given the look in his eye, his suggestion was perfectly clear. "And to think for a moment," she responded, rising to her feet. "That I nearly forgot you were a rogue and only half a gentleman!"

He rose as well and took the small glass from her hand. Setting their glasses on a table near the sofa, he queried, "And is that why you wore a gown today which, though I find it utterly charming, is the most scandalous morning gown I have ever seen? I can only wonder that your mother permitted you to leave the house."

His amused expression and the choice of his words caused her to feel like a schoolgirl who had gotten caught dipping into her mother's rouge-pot. She also felt like a perfect hypocrite.

"You are right to upbraid me," she responded, looking up at him candidly. "For I was hoping to appeal to you, perhaps in every sense today, in order to *persuade* you to give a ball. And though my mother knows of this gown, and though she was rather shocked, she would of course say nothing to me since I am of age."

He narrowed his eyes at her, the hint of a smile on his lips. "But you are most intriguing today," he whispered, drawing very near to her, so near that she could see light brown flecks in his hazel eyes. "So forthcoming and honest. Only pray tell me now *why* you wish me to give a ball?"

Alexandra had already considered her answer carefully. She knew Launceston fairly well and had already decided that to tell a whisker wouldn't fadge, nor could she tell him the truth, so instead, she responded, "Because I wish for it." Again she held his gaze squarely and firmly, but refused to say more.

"You wish for it and because you wish for it you think I ought to simply oblige you?" he queried, taking another step toward her so that his striped wool trousers actually brushed up against her royal blue skirts.

He was far too close to her, especially since more than once he permitted his gaze to drift over her hypocritical bosom. She was finding it difficult to breathe and equally as difficult to continue looking into his hazel eyes. Images of the manner in which he had kissed her two summers past, kept flitting through her mind. "Y-yes," she stammered, her heart beginning to sound in her ears.

"I'll wager you for it," he said, holding her gaze steadily.

"A wager?" she responded. "And just what sort of wager would you propose?" His lips were scarcely a breath away. Her thoughts would not order themselves.

"I'll wager you that I can guess the number of petticoats you are wearing. If I am correct, you will give me a kiss. If I guess incorrectly, you shall have your ball."

"Done," was her reply, offered without thinking, without considering the consequences.

"You are wearing six," he responded triumphantly.

She shook her head. She wanted to smile, but for some reason she was utterly captivated by the nearness of him, by the smell of his shaving soap, by the way she could hardly breathe simply because he was standing so close to her.

"I don't believe you," he cried. "I was given it on the best of authorities that women always wear six. How many, then?"

"Only five."

"Show me," he commanded, smiling.

The whole of it was so scandalous that Alexandra first could only blink up at him. "I cannot! You will have to take my word for it."

"I won't give you the ball unless you prove to me you are wearing five petticoats."

Only then, when the wager took a more serious turn, did she find his spell breaking a little. "Very well," she said, taking up her seat again on the sofa. She set her hands on her knees and with the smallest of movements crumpled her royal blue velvet gown in each hand—just a mite—and suggested he count them for himself.

Launceston's crooked smile gave way to a broad grin as he dropped on one knee before her. As he looked down at the rows of ruffles, he said, "I can hardly see anything. Pull your skirts up higher."

Alexandra felt another blush begin creeping up her cheeks as she crumpled another few inches of the velvet into the palms of her hands.

"One," he began slowly, peeling back the velvet of the gown, then the first petticoat. "Two. Very pretty. Do you always wear this plaid taffeta tucked between two white muslin petticoats?"

Since he looked up at her, she met his gaze and again felt her breath desert her. Would to God he was not so dreadfully handsome, she thought. She nodded in response to his query.

"Three. Four. Five. And what a prettily turned ankle you possess, Lady Alexandra." Much to her surprise and consternation, she felt his hand on her ankle, just above the top of her half-boot but below the ruffle of her pantalette. His fingers were warm against her silk stocking. For the longest moment, the feel of his hand kept her stilled like a rabbit caught in the garden by rush-light. Her breathing was strangely shallow and a dizziness—very much like the sensation she felt when Anteros was working his wiles—was overtaking her mind. What was he doing to her? A seduction, perhaps? No, she wouldn't permit such a thing to happen to her.

"You mustn't," she whispered, panic suddenly seizing her. She quickly drew her legs back, let down her skirts, and rose all at once. "Are you satisfied?" she asked, taking two steps away from him as he gained his feet. She was frightened, frightened by how much pleasure the mere touch of his hand on her ankle had given her. She knew she had to leave and she began backing away from him. "Are you satisfied?" she queried again as he began to walk toward her.

"Not by half," he responded throatily. Before she could place herself beyond his reach, he caught her, took her forcibly in his arms and kissed her hard on the mouth.

She struggled, but only for a fraction of a second. A wave of desire, profound and overwhelming, crashed down on her. She was utterly caught up in a frothy sea of pleasure from which she had no desire to escape. She remembered in quick succession the kiss of the summer prior, then the manner in which she had wanted him to kiss her on the streets of Stithwell only the day before, and how, a moment earlier the merest touch on her ankle had thrilled her.

Now she was in his arms, his lips bruising hers in a painfully sweet manner. She slipped her arms about his neck and returned kiss for kiss. Her breathing became labored and as she parted her lips, he took possession of her mouth. Her knees grew weak, her pulse thrummed in her throat, as she clung to him. His arms were tight about her waist and even through her five petticoats she could feel his firm muscular legs pressed hard against hers.

She had believed the first kiss with Launceston could not have been exceeded in excitement or pleasure but she was wrong. Perhaps it was because they brangled so, or perhaps it was because images of India flashed vividly through her mind as he kissed her again and again, but whatever the case, she could not seem to keep from giving herself fully to his embrace, to the pleasure of his kiss, to the unequaled thrill of being held so firmly in a pair of strong, masculine arms.

After a moment, he drew back from her and searched her eyes.

"Oh," she breathed, releasing her arms from about his neck. She didn't want to let him go but this could not continue. She couldn't give herself to Launceston, she despised him and he was a confirmed seducer of women.

"Don't go just yet," he whispered, still holding her tightly about the waist. "Alexandra, perhaps—"

"You are such a wicked man," she interjected, pushing away from him, giving voice to her thoughts. "I must go. Nothing can come of this. I know who you are—a libertine—I must go." She turned around and began walking unsteadily toward the door.

"So I am wicked, is that it, is that how you view me?" he called after her. She heard him approach her quickly and was not surprised when he stopped her abruptly from leaving by taking her arm in a firm grip at the elbow. "How is it I earned this low opinion? What is it I have ever done to you—or to anyone?"

She blinked several times and found that the anger etched into his face was having a calming affect on her overwrought state. "Tell me, Launceston," she began unevenly, "why was it that last summer after you—you assaulted me—though to be fair, not uninvited—you never sought me out again? I know that my maid informed you of my identity so you can have no excuse on that head."

"Is that how it is with you? A gentleman makes your acquaintance and because he does not immediately pursue you, you consider him a wicked creature?"

"It was not only that—though I must say I rather thought that after the way in which you kissed me that day, you might have shown some interest in me—but it was other things. When you didn't even have the courtesy to call on me, and when I learned that you apparently were somewhat in the habit of breaking hearts, I grew to suspect you of harboring a cold, unfeeling soul. You may tell me otherwise if you wish to, but I suspect you know what I say is true. To prove as much, tell me what possible reason you could have had for kissing me just now when you had already lost the wager?"

"You are so deuced pretty!" he cried, irritated. "A man hardly needs another reason. And just why did you throw your arms about my neck and permit me to continue? Tell me what *your* motives were?"

"I—I—" She wanted to tell him the truth, that she had found herself completely undone by his company today, by his tales of his life in India and on the high seas, and because she found him amusing and handsome and an agreeable companion, but she couldn't. Instead she lifted a brow and said, "To ensure the ball, of course."

"You do not consider me a man of honor, then?"

She shook her head, but could no longer meet his gaze.

He released her elbow and threw up his arms in exasperation. "Have it as you will, then. I am wicked and you are self-serving. You shall have your ball but I warn you, Lady Alexandra, I have not done with assaulting you yet. From this moment on, I intend to do everything I can to prove your unhappy opinions correct, that I have none of the finer qualities, that my intentions toward a lady must always be lascivious. In short, I intend to break your heart, that is if you even have one."

Alexandra found herself as mad as fire. If *she* had a heart. Well! If that wasn't the pot calling the kettle black! "I shall return tomorrow," she said frostily, "to discuss plans for the ball and to make up a list of guests who I intend to contact personally. We've a lovely society gathered about Falmouth and Stithwell and I'm certain we shall not lack for guests. Good day."

He growled in response, then led her through the castle to the front door without saying another word.

When Alexandra returned from the castle, she went to her bedchamber immediately, fearing that either her sisters or her father would see her scandalous gown. At the same time, she summoned Lydia and bid her to personally fetch a bowl of turtle soup for her from the kitchens.

Psyche had been exceedingly grateful for the soup and while she had dipped her spoon into the deep bowl, Alexandra examined her guest's unhappy ankle. It was still considerably swollen.

"You actually saw Anteros at Castle Porth?" Psyche queried.

Alexandra nodded, as she carefully propped her guest's still swollen ankle up with another pillow. "Yes," she said. "I was never more frightened. I kept hearing a dreadful scraping sound, and for the longest time Launceston did not come to the hall. I finally left the great hall and followed the sound. Of course what was strange was that I ended up mounting a short flight of stairs and peering through a pretty stained-glass window into the chapel ruins. Launceston was there. He had been following the noises as well. Isn't that curious?"

"What do you mean?"

Alexandra crossed the room to dip the white linen into the bowl of cold water beside her wardrobe. Wringing it out thoroughly she continued, "I have only now just considered how odd it was that he and I were both led about by the noises. Why would Anteros have set about to intrigue Launceston as well?"

"I don't know," Psyche said. "But he can be quite devious."

Returning to the bedside and laying the cloth on Psyche's ankle, she continued, "Anteros approached me and again bid me come to Olympus with him. He heard Launceston's steps, however, and faded from sight. Only tell me, Psyche, are you in terrible pain still? I can fetch you a little laudanum if you wish for it."

"If I keep my leg perfectly still I am quite comfortable I assure you. And thank you for the soup. It was delectable."

Alexandra glanced at the empty bowl and wondered how she was to continue having food brought to her chamber without giving rise to suspicions. She supposed she would just have to pretend to be experiencing an inexplicable increase in appetite.

Psyche continued, "Only tell me of your conversation with Launceston. How did it come about he actually agreed to the ball?"

Alexandra gently pressed the damp cloth about Psyche's ankle but for a long moment remained silent. She drew forward an oak chair covered in a button-tuck red velvet and wondered how much of what transpired she ought to reveal to the pretty immortal.

"What is amiss?" Psyche queried sympathetically. "For I can see that you are distressed. Pray tell me, Alexandra. I hope you know that you can tell me anything—I won't judge you or give you a dressing down if that is what you fear."

At that Alexandra could only smile. She could not imagine sweet-natured Psyche giving anyone a dressing down. When she met her gaze, the understanding which she found in Psyche's gaze prompted her to tell her everything. She even revealed her quite inexplicable response to Launceston's assault. "For I don't even like him!"

Psyche nodded and appeared to be ruminating on everything Alexandra had told her. Alexandra sensed that she was restraining some thought or other so that she felt compelled to say. "Please speak your mind—tell me what you think? Am I—am I perhaps an unnatural sort of female?"

Psyche trilled her laughter. Alexandra thought it was the prettiest sound she had ever heard. "No, not by half!" Psyche returned. "Indeed, from all that you have told me, I would only wonder if you had not fallen into his arms."

"But what does it mean?"

"Well, as to that—"

But she got no further, for the door opened and Lady Brandreth, her deep brown hair dressed in a chignon at the back of her head and charming ringlets dangling at either side of her still lovely face, appeared. "I heard laughter," she said, "the prettiest sound." She looked at Alexandra quizzically. "And not at all like you, my dear. I thought perhaps you had company."

Alexandra blinked at her mother who was gowned elegantly for dinner in purple silk, and responded uneasily, "N-no, Mama. There is no one here, just me." Only with the greatest effort did she keep from glancing toward Psyche. It was evident her mother was unable to see Butterfly.

"Evanthea," Psyche murmured. "How handsomely she has aged. When I knew her, she was not yet thirty. But she cannot see me and I don't think I am able to help her see me, or hear me! How very much I wish I could speak with her. How I have missed her! We used to be excellent friends."

A strange expression overtook Lady Brandreth's face. "I know I have heard that laughter before," she murmured, as though to herself. She glanced about the chamber. "Yet there is no one here." She laughed and gave her head a shake. "Perhaps a ghost has come to haunt our halls, either that or I am growing addled before my time. But enough of this. I can now see that you are not yet attired for dinner. You must hurry—you know how Cook frets if we keep her cuisine waiting. And pray, above all things, do not let your papa see that gown!"

Alexandra rose from her chair. "Of course not, Mama."

Lady Brandreth cocked her head. "Why were you sitting over there, on the other side of the bed? Alexandra, you have been behaving strangely of late. And what is this? Soup before dinner. My dear, are you feeling well?"

"Indeed, yes," she responded, rising quickly and moving briskly across the room to ring for her maid. She was afraid that if her mother began to press her about her odd conduct, she would be forced to reveal her involvement in a situation which Lady Brandreth could only interpret as madness on Alexandra's part. She explained the soup by saying, "It is just that I remained at Castle Porth longer than expected. I was so hungry when I returned that I begged Cook for a little soup. Did I err?"

"No, of course not. But with regard to your visit I feel I must warn you that your father was very distressed since you attended his lordship without informing either of us and that you paid your call without benefit of even a maid to lend you countenance. Even if you are not in the first blush of youth, you ought to have at least taken Lydia with you. Papa is quite protective of you, as you very well know, and will remain so, I suspect, so long as he lives." She then smiled at her daughter, searched her eyes and added, "Did you—did you enjoy your time with him?"

Alexandra was startled by her mother's question and in particular by the hopeful gleam in her eye. Was it possible her parent thought a match between them a possibility? Oh, dear. Well, she certainly did not want to encourage her mother down that path. She thought it wise, therefore, to respond with some indifference. "He was sufficiently congenial, I suppose, but you know we cannot be in the same chamber without arguing."

"You argued with him?"

"Yes, but I believe it was mostly my fault. I made him agree to give a masquerade ball, you see."

"You made him?" she queried, clearly stunned. "A ball? Whatever for?"

At that moment, however, Lydia arrived, rapping on the door and interrupting their conversation. She was a little out of breath and as she dropped a curtsy she said that Cook was pinching at everyone because she was afraid dinner would be put-off on account of *one* of the young ladies not having even summoned her maid. Cook had prepared her recipe for woodcock along with salmon and oyster patties and was afraid her entire dinner would be ruined.

Cook was a formidable woman, with large forearms and a culinary gift exceeding none that Alexandra had ever experienced in any other home. She was also easily offended and Lydia's demeanor convinced both Lady Brandreth and Alexandra that the conversation ought to be continued at a later hour.

At dinner that evening, with the family gathered about the dining table, the subject was again taken up and Alexandra felt Victoria's glare heavily upon her.

"You will plunge us all into scandal!" her sister cried, stabbing her peas with her fork, her lower lip quivering. "Two hours!"

Alexandra, who had just set a morsel of salmon on her lips, and who had been letting the sumptuous fish sit readied just beyond reach of her tongue, blinked at Victoria in astonishment. She had not considered before all the possible ramifications of her conduct. Slowly she let the salmon pass her lips and began chewing slowly. She knew her father's eyes were upon her as well and she could not prevent a blush from creeping up her cheeks.

"How is this?" he queried, a frown creasing his brow. "Alexandra, do you tell me you were at Castle Porth for two hours, alone, in the company of, of Launceston?"

A silence fell over the table. Alexandra glanced at her mother and saw that she was appearing quite concerned.

"He was a, a gentleman," Alexandra responded, cutting into an oyster patty and avoiding her father's piercing gaze. She had meant to say a *perfect gentleman,* for that much he had not been. She was in a quandary as to what to say next to her family, to her father's accusing glare, to her mother's concerned brown eyes, to Julia and Victoria's reproachful gaze. She tried not to recall the scandalous kiss Launceston had placed on her lips, nor the appearance of Anteros in the hallway, but the images would not disappear and instead no doubt deepened the blush on her cheeks. She spoke in an effort to keep her thoughts from revealing themselves in the expressions of her face.

"The truth was, I, I begged his lordship to give a masquerade ball on Wednesday next. I know it was improper, but I thought it would be such fun and, and he proved most agreeable to my scheme. It would seem he is most anxious to make the acquaintance of his neighbors."

She swallowed hard and glanced at each of her siblings and parents in turn. Would they believe her?

Victoria pouted and addressed the true point of contention. "How could you have gone to Castle Porth without me? Julia, I can well understand for she makes such sheep's eyes at Launceston as to appear revolting. But you know that Launceston is in love with me. We are to be married and—"

"What?" Julia cried. She was seated next to her sister and with these traitorous words, her ability to keep her temper was lost. "Launceston would no more wed the likes of you than he would, well, than he would Alexandra and you know how much he despises her! You tell such whiskers! How very much I despise you, Victoria!"

"Now that is quite enough!" Lord Brandreth cried, slamming his fist on the table, the blow softened by the white linen table-napkin curled within his hand.

Both Julia and Victoria jumped backward in their seats, their complexions turning ashen at the sight of their father's choler. "I beg your pardon, Papa," Julia said hurriedly.

"I, too," Victoria added. Lord Brandreth might take great delight in his daughters, but he never permitted such outrageous manners. Each lady appeared considerably abashed, even sitting with primly folded hands like two schoolgirls caught in mischief.

Seeing that his daughters had taken his reproach as they ought, he turned his attention fully to Alexandra. "You have always shown such uncommonly good sense, and rarely display the wont of such, that I am reluctant to admonish you, Alexandra. Only can you explain to me why you remained such a long time in company with Launceston and why you did not even see fit to take your maid with you? Though I do not hesitate to say that I find your having pressed Launceston into giving a ball a most incomprehensible act!"

Alexandra glanced at her sisters across the table and saw the resentful smirks on each pretty face. But she could not be cross with them, how could she be? She alone was at fault for having let two hours slip away from her.

"I don't know what happened, Papa," she said, at last, ignoring the rather startled expression on her sisters' faces. "We, we began to speak of his childhood and mine. He told me a great deal of his voyages since he was quite young. I vow I found myself utterly fascinated. Did you know for instance that at one time he was able to climb the main mastpole of his ship faster than any other midshipman? Silly, I know, but I found myself caught up, I think, in his adventures. It was like reading Byron by flashes of lightning. I know it was wrong of me to forget the hour and you are very right to take me to task for it. I can only promise you it will not happen again. As for the masquerade," and here she paused, forming a swift whisker in her mind, "I thought it would be vastly amusing since it is nearly All Hallow's Eve, and, and I had just learned this morning from Lydia that the servants at Castle Porth are exclaiming over the presence of a ghost."

Julia and Victoria gasped.

Lady Brandreth expressed the astonishment of all. "A ghost? At Castle Porth? Is this possible?"

"Yes," Alexandra answered. "And even I, when I was awaiting Launceston, heard such scraping noises in the hall beyond the great hall that I was nearly overset. I know I shouldn't have, but I followed the noises and, and I came upon the most incredible being—he was garbed in black clothes, was quite handsome, and had silver hair."

Lord Brandreth queried, "And has Launceston seen this ghost?"

nonentity, but this is a different woman. I don't know this
woman. Who is she? She's going to drown all of us." I
took one of Gary's guns and shot holes in the boat and as
it sank I started to swim to shore. Paul Tyson helped me
when I grew tired.

After she finished writing down the dream Margaret
read and reread it trying to puzzle out the various parts.
She folded it and put it in her pocket when there was a
light tap on the door.

"Yes," she said. Lizanne entered.

"Do you want breakfast in here, Miz Oliver? Mr. Bennett said I should ask."

"Coffee," Margaret said absently. She had never asked
for any special service before, had always appeared at the
table when meals were ready, always refused any special
attention. Lizanne nodded, not so much in response to
Margaret as in confirmation of her own secret suspicions.
She left. I listened to her in the hall outside the door. Very
quiet whispers, hers and Arnold Greeley's. They retreated,
but I could still hear them, whispering, agreeing that
Margaret was changed, that she was being secretive about
something. Moving out of range then, no, stopping because Bennett had appeared. Arnold and Bennett talking,
Arnold suggesting that Margaret shouldn't be left alone,
that she didn't look well. Bennett agreeing, relief in his
tone of voice.

When Bennett came in he was carrying the coffee that
Margaret had asked for. She was dressed now, in slacks
and a sweater. He had two cups on the tray. Before he
could say anything, Margaret said, "I had a curious dream
last night. In it you and I were quarreling over Lizanne. I

told you that I would fire her if she didn't catch the bus back to the city, and you said I couldn't fire her, that she was your cook, your housekeeper." She poured coffee.

Bennett said, "I don't want her to leave you here alone, darling. I did tell her to plan to remain until you're ready to go back to the apartment."

Margaret nodded. *"Déjà vu.* Strange, isn't it?"

"Not at all. You passed out, or something last night. Obviously I wouldn't leave you alone. You sensed that and dreamed that dream. Wish fulfillment on your part. You really don't want to be alone right now."

"But I do, Bennett. And I will. In the dream, I said that if she stayed, I'd go to a hotel."

"Margaret, don't be childish. I have already told Lizanne to stay with you. Don't make a scene over it." In the past the matter would have ended right there. How many times, Margaret wondered, had she given in to him not because of anything he said, but because he used that particular tone of voice? She sipped her coffee, watching him over the cup, waiting for him to finish. "Arnold and I plan to leave about two or three," he said. "Come on out and behave now."

"I'l fire her, Bennett," Margaret said calmly. "I really will. And if she won't leave then, I'll call the police and have her arrested as a trespasser."

Bennett blinked and removed his glasses and polished them hard. After a moment he said, "You know you can't fire her. You already admitted that. She's been with me since I was a kid; she took care of me all my life. I know that servants are usually the woman's prerogative, but in this case, I'm afraid your dream was right. She is my cook, my housekeeper. She would laugh if you tried to fire her."

"Yes. The servants as well."

"By all that's wonderful!" he exclaimed. "I've heard of such things—but I've never seen a real spectre! Silver hair, you say?"

"Yes." Alexandra felt faint with dread. Would her parents now think she was going mad like Lady Elle? At least the servants and Launceston could confirm her own experience.

"Oh!" Lady Brandreth cried, patting and rubbing her arms as though she had gotten a chill. "You have given me such gooseflesh. Imagine! A ghost at the castle! How very intriguing! But to own the truth, I do love a good scare." She then broke into a broad smile. "Well, I believe there is only one thing for it! Launceston must give a masquerade ball. You were very right to propose such a scheme to him." Since she lifted her goblet of Madeira, a toast was proposed and in spite of a slightly worried frown on Brandreth's brow, the ball was given her approval. Once given, Julia and Victoria immediately began to argue over which of them Launceston would dance with first and Alexandra was no longer the object of her parents' scrutiny.

If she was a little surprised by her mother's quick acquiescence to the masquerade, she did not mistake the penetrating glance her parent cast toward her father. She knew her expression well and that it meant Lady Brandreth intended to discuss the whole of the scheme with her husband when they had a private moment together.

Later, Brandreth addressed his wife's hasty agreement to the ball. "I cannot believe you agreed so readily. Your own opinion of Launceston is not particularly high, nor have you been the least content with either Victoria's or Julia's absurd infatuation with the fellow. Now you are permitting a ball, and if what Alexandra told me over our game of piquet is true, she intends to spend a great deal of the next few days at Castle Porth in preparation for the event."

"That much is true," Lady Brandreth said. "Since Alexandra suggested the ball to his lordship, she feels obligated—and that most appropriately—to oversee the preparations. I supported her in this wholeheartedly."

"But this is most improper!"

Lady Brandreth merely smiled up at her husband and placed a kiss on his cheek. "I know it is most improper and that is why I have insisted that Victoria and Julia accompany her."

"But you are speaking of our daughters fixing themselves daily within a bachelor's establishment."

"Well, it won't be a bachelor's establishment for long, if my suspicions are correct," she murmured as she brushed passed him to retire for the night.

"I still can't believe you agreed to this!" he called after her. "And I am persuaded he doesn't give so much as a flying fig for the happiness of any of our daughters!" But since her door had already closed, he strongly suspected she did not hear a word of his final parting shot.

Eight

Walking toward his own bedchamber, Brandreth decided that the only way he would have a moment's peace was to address the matter with Launceston himself. Tomorrow, perhaps.

A kitchen maid bearing a covered tray appeared at the top of the servants' stairs but he hardly noticed her. His mind was wholly consumed with his family, in particular his three daughters. How had it come about that each one of them, especially Victoria and Julia, had grown completely enamored of Lord Launceston? Not that Alexandra was caught in the throes of love, for to all appearances she held Launceston in profound dislike. But what in the name of Jupiter had prompted her to pay a morning visit upon his lordship—and for two hours, nonetheless—and ask him to give a masquerade ball!

Really, the whole of it was incomprehensible to his masculine mind.

The maid bearing the tray passed by him and he caught the aroma of warm bread. Bread?

"Susan!" he called to her, turning about at the same time.

The young maid also whirled about, dropping a slight curtsy, her cheeks suffused with an embarrassed blush. "Yes, m'lord?" she queried, her brow furrowed in distress.

He stepped forward to close the distance between them. "I didn't mean to startle you but what is it you have on your tray?"

She balanced the large tray on one hand and with the other lifted back a clean, starched linen cover. Warm bread dripping with butter, a bowl of turtle soup, several slices of roast beef, and a dish of cooked, cinnamon apples greeted his eyes.

"Who is this for?" he asked, dumbfounded.

"Lady Alexandra," she returned in a small voice. "Should—should I take it back to the kitchens?"

Lord Brandreth spoke more to himself than to the maid. "But I watched her at dinner. She ate a generous portion of the salmon, two oyster patties—they were always a favorite with her—broccoli, rice, and two rhubarb tarts. But not much of the woodcock—I think the woodcock was a bit off. And now she wishes for what I can only describe as another meal." He lifted his gaze to look into the maid's frightened blue eyes and smiled, "I shan't come the crab, Susan! I am merely astonished."

The maid smiled nervously in return and replaced the linen cover. "N-no, m lord. Of course not! It is just that, well—"

She appeared loath to continue.

"Please, speak your mind. Is something afoot which I ought to know about?"

"I don't—that is, Lady Alexandra has always been kind, and I wouldn't want to—well, I'm not sure if I ought to say anything."

Lord Brandreth nodded. "I am concerned about my daughter, Susan, so if there is something you or anyone else feels I ought to know I hope you will be forthcoming."

His speech did not appear to relieve each wrinkle from the young maid's forehead, but she did at least open her budget. "Cook was saying that since yesterday, this is the fourth meal Lady Alexandra has ordered to be brought up by tray—and that after having partaken of a substantial meal with the family."

Brandreth was again dumbfounded. "You're sure about this?"

"Indeed, yes," Susan responded. "I have taken each one to her bedchamber myself and when the tray has been retrieved, not a morsel remained."

"I see," he said, thinking that the moment his wife's surgeon arrived, he would recommend the good doctor have a look at his eldest daughter as well. For the present, he extended his hands toward Susan. "I'll tell you what. Let me have the tray and I shall tend to Lady Alexandra myself."

"Very good, m'lord," Susan responded quietly, the frown now deep on her brow.

"Never fear! Am I such an ogre in my own house that you must look as though I would eat my daughter alive?"

At that Susan smiled. "Not by half, m'lord." She then dropped a curtsy and walked quickly back down the hall toward the servant's stairs.

Brandreth continued down the hall until he reached Alexandra's door. Scratching lightly on the ornately carved wood, he waited to hear her permission to enter. When she did not immediately respond, he called to her, "Alexandra, it's your father. Pray open the door."

Alexandra heard her father's voice and felt her heart quail in her breast. "One moment, Papa!" she called to him, panic-stricken.

She looked first at Psyche, who was in tears and who was holding a candlestick aloft, preparing to throw it at Anteros, then turned her attention to Anteros who was standing beside the figurine of a small, winged boy—Cupid as a babe—at which he was laughing uproariously. "Will you please stop funning, Anteros!" she called to him in a firm whisper. "You are making Psyche cry!"

She turned to Psyche and with her arms thrown pleadingly wide, said, "If you don't put the candlestick down, how will I explain the presence of a silver object floating in the air?"

When Anteros appeared to oblige her and when Psyche had set the candlestick on the table by the bed, she quickly crossed the room and opened the door. She had put on her best smile but when she saw that he bore Psyche's dinner in his arms, she felt the smile grow stiff on her lips. "Whatever are you doing, Papa?" she queried. "Where is the maid?"

"May I come in?" he asked.

Alexandra's heart sank. She knew her father well for they had been great friends for a long, long time. His face was etched with parental concern. "Of course," she said, stepping away from the doorway and holding the door for him.

"Where would you like this tray?" he asked.

"Over here!" Anteros called, his expression sardonic as he gestured toward the bed. "Poor Butterfly is famished."

Because her father's back was to her, she glared at Anteros and said, "Here, Papa. Let me clear the table."

Near the window sat a round table of mahogany inlaid with mother-of-pearl in a floral design. The design, however, was quite invisible since the top of the table was covered with a variety of objects—a potted fern, shell flowers under glass, a bronze cup and fringed cover, a long-necked glass vase, a crotchet box and several china figurines of mythological characters—one of which was the offending Cupid.

"Let me help you," Anteros called as he came up behind Alexandra.

She knew she couldn't answer him. She could only grind her teeth together and begin removing the various articles from the table. "I ought to have another table in my room with not so many adornments on it for, for just such occasions," she said, stepping sideways and catching Anteros's arm with her elbow by way of keeping him from attacking the little figurines. She then gathered them up in her hands.

"So it would seem," her father said, turning toward her as he watched her place the objects on her nearby dressing table.

"Oh, do let me help you, Alexandra," Anteros whispered mockingly in her ear.

"My pet," Lord Brandreth said. "I know that you are a lady all grown up, but what I have just learned has quite disturbed me."

"And what was that, Papa?" Alexandra said, holding tightly onto the tall, glass vase since Anteros was trying his best to pull it from her fingers.

Lord Brandreth extended the tray slightly toward her and said, "Tell me what this means? Was it possible you left the dining table still hungry?"

Alexandra glanced at the tray, but did not answer her father right away. Anteros still had a hard hold on the glass and she was afraid it would break. She whirled suddenly away from him and fortunately he released the vase at the same moment.

"You are too clever for me," Anteros said, laughing as he backed away from her and threw himself down into a red velvet chair which bore short legs and ball and claw feet.

"Do leave her alone!" Psyche called to him. "Anteros, don't you realize that if you make Alexandra appear as though she is as mad as Bedlam, her parents will take her to Bath to drink the waters and then where will your schemes be? For I promise you that if she leaves Roselands, nothing shall prevent me from returning to Olympus at the appointed hour. And that is your purpose, isn't it, to see that I fail to return?"

Alexandra turned to remove the fern from the table and stole a glance at Anteros. The smile was gone from his face and he stared at Psyche as though he wished her turned to stone.

When Alexandra had returned to her bedchamber following dinner, she had found Anteros alone with Psyche and caught up in a heated argument. She had sensed Anteros's hostility the moment she crossed the threshold and was not surprised that her arrival failed to defray their quarrel. Psyche accused him of scheming with Aphrodite to separate her from Cupid for all time and he admitted to it, without blinking an eye. Even though she had tenderly begged him to tell her in what way she had so grievously offended him, Anteros refused to answer. That was when he began to tease and provoke her about her love for Cupid, taunting her with the white, ceramic figurine of Cupid portrayed as a winged babe.

Now, as he watched Psyche with his former dislike evident in the twitching of the tips of his black feathers, he rose swiftly and vanished through the wall near one of the windows.

Grateful he was gone, she addressed her father's concerns.

"You may set the tray down now, Papa," she said, able to breathe easily at last. "The truth is—and I can't begin to explain why— but of late, yesterday in fact, my appetite has increased extraordinarily. The weather turned recently. Perhaps I am like a little forest creature convinced I must thicken my coat before the onset of winter." She was rambling, but hoped her silly answer would satisfy him.

He stood looking down at her, for he was of a height with Launceston, and scrutinized her face as though searching for some sign of illness. "I have sent for your mother's physician. He will be here tomorrow and I would like him to take a look at you. Yes, yes, I'm sure you are perfectly stout, but you must admit I cannot but wonder at your sudden change."

"Really, Papa, it isn't necessary to bring the doctor all the way to Roselands because, because I am eating too much."

At that, his face crumpled slightly. "It isn't you," he said. "I have requested the doctor for your mother's sake."

"Oh, no," Alexandra cried, forgetting her troubles for a moment in view of her father's obvious distress. "Is she—unwell?"

"Yes," he responded, sliding into an antique Empire chair next to the table. He leaned forward, his elbows on his thighs, his hands clasped between his knees. "That is, I'm not sure. We don't know. She has claimed some indisposition which, which remains inexplicable. We will know nothing until tomorrow when the doctor has promised to visit us. Please say nothing to her. She didn't want to overset her daughters with fears which will probably amount to nothing."

"Of course not," she said, rounding the table to place her hand on his shoulder. "I'm sure she's fine, Papa. You have only to look at her to see that she is healthy. In fact, of late I thought her complexion was quite alive with health and vigor—she was almost *glowing.*"

He nodded, patting her hand. "She always enjoys returning to Roselands."

"And as for my own curious appetite, I'm sure it will pass in a day or so."

Lord Brandreth reached over to the tray and removed the linen cover. "Well, I will not allow your soup to grow cold. Pray begin your meal then, but if you don't mind I should like a word with you about Lord Launceston."

Alexandra took a deep breath and wondered how she was to eat the meal before her when she was still full from dinner and her corset was cinched tightly to create her twenty-inch waist. She sat down opposite her father, in a similar antique chair and began taking slow sips of the turtle soup. All the while, she ignored Psyche's gentle murmurs of complaint. She had not eaten since midafternoon and since the clock upon her mantel was striking eleven, Alexandra knew that the poor young woman was famished. She ate slowly therefore and attended carefully to her father's many concerns about each of his daughters' apparent *tendres* for a man he felt was quite indifferent to the marital state.

"His prospects are quite acceptable," Brandreth said. "But he casts his eye about as though he was a young buck of twenty instead of a man of thirty."

Psyche entered the conversation with a giggle. "Launceston reminds me of your father just before he fell in love with Evanthea."

Alexandra bit back a smile recalling to mind Psyche's story of their courtship and how Evanthea Swanbourne and the Marquis of Brandreth had been at daggers drawn until Cupid's arrows had finally taken their toll.

"Why are you smiling?" he queried, his eyes full of affection for his daughter.

"I have always wondered what you were like, Papa, before you fell in love with Mama."

He seemed taken aback as he leaned back in his chair. Clearly he had not considered the matter before. "Well, I don't know," he offered, scratching his head slightly. With a smile that became almost a grin, he continued, "A bit like your Launceston, I suppose. Your mama was used to say I was set up in my own conceit."

Alexandra took another sip of turtle soup, which she had difficulty swallowing. "And were you?" she asked, wondering at the same time how she was supposed to eat all the food on the tray and whether or not she could somehow encourage her father to leave her bedchamber without discouraging the gentle discourse that was presently flowing between them.

He blew a huff of air out his cheeks. "I suppose perhaps I was," he admitted. "I'm not proud of it, but unfortunately when you've been graced with a title and a fortune—"

"Not to mention a handsome face and figure."

"I will bow to your taste in such matters, my dear," he responded, smiling with pleasure. "But as I was saying, the devil of it is, you're pursued by every fortune or handle-mad female about and I suppose there's nothing for it but to forget to check your hat size once in a while."

She finished the turtle soup and began nibbling on the bread which was now cold. Brandreth looked at the remaining repast and shook his head. "And you really are hungry?" he queried.

"Isn't it strange," she responded with a bemused tilt of her head. "But don't feel you must keep me entertained, Papa, for I have little doubt you were headed for your bed when you came upon one of the servants bringing me my tray."

He nodded, the fatigue of the day suddenly settling into his features and over his shoulders. "I was in the saddle for four hours this morning," he said. "And this afternoon I walked through the entire house with your mother's architect, reviewing all her schemes—and they are quite admirable, if I may be permitted to say so. Unfortunately, my legs are stiffening up just sitting here. I must be getting old, Alex." With a laugh, he rose from his chair and added, "I shall tell you what Lady Elle was used to tell me."

"And what was that?"

"Don't get old, Brandreth." He remained looking down at her, a fond light in his gray eyes. "Be careful in your associations with Launceston. He has the devil's own reputation."

"I know Papa and I shall take care—you need have no concerns on that score." She took another bite of the bread which stuck to the roof of her mouth in utter rebellion. She rose to join her father, working the bread free with her tongue, and hooked her elbow about his as she swallowed the offending morsel.

"I love you so, Papa," she said, walking him to the door. "Thank you for being worried about me."

He looked down at her and smiled. "You will always be my pet," he responded sweetly. "At what hour do you intend to go to the Castle, tomorrow?"

"Quite early. Ten o'clock."

He nodded. "The doctor will be here about four o'clock."

"I'll be ready to see him," she responded.

When she had shut the door on him, she finally breathed a sigh of relief and immediately turned toward Psyche. "The soup is all gone," she whispered woefully. "But there is a bit of bread left, some roast beef and apples."

"It's all right," Psyche responded. "The truth is I didn't consider how it would look for you to be eating so much."

Alexandra laughed as she returned to the table, retrieved the tray and carried it to Psyche. "I can't imagine what Papa would say if he knew the truth—that you were lying on my bed with a sprained ankle."

At that, Psyche's pretty face crinkled into a smile and her trilled laughter filled the chamber.

As Brandreth reached his door, the strangest sound greeted his ears, of a young woman's laughter coming from somewhere behind him. A chill went down his spine, for it wasn't just that he knew the laughter did not belong to any of his daughters, but that it seemed somehow familiar. He looked up and down the hallway, but no one was there.

A ghost perhaps?

Was Roselands haunted as well as Castle Porth?

How singular!

* * *

Aphrodite blinked twice and did not at first apprehend where she was. From the blurred image of a nearby window she could see that the hour was sometime in the early morning, perhaps even near dawn, but her mind was so fuzzy she couldn't quite place where she was or even what day it was. What she did know was that something very coarse and prickly was beneath her neck. In fact, she was reclining against it.

"Mama." She heard a voice call to her from what seemed like a great distance, as though she was standing within the recesses of a mountain, deep within a cave, and the voice was coming to her from the entrance of the cave.

"Mama, can you hear me?"

"Anteros?" she whispered, her mouth feeling very dry. She felt a strange sensation on her lips, an oil perhaps, which smelled of sage and thyme. In the confusion of her mind she thought it bore a resemblance to her antidote-to-love potion but that was impossible.

The coarse sensation on her neck was now beginning to irritate her fine, sensitive skin. She reached behind her neck to remove the stiff blanket, or whatever in Hades was prickling her neck, but she could find no edge to the blanket. She opened her eyes and sat up, wondering what on Olympus she could be reclining against and as she craned her neck to see, she discovered a pair of hooves and the monstrous, black flanks of, of— oh, dear Zeus!—a centaur! *The* centaur! *Jupiter's centaur.*

The memory came back to her in a flood—of Eros's terrible prank, of pricking her with his secret blade, of falling into the eyes of the centaur, of hearing the roar and laughter of the crowds and all the while not caring a single whit because she had tumbled in love with the ugliest creature—next to Vulcan, of course!—in the whole of Olympus.

She shrieked and would have awakened the centaur who was fast asleep and snoring gently in his stablelike quarters behind Zeus's palace, but a pair of black wings enfolded her quickly and covered her face. Before she could utter another sound, Anteros had swept her from the stables and into the night sky.

"I shall murder my own child!" she cried out, once she was safely out of the hearing range of any of the Olympians below.

"Stubble it, Mama! What did you expect Cupid to do once he discovered the truth of our schemes?"

"I suppose you are right—but a centaur! I am ruined! I shall be the laughingstock of Bacchus's fêtes for at least two decades."

"But a small price to pay, don't you think? Once we are rid of Psyche, you will be admired for your cunning. If I might prevail on your patience for a moment, Mama, I need your help in one small deed before the night is through. I know where Cupid is for the night—I stumbled upon him quite by accident earlier today when I was beguiling the woman called Alexandra. I was following her, waiting for the right moment to cast my spell over her, when I discovered that for some reason he was making these silly scraping noises all over the castle. I think he is pretending to be a ghost, or some such nonsense.

"At any rate, I followed him throughout the day and found where he hides—a closet near the ballroom. I am convinced he leaves his quiver there. If we can steal his arrows, he will not be able to cause Alexandra and Launceston to tumble in love— but I need your assistance."

"Of course, my darling. Though I would ask that you take me home first—I will want my chariot and doves. You are very strong, but I daresay you would grow fatigued if you had to carry me to England and back."

"I am perfectly capable of doing so," he assured her.

"Even so, you will want to remain at the castle and I will want to return to Olympus. You know I can't abide being gone from home for days at a time."

"Of course."

"Anteros, you will see to everything, won't you? I have so longed to be rid of that female!"

"I will indeed, Mama."

"And you do not still harbor a *tendre* for her, do you?"

He laughed bitterly. "Of course not. In truth, I never did. I merely enjoyed provoking my brother now and again by pretending to be in love with her."

"Excellent," was her murmured reply as she placed a kiss on his forehead. She then shuddered, "I can now recall that I actually tried to kiss the centaur. Oh, I think I shall be ill!"

At ten o'clock on Tuesday morning, Lord Launceston stood on the landing at the top of the stairs and regarded the beautiful Staple sisters before beginning his descent. They were situated in the entrance hall below, their attention caught by something or other in the long gallery. His butler, Cuthbert, was about to direct them to the great hall, but Launceston waved away his servant and gestured not to disturb them for the present.

Cuthbert bowed to him and disappeared quietly between the suits of armor, down the arched hallway, toward the back of the castle. Because the ladies were so completely intrigued by whatever it was that had captured their attention, he was able to observe them unnoticed and to try for a moment to determine why it was that the mere sight of Alexandra, in particular, had served to cut up his peace all over again.

When she had left the day before, clearly on her high ropes, he had been able to revert to his original opinion of her—that she was a Frost Queen born and bred. Nothing it seemed was going to move her from such a cold, unfeeling state—neither the quite pleasant conversation which had flowed between them nor the passionate kiss they had shared. He recalled to mind the manner in which she had responded to his embraces and desire flowed over him. She had returned his kisses as though her whole being had been fixed for a particle of time solely on him. The experience had been intoxicating for there was nothing quite so delicious to him, or to any man perhaps, than to be attended to, however temporarily, as though he was the center of the world.

But the kiss had ended and she had accused him of roguish
conduct toward her and toward their society in general, she had
mocked his character and treated with contempt the kiss they
had enjoyed together by saying she had used him to a purpose—
to secure the masquerade ball. He had been very angry but
when she had left, eventually his temper had calmed and he had
been able to think of her quite dispassionately—until now, when
she was in his home again. He was piqued by her opinions of
him for he didn't feel they were deserved. Yet what more could
he expect of her opinions given the nature of gossip among the
beau monde?

He knew he had a reputation, but the whole of it was built
on lies and jealousies. He would no more seduce an innocent
than he would cut off his leg. As for breaking the hearts of the
ladies of his acquaintance, he was not certain he could be held
to blame for that—young ladies were so fond of fancying themselves in love with any hopeful matrimonial object that was
there any wonder, given his rank and fortune, that his path had
been sprinkled with the tears of disappointed females? God
knows he had tried to keep the silliest of them at bay, but he
had not always been successful in his efforts.

And unfortunately, both Alexandra's sisters were examples
of his failure to do so though to be fair, they were certainly not
as lacking in intelligence as most.

He took a deep breath and resigned himself to the fact that
his relationship with Alexandra was something of a coil, in part
his fault, in part hers, in part nobody's.

As he descended the stairs, therefore, his left hand gliding
along the polished oak wood of the banister, he let his gaze
sweep appreciatively over the beauties before him. He watched
them with some amusement since their attention was still held
captive by something or other—perhaps the new ghost who had
appeared this morning to many of his servants—at the end of
the long gallery. They were still turned toward the doorway
which held a view of the long gallery lit by autumn sunlight
streaming through five arched windows. A massive dining hall

could be reached from the hall and at the end of the gallery was a narrow staircase leading upward to a tower. At the base of the staircase and to the left was a hallway which led to the Green Salon, the expansive kitchens, and the housekeeping offices.

The ladies stood in similar poses, a strong indication of their familial relationship. Each leaned slightly toward the right, bonneted heads cocked, hands clasped into fur muffs, each pair of kissable lips parted prettily. Had he been a more susceptible man, he would have purchased Castle Porth for the sole reason that three such exquisite young beauties resided across the valley from him. As it was, he could only thank Fate that his love and fascination of the ancient, partially ruined castle had also permitted him the enjoyment of all the pleasures which would accrue with the mere presence of Ladies Alexandra, Julia, and Victoria.

Alexandra stood slightly behind her sisters and was gowned in a dark blue plaid taffeta skirt with a short, midnight blue velvet jacket which was pleated about the waist in a peplum of a style not unlike the castellated rooftop of Castle Porth. She was taller than her sisters and in her bearing was a queenly demeanor he had always found quite appealing. She was indisputably the Beauty, though neither Julia nor Victoria fell too far short of her comeliness.

Lady Julia, who he knew to be the next eldest sister, was nearest the stairwell. He paused and scrutinized her profile. Her nose was slightly retrousse—quite different from Alexandra. Her chin was pointed and her smiles infectious. She was the shortest sister though not by any means too small. Of the three sisters, she laughed the most but at the same time displayed the quickest temper. If she was quixotic, not less so than because there was also a part of her that tended to weep in sympathy at the smallest provocation. He remembered during the last season that a friend of hers had lost a favorite pet, an ugly pug dog if memory served, and Julia had draped her arms about her friend's neck and wept with her in her grief.

He understood Julia to fancy herself violently in love with

him. She had once even begged him to kiss her, raising her lips
to him, closing her eyes. She had been deuced pretty that night,
her dark brown hair draped in ringlets about her heart-shaped
face. She had led him into an orangerie during a heavily attended ball and had thrown her arms about his neck. Anyone
could have witnessed such a kiss had he permitted it. But he
hadn't. Instead, he had refused to oblige her, had disengaged
her arms from about his neck, but softened his rebuff by going
down two sets with her. He knew by the triumph in her eyes
that she had believed she had won a victory.

His gaze drifted to Lady Victoria who he realized was a different woman altogether from her two sisters. The youngest,
she had recently celebrated her nineteenth birthday. She shared
the same wide blue eyes with Alexandra and Julia, but her face
had a melancholy cast to it which he knew had intrigued more
than one poetic young man. She had the fairest complexion, the
firmest jawline and her face was a little longer than Alexandra's
which was offset by a fluff of curls on her forehead. She was
deeply moved by beauty, he had discovered, whether in the
paintings in the Royal Museum, or by an exquisitely rendered
interpretation of a Haydn sonata, or by a full moon rising in a
cloudless sky. If she frequently pouted when she did not get her
way, her perfection as a partner for the waltz would easily gain
her forgiveness. She, too, had once begged for a kiss after he
had kept her beside him along the walks of Bath's famous Orange Grove until the paths were deserted. He almost kissed her,
too, for he had just caught sight of Alexandra's disapproving
expression as she appeared at the end of the path, and he had
known an impulse to provoke her by kissing her sister. He had
restrained himself, however, since he knew such a display would
go too far in confirming Victoria's belief that he was tumbling
in love with her.

So instead, he thought with an inward, ironic laugh, though
he had controlled his impulses to kiss Julia and Victoria, the
moment he was alone with Alexandra, he seemed to cast all
caution to the wind and permitted his impulses to run riot. *Why*

was that? he wondered as he approached the bottom of the stairs. Why was it that he had but to look into her eyes and he wanted nothing more than to draw her into his arms? Could it be he had somehow gotten caught up in a stupid schoolboy's *tendre* for the elusive Frost Queen or was he just piqued by her unhappy opinion of his character?

Whatever the case, he thought as he again cast his gaze over her fine person, he had a wager to win. Trenear had even taunted him last night by showing him the unequaled ruby brooch. He had been utterly enchanted by the sight of the deep, wine-colored stone which had come to represent the impossible to him. No one had ever bested Trenear in one of his wagers and no one had ever won the heart of the Frost Queen. For the present, he could think of nothing that would please him more than achieving both objects with the casting of one stone.

So, with these thoughts holding reign in his head, he stepped onto the entrance hall floor of worn granite stone, and addressed Lady Julia first. "How glad I am that you've come," he said, making himself known to all the ladies for the first time since their arrival. He watched with a smile as each of the ladies jumped. He immediately moved toward Julia and possessed himself of her gloved hand. "Why are you frightened, or can I guess? Have you seen our beautiful lady, then, as many of the servants have this morning?"

Julia nodded, clearly caught between a state of fright and amazement. "Indeed, yes—she is exquisite beyond words. But do you mean to tell me she is—she is not real? Is she a ghost?"

"So it would seem," he returned, turning slightly to peer up the hall. The autumn sunlight had drenched the stone hall, setting off to great advantage the ancient portraits of his forbears which had been hung in the long gallery only the night before, but nowhere was the beautiful lady to be seen.

Earlier that morning, his valet had informed him that another ghost had been witnessed by the servants. Launceston had not been surprised when he received a description of the new spectre—a woman of exceptional beauty. So, they were both still residing at Castle Porth, he mused. How odd that he was not disturbed by that fact, almost as though some part of him had already accepted that they would one day reappear to him—and now that day had come. "I apprehend you all saw her?"

"All of us," Victoria chimed in, moving to stand beside Julia.

At the sight of her whiter than usual complexion, he took advantage of her fright by possessing himself of her hand as well. "I am so very sorry you are distressed by these extraordinary events in my poor home. For some reason, even before my arrival of the day prior, the castle has become most seriously haunted."

"How very strange," Victoria returned, "that such a haunting should occur so very suddenly, for Cuthbert was just telling us that these ghosts were not noticed much before two or three weeks past."

He shook his head. "So it would seem. Though I know of another instance, some years past—"

He let the words hang hoping to further frighten the younger ladies since their tremblings would afford him many opportunities to console and to comfort. His consolations would in turn irritate Alexandra.

"Yes?" Julia queried. "When did this happen? How do you know of it?"

"Well, I have never told anyone of my experiences before, but there was a time when I visited my distant relation here many years ago, that I saw ghosts in the chapel ruins. Of course, I only saw them once, the woman such as you have described and the black-winged man."

He chanced at that moment to glance at Alexandra and saw to his surprise that her expression was one, not of fear or apprehension, but of pause, as though she had started to say something but then caught herself.

"What is it?" he queried, withdrawing his hand from Victoria successfully, but finding that Julia was refusing to permit him to disengage his hand. Unwilling to let her divert his attention completely, he admonished her with a friendly scowl and a shake of his head and making use of her hand, he gave her a quick twirl on the stone floor. She giggled, her wide skirts of a pretty apricot silk billowing out all about her.

Only then did she release his hand and return hers to the depths of her sable muff.

When Alexandra didn't answer his question, he pressed her. "I know you were going to say something just then—before Julia began to dance—but what? What did you mean to say?"

Alexandra gestured toward the hallway. "I merely find my curiosity aroused, Lord Launceston. Do you say it was the same woman who you saw many years ago?"

He nodded, slipping his hands behind him since Julia had again withdrawn hers from her muff and was seeking his fingers with her own, the minx.

"And you have seen her yourself this morning?" Alexandra asked.

"No, but by the descriptions I have heard, I have reason to believe she is the same one. Her beauty is something quite out of the ordinary."

Alexandra tilted her head and regarded him closely. "You are not in the least disturbed by the presence of either the lady or the black-winged man, are you?"

He shook his head. "I suppose not," he answered. "They don't seem bent on mischief. Ought I to be afraid?"

A frown rippled Alexandra's brow. "No, I guess not," she responded. Why did he have the feeling she was greatly unsettled by the haunting, unsettled in a manner quite different from her sisters.

She scanned the long gallery again and finally murmured, "I believe she is gone. Perhaps we ought to turn our attention to the many duties waiting to be accomplished."

"Well, then," he said affably. "Let us hope our visitors are harmless and have no greater intention toward us than to give us each a comfortable fright." He smiled as the younger sisters drew close to each other and shuddered. "Pray make yourselves at home. You may set your bonnets and gloves over there," he gestured toward a tall, long table to the side of the entrance hall, "and I shall lead you to the great hall. With only nine days until our ball, I have little doubt that there remains a great deal to be done."

The ladies began removing their charming bonnets, Alexandra's of a dark blue velvet, Julia's of an apricot silk to match her gown, and Victoria's of a forest green velvet, overlaid with an exquisite white ostrich feather, in contrast to her gown of beige, brown, and forest green plaid wool. When the bonnets were properly arrayed on the table, like three plump, colorful pheasants, Launceston graciously guided them into the great hall.

"Eros!" Aphrodite called out.

Cupid heard his mother's voice, but refused to respond. He had secreted himself into a hidden priest's hole between the ballroom and an adjoining antechamber. He had heard the sounds of her doves long before her arrival, for there was only one noise in the world like several hundred doves in flight. The measured beat of their wings as they drew her chariot forward had sent a clear warning to his ears. He suspected Aphrodite had been released from the spell of his arrow probably through his brother's efforts and one of her own potions. He trusted she would quickly lose patience with her search for him and turn the whole of her schemes over to Anteros. He wanted her to return to Olympus as quickly as possible since her potions, should she choose to employ them, or her famous Cestus, could seriously hinder Psyche's efforts in trying to bring Launceston and Alexandra together.

"He is not here," Anteros called to her.

The sound of his brother's voice, and that so near him—faith he must be on the other side of the secret panel in the ballroom itself—startled him.

"Anteros! You naughty child," Venus returned. "You gave me such a start. Were you laying in wait for me this whole time?

Did you know I had arrived? And what do you mean *he is not here?*"

"Cupid is not here," Anteros responded, ignoring all her other questions. "I don't believe he intends to come to rescue his wife this time. I have looked everywhere for him, both here and on Olympus. He's not to be found anywhere."

"And have you found our little *butterfly?*"

Cupid heard the malicious tenor to his mother's words and ground his teeth together. What a fool he had been to have supposed Venus had finally come to accept and love his dear Psyche! He found himself angry all over again, nearly as angry as he had been when he had first discovered how his mama had maneuvered Psyche into returning to earth. He felt the tips of his wings begin to pulse. If he wasn't careful, his wings would subdue the cramped confines of the chamber and whether he wished for it or not, he would pass through the walls. He took a deep breath, then another and forced himself to concentrate on their discussion. Better to listen to their schemes than to lose his temper and expose his presence.

"She is at Roselands—she has secluded herself in Alexandra's bedchamber. Alexandra, if you may recall, is Evanthea Swanbourne's daughter."

"Yes, yes, I know all about her marriage and her progeny. But tell me why Psyche is not here trying to accomplish her mission, for I just saw Alexandra and that fellow Launceston not a moment ago. One would think with the press of time, that she would make haste to bring them together."

"Because, Mama, Cupid's little ninnyhammer turned her ankle coming through the portal. She can't walk or in any other manner move about."

Silence reigned for a brief moment beyond the wall, then both his parent and his sibling burst into a loud, raucous laughter. Again Cupid's choler rose and the tips of his wings began to pulse and thrum. At the same time, he was stunned by the news Anteros had unwittingly related to him. When he had first found his wife upon arriving in Stithwell, she had been in bed, asleep. He had no idea she had been injured! His heart constricted at the thought of her discomfort. And how cruel of his brother and mama to be laughing at her misfortune!

"How utterly perfect," his mother cooed between trills of mirth. "She turned her ankle! She will now be able to achieve nothing!"

"She always was a birdwitted female. Imagine not being able to navigate through a portal? I have given myself over to uncontrollable fits of laughter more than once thinking on it. We shall prevail this time, Mama. We shall! Psyche can do nothing now and so long as Cupid does not attempt to help her, we shall prevail!"

Cupid could no longer control his anger. Knowing that his wings were about to unfurl and that his hands would just as quickly be about Anteros's throat if he surrendered to the rage which poured through him, he leaned against the opposite wall and let himself fall into the empty hallway beyond. He took another deep breath, and began running in the direction of the great hall, away from the ballroom as quickly as he could. Once in the great hall, he unfurled his wings and with a single mighty beat, lifted off in the direction of Roselands, passed through the thick granite wall of the castle and hurled himself into the air. A moment later, he had disappeared into the woods to the east of Roselands and circled back toward the house.

Psyche was hurt!

Zeus help her, his mind cried. She had to succeed in this absurd task or he would lose her forever.

Anteros bid goodbye to his mother and after kissing her softly on the cheek waited until her chariot had disappeared from sight against the deep blue sky of the October day, before returning to the ballroom on a dead run. His brother was such a fool and if he knew him, he had left his bow and arrows behind in the priest's closet.

When he arrived at the ballroom, he slipped through its thin wall and found the chamber deserted just as he suspected it would be. He knew his brother well, that once having learned of his wife's injury, Cupid would waste no time in going to her side.

Now, as he let his eyes adjust to the darkness of the chamber, he dropped to his knees and with his hands began searching for the quiver, the arrows, and the bow. The feel of soft velvet drifted over his fingertips and he smiled. He lifted the cloth and with both hands found the bow and quiver full of arrows—the new ones from Vulcan, truer to the mark than ever. A moment later, he was rising through the ceiling of the small chamber into the bedchambers above, on and on until he left the castle itself. Once in the open air, he paused, gained his bearings and proceeded to the small turret which overlooked Roselands. For the present he had made his home in the tower which rose from a narrow set of stairs at the end of the long gallery. He slipped easily through the wall. Using a piece of linen he had retrieved from his home in Olympus he wrapped up the bow and arrows. Afterward, he returned to the air and flying swiftly to the beech forest to the south of the castle, hid the arrows deep within the rotted trunk of an ailing tree and packed the opening with moss. Satisfied that the arrows could not be discovered easily, he returned to the solitude of the tower where he intended to rest for a time. Bringing his mother to Castle Porth had greatly fatigued him.

The round chamber which was his home for the present was quite small and housed only a bed of straw, a table, and a stool. Round, iron rings, about shoulder height and shoulder width were stuck in the wall but for the life of him he couldn't determine what their purpose might be. Of course, Psyche would know and probably Cupid for both of them had frequently visited earth over the centuries, until Zeus's recent ban, of course. But for himself, he found mortals to be a dead bore. They were always tumbling in love, for one thing, then living unhappily for several decades after with their chosen spouses.

She almost fell. Bennett! Hurriedly she pulled on her robe and went into the living room.

"Bennett, what's the matter? Is something wrong?"

"I should ask you that. I called and called, first it was busy, then no answer. Where've you been?"

They stood on opposite sides of the room hurling questions at each other, and both fell silent at the same moment. Margaret shrugged and turned first, going into the kitchen. She said over her shoulder, "I went shopping. I was gritty, so I showered before putting the things away. Do you want a sandwich or something?"

"No." He followed her and watched as she emptied the bag. His gaze kept returning to her face, and he said abruptly, "Margaret, stop all that. Sit down a minute. Why did you have the phone off the hook?"

She sat down by him at the small kitchen table. "I found it off at about ten," she said, "and put it back. I must have knocked it off earlier without noticing. And today I drove awhile, then shopped and came home." She felt momentarily that she was leaving something out, but whatever it was, it was gone, and she waited.

Bennett suddenly stood up and went to the door, making certain it was locked. "Do those two come right in when they get ready? I saw the kid starting to come up the back stoop when I drove up. He saw me and left. What are they doing?"

"I don't really know. Research into the work of Paul Tyson. I will let them take out only one notebook at a time, and when they finish it and bring it back, I give them another one. They're working in the apartment over the garage."

He wasn't really listening. He looked at her again, and

quickly averted his gaze. "I feel such a fool," he said after a moment. "I never had a suspicious moment before, not until Arnold Greeley planted the idea. But now, with you, I feel like an idiot. Have you been crying?"

"Soap," she said.

He nodded. "You . . . you're looking very beautiful. And you act differently somehow. You're not ... I mean, Margaret, are you pregnant?"

She was startled at the thought and shook her head. Bennett came up to her and touched her cheek lightly. She didn't move away, but he passed on behind her chair and, standing behind her, his hand caressed her neck, then slid down her robe and inside it. He stopped when his fingers came in contact with her nipple that was still hard and upright. His hand tightened and his other hand on her shoulder dug in hard. He squeezed her breast, hurting her, then withdrew his hand and said, in a thick, almost unrecognizable voice, "Get dressed. I'll take you to an early dinner down in Hampstead. I know a nice place. We'll come home early and get some sleep. And in the morning I have to catch a flight back down to Atlantic City."

Margaret felt the blood suffuse her face and neck at his touch, then drain away, leaving her almost faint. She stood up unsteadily, and turned toward him. "Bennett . . ." She was holding the chair back to keep her balance. If he would take her now, she knew there would be an end to so many things. If only he would learn her sexuality, her needs that were as great, as bad, she thought first, as his own, or even more powerful maybe than his. Take me to bed and make me come again and again and again, she cried silently. Please, Bennett.

He turned from her and said, "Is there any Scotch

He threw himself on the bed, wrapping his wings tightly about his body and resting his hands behind his head.

He thought it likely being leg-shackled to Alexandra would be pleasant, but only for a brief time. She wasn't so bad in herself, it was just that for as long as he could remember, only one lady had ever caught his fancy.

How quickly his spirits fell as his thoughts turned toward Psyche. A fire burned within his chest until even breathing caused him a kind of pain so great it was all he could do to keep from screaming.

How ironic, he thought, that he was the god of unrequited love and he had fallen in love with a woman he would never be able to possess.

Well, if he couldn't have her, then Eros couldn't have her either! Before nine moons crossed the sky, he would see Psyche bound to earth, and therefore to the fading of her immortality and to the eventual destruction of her temporal body. At the same time, he would take a wife to himself, if only to torment Cupid.

Perhaps then he would finally know some peace.

Nine

Psyche reclined upon several plump pillows and squinted through the spectacles she had found while rummaging through the drawer of the table next to Alexandra's bed. She held the novel she had been given to read at an even greater distance than before but she still could only barely make out the word, *Ivanhoe,* and let out a trill of laughter.

"What are you doing, my love?"

Psyche was so startled by her husband's sudden appearance at the foot of her bed, that she gave a little shriek, dropped the book on her lap and placed a hand at her chest as though to protect herself from him.

"Oh, it is you," she breathed with a great sigh of relief. "Eros! How happy I am to see you? But however did you get here? Oh, silly me. You are a god. You don't need to use a portal like us mere half-mortals."

"I've come to help if I can," he said, carefully stealing about the bedpost and settling himself by her wounded ankle. Lifting the cloth, he winced when he saw how swollen it was. "I only recently learned you were injured. My darling, are you in very much pain?"

"Only when I try to move my leg, which is frequently since I am getting very sore lying here hour after hour." Her smile faded completely as she recalled the moment she had been injured. "The journey through the portal was so very painful," she whispered. "I fell from the ceiling to the floor."

Cupid looked up at the tall ceiling and whistled low. "You

were fortunate not to have broken a bone. Are you certain you didn't?"

Psyche nodded. "As painful as this is, it isn't anything like the time I climbed about the peach orchard and broke my arm. No, I'm certain it's only a sprain." She then looked up at him and her heart filled with affection for the man she loved. "I have to do this," she said.

"I know," Eros returned, sadly. "But I will help you. At first I meant to let you do what you could by yourself, but now I see that you can't. I've brought my arrows and as soon as I can find Alexandra alone with Launceston, I shall see the job done. Then, at the appointed hour on All Hallow's Eve, I shall whisk you away to the portal."

"Thank you, my darling," she said, sighing with pleasure. "I had hoped to accomplish the task myself, but I hadn't expected to be hurt."

A frown rippled Cupid's forehead. "They wish us separated forever."

"I know," Psyche said, tears starting to her eyes. "Why do they hate me so?"

Cupid rose from the bed very gently and came to kneel beside his wife. "Do you know," he said softly, stroking her hair with his hand, "I think they are jealous of you for several reasons, but not least of which is because I am utterly devoted to you. You know what my mother is, she may be the goddess of love, but jealousy is her handmaiden. As for Anteros—I don't know. I was used to think he was in love with you himself, but why then would he want to see you bound again to earth? He must know you would soon wither and die."

Psyche shook her head, as perplexed as her husband about Anteros's motives. She lifted her hand to touch her husband's cheek. "So long as you are with me, Cupid, I don't give a fig for why they dislike me."

He leaned forward and placed his lips on hers. Psyche took in his breath and felt her whole body begin to tingle as it always did when he was near. She felt the tips of his feathered wings touching her arms lightly and she sighed yet again. Her heart went out to him as it always did when he was close to her. She loved him so very much and still his touch pleased her as though he was touching her for the first time instead of the ten thousandth.

After a moment, he drew back and regarded her lovingly. "I know that even at this moment, Alexandra is at Castle Porth and I assure you I intend to begin at once."

"But you already have, haven't you?" Psyche returned, smiling secretively.

"What do you mean?"

"The scraping noises?"

He chuckled. "Yes, that was me."

"He kissed her, you know," she said, slipping an arm about his neck. "Like this." She then drifted her lips over his and to her delight felt his immediate response as he kissed her very hard in return, murmuring his pleasure all the while.

After a long, lingering moment, he finally drew back from her and shook his head. "I wish you weren't hurt, my dear. For I vow I have the strongest inclination of the moment to sweep you into the woods nearby."

Psyche giggled. "And I would go with you."

When he got just that particular glint in his eye, she quickly set a hand on his chest and pushed him playfully away. "You had better go!" she cried. "At once!"

He growled at her, but after placing one final and very quick kiss on her lips, he lifted into the air and disappeared through the stone wall heading south to Castle Porth.

Alexandra was seated in a tapestried prie-dieu chair by the window, the morning light pouring from between the crimson velvet draperies to illuminate her scribblings over her left shoulder. Every now and then she would glance through the window to enjoy the view of the rooftops of Stithwell in the distance. She held a pen in hand and a small lap desk settled firmly before her, her feet propped up on a small footstool. She was making out a list of guests to invite to the masquerade ball while her sisters were sitting in a *tête-à-tête* chair near the rosewood pianoforte and penning the invitations.

She lifted her head from her scrutiny of the list of names she was compiling and again gazed at the rise and fall of Stithwell's skyline in the distance. Her thoughts, however, were not fixed on the small market town, but on Launceston.

They had kissed and quarreled yesterday, but this morning it was as if nothing untoward had occurred between them. She realized that regardless of her need to encourage him in order to thwart Anteros's assaults on her, the flow of her relationship with the viscount was an utter mystery to her. It seemed to her that no matter how many times she tried to devise a sort of neat little box for Launceston, the next time she saw him, he would burst out of the box and surprise her.

This morning he had done no less since from the moment he greeted her at the bottom of the stairs, he had treated her with a friendly, agreeable demeanor even though they had each spoken harsh words to one another on the day before. Somehow she had expected him to still be angry with her, but when they had entered the great hall an hour earlier and Julia and Victoria had exclaimed over the decor of his principal receiving room, he had whispered to her, "Will you forgive me for my conduct of yesterday? I should not have kissed you and having kissed you it is no wonder you upbraided me for my lack of principles."

She could only stare at him, wonder, and wonder again. Never would she have expected him to have humbled himself to her and because he did so when she was as much to blame as he for the indelicate kiss they had shared and the brangling which followed, her heart softened toward him immediately.

"Of course," she had responded warmly. She had wanted to say more, but the next moment both Julia and Victoria swarmed over him, begging him to explain where he had found such exquisite sofas and whether or not he would sit with one or the other in the fashionable, and exceedingly romantic, *tête-à-tête* chairs.

Now, as she added another name to the list of guests, she found herself oddly content in both her task and to be in his home. He was for the present sitting on the sofa facing the windows and amusing himself by reading the *Gentleman's Magazine*. The numerous bids for attention he received from her sisters he responded to by answering their questions and hints with generous affability.

She was just adding the honorable Mylor Grampound to the list, when she heard, just for the barest moment, a scraping noise coming from the direction of the three arched windows and sounding very much like those of the day before.

She turned her head toward the tall, arched window behind her, the October light now full on her face, and wondered if she had indeed heard the strange noise. At the same time she thought it possible that Anteros had arrived to give them all a fright and to continue his devilish schemes.

In her many cogitations about the extraordinary events of the past two days, she had become convinced that the god of unrequited love had orchestrated the scraping noises himself for the purpose of placing her in a vulnerable position in order to steal her from England. From what Psyche had told her, and indeed from what she had sensed from Anteros himself, he was an exceedingly lonely creature who wished for a companion. She certainly did not begrudge him his happiness, but she took strong exception to the fact that his pursuit of contentment involved her so nearly.

As she continued to listen for more scraping noises, she wondered what would happen if she tried to speak with Anteros about his need and wish for a wife. Perhaps he was not beyond reason and with a few carefully chosen words she might be able to direct him into a different mode of thinking.

For this reason, she secured the lid on her silver filigreed inkpot, returned her pen to its tray and rose to set the lap desk on the table at her elbow.

She felt movement behind her and whirled around to see if Anteros was there, playing at his tricks, appearing and disappearing, but she saw only Launceston. He had risen from his seat on the velvet sofa and was certainly too far away from her to have created the faint rush of air which brushed across the back of her neck.

He met her gaze, a questioning expression in his eye. Another scraping sound ensued from the antechamber beyond, this time causing both Julia and Victoria to glance toward the doors of the great hall, opposite the window, from which direction the sound had emanated.

"That is what I heard yesterday," Alexandra said, addressing her sisters.

"The ghosts again!" Julia and Victoria cried in unison, their own pens held poised in mid-air, their blue eyes wide with fright.

"Alexandra, where are you going?" Victoria asked, a frightened frown on her brow.

Alexandra, who had immediately begun walking toward the doors, turned back and said, "I must confess to more curiosity than may be wise for me. If Lord Launceston doesn't mind, I wish to discover for myself if, if the beautiful lady has returned."

"I can have no objection," he said. "In fact, I shall come with you. I think it time I meet the spectre or spectres who have taken to haunting my home and frightening my guests."

"Well, I for one, intend to remain here," Julia cried, "since it would seem your ghosts have already passed through this chamber."

Victoria slipped her hand in Julia's and after swallowing hard, said, "I am staying with Julia. But pray, once you have found your ghosts, please tell them to leave. I am not of such a romantical turn that I find these scraping sounds in the least soothing."

Launceston bowed to her and promised her he would do all

he could to discourage his ghostly visitors from remaining within the bounds of his castle walls.

Cupid reached his priest's hole intent upon seeing his task accomplished with all speed. He had been immensely pleased to have found Alexandra and Launceston together in the great hall, and decided that two arrows would suffice to begin his redirecting of their hearts. He would place the arrows with great precision in the bosom of each of his victims, the blossoming of love would follow as it always did, four additional arrows would be dispatched for both of his victims on two successive days, and the deed would be done!

Slowly he dropped to the stone floor, feeling his way since the small, secretive closet was as black as a raven's feather. Once on his knees, he began to search for his velvet-cloaked bow and quiver of arrows, but he found nothing. Again he searched the stones, carefully feeling every space, every corner. Still nothing.

Three times he spun about on his knees scrutinizing every inch of the priest's hole, but his quiver and bow were not to be found.

When the reality of his loss struck home, a blow across his face could not have been more stunning. The arrows were gone.

Somehow Anteros had discovered his hiding place and had stolen his precious weapons. He recalled the conversation between Anteros and their mother and groaned aloud. Like actors they had staged their exchange—informing him of Psyche's injury, speaking of her with such malice—so that of course he would lose his head and leave his arrows unattended! He felt ill and utterly stupid at having been duped by his brother.

Zeus take it! What in Hades was he going to do now? Vulcan had required three weeks to fabricate his new arrows since the love potion had been carefully poured, in successive stages, into the molten metal before the arrows were even cast. And he had already had his old arrows melted down!

He turned and sat down, leaning his back against the cold

stones, his wings a comfortable cushion against the hard wall. He drew his knees up and clasped his hands about them burying his face into the palms of his hands.

What was he to do now? The only other potions that would have any effect upon the hearts of either Alexandra or Launceston belonged to his mother. At that, he lifted his head, a rather wicked scheme rising sharply in his mind. She had several love potions which, according to Psyche who had stolen them two decades prior, she kept in her wardrobe. He smiled to himself. Given his mother's despicable conduct toward his wife, he had no misgivings in deciding that next he ought to pay a secretive, nocturnal visit to his mother's palace, in particular, to her wardrobe!

He would have given himself over to planning precisely how and when he would steal his mother's potions, but voices interrupted his reveries. A moment later, he grew to an awareness that Launceston and Alexandra had entered the ballroom.

He listened to them for a moment and realized that Launceston was teasing her about some event which must have occurred in the past.

"You wished for it!" he cried. "Admit it is true!"

"I wished for nothing of the sort," Alexandra responded warmly. "When you came upon me I was merely taking a stroll along the River Avon, which summer visitors to Bath are wont to do. And I did not invite you to kiss me. I did not!"

Cupid listened to the tone of her voice and heard neither distress nor anger. In fact, the lilt of her words was almost playful. A flirtation, perhaps? This was promising indeed!

"You most certainly did!" Launceston countered. "The truth is, I have never held a more willing lady in my arms."

"I find that very hard to believe and you may take that roguish smile from your lips. You were mistaken in everything! I'm sure when you appeared on your horse the sun was in my eyes and if you saw anything in my expression of, of desire, it was undoubtedly due to my sincerest hope that I would not go blind from the strong sunlight."

"The sun was at your back."

"It was not."

So they had shared a kiss, and a rather forbidden one at that if what he was hearing was true. Well, this at least gave him cause to hope and furthermore, the nature of their discussion indicated Alexandra's sisters were not presently with them.

If only he had in his possession his bow and arrows! How easily his task might be achieved!

Ah, well, he thought, better not to dwell on what he didn't have and concentrate instead on what might be done, especially since for these few moments Alexandra and Launceston were alone together. He knew enough of life in earth's nineteenth century to know that unmarried ladies were rarely permitted to be alone with their beaux. He therefore began to search his mind for ways he might press to advantage the unique situation before him.

When he could hear their footsteps and the sounds of their voices diminish, he knew they were leaving the ballroom. He rose to his feet, intending to follow them. For though he might not know precisely what he could do to advance their budding romance, he intended to be ready for an opportunity to act should one present itself.

He kept himself invisible as he slipped through the wall and followed them into the hallway opposite the ballroom which would lead back to either the great hall, the entrance hall, or the chapel ruins. An idea came to him and bounding ahead of his prey, he entered a central antechamber which contained the most peculiar table whose legs were actually a statue of what looked like Atlas supporting a table top upon which sat a simple oil lamp. Ignoring the strange table, he purposefully dragged his sandaled foot across the stones and a moment later had the satisfaction of seeing Alexandra appear in the doorway of the intersecting hall and stare straight through him.

Alexandra had heard a distinct scraping noise and now stood at the intersection of a hallway and a small antechamber. She realized she was looking at the gladiatorial table which she had encountered on the day before. Beyond the table, directly ahead of her, was the long narrow hallway and the short flight of stairs which led to the chapel ruins. So this was where the hallways merged—from the ballroom to the chapel.

"Did you hear that?" she queried, glancing at Launceston who was now standing beside her.

"Yes," he responded. "Our ghosts again. But what do they want of me, or of my guests, or of my home? I am completely baffled."

Lord Brandreth stood in the entrance hall of Castle Porth and stared in some astonishment down the darkened, arched hallway below the landing of the stairs and could not for the life of him determine what could have caused the sliding noise he had just heard. Gooseflesh travelled all down his spine and he thought yet again that ever since yesterday the calm of his world had been overset. Firstly, ghosts were reported at Castle Porth and suspected at Roselands, then his eldest and most sensible daughter paid a scandalous call upon Launceston, then he learned his wife was suffering from an unexplained malady requiring the attention of her physician, then he discovered that Alexandra was eating no less than six or seven meals each day!

Was it any wonder such a peculiar scraping sound should set his nerves on edge?

Only where were Launceston and Alexandra?

He had arrived but a few minutes earlier and Launceston's butler had announced him to his two youngest daughters. Even the butler had been astonished to find that the viscount was not present in the great hall nor the marquis's eldest daughter.

Julia and Victoria quickly explained the absence of their sister and their host—they had gone in search of a ghost they had seen earlier, some drivel about a beautiful woman and a scraping noise.

He had dismissed their high complexions and fretful manners

believing both of his daughters were suffering the familiar symptoms ladies frequently did when they had been engaged in reading far too many novels. But now, as he stared down the hallway, waiting for what he knew not, he was not so certain that Julia and Victoria had been mistaken in exclaiming over "scraping sounds."

Waiting for what seemed like an eternity but could only have been a minute, another sound ensued, coming from the same direction. A moment later, he saw Alexandra pass by the end of the hallway, with Launceston in tow. Neither of them saw him, and it was clear each was intent on precisely what had caught his own attention—the sliding, scraping sound. He proceeded to walk slowly toward the hallway.

Alexandra reached the short staircase and turned back to Launceston who was right behind her. "Dare we go into the chapel?" she queried.

"Perhaps we are being summoned there," Launceston suggested, not without a smile.

Alexandra looked up at him for a long moment, and the thought struck her that when he was being as sweet as he presently was, she found herself enjoying his company immensely. His hazel eyes were lit with amusement and she knew he was teasing her, as he had been in the most delightfully flirtatious manner ever since they had left the great hall some few minutes ago.

Psyche had suggested she get up a flirtation with Launceston and perhaps for that reason she had not immediately rebuffed him when he had first begun talking nonsense with her. And it was nonsense, all of it. First he had complimented her on the peplum of her snug-fitting midnight blue coat, then he had praised the courage she was displaying in wishing to follow after the ghosts, then he had quite scandalously accused her of having begged to be kissed when he had first chanced upon her by the River Avon.

She had never been led such a pretty dance before, nor had she ever permitted herself to be led down such summery, flowery paths. But here she was, looking into his eyes and feeling her heart warm to him, to his words, to the amusement lighting his face, to how close he was standing next to her.

The scandalous thought came to her that she wanted him to kiss her again and she quickly pushed the thought away. She couldn't be forever kissing Launceston! She couldn't! She might need to flirt with him in order to keep Anteros from stealing her away from England, but if she continued to permit him to assault her whenever they were alone, he would soon begin to develop a wretched opinion of her character.

"What are you thinking about?" he whispered, leaning toward her slightly.

"N-nothing," she replied, also in little more than a whisper. She felt his hand on her arm and her heart leaped at his touch.

"Tell me," he murmured, leaning closer to her yet, his breath just touching the temple of her forehead. "Were you thinking of yesterday or perhaps two summers past?"

"You shouldn't be reminding me of things that should never have been," she said, not daring to look at him. She was persuaded if she did so, she would again fall into his arms. "Nor should you be prompting what ought not to be."

She felt the faint touch of his lips on her temple. "I am beginning to think you are just the sort of woman who enjoys being reminded of what ought not to be."

"Oh," she said, swallowing hard. Why were his forbidden words so pleasant to hear and how was it possible his nearness could cause her to so easily forget that she despised him?

But this won't do, she adjured herself. If she must flirt with him, so be it, but she couldn't permit him to kiss her again and by all appearances, he was fully prepared to do just that!

So, with some reluctance, she took a step away from him, and taking up her plaid skirts in hand, began to ascend the steps, very slowly. "I think we ought to go into the chapel and see what we might find, don't you?"

"As you wish," he said.

"I'm sure I heard a noise coming from here yesterday," she added. She reached the small landing at the top of the short flight of stairs, turned to see if he meant to follow her and the next moment she felt a strong push at the small of her waist.

"Oh!" she cried, as she fell forward. At the same moment, Launceston, waiting at the bottom of the stairs, braced himself and caught her neatly in his arms, lifting her up at the same time so that she would not injure her feet or ankles on the steps.

She was so frightened that when he held her tightly to his chest, she made no effort to pull away from him but breathed her thanks at his having caught her as he did.

"You were pushed!" he cried, astonished. "I saw it plainly."

"Indeed, I was," she breathed, her heart racing. Why would Anteros do this to her?

"There, there. You are all right now." He was patting and stroking her back, comforting her. One of her arms was draped about his neck and holding him fast.

"Launceston, I'm afraid," she murmured into the lapels of his gray wool coat. "I've—I've *seen* the, the ghosts, but I've never had one try to *harm* me before."

Her heart was still pounding in her chest and for a long moment she did not try to draw away from him. He murmured soothing words of comfort into her ear and held her tightly about the waist. He rocked her gently and time became a passing breeze, cool and welcome, a soothing balm. Her heartbeat began to slow, and the warmth of his shoulder calmed her frayed nerves.

When at last she felt less agitated, she tried to draw away from him, but he would not permit her to do so. He looked down at her and shook his head. "Your deathly complexion tells me if I let you go, you will faint," he said firmly.

She was feeling quite dizzy and nodded to him, letting her head again rest on his shoulder. "Thank you," she murmured. "I believe you may be right."

After a time, she lifted her head intending to begin the delicate process of withdrawing politely from his arms, but his lips were too near her own to make it possible for her to continue with her initial resolution. His face grew dark with passion and for a reason she could not explain she found herself responding to him, yet again.

"Launceston," she whispered, a desire to be kissed by him overcoming every dictum of modesty and propriety.

He seemed to need no greater invitation and the next moment his lips were pressed against hers in a soft, sensual touch that quickened her pulse and took her breath away. Her mind grew very distant, as though separated from her body somehow. If she knew that what she was doing was very, very wrong, she dismissed these traitorous promptings of her conscience and let her mind drift to a place of perfect peace. She had no thoughts, she could only feel the softness of his kisses—so very different from the last time—and the strength of his arms surrounding her.

Was this what love felt like, she wondered?

She parted her lips, as before, but this time his search of her was sublimely gentle and she wished he would go on kissing her forever and ever.

She disappeared entirely and felt as though she was floating freely, the gentlest of breezes carrying her from one pillowy cloud to the next. She cooed her pleasure and felt the smallest shift of his arms about her waist, tighter, stronger, safer. A warmth flowed through her, so enticing, that she drew closer to him still, turning into him fully and slipping her other arm about his neck.

Lord Brandreth returned to Roselands without having addressed either his daughter or Lord Launceston. He had been so overset by the sight of Alexandra kissing the viscount—and that so very passionately—that rather than follow his immediate impulse to plant the man a facer and drag all three of his daughters from his home, Brandreth called for his horse and quickly

left Castle Porth. He wanted to speak with his wife first about
what he had witnessed and what such a kiss could possibly
mean rather than go off half-cocked. She knew Alexandra far
better than he and would have her own ideas about what ought
to be done next, if anything.

For himself, he was completely bemused. Why had Launceston chosen to assault his sensible Alexandra and why had she
submitted to his rather fulsome embrace when it was commonly
known they were at daggers drawn? Was it possible his daughter
was tumbling in love at last? Or was Launceston working his
wiles upon her untried sensibilities? Whatever the case, he
wanted his wife's opinion first before intervening in the quite
unacceptable affair. That he himself had several times assaulted
Evanthea before ever expressing a genuine love for her, was
the chiefest reason he hesitated. To call Launceston a libertine
for kissing his daughter would be doing it a bit too brown for
his own conscience's sake.

For that reason, he sought out his wife for the strict purpose
of laying the whole of the matter before her. He found her in
her bedchamber of blue velvet and gilt, resting on her bed, her
eyes heavy with fatigue. "You didn't sleep well?" he asked,
momentarily setting aside his concerns for Alexandra in the face
of his wife's mounting illness.

"I have been so sleepy of late—I can't account for it. How
grateful I am I permitted you to summon my physician for I
can't for the life of me determine why my usual buoyancy has
failed me."

He drew a chair forward next to the stately tester bed. Seating
himself, the long gold fringe of the royal blue velvet bed curtains brushed his cheek as he leaned forward to possess himself
of his wife's hand. She turned on her side to better see him and
the light pouring over his shoulder from the windows behind
him illuminated her lovely face. She was nine and forty but had
all the youthful beauty of a lady in her thirties. He loved her
so very much, he thought, as he looked down at her. He was
glad too that he had sent for Dr. Newquay, for he could now

see that bluish circles lay beneath her eyes in contrast to her otherwise rather healthy complexion—her cheeks were even tinged with an apricot glow.

He caressed her face with his hand and ran a thumb across her chin. "I adore you, Evanthea," he said softly, smiling at the way she squinted at him as he spoke. She wasn't wearing her spectacles and he suspected she could barely see him.

Her affectionate smile deepened, however, and her brown eyes narrowed as she laid her hand over his, then turned to kiss the palm of his hand. After sighing with what he perceived to be her contentment, she queried, "You have returned so quickly from Castle Porth? Did you speak with Launceston? All is well, I trust?"

At that he sighed heavily. "I don't know," he said. "You see, I found our daughter in the arms of our new neighbor."

"Which daughter?" she queried, her brows lifted in surprise.

He chuckled softly. "Not the one you would imagine," he said.

"Ah," Lady Brandreth murmured, her eyes taking on a curious gleam. "So, Alexandra has fallen in love with him. I thought as much."

"As easily said as that," he returned, dumbfounded. "Without even a shade of doubt in the timbre of your voice! *Alexandra has fallen in love with him.*"

"Why are you so piqued? Because you did not perceive it before me?"

"Well, I am her father," he said. "And we do share a most excellent camaraderie."

"That you do," she assured him. "But to own the truth, I only began to suspect Cupid was at work when she wore that rather daring gown yesterday."

He lifted a brow, withdrew his hand from her cheek and leaned back into his chair. "Which gown?" he queried, his fatherly concern now taking an entirely new turn. He saw his wife bite her lip and knew she was regretting her revelation.

"I had not seen it before yesterday," she said. "A new gown, perhaps, or—now that I think on it, I begin to wonder if she did not have her blue velvet gown cut daringly low across the bosom."

"What?" he exclaimed. "Exposing her bosom in the afternoon? I am shocked!"

Lady Brandreth nodded and swallowed visibly. "Now pray don't take a pelter. If I recall correctly, when I began to view you with an amorous eye, I also changed my costume considerably. You were quite moved by the sight of my gowns, if I remember correctly."

"Don't be absurd. I don't recall anything of the sort except that for a time, before Annabelle got her hands on you, you were something of a dowd and then you became fashionable and very, very pretty."

She turned her head and eyed him suspiciously. "And not once were you moved by the décolleté of one of my gowns? You are such a hypocrite, Brandreth, and well you know it!"

He huffed a little, and would have protested, but he knew she was right. "Damme, but you always could see through my pretensions and stupidity. What man isn't charmed by a woman's *charms.*"

"Precisely so."

"But when, exactly, did Alexandra decide to begin *charming* our new neighbor, that is what I wish to know. I mean, they always despised each other. There is something about the whole of this business, including the masquerade, which I find completely baffling." He crossed his arms over his chest and directed his gaze to the bird's-eye maple wardrobe which was across the chamber and situated next to the door. He sighed again.

He was quiet for a long moment, turning the matter over in his mind for several minutes. Finally, he said, "Well, when she returns for the doctor's visit, I shall speak with her, warn her against setting her heart on an object which may not be capable of returning her affection. But tell me what you think, my dear, should I ask her about—" As he looked down at his wife, however, he saw that she had fallen into her slumbers, her eyes were closed, her breathing was slow and even, her soft hand was tucked beneath her cheek, her lips were parted just so.

He was overwhelmed suddenly with affection for her. "Oh, my darling Evanthea," he whispered. "Pray don't be ill, for I don't know how I would get on without you."

"It is called a stethoscope," Alexandra murmured, as the door closed upon the doctor. Psyche had been curious as to what the instrument was the physician had used to examine her. It was a small object, about ten inches in length, each end opened and belled though of differing bell-shapes. The larger bell had been pressed against her chest and the smaller opening held to one of his ears. "He listened to my heart and to my lungs and apparently can discover my ailments by the sounds he hears. I think it is pure humbug, of course, but Dr. Newquay has a very fine reputation in Falmouth."

"I saw you jump," Psyche said. "Did it hurt you?"

Alexandra smiled. "No. It was just very cold. But I don't see how I am to go to bed for a week. I only hope Papa does not insist I obey the doctor's orders." She then looked back at Psyche and said with a smile, "But never mind that! He kissed me."

Psyche opened her eyes wide. "The doctor?" she queried.

Alexandra laughed and shook her head. "No. Launceston. He kissed me yesterday, too." She rose from her seat on the bed and slowly progressed around the foot of the bed to tend to Psyche on the other side. "How is your ankle?" she asked, lifting the cloths and noting that some of the swelling had diminished.

"Better, I think. But I still want to cry out in pain every time I but barely move it. With only nine days until the ball I wonder if I will be able to walk."

Alexandra looked down at the delicate beauty and said, "Don't fret yourself yet. Nine days can heal a body quite well, you'll see."

Psyche then gestured toward the red velvet and oak chair by her bed. "Do sit down, then, and tell me all about these kisses of yours."

Alexandra seated herself as she was bid and for some reason felt perfectly comfortable in relating the whole of the morning's experience, ending with how Launceston had comforted her when she had been pushed—undoubtedly by Anteros!—down the stairs.

"What I don't understand though," Alexandra said, after completing her detailed accounting of all of the events, "is why I continue permitting Launceston to kiss me. I know he hasn't the smallest proper intention toward me and what of my own motives? I have no interest in, in marrying him. He would not in any manner make a proper husband—he is arrogant and immodestly self-assured with the ladies, his years in India must by their nature be suspect, and he argues with everything I say to him. Really, the whole of it is a mystery to me."

"Love is always that way," Psyche returned, giving her brown curls a shake.

"But I am not in love with him," Alexandra returned firmly.

"As to that, I believe the reason you feel almost compelled to kiss him is that to a small degree you are experiencing a form of love, if not one that will mature into marriage. But I think what I wanted to say is that no relationship, before or after marriage, proceeds without any number of complexities, breaches of understanding, and passionate episodes.

"I remember when I was helping your mother and father to tumble in love, I was also at the same time having the most dreadful breach with Cupid over some stupid misunderstanding of nearly a half-century past. You see, I danced with Anteros and he, well, he sort of kissed me and somehow Cupid saw us at that moment and believed I had given my heart to his brother. Can you imagine anything so absurd?"

"You kissed Anteros?" she asked, shocked.

At that Psyche shifted her gaze away from Alexandra. "Cupid had been flirting with a tavern wench, here in England, and had been ignoring me one year out of two and I guess I thought I might take a little comfort in Anteros's interest in me."

"His interest in you?" Alexandra queried.

"Well, yes. I think he had developed a sort of *tendre* for me, but nothing to signify. At any rate, after he kissed me, I realized I could not oblige him further and so I broke with him in that very moment. But Cupid did not know as much and came to suspect me of the very worst of wifely transgressions. Month upon month he grew more and more distant, more belligerent and month upon month my heart fell to a place of despair so deep I thought I would never return from it. That was when I came to Flitwick Lodge, where Lady Elle originally resided, and decided to forget my troubles by involving myself in your mother's affairs."

Alexandra smiled. "Do tell me all about it," she said. "Lady Elle told me the story, but I do so wish to hear it again, of how you stole your mama-in-law's Cestus and how Cupid shot Annabelle and she fell in love with the vicar, Mr. Shalford."

Psyche's laughter trilled to the ceiling. "I had forgotten about Annabelle, poor, beautiful, rich creature that she was. Well, it all began when your mother found me by the pond . . ."

"So tell me, doctor, how is she?" Brandreth queried as he met the physician in the hallway outside of Alexandra's bed-chamber. He had been waiting anxiously belowstairs for the doctor to come to him but his impatience got the better of him and he left his study to go in search of him. He saw the deeply concerned expression on the good doctor's face and his heart sank. "Please, tell me the truth. Then I was right to have you see her?"

"Yes, very right to have done so," he said. "But I can't begin to express the grave concerns I have for her, in this quite, quite extraordinary situation. But is there somewhere we might go to speak privately. I wouldn't want what I have to tell you to be overheard by gossiping ears."

"Of course, of course," Brandreth said. He was grievously alarmed as he immediately guided Dr. Newquay down the stairs and into his study.

The small chamber was situated facing the low hills to the north. The walls were wainscoted in a fine mahogany, the single but quite large window was flanked by deep blue silk damask curtains, a carved bookshelf lined the wall behind a desk also of mahogany and two winged chairs in a wool plaid sat to either side of a brick fireplace. The rest of Roselands might be littered with the current mode for collectibles of every shape and size, but his private chamber would remain simple and tidy, a refuge for him in times of trouble such as this moment.

From an inlaid table by the door he quickly poured out two glasses of sherry and did not mistake the grateful light in the good doctor's eye as he received his glass and at the same time took up a seat on one of the winged chairs.

Brandreth took a sip of the fine sherry, hardly noticing the faint burn as the wine slipped down his throat. His mind was fixed solely on the doctor's weathered face, the deep creases on his forehead, the white of his hair, and the kind blueness of his eyes. He had not believed anything truly serious could be wrong with his daughter until he had seen the deep frown on his face as he stood with bowed head outside of Alexandra's bedchamber.

His daughters were the lights of his life, he realized with a start. The thought that Alexandra might have contracted a grave, perhaps even fatal illness, so overwhelmed him that he hardly knew how to encourage the doctor to speak.

"Will she be all right?" he asked at last in a small voice.

"There, there, man," the doctor exclaimed. "I can see by your expression that I have overset you and that was not my intention. Perhaps I have been too serious in the representation of my concerns for her and perhaps I am troubled beyond reason, but I am very fond of her you see. She has been a patient of mine for, well three and twenty years."

"So she has," Brandreth returned, remembering that the good

doctor had been present at her birth. He swallowed hard and asked the question he did not want to ask. "So, tell me plainly, what is afflicting her?"

"I have not said as much?" he queried, a little startled.

Brandreth shook his head.

"Forgive me, it is just that I am shocked by it. It is quite unusual, you know. The fact is, my lord, she is increasing. I would say three, possibly four months now. Her confinement should take place some time in April."

For a long moment, Brandreth could not speak. He had felt the air rush from his chest and now he could not so much as breathe.

Alexandra to have a baby.

At last he drew in a long, deep breath then bellowed, "What?"

"Easy, my good man!" the doctor exclaimed, jumping slightly in his chair. "I was never more shocked myself, but these things do happen and there is no sense flying into the boughs at this late hour."

Brandreth no longer heard the doctor's voice. All he saw was his daughter in the arms of that, that scoundrel!

"You must excuse me," he said, turning on his heel and parting from the doctor quite rudely. "But it would seem that I have some business to attend to immediately."

"But of course," the doctor's voice floated after him as he charged from the chamber. "I'll just have a little more of your sherry, then I'll be on my way."

A moment later, Brandreth was knocking harshly on Alexandra's door. Without waiting for permission to enter, he opened the door just as she was buttoning the top button of her gown. She was sitting on the edge of her bed and her face seemed quite pale. She looked up at her father and said, "The doctor wishes me to go to bed for a sennight, but I cannot. I have so much to attend to—with the masquerade ball, the guests, the decorations. Papa, won't you please speak with him and—my goodness, whatever is the matter? You seem quite angry, but why? Are you angry with me?"

"With you, yes, of course I am! What parent wouldn't be! And with, with *him!* Alexandra, how could you? You know how important this is!" he dragged a hand through his lightly silvered hair.

Alexandra appeared confused. "I know I haven't been getting enough rest of late! But—"

"Getting enough rest!" he cried, unable to credit she would treat with such disdain her condition, not even addressing the issue at hand but rather her need to care for herself while she carried a child within her. "Forget that for a moment!" he cried. "Just tell me this—when, how was it that, where? In heaven's name child, tell me the truth?"

"Papa, what are talking about?"

"When did you first *kiss* Launceston!" he shouted at last. When a deep blush suffused her cheeks, he was satisfied that he was at last getting to the truth. "So it is true! The man had the audacity to approach, to violate a complete innocent!"

"Well, it was as much my fault as his. My maid was not with me at the time and, and I was not using my head. And he was dreadfully handsome and I had been skipping stones on the River Avon—"

"In Bath, then, this summer past?"

Alexandra nodded, her head cast down in shame. "But I never—you mustn't think."

"It only takes one time for a woman to pay forever for this sort of—of scandal."

At that Alexandra looked up and blinked at him. "But Papa—"

"Don't you dare attempt to make light of this, young lady. I'm still utterly appalled and devastated. I trusted you, I've always trusted you. I might have expected Julia, who is shatterbrained, or Victoria who is far too receptive to the compliments of any gentleman, but not you, not my good, sensible Alexandra!

But never fear, I shall make this all right and tight, so you needn't worry. I intend to call on him immediately."

With that, Brandreth swept from the room.

Alexandra watched him go, dumbfounded by his curious demeanor and conduct. She looked at Psyche, wondering if her new friend could explain her father's strange speech, but the young immortal merely shrugged her shoulders, her eyes wide with astonishment. The doctor had told her she was suffering from a humor of the blood and required rest, that her appetite had been a reflection of her weakened state. But her father had stormed into her bedchamber, in a state of passion which did not quite seem fitting for the doctor's diagnosis of her condition.

As she rose from her bed, it struck her that she rather thought he had accused her of something more than the innocent kiss she had shared with Launceston. In fact, the more she thought on it, the more it seemed to her that her father believed the viscount had violated her as a man might violate a maiden.

As awareness dawned on her, she felt her former blush return to her cheeks and burn fiercely in her embarrassment. He—he must have thought she had and that she was now—goodness, she couldn't even form the thoughts in her mind.

If, somehow the doctor had communicated such a notion to him, unwittingly, then her father was even now on his way to—oh, dear God, to, to force Launceston to make an honest woman of her when Launceston knew he had not—and what would he now think of her if her father told him she was, if she was *increasing!*

These thoughts so twisted her mind about that before she knew what she was doing she had left her bedchamber and was running to her mother's room who she knew the doctor had also examined. But even as her silk-slippered feet pounded the thick carpeted hallway runner, another thought occurred to her, namely that there could be another, quite reasonable explanation as to why her Papa might possibly think she was with child. The doctor might have informed her father of his wife's condition instead of her own.

Therefore, when she reached the door of her mother's chambers, instead of entering in a wild state, she scratched lightly on the door and waited for her mother to bid her enter. Upon hearing her mother's quiet voice, she opened the door slowly and saw by the smile and the glow on her mother's face that what she now suspected was true. She was standing by the window, framed by the light of the late October afternoon, tears coursing down her cheeks. She now looked at her mother's figure and realized that a certain stoutness characterized her body.

"It is true then?" Alexandra murmured as she closed the door behind her and crossed the chamber.

Lady Brandreth nodded, more tears flooding her eyes, which she wiped away with a lace-edged kerchief held tightly in her right hand. "I always wanted a dozen children, Alex. Well, perhaps not always but certainly from the time I married your father. I didn't think it possible, but oh, my darling daughter I'm frightened. I'm very old now and my two sons—"

Alexandra quickly slipped her arms about her mother's shoulders and held her close, not knowing what to say to her but certain she was justified in her fears.

"It never occurred to me I might be with child. I had thought I was greatly past my time. And how much I want a son." She then dissolved into tears, accompanied by deep sobs.

Alexandra knew her mother well that—though she had never said as much, she had always felt she had failed her husband in this most unpredictable of duties—the birthing of a son and heir.

"Father will not give a fig about that," she said, trying to reassure her mother.

"I know, that's what makes it so hard to bear. He has loved his daughters so much and has never said a word of reproach. Oh, that you might be blessed with such a husband."

For some reason these last words had a sobering effect on Alexandra and she remembered the reason she had come to her mother in the first place. "Mama," she said, her fears rising to take her breath away. "I—I think it possible Papa misunderstood the doctor. Does he know you are increasing?"

"The doctor said he meant to tell him."

"Well, I believe there has been some mistake for Papa came into my room and, and accused me and Launceston, of—" she couldn't speak the words, but continued, "I told him the doctor said I needed a great deal of rest. He grew furious and asked about Launceston, whether he had ever importuned me and I recalled something of summer last, I mean not this summer past, but the summer previously—oh, my goodness he thought I meant a few months ago which would—Mother, he's gone to accuse Launceston of getting me with child. But all he did was kiss me. P-please don't faint. Don't be ill."

But Lady Brandreth began to laugh and couldn't stop. "He must have asked the doctor how you were," she cried, swiping at her tears, "And, and then the doctor must have indicated *you* were increasing, which of course the doctor was referring to me, but your father, who saw you kissing Launceston only a few hours ago, has been quite concerned about you—" She caught her breath suddenly and her expression changed to one of sheer horror. "He will kill Launceston."

At that, Lady Brandreth gathered her red wool shawl off the end of her tester bed and racing toward the door, cried, "We've got to stop him!"

Ten

Launceston had just risen from a steaming bath in preparation for dressing for dinner, when he received word that a rather inflamed Lord Brandreth had come to call. The hour was nearly five o'clock, and like many Londoners he had come to accept the earlier dining hours found in the country and preferred it. Hence, he had just completed bathing when he was informed of his lordship's unexpected arrival. According to Cuthbert, the good marquis's face was splotched with red patches that had more to do with his choler than with the increasingly cold temperatures out of doors. Whatever could Brandreth mean by it?

Launceston's state of undress, however, made it impossible for him to attend to the marquis immediately as was his initial impulse and desire. It was therefore fully half an hour before he walked briskly down the stairs, attired in a black coat, a burgundy and black striped silk waistcoat, dark gray wool trousers, a white shirt sporting low points, and a narrow burgundy silk cravat tied in a bow.

He found his lordship in the small Green Salon which served as his office and was located at the end of the long gallery and set back just beyond the narrow staircase on the ground floor. A warm fire was glowing on the hearth, and a northwesterly view of the valley and of Roselands could be seen from the two stone-rimmed arched windows. The chamber was somewhat dark, the last rays of a setting sun just catching and setting aglow the forest green velvet draperies which flanked the windows.

Standing in the doorway and observing his guest for the first time, Launceston's mouth fell agape. Lord Brandreth, his features stony with hostility, was sitting in one of two winged chairs, each covered in a tapestried fabric and placed slightly facing one another in front of the fireplace. Across his knees lay a fencing sword, one of a pair, the other of which was still mounted over the mantel.

The odd circumstance of the marquis being in possession of one of the swords, Launceston could have explained as mere curiosity, since the swords were quite ancient. But what could not be so easily explained was why the marquis had removed his coat of dark green wool, nor why he looked at the viscount as though he meant to run him through.

As Launceston advanced into the chamber, Brandreth rose to his full height, a height which matched his own. He took a step to the right toward a nearby desk of gleaming mahogany, Launceston took one to the left.

"What is the meaning of this, my lord?" Launceston queried firmly, his gaze drifting first to the practiced manner in which Brandreth began to wield his sword, then flashing to the second sword mounted above the mantel. "I take it you hold some grievance against me?" He walked carefully toward the mantel and was not surprised when Brandreth matched his steps giving him a wide berth, circling behind the desk.

Launceston thought of Julia and Victoria and the whiskers they were wont to tell with regard to his supposed affections for one or the other. But he doubted that either young lady was likely to impart something so scandalous to their papa as would cause him to apparently desire to hasten his death.

"You know very well what you've done, you cur!" Brandreth cried with such vehemence that Launceston started.

"Good God, man!" he returned with a scowl. "I cannot begin to conceive of what I might have done to have earned your wrath."

"Take up your sword!" Brandreth cried, flipping his own blade in the air the direction of the mantel.

"I will not," Launceston returned flatly, still he edged closer to the fireplace.

Brandreth completed his circling of the desk and with great speed leaped toward Launceston and pricked him on the arm. The blade easily cut through the fabric of his black coat and through the fine white linen of his shirt. By the stinging sensation which followed he knew his white shirt was undoubtedly now stained with a pretty circle of blood.

"Damn and blast," he murmured, scowling further, his own choler rising at this marked provocation. "You've cut me! Though I question your right to do so, I'll not take that from any man." He quickly retrieved the other sword from the mantel, leaped away from the fireplace and the chairs and faced his enemy.

"Scoundrel!" Brandreth breathed as he began to circle the desk again, forcing the viscount to back up against the windows as he thrust toward him. The tip of the blade touched stone in a delicate clink. A little more force and the tip would have snapped against the hard, gray granite. "Do you tell me then that you were not kissing my daughter this morning?"

Launceston opened his mouth then immediately clamped his lips shut. Of course he had kissed her. "I will not deny it," he responded. "I stole a kiss, will you require my life for it?"

Launceston moved swiftly back toward the fireplace and slid between one of the winged chairs and the hearth. Brandreth lunged at him again. The blade caught the tapestried fabric and tore a gaping strip along the winged edge. "You've kissed her more than once, you rogue!"

Launceston could not deny it for it was true. Yet, he couldn't credit that Brandreth meant to kill him for it. "In perfect innocence, I assure you!" he responded, trying to justify actions which truly could not be justified. He moved to the right, keeping the chair between himself and the marquis.

Brandreth's mouth turned down bitterly as he reached forward and with a mighty pull of his hand and arm, dragged the chair away from Launceston. Behind the chair and to the right was a tall bookcase which now pressed itself into the viscount's back. As Brandreth lunged again, Launceston lifted his blade and caught the marquis's sword near the hilt. Brandreth pressed his advantage and maneuvered his blade until it was pressed against Launceston's neck. "You shall pay for this, dearly, Launceston. You have stolen Alexandra's innocence and denied doing so. Had you confessed your misdeed immediately and perhaps begged for mercy I might have been able to forgive you. But that you looked at me in such astonishment and pretended only kisses when you know very well no man of honor will have her now—"

Launceston choked against the pressure of Brandreth's fist and hilt into his neck. "What—what the devil are you at, my lord?" he whispered. His eyes were watering and he was having trouble breathing. For all his youth and strength he was no match for Brandreth's rage.

"She is with child!" he cried.

"So I am," a feminine voice called out. "My love, whatever are you doing to poor Launceston?"

As Brandreth turned around, his sword slipped away from the viscount who took the momentary breach in their conflict to give the marquis a shove into the back of the winged chair. Brandreth lost his footing and slid to the floor. Launceston watched as a now red-faced Lady Alexandra and a faintly amused Lady Brandreth, entered the small chamber.

The marchioness crossed the room, her booted heels silent on the thick carpet bearing a pattern crowded with pink roses on a dark green background. She moved to stand over her husband and peered down at him. "Whatever are you doing, my darling? Why are you unclothed in Launceston's home? Where is your coat? Oh, I see there it is, sitting crumpled on that small *papier-maché* table by the door. Alexandra, will you fetch it for your father?"

"Of course, Mama!"

Launceston watched in some bemusement as Alexandra quickly retrieved the coat and brought it to Lady Brandreth. His gaze swept over her figure, her small waist not even remotely indicative of her current condition. He could not credit it was true! Alexandra with child!

He knew he wasn't the father, but who was? And what was it Lady Brandreth had said while standing in the doorway? He was confused. Still, he could not but watch Alexandra who he found refused to meet his gaze. Her cheeks were aflame. She was with child. But whose? Mylor Grampound's perhaps? Trenear had spoken of her affection for him.

"Mylor Grampound!" he cried aloud, staring hard at Alexandra.

"What?" Alexandra asked, her gaze flitting to meet his at last.

Launceston didn't know how it was, but the thought of Mylor Grampound and his tall, bony frame, his wide smile, and sluggish eyes, his lips, his hands, his arms possessing Alexandra threw him into a fit of rage. As Lady Brandreth extended the coat to her husband, he stepped on it and pulled it to the floor with his foot. He addressed Alexandra. "You permitted that— that fish-eyed, clumsy, nitwitted bore—Alex! It's unthinkable, unbearable! How did you—? How could you have—? This is beyond bearing!"

He saw her blinking at him in amazement. "You actually think that I—that Mr. Grampound—that we—! Oh, you are the most vile, the most hateful of men. I despise you, Launceston, beyond words! It is just like you to accuse me of something so utterly wicked, when it is you who have no conscience, no fine sentiments, no nobility of heart. You are the one who has been kissing me and teasing me, not the honorable Mr. Grampound! You are a wretched man and always will be!" At that, he watched tears spring to her eyes, her hands dip into her skirts and once the fine fabric was in her hands, she whirled away from him and left the Green Salon.

He remained standing in the middle of the room, staring at the empty doorway, his sword still in hand, for a long, long moment. Why was she denying the truth? He would probably have remained staring at the doorway had not the sounds of Lord Brandreth's exclamations met his astonished ears.

"Oh, my darling! My dearest one! Tell me again, is it true?" He had risen from his place behind the chair and was even now standing beside his wife in front of one of the arched windows, his hands gripping her shoulders tightly. On his face was an expression replete with pleasure, astonishment, and joy.

What the devil, he thought.

"Yes, it's true," his wife was saying to him.

"I can't believe it."

"Nothing short of a miracle, I promise you."

Launceston now felt perfectly addled. Why was Brandreth now professing great excitement over Alexandra's scandalous predicament?

"You shouldn't be here," he said, sliding his hands down her arms, possessing himself of her hands and lifting them to hold them tightly against his chest. "You should be lying abed and taking care of yourself."

"Silly man," she said, smiling up into his face. "I had to come here to keep you from killing our new neighbor!"

He laughed, the lines about his eyes crinkling and deepening with his pleasure. "Have I ever told you that you are the best of women? Have I ever told you as much, my love?"

"A hundred times, but you may say it again."

He didn't speak the words, but instead he drew his wife into a close embrace.

Launceston was watching the Marquis of Brandreth kiss his wife, quite passionately, before he knew what was happening. His mind was working painfully slow, perhaps because just a moment ago, the same man was fairly choking him to death, and he didn't know how to respond to what was happening all about him. Gone was Brandreth's anger and in its stead was a happiness so real that Launceston felt it as though it was a tangible thing.

When the marquis finally completed the rather fulsome salute, he again gathered up his wife's hands to his chest. "When does the doctor think you are to be confined?"

"April," was her soft, sweet, glowing response.

"Yes, of course, now I remember."

Upon that solitary and joy-filled word, Launceston finally understood the truth.

His sword slipped from his hand and bounced in two thuds on the carpet. He wheeled around and wondered now how he was to make amends with Alexandra. But as he entered the long gallery which led back to the entrance hall, he stopped cold, his thoughts full of one particular portion of the previous quarrel. Why had he been so angry at the thought of Grampound's hands clutching at Alexandra? He hadn't just been piqued or disturbed or mad, he had been outraged, like a man who already has a claim on a woman.

He didn't know what to make of it, except that if he didn't know better, he would have thought himself actually jealous, possessively so, of Alexandra. Curious that. He had no claim upon her, no interest in her except in winning a ruby brooch from Trenear by breaking her heart.

Slowly, he began walking up the hall, his shoes resounding in a firm step along the stone floor. No matter what he thought of his surprising sentiments, he owed her an apology of no mean order. But when he arrived at the entrance hall, he found she had already left his home having chosen to walk the distance across the valley instead of waiting to travel in her mother's carriage.

Cuthbert explained, "She slapped her bonnet on her head, her shawl about her shoulders, and had opened the door before I could make my way across the entrance hall. I do beg your pardon, m'lord, but I fear she was that mad."

"She was, indeed," Launceston murmured.

"My lord!" Cuthbert then exclaimed. "You've hurt yourself! You're bleeding!"

Launceston glanced indifferently at the tear in his coat sleeve, then at his hand which bore a narrow rivulet of blood. "So it would seem," he responded.

"But m'lord!" Cuthbert protested.

"A mere scratch," Launceston assured him. "Lord Brandreth and I were testing the swords in the Green Salon, nothing to signify."

With that, Cuthbert had to be content, though he left his master standing in the entrance hall and stared blankly at the front door.

Cupid enjoyed viewing Olympus from high in the air because twilight saw the lighting of dozen upon dozen of oil lamps all throughout Zeus's magnificent kingdom. Just as the stars appeared in the sky, so did the lamps appear, twinkling over the city like diamonds embroidered on a colorful scarf.

He loved Olympus which had been his home for centuries. He knew every corner of the kingdom by heart and many of the people and gods under Jupiter's command had filled his life with the pleasures only long and loyal friendships can bestow.

Vulcan was among his chiefest friends. He had already called upon the formidable god, whose lameness and ugliness was well known throughout the land. He had begged Vulcan to fashion at least one new arrow for him, adding that he would place the love potion on the tip by hand as in former times, but Vulcan had informed him of a recent vandalizing of his workshop—all of Cupid's arrow molds had been destroyed, crushed by a heavy hammer. The soonest Cupid could expect a new arrow was in three months.

He had left his friend, dismayed at what he had learned. Earlier, he had been curious as to why he had not stumbled across Anteros anywhere at Castle Porth during the remainder of the day. At first he had believed that his brother would be afraid of his wrath once he had discovered his arrows were missing. But now, he suspected Anteros of an even greater treachery, of having returned to Olympus in order to destroy the arrow molds.

Now, as he flew toward his mother's palace, he realized his brother was more intent on keeping Psyche bound to earth than he had previously been willing to believe. Stealing his arrows from the priest's hole certainly indicated part of his intention, but returning to Olympus and smashing the arrow molds revealed the depth of his animosity and purpose.

When he neared the palace, he circled high over head to determine if his mother was home. But by the lack of activity in her carriage house and the absence of her doves, he knew she was not at home. He smiled as he began his descent recalling with great irony how three and twenty years ago he had given his dear wife a severe dressing down for having committed the very crime he himself was about to commit—the theft of his mother's potions.

As he settled on the back terrace and noted that the house was dark, that there wasn't a single oil-lamp burning, he hurried into her august mansion. A moment later, he was in her wardrobe where he knew she kept her potions, and he retrieved a bottle of rose-oil which he knew contained the potion designed to create love where there was none before. Another bottle, situated beside the love potion, was tinged a green color. He removed the stopper and smelled the pungent aroma of sage—her antidote for love. But there was also present a third bottle which upon inspection proved to be amber in color. When he removed the stopper, he took a careful whiff and immediately felt dizzy with sleep. He secured the glass stopper with a quick, grinding twist, left the wardrobe and drew in a deep breath of fresh air. His mind began to clear rapidly, but a new idea entered his head and for the first time all day he began to feel lighter at heart. He knew now what he could do to Anteros to help ensure the success of his schemes. All he needed now was a large needle. A few carefully chosen words placed within distance of his brother's hearing to entice Anteros back to the priest's hole, and his task would be accomplished.

He quit his mother's mansion and rose swiftly into the air with a single long beat of his majestic wings and flew eastward. How many days left? Seven. Seven to bring about a miracle so that his darling wife could return to Mount Olympus with him. How his heart constricted in his chest, for if he failed to help

Alexandra and Launceston discover their love for one another, he would lose his beloved Psyche. What then would Olympus be to him without the wife of his choosing by his side? An inhospitable land, without pleasure, without love. For all of its kind associations and its beauty, Mount Olympus would be nothing without his darling Butterfly by his side.

The following day, as agreed upon, Alexandra sat in Lord Launceston's carriage, opposite Julia but next to Victoria. Her sisters were keeping the viscount happily entertained for he was sitting next to Julia and opposite Victoria, and from the time the giddy, younger sisters entered his large, travelling coach, each had been intent on winning his smiles, on stealing the majority of his conversation for herself, on capturing his heart.

The ladies were fashionably dressed in carriage gowns, Alexandra in cornflower blue silk trimmed with ermine about the full sleeves, Julia in a russet velvet with white lace at the throat and at the wrists, and Victoria in a dark brown velvet jacket over a taffeta skirt in autumnal shades of reds, rusts, and browns. Each wore modest poke bonnets trimmed with ribbons to match their gowns.

When crammed into the carriage, the full skirts of their gowns overlapped one another and created the appearance of the ladies being waist deep in a sea of fine fabrics. They did not lack for warmth being cloaked in so much silk, velvet, and the ruffles of nearly a score of petticoats. Even Launceston's gray-striped trousers were hidden by their skirts.

He was dressed immaculately, as always, in a dark gray wool coat, and matching waistcoat, black wool trousers, a black silk cravat, neatly starched shirtpoints, a well-brushed beaver hat, and glossy black shoes.

Despite his elegant appearance, for the most part, Alexandra ignored Launceston. She was still angry that he had so quickly believed the worst of her yesterday. Of course he had apologized. After seeing her sisters safely stowed in his carriage, he had held her back for a moment and begged her to forget all that he had said. But he had so twisted and turned his apology that by the end of his speech she was convinced he was blaming her for the whole of the incident since she had succumbed to his kisses so readily.

"I see," she had responded in a frosty whisper, not wanting either her sisters or the postillion to hear their conversation. "So what you are saying is that had I not succumbed to your advances on the three occasions in which I permitted you to kiss me, then of course you would have believed me innocent."

He had opened his mouth, but couldn't speak for she had dumbfounded him. "I didn't mean it that way," he said with a frown. "That is, I suppose it is true in one sense, but I—"

She had turned on her heel at that and left him stammering by himself. Of course, he was not left to his devices for long. Julia and Victoria were quick to beg him take up his seat and before long she observed that he was as puffed up as ever in his conceit. The lazy look had reentered his hazel eyes whenever her glance crossed his line of vision and his lip curled sardonically whenever the subject touched upon matters of the heart, of flirtation, or of the mysteries of love and affection.

She despised him so much, beyond words.

Well, she had only seven days, including today, in which she must endure his company. Then she would see Psyche safely returned to the portal in the chapel ruins and she would take up a new scheme, that of securing lodgings in Brighton, with a companion of course to lend her countenance, where she intended to further her study of the art of watercolors and oils.

She enjoyed seascapes which the environs of Falmouth Harbor provided in abundance and Brighton, especially with its view of George IV's famous Pavilion, would provide a new aspect to study and master.

She loved the sea, she thought as she lowered the window next to her. The smell of salt air swept through the opening and freshened the air within the carriage. She and her sisters had several destinations today in order to see that all their invitations were delivered, but their first call would be upon her dearest friend, Mylor Grampound. She smiled at the thought thinking how Launceston had actually accused her of carrying Mr. Grampound's child. It was fitting then that they call upon the honorable Mr. Grampound first.

Julia interrupted her satisfying reverie by complaining that her lowered window had set a chill in the air. But since this afforded her the opportunity of scooting closer to Launceston and dimpling her smiles up into his face it was Victoria who forthwith began to caterwaul about the unhealthfulness of fresh air.

Alexandra chose to ignore both of her sisters and continued to stare out the window. Her thoughts turned again toward the sea. She realized suddenly how very much she loved the ocean, the sounds of the surf pounding against the sand, the gulls crying out and sweeping over the water in search of a morning or afternoon meal, and the way the ocean seemed to settle down in the late afternoon as though it had worn itself out.

Sometimes in summer, when her family would walk along the beaches and find a deserted cove, she would remove her boots and stockings and enjoy the thrill of the water on her feet and the sensation of the muddy sand enveloping her toes. Sand was such an odd thing, almost as though it had a life of its own and was determined to take that life with anyone who came close to it. She smiled thinking that after a day at the beach, she would find sand everywhere for a full sennight afterward, stuck to her petticoats, in between her toes, in her hair, tucked into every crevice of her clothing.

Two gulls flitted by her window and passed overhead. Mr. Grampound's home was nearer the sea than Roselands. She turned her head to look out the other window in order to watch the gulls come again within view then disappear as the coach took a turn to the south into the woodlands near Mr. Grampound's home. Her gaze naturally landed upon Launceston's handsome face and she was surprised to find that not only was he looking at her but that the sneering expression was gone from his lips as well as the lazy droop to his eye. Presently, Julia was arguing with Victoria about how small her waist was and it was clear to Alexandra that Launceston had not been attending to either of her sisters for some time.

She found herself trapped by the expression on his face. She felt as though he was speaking to her, asking her something, but she couldn't make out the question.

"What is it?" she whispered.

He appeared as though he wished to speak, his lips parting slightly, his eyes narrowing, but he seemed reluctant. He then glanced out the window next to her then as quickly returned to look into her eyes. She caught her breath at the intensity of his expression. What was it about him that brought her heart beating so strongly in her breast?

"What?" she whispered again, tilting her head slightly.

But this time he smiled softly and shook his head. Since Julia now realized that his interest had waned, she immediately began to flirt with him. "Do tell us again, Launceston, about the storm. Did you really climb to the top of the main mast pole in order to secure the mast?"

Alexandra could see that Launceston did not want to regale Julia of his exploits again. "Perhaps another time or you will have me sounding like a bore."

"Oh, you mean like Mr. Grampound," Victoria stated as she pulled a face.

Alexandra looked at her. "How unkind of you," she said. "And Mr. Grampound does no such thing. It is just that—that—he is so very accomplished and precise in his manners and speech that he does not have your liveliness nor Julia's."

"Sounds like a bore," Launceston intoned, the teasing expression in his eye intended to disrupt Alexandra.

Julia broke into a trill of laughter. "Oh, he is, ever so much. You will not like him—I am persuaded of it. Mark my words, he will begin lecturing you the moment you but give him the smallest opportunity."

"You are the only one he lectures," Victoria responded. "And rightly so, I'm sure. For he only tells you what all of us know, that you are too vain and talk too much about nonsensical matters."

Alexandra saw Julia bristle immediately as her fur muff rose to a pyramidical shape. She could see the outlines of Julia's hands lifted in the manner of cat's claws, ready to attack her sister.

"And what of you, Victoria?" Alexandra said, intervening quickly. "Do you always say what is proper?"

She watched a quick blush rise to Victoria's cheeks and was satisfied. Victoria's eyes shifted toward Julia, then Launceston, then back, like the rocking of a boat. Properly chastened, she addressed her sister, "I do apologize, Jules. I shouldn't have said such a mean thing."

Julia pinched her lips together. "Oh, never mind," she said, agitated. "Perhaps I am a little vain, for I am so enchanted by the latest fashions and jewelry and I find glittering objects much to my preference. And I do talk too much, even Mama says so, but I still don't like Mr. Grampound—no matter whether Alexandra dotes on him or not."

At that, perhaps because Julia's expression was so childlike and honest, Alexandra smiled, Victoria laughed outright in a pleasant manner, and Launceston, much to his credit, told her that if Mr. Grampound began one of his dressing downs, he would personally plant the man a facer.

Mr. Grampound may not have been a favorite with the younger sisters, but in one respect he pleased them immensely since he was very much fond of society. When Julia extended their invitation to the masquerade ball he immediately expressed a sincere delight in the prospect of such a ball. Upon learning that the theme for the masquerade was to be the previous generation's style known as the Regency style, he exclaimed that he knew his parents had stored up any number of garments from which he was certain he would be able to choose a proper costume. "For m'father and I are much of a height and when he was younger he was not so stout as he is today." He seemed to recall a particularly fine representation of the period which included a pair of pale yellow breeches, a fashionable waistcoat of blue and white stripes, and a cutaway tail coat in a dark blue fabric. The ladies groaned at such an absurd image. He continued with a smile, "Silk stockings, a pair of ballroom slippers, perhaps a wig—for from the portraits I believe the hair was worn quite short and swept forward along the temple like the ancient Greeks and Romans—and I will defy anyone to appear to greater advantage."

Everyone laughed at his descriptions, more so still when upon rubbing his sidewhiskers, he lifted a brow and said, "But not for the Queen herself will I shave off my whiskers!"

Mylor Grampound was taller than Lord Launceston and very thin. Alexandra couldn't help but wonder just what his thin legs would look like in the white silk stockings so fashionable during the years when the Prince Regent reigned in London and in Brighton. She rather suspected, and that most disloyally, that he might take on the appearance of a crane.

She kept her smiles and her amusement to herself, though she didn't for a moment fear he would take offense even if he knew the nature of her thoughts for he was a kind, unselfish man who knew little if nothing of vanity and narcissistic self-interest. He was a good friend, a welcome addition to any drawing room, and a gracious host. Even from the time they had entered his lovely, small manor house, littered with dozens and dozens of fresh roses scattered about the drawing room, his attention had been all for the younger sisters. They might decry his general temperament as boring, but Mylor Grampound was every inch a gentleman.

The chamber was a reflection of his mother who had passed away a year prior. Besides the presence of roses in soft yellows, peaches, pinks, whites, and reds, the two identical sofas, situated opposite one another, were covered in a lively chintz, matched by the fabric of the draperies. The fireplace, housing a pile of logs and kindling in preparation to be lit for the evening hour, was painted a glossy white along with the wood mantel and the panelled wood above the mantel. A painting of a clear glass of roses, with a single rose lying on a lace tablecloth next to the vase confirmed the cheerful meaning of the chamber. Mrs. Grampound had not succumbed to the current fashion of the day which dictated closed blinds, dark fabrics and a scattering of collectibles over every surface, all of which tended to diminish the size of the chamber. Instead, she had held steady to her own preference for air, for light, for colorful roses, and for comfort.

Alexandra enjoyed this chamber as much as she had adored Mrs. Grampound. Mylor had been very attached to his mother and had suffered considerably in the first few months following her death. But the steadiness of his mind and of his faith made his recovery inevitable. Month by month, he had become as animated and as convivial as in former times.

He was no less now as he begged them to see the rose garden which was still, as was evident by the number of roses in the chamber, still in considerable bloom though it was late October. In planting her gardens, the late Mrs. Grampound had taken advantage of the mild, temperate southeasterly coast of Cornwall which was a protected part of England's coastline, unlike the westerly coast which took the full brunt of the Atlantic's wintry distemper. A tall, thick yew hedge about the garden had further extended the blooming months.

When Mr. Grampound offered Julia his arm, she cast Alexandra a despairing glance, but there was nothing to be done. To have refused him would have been an unacceptable, ungracious act.

"But this can't be," Mr. Grampound added, extending his other arm to Victoria. "You must take my arm as well." She readily accepted his invitation and the three of them passed through the wide double door of the drawing room and began a pretty progression toward the back terrace and the rose garden.

Alexandra would have followed after them, but she felt Launceston's hand stay her arm just at the crook of her elbow. She looked back at him, her brows lifted in surprise.

"Will you forgive me?" he asked bluntly.

Eleven

"Forgive you?" she queried.

"Yes, for having believed for even a second anything so absurd as—as, well as what your father gave me strong indication I was supposed to believe. And pray don't pretend you already have forgiven me, for I know you haven't."

Alexandra looked away from him, still smarting from his words of yesterday and equally embarrassed by the nature of the subject.

He took a step near her and now gripped her elbow firmly. "Confound it, you are the most stubborn female. Of course I know you are an innocent, Alexandra. I am well-versed with your character. And I don't know how it was, but when your father made his accusation, with a sword tip directed at my heart, and when he said the doctor had told him it was so, all I could see was Mr. Grampound's face and wondering if he was the father of your, your child!"

Alexandra felt a blush burning her cheeks. Such things were rarely spoken of, even between women.

He lowered his voice and because he was standing so near to her she felt his breath on her ear, her cheek, her neck. "I don't know how it was," he reiterated, "but that particular vision enraged me."

At that Alexandra turned to look into his hazel eyes and drew in a sharp breath. "Of, of Mr. Grampound, and, and me?" she breathed, a well of laughter rising in her throat. "Oh, dear! I wish you hadn't said such a thing to me!"

The image which then took hold of her, of her dear, rather formal friend—who was in truth always correcting poor Julia—making wild, passionate love to her and robbing her of her innocence was proving too much to bear. Her first laugh came out as a squeak, then a tremolo of laughter followed which she simply couldn't stop.

She turned and drew quickly away from him, picking up her cornflower blue skirts. She followed in the wake of her sisters and her supposed lover, her giggles apparently infectious since she heard Launceston's laughter coming from behind her. He caught up with her as she walked quickly past the stairs and entered the long hallway which led to the back terrace.

"I knew it," he said, whispering in her ear. "You are as incorrigible as me."

Alexandra felt very strange hearing him say so and she realized in that moment that he was speaking straight to her heart. She paused in her steps and looked up at him, holding his gaze steadily. "Launceston," she began, introducing an entirely different subject, but one she thought was to the point, "when I was very young, I was used to imagine what it would be like to be a boy—a man—unfettered, free to roam the woods hereabouts, or the county, or the entire island, or even the world. I admit it was a great sorrow to me when I learned what my true duties in life would be. Ever since you spoke to me of your life on the high seas and in India, I believe that earlier child has begun to awaken. How else can I explain why I have let you kiss me? I can't even explain it to myself. Of course I will forgive you, if, if you will not think too badly of me."

Launceston looked down at her trying to imagine her as a little girl, with her hair in braids and her knees muddied after a morning's adventures. "Did you frequently escape your nanny?" he asked, a warm smile on his lips.

Alexandra nodded, her heart softening to the memories which his question culled forth from within her. "She would come the crab with such vehemence as though I had been terribly wicked by playing in the woods instead of just bored to tears with my letters and my embroidery stitches."

She turned and began walking again toward the terrace.

"I wish I could have known you then," he said. "It would seem we have for years shared something in common."

"A dislike of the schoolroom?" she ventured, slowing her steps as she approached the French doors which led onto the terrace. Unwilling to end their conversation by joining the others, she drew to a stop before the doors and turned to look at him. The light through the windows of the doors illuminated his face and his hazel eyes appeared almost green.

"No, for I am well enough acquainted with you to know that you have a love of books, as do I. I was thinking more at a love of adventure, of freedom, of choices."

She heard something sad in his voice. Somehow the intimacy of the conversation had permitted him to expose a sentiment she was sure was of no small significance. "Of choices?" she asked, holding him back when he moved forward to open one of the French doors.

He let his hand drop away. "I was in love once," he said, holding her gaze steadily. She heard an edge to his voice that surprised her and caused her to wonder.

When he ventured nothing more, but just looked at her, her wondering became more acute. Why did he seem angry in this moment when he spoke of having been in love once? Disjointed thoughts of him, of his attitudes, suddenly coalesced in her mind. She thought she was beginning to understand him a little. "She was not of our class," she stated. "Was she?"

"She was not," he said. "But she was far more a lady than any I have met. She was sweet-tempered and kind, her hand was always outstretched to the needy."

She knew he did not realize he was being offensive. Nor did she understand precisely how it was she could forgive him entirely for saying such a rude thing to her. He was looking into the past, his thoughts locked away from her. Finally, he sighed and again lifted his hand to turn the door handle, but she placed her hand on his and again prevented him.

She felt odd tears sting her eyes as she spoke. "The injustice you serve me, Launceston, is so unfair," she began but not unkindly. "I have frequently noticed that ladies in the lower classes have a far greater capacity to enjoy their lives than many of us do. Even you were quick to judge me capable of conduct of the most irresponsible and wanton because in two or three unguarded moments, I gave into an impulse to enjoy a kiss. Admit it's so."

He was staring at her as one astounded. "I never meant—"

"I am not offended, but don't you see how you have despised me because for the most part I do behave as I am expected to behave—indeed, as even *you* expect me to behave—and yet you have condemned me for the one spontaneous, abandoned act that I succumbed to beneath a beautiful summer sky so long ago. What do you want from me? Shall I give in to all my impulses and be cast from society forever? Or shall I continue to mind my conduct and my manners so that you will not have cause to think me slatternly? Tell me what you think I ought to do."

He turned away from the doors, overset. "Dear God, you are right, a thousand times you are right. Ever since I returned from India, I have borne a chip on my shoulder. Life was not meted out to me in easy measure. Since I was thirteen, and my father perished leaving me penniless, I have felt as though I have fallen from the top of a tree, striking one branch after another. I don't think I realized until now how bitter I had become. But when I am in company, and I listen to the prattlings of spoiled young ladies, and the discompassionate boasts of men who have never seen the squalor of the world in which most people reside, I am sickened, do you understand?"

Alexandra nodded. "Perfectly."

"When Susan entered my life—she was in service in my household in India—I had planned never to return to England since I intended to marry her. But she died of the cholera having cared for a family with the dreaded disease only a few days prior."

Alexandra watched him, her heart yielding and warm toward

him. "I'm glad you've told me," she said. "You do not seem so formidable to me now."

He seemed surprised. "Me—formidable?"

Alexandra laughed. "Don't you realize that when men boast, it is because they cover their insecurities, especially around someone like you. There isn't a man I have met who does not watch you pass by without awe in his eyes, or jealousy or fear. Every untried man is frightened of discovering he is unworthy of his rank or fortune. But you, you are tried and tried again, by fire as it were. You command respect merely by setting your foot in another man's house. Do you not understand as much?"

"You seem to hold me in a measure of esteem which surprises me."

Alexandra could not keep from taunting him a little. "I am speaking of men. As for my opinion, I find you arrogant and frequently unkind in your manners and addresses, so don't think I am merely pandering to your vanity by explaining how I perceive your peculiar situation in society."

"That is much better," he said with a crooked smile. "I was beginning to fear you had begun to like me."

"That is impossible," she responded, a faint smile on her lips. "Now, prepare yourself for beauty unequalled." She then gestured toward the French doors.

"Dear Zeus!" Launceston murmured as he ventured onto the terrace and placed his hands on the curved, granite wall before him. "I have never seen anything of the like before. It is exquisite."

"Mrs. Grampound was a gifted horticulturalist. She was adored by everyone and is sorely missed in our little circle."

"No wonder there are so many roses in the house," he said.

The rose garden was just as its name implied, and stretched for a full acre toward the sea. The house was situated on a rise and the shimmering silver line of the ocean could be seen not a mile distant. Woodlands bordered the house on the right and left cradling the garden and the small manor house in the faintest dip of the land.

Launceston watched her descend the shallow tier of steps and move onto the gravel path that led to the center of the rose garden, but he did not immediately follow. Instead he watched her, his senses alive to her as they never had been before. The thought struck him that he could love such a woman. He found himself completely stunned by such a thought. He? In love with the *Frost Queen?* Impossible.

Yet each time he had kissed her, he had been acutely aware of her responsiveness, of the way she would hold him tightly, of the gentle murmurs in her throat, of the way she unwittingly pressed her body against his, always igniting his own passion.

Yet, what did you she want from him? Or did she want anything except a masquerade ball? He still didn't know why she had asked such a thing of him or why she had been willing to wager him for it. He narrowed his eyes, his suspicions of the Fairer Sex beginning to overtake what for a long moment had been a succession of distinctly tender and warm sentiments toward her.

She was an enigma, to be sure. But she was above all, a lady of his class and therefore bred with certain quite specific expectations in her mind and heart—a wealthy husband to sustain her mode of living, a nursery full of children, a fine country house, a London season, holidays in Bath and Brighton. He felt his heart growing painfully cold as he stared out over the beautiful roses and the silvery sea beyond.

When was it, he wondered, that he had become so vilely cynical?

On the following evening, Mr. Trenear regarded his host with lazy eyelids as he sipped a glass of port. "You've made amazing progress, then," he said, and with a half-smile added, "You are to be congratulated."

Lord Launceston was stretched out on his stomach, lying on one of the scarlet sofas, a forest green, down-filled pillow scrunched up beneath his chest and chin. He was staring into a blazing fire but at his friend's sardonic words turned to scowl at him for a brief second only to revert his gaze almost as quickly to the flames licking at the several thick chunks of wood stacked high in the massive hearth. The heat was delightful and was being kept penned in their small circle by three carefully placed screens, each of which had been recovered from the attics and sported scenes of Medieval life—the hunt, elegant ladies at weaving looms, dancers on straw-covered stone floors. Mr. Trenear knew very well he had failed to increase his hold on Lady Alexandra's heart.

"I've been trapped in time, here," he said cryptically, not certain what even he meant.

Trenear took another sip of port. He was situated on the opposite sofa, reclining against several pillows, his feet shoeless, his legs stretched out comfortably in front of him. Both men, as was the fashion, were dressed fully in black, save for white shirts—trousers, coats, waistcoats, black cravats.

Mr. Trenear sighed. "I never could quite comprehend why you had chosen to purchase this dilapidated collection of stones when you could've had a house of your liking built for you."

"I don't know why I became obsessed with Castle Porth, but I love the land down here, so close to the sea, not so rugged as the western coast of Cornwall, the natives so passionate."

"You sound as though you are describing India and not Falmouth."

Launceston laughed. "You need to begin looking beyond the fashions people sport," he responded, thinking of his curious conversation with Alexandra for the hundredth time. "Have you never noticed, for instance, when we go to Falmouth, how bright and lively the ordinary people of the town are—how fervently they discuss the weather, or how many fish they caught that day, or, or whether it is likely trains will actually reach so far as their fair town? I don't know how it is, but I am enamored of the land and the people here."

"And the ladies?"

Launceston turned on his side to fully hold Mr. Trenear's gaze. "The ladies?" he returned.

Mr. Trenear took another sip of port and let the rich wine rest fully in his mouth for a long moment before swallowing. "I refer of course to the inmates of Roselands. They labored very long here today—all of them."

"What are you saying, Trenear? You may speak plainly to me."

Mr. Trenear gestured gently with his glass of port. "Only this much, that you seem to have made at least two conquests but not the one you need—at least not if you are to come into possession of my brooch."

Launceston rolled back onto his stomach, again adjusting the pillow beneath his chest by punching it several times. He was irritated. After his trip on the day prior to deliver a dozen invitations—and more particularly, after delivering Mr. Grampound's invitation—he had felt more secure about his chances of actually winning Alexandra's affections within the requisite period of time.

But today, she had been less generous with her conversation and gestures. She seemed somewhat remote and inaccessible. What had occurred, he wondered, during those four and twenty hours, to have caused her to return to her rather frosty demeanor? He had truly supposed that after having shared such a series of intimate exchanges with her that he would be able to progress easily in his designs to break her heart. But instead of finding her responding to his welcoming smiles and enthusiastic compliments over her ideas for decorating the ballroom she had hourly become the withdrawn, reticent, cold fish he had known in London.

He sighed. "She makes no sense to me—none at all. One moment, she is completely open and engaging and the next moment she treats me as though I've contracted the plague."

"Well, perhaps she sees through your motives," Mr. Trenear suggested softly.

"How could she?"

"Braggart," he responded.

"Well, I don't mean to boast, Trenear, but I am an old hand at this business."

"I think it likely you underestimate your prey. Lady Alexandra, as I have observed, is a woman of keen intelligence and perception. I would suppose she would know when she was being trifled with and when she was being pursued with honorable intentions."

At that Launceston again regarded his friend, turning his head toward him and resting his head on his crooked arm. "It would seem then, if your theory should prove correct, that I am destined to lose this wager."

"Do you concede now, for I will happily arrange to have your horses driven to my home in Berkshire on the hour?"

"The devil you shall!" Launceston returned. "I am not persuaded you have the right of Lady Alexandra, that's all. I just need to reconsider my approach. I suppose what I have learned from today's misadventure is that she is not to be won as her sisters were so easily won."

"Well, I could have told you that, my good man."

"Oh, and you such a favorite of the ladies," he returned facetiously.

"One does not need to be a master to state the rudiments of any course of study."

"Oh, Psyche, I don't know what to make of him," Alexandra complained. "For a moment, yesterday, it seemed as though we had glimpsed one another's hearts, fully and openly, but today he was so altered and disgusting, praising me as he does Julia or Victoria and expecting me to gush my adoration of him. I was never more revolted nor—"

"Nor more disappointed?"

Alexandra sank onto the side of the bed, her gaze fixed on the red and gold floral wallpaper in front of her. Her skirts of a soft Merino wool, in the shade of Yorkshire heather, were bunched out on either side of her hips. "What was he thinking?" she asked. "That I would enjoy such absurd compliments? He even said my hair was as beautiful as a raven's feather."

Psyche, who was sitting up and eating a bowl of turbot soup, sighed heavily. "What sapskulls men can be." She then glanced to her left as though seeing some invisible object, blinked twice, hid her smiles and quickly returned her gaze to Alexandra.

"Can't they just," Alexandra agreed, still looking absently at the wall. "But enough of them. How is your ankle?"

Psyche frowned. "A little better, but the swelling is still the same, I fear."

Alexandra forgot her insignificant concerns and rose from the bed to lift the cool, damp towel from Psyche's ankle. "If you are not able to walk, I don't know how you shall go to the masquerade ball."

Psyche smiled. "I have been giving my dilemma a great deal of thought. If you were to secure a large wicker basket in which I could fit, I believe you could steal me away to the castle quite easily."

"Of course!" Alexandra cried. "I could drape several linens and lengths of cloths over you, two footmen could carry you downstairs, and the basket could be placed into a cart with no one the wiser. Even if they wondered at the weight of the basket, they would not have the impertinence to ask me why it was so heavy!"

"The privileges of rank!" Psyche cried.

Alexandra replaced the damp towel on Psyche's ankle. "Now that we have a plan of some sort for the night of the masquerade in case you cannot walk, I can be a little more content. But right now, I must join my family for tea. I hope you are not too lonely here, by yourself, hour upon hour."

"Not by half!" Psyche assured her, still sipping Cook's delectable fish soup. "Please, do not concern yourself with me. I have *Ivanhoe* to read and I frequently fall into little dozes throughout the day, probably because of my ankle. Only, when you return, you must tell me how your mother fares. I am still so delighted she is to have another child."

"She and Papa are simply *aux anges,*" she said, crossing the room and lifting her black knit shawl from the back of the chair by the door. "They are like children in their excitement. I can't tell you how wonderful it is to see." She then blew Psyche a kiss and was gone.

Psyche leaned her head against the cushioned back of the tester bed and looked at her husband who was reclining on the bed next to her, stroking her arm gently with his soft wings. "You heard her story, my love," she said. "Whatever are we going to do to bring them together when Launceston insists on behaving like a perfect nodcock!"

Cupid rolled over on his back and sighed. "I shouldn't even be speaking to you," he stated. "You called me a sapskull!"

Psyche giggled and dipped her spoon into the tasty broth. "Well, occasionally the appellation suits you."

He gasped, but since she wore a teasing smile on her lips the only appropriate response was to kiss her which he did.

When he leaned back from her and smiled lovingly into her eyes, she said, "I withdraw my criticism. You have never behaved like a sapskull."

He let the tips of his white wings brush her cheek. "Only two days out of three. No, no, don't try to argue for we both know it's true. I still ignore you far too much when I am busy at Vulcan's forge, or trying to restore love to a faltering Olympian marriage, or attempting to create a new, stronger potion for my arrows. You are very right to say the appellation suits me. But I want you to know how very happy I have been these past three and twenty years, more than you will ever know."

"Oh, Eros," she murmured, tears brimming in her eyes.

"As have I, you can have no notion!" She sighed, then addressed the former subject. "But whatever can we do about Launceston?"

"You would think he was little more than a halfling. Imagine trying to flatter her as he does her sisters!"

"What a simpleton! If only you had your arrows. Have you searched the entire castle yet?"

"Every square inch, I promise you. But don't think I mean to give up, my pet. So long as I have breath, I shall continue to look for my arrows. And don't worry your head about getting to the portal in time. I will easily be able to transport you to the chapel ruins at the proper hour, make no mistake."

A tear slid down Psyche's cheek. "I know that my love—but I have this terrible fear that neither you nor I will be able to bend Alexandra's heart toward Launceston in only six—no five days beginning tomorrow! I have no doubt, given everything she told me of yesterday's events that time would see them joined together. But five days! Oh, Cupid, whatever are we going to do? I can't bear the thought of living on earth without you."

He scooted closer to her and lifted the bowl of soup from her lap, setting it on the table next to the bed. He then overlaid her with one of his wings, embraced her and kissed her. "I know that together we shall contrive something and tomorrow, I shall not let the sun go down without the pair of them having fallen into one another's arms again." He then paused for a long moment as though listening intently. "Besides," he said, in a voice markedly louder, "I have secreted Mama's love potion in a—a safe place. I promise you, I shall soon see the task accomplished."

Anteros watched the happy reunion of husband and wife and found bile rising in his throat. He did not wait to hear further of his brother's endearments and turned to slip silently through the stone wall. So, Cupid had stolen a vial of their mother's love potion and had hidden it—but where? Certainly he would not have placed it in the priest's hole, or would he? His brother was not the most cunning of gods and perhaps he would suppose the vial would be safe in a place where his arrows had not? Whatever the case, though he would begin his search in the priest's hole, he would not rest until he had found the vial and destroyed it. This time, the whole of his schemes would succeed—he would keep Launceston and Alexandra apart, Psyche would be bound to earth to await her death, and at one minute past midnight on All Hallow's Eve, he would take Alexandra to wife.

How he despised his brother, he thought bitterly as he flew toward the castle. So handsome, so confident, so blessed in his happiness with his beloved Butterfly! No man should be permitted such contentment. He beat his wings angrily through the dusky air, moving swiftly toward the horseshoe-shaped outer court and just as swiftly through the walls of the entrance hall. A moment later, he was within the darkened priest's hole. Much to his disgust at his brother's stupidity, he found a soft, velvet pouch lying in one corner of the secret closet. The love potion, no doubt.

He lifted the front flap of the pouch and reached within. He felt several soft cloths, but not the vial, then suddenly something very sharp pricked his finger. He cried out and in the next moment felt a familiar dizziness assail him.

"Oh, for the love of Zeus!" he shouted in frustration as he slowly and unsteadily rose up into the air, "Mama's sleeping potion!" Through a fog of growing sleepiness he sought his tower and his bed. Just as he passed into the round chamber, and reached his straw pallet, he fell hard against the mattress and tumbled into a deep sleep.

When Eros found him two hours later he was pleased that his mother's potion had worked. He could now advance his schemes without hindrance from his brother.

Saturday arrived with a rain so hard that Alexandra, Victoria, and Julia stood at the large, multi-paned window of the central drawing room and stared gloomily across the shallow valley at the barely visible image of Castle Porth.

"It might as well be a thousand miles distant," Victoria whined. "How are we to get to the castle without being soaked through? I have not seen it rain so hard in years!"

Each lady wore her favorite color, Alexandra in a royal blue which always set off to advantage her black hair, Julia in a handsome fuschia and Victoria in an exquisite forest green. The common thread was velvet and grouped together, as Alexandra glanced from one sister to the other, she couldn't help but think they looked like a row of spring pansies.

She said as much which caused her younger sisters, Julia on her right and Victoria on her left, to slip their arms affectionately about her waist.

Julia expressed the disappointment of all the ladies. "Why did it have to rain like this today when we were to clip the yew hedges and make garlands for the ballroom?" Launceston's yew maze was so badly overgrown that he had been delighted with their scheme of decorating the ballroom with clippings from the rangy maze.

"I only wonder that we will have enough to occupy our time today without the garlands," Alexandra said. "They must be constructed first before we can proceed with the remainder of our decorations."

Julia pouted, turning to look behind the ladies at several baskets and trunks. "And everything ready—our dried flowers, laces, ribbons, and silks!"

Alexandra turned around as well. The containers sat in a forlorn jumble, lit in dappled dark gray shadows as the rain continued to pelt the windows. "Well, we shall simply have to make the best of it," she said. "Perhaps we can spend part of the day searching the Castle's attics for more treasures to place in the ballroom."

Julia winced. "Do you really wish to be poking about Castle Porth when ghosts are already rampaging through the halls? I for one do not, I assure you! I intend to remain in either the great hall or the ballroom—you may stroll through the remainder of the narrow hallways and passageways, but I shall not!"

Since at that moment two of Lord Brandreth's largest town coaches drew in front of the steps, the ladies let the subject drop. The trunks and baskets were placed in one vehicle and the ladies were guided with great care beneath large black umbrellas into the dry confines of the second coach.

The rain continued to pound the roofs of the coaches the entire distance to Castle Porth.

Twelve

Alexandra scanned the ballroom of Castle Porth with satisfaction. The empty chamber was in excellent condition due to the previous owner's exacting care of the untainted portions of the partially ruined structure. Planked, grooved, pegged, and recently waxed, the floor of the long; rectangular room was ready for dozens of dancing slippers. The walls were covered in a beautiful green silk-damask fabric—a fashionable wall-covering from two decades prior—and were a perfect canvas upon which Alexandra and her sisters could employ every decorative whim in preparing for the masquerade.

Both Launceston and Mr. Trenear showed them to the ballroom. But Mr. Trenear, after wishing them well in their exploits, retired to the billiard room which was situated up a short flight of stairs off the ballroom itself. The castle was full of such oddities of arrangement, though in some respects, a billiard room so close to the ballroom had its own advantages, primarily that of lending a few gentlemen, without the skill to partner ladies about the floor, a happy diversion.

At the far end of the ballroom was a raised alcove—opposite the main doors—in which the orchestra would sit. To the right of the main doors along one of the longer walls, were two very tall, double doors panelled with glass each of which led onto a narrow terrace on which, especially during the summer months, the air could be taken as needed.

As Launceston pointed out the various advantages of the ballroom, the rain continued to pummel and rattle the windows.

Julia stood beside one of the windows, the gray rain-light dappled over her pretty, pouting features. "Now we shall have to wait at least until tomorrow before bringing the yew branches in," she complained.

"Yes," Launceston drawled, his brow lifted provokingly as he glanced toward Alexandra. "It is most unfortunate that your sister did not have sufficient foresight to see the task completed before today."

Alexandra turned wide-eyed to stare at Launceston, instantly on her mettle. "I am capable of a great many things, my lord, but if I am not able to predict the weather I don't know how it is you must chide me for it."

He clicked his tongue. "I do so enjoy how easily you rise to the fly." He then laughed and waved toward the entrance. "At least one of us was not so completely careless of the weather."

Alexandra, uncertain whether to be miffed or mystified, turned toward the door and saw that Launceston's butler was just then directing several footmen to bring in at least a dozen bound bundles of cut yew branches. "Oh," she remarked intelligently.

"How very much like you, Launceston," Victoria cried, moving to stand beside him and beaming up into his face.

"Indeed, yes!" Julia cried, quickly crossing the room to take up his other side. "We are so very grateful!"

Alexandra watched her sisters and only with the strongest effort restrained her impulse to box each set of ears. She could not bring herself to meet Launceston's gaze which she knew was probably dressed in an utterly triumphant expression and so instead turned her attention to the yew branches.

"Well," he said. "I shall leave you to it then. Only pray inform Cuthbert of anything you might require—anything. I have also taken the liberty of having Cook prepare nuncheon to be served at one o'clock."

Only as he began to leave the chamber and her sisters had attacked the trunks of fabrics and the bundles of yew, did Alexandra bring herself to thank him, albeit stiffly, for his efforts and for his foresight.

He paused in the doorway and looked at her, his eyes narrowed slightly. "Have I offended you?" he asked with more sincerity than Alexandra was used to hearing from him.

Taken aback, Alexandra gave a quick shake of her head. "No, of course not. No."

His smile was warm as he nodded briefly in response, then slapped the doorjamb with his hand before departing. Alexandra stared after him wondering why it was he had the ability to so thoroughly discompose her.

By the time nuncheon was served, Alexandra had seen the ballroom transformed into a workshop. Cuthbert had been of enormous assistance, providing her with the strong arms and considerable woodworking ability of three footmen. Long tables, set up on wood-horses provided the ladies with ample space for designing the garlands which would run at eye-level the length of each of the four walls. Three serving maids, skilled with needles and fabric, were also employed taking the directions of the ladies and adding their own useful suggestions as to how each rosette, garland, and bow might be better accomplished.

When Launceston arrived to fetch both the ladies and Mr. Trenear—the latter of whom had fallen asleep in the billiard room with *The Times* spread over his face—he found himself staring at an industry which stunned him.

"Good God!" he cried.

Since Alexandra was standing near the doorway and trying to determine with one of the maids just how the garlands might be arranged so as not to injure the silk-damask on the wall, she heard his exclamation most acutely.

She found herself pleased knowing that of all the gentlemen of her acquaintance, he was the hardest to stupefy. "Have you never seen ladies prepare for a ball before?"

He turned to stare at her and blinked. "Yes—that is, no, suppose I have not. And I don't know precisely what I was thinking but, but this was far more effort than I had supposed must occur."

"You are just shocked because you think of us as pampered, indolent creatures." She had meant her words to be a jest but the slight confusion on his face reminded her that he indeed had no great opinion of the ladies of his society. "Actually," she added, placing a hand theatrically upon her brow and sighing with feigned weariness. "I must confess that I am utterly fatigued by the labors I have endured of this past hour and more." She then dropped into a chair by the door and released another long-suffering sigh.

"Oh, stubble it, Lady Alex," he returned, scowling down on her, a smile twitching his lips. "You've again proved my opinions inadequate."

Alexandra looked up at him. "Have I?" she queried. Rising to her feet, she beamed on him. "You begin to give me hope, Launceston. Indeed, you do!"

A considering expression overtook his face as though he was attempting to adjust his thoughts about her, but chose not to give voice to those thoughts. After a moment, he stated his purpose in coming to the ballroom and after rousing Mr. Trenear from his slumbers, led the ladies to the morning room where a small, cozy table had been prepared and a sideboard laden with sufficient delicacies to tempt all their appetites was ready to be attacked.

The fine food, the labors in the ballroom, and the prospect of a masquerade so firmly on the horizon, provided a convivial atmosphere about the table. Ideas flowed among the ladies about further plans for transforming the ballroom and in between these ideas, Mr. Trenear was happy to recall to mind the decorations of every ballroom he had ever had the pleasure to grace with his presence, all of which kept the conversation light, lively, and gay.

When the last droplet of lemonade and Madeira had been consumed, Mr. Trenear offered his arms to Victoria and Julia who, because of his persistent compliments to each of them throughout nuncheon were not reluctant to oblige him. They only mildly protested when Launceston said he must take Alexandra to speak with his housekeeper about the dinner he would be serving.

Alexandra presented her menu to Launceston's housekeeper, Mrs. Morstow, and at the same time offered to that good lady, on her mother's insistence, the use of the staff at Roselands. Mrs. Morstow stated with a twinkle in her eye that Launceston had gone so far in obliging the beautiful Lady Alexandra that by tomorrow her kitchens would be overrun with newly hired servants. She had interviewed them herself not two days past.

Alexandra was stunned and not a little distressed by this news. After expressing her appreciation to the good-natured woman of middle years, who she found to be warm and friendly, she left her office only to find Launceston waiting for her in the hallway which led to the long dining room, the Green Salon and the long gallery.

When they were well down the hall, he leaned toward her and asked quietly, "What is wrong, you seem overset? Are the arrangements not to your liking? Was Mrs. Morstow uncivil to you?"

She looked quickly up at Launceston. "You know very well she was not. I am persuaded that excellent woman could never be uncivil to anyone. What a fine servant you have in her."

The expression on his face was considerably arrested and his lips were parted as though he wanted to speak but didn't know precisely what it was he wished to say. Finally, he arranged his thoughts. "I am exceedingly pleased with Mrs. Morstow and from the first of my acquaintance with her, some nine years past, she has been just as you have described her."

"You knew her in India then?" Alexandra queried, astonished.

"Yes. She was a spinster governess at one time to the children of a Lieutenant-Colonel and his wife. She chanced, most propitiously for me, to fall in love with my valet. Since I was just beginning to prosper at that time, I suggested, if she wished for it, she might take over the duties as my housekeeper. She certainly was qualified in every respect for the position and I was fortunate to be able to keep my valet content."

"He is no longer with you?" she asked.

"He died a year before my return to England," he said, as they moved into the long dining room. He touched the back of each chair as they strolled by. "He was carried off by the cholera. My house was decimated, we burned nearly everything." His face grew pinched and distant. "I have never known such fear."

Alexandra felt very strange and very small in that moment. "It is no wonder you despise us," she said softly, her eyes filling with tears. "I had the measles once and thought I should perish from the itching." She then laughed, a little too brightly.

He quickly took her by the arm and turned her toward him. "Now I have made you cry," he said. "I did not mean to overset you or to take you to task for having lived a comfortable life in England. When I have daughters, will I want them exposed to the plague—by no means. I have not been fair to you, Alexandra, and for that I apologize."

"Nor have I, Launceston. Mrs. Morstow told me you have hired an army of servants in order to accommodate my truly reprehensible request that you give a masquerade ball. I am sorry to have inconvenienced you in this manner. Truly I am."

He smiled. "As I recall, you did not request a ball at all. You wagered for it and won the wager."

She lifted her chin slightly. "As I recall, we both won that wager."

His smile broadened and he laughed, "So we did." He then slipped his arm about hers.

"Oh," Alexandra cried suddenly as she reached up and touched her lips. The fragrance of roses was suddenly all about her and a familiar oil was again on her lips. She felt dizzy and exhilarated all at once. "Again?" she murmured.

"What is it?" he cried, turning toward her just as he reached the doorway.

Alexandra looked at the viscount and saw him through a strange, golden haze. She blinked, trying to clear her vision. Her heart was beating suddenly very quickly in her breast. She walked toward him, feeling a strange warmth enveloping her, swirling about her senses, her heart now madly on fire. She walked into his arms, threw her arms about his neck, and within a deepening fog felt his lips touch hers.

She knew he was kissing her, wildly, deeply. She felt him turn her and press her against the wall. Pleasure, love, desire rolled over her in wave after blissful wave. She heard him speaking, but couldn't discern a single word, except her name. He kept speaking her name passionately into her ear. *Alex, Alex.* She felt her mind tumbling inward. She was falling, falling, falling.

Launceston caught her in his arms before she tumbled to the floor. "What the devil—" he murmured. Good God, had the sudden passion which had sprung up so violently between them killed her?

Lifting her up and holding her in his arms, he pressed his neck against hers and felt her pulse, steady and strong. He quickly carried her back to the housekeeper's office. Mrs. Morstow immediately rang for a maid but bid him to continue holding her in his arms. "Sit in my chair by the fire," she added. "There is no place for her to lie down for the present. She looks almost like an angel," she added, bending over Alexandra and peering into her face. "How did you say this happened?"

Launceston was loath to explain. He swallowed hard. "She kissed me," he admitted at last.

"Ah," Mrs. Morstow nodded without the least embarrassment or surprise. "It is these dreadful corsets," she explained. "I don't like to bring forward so delicate a subject, my lord, but in my time fainting was an art to be employed to a purpose. But with these corsets a woman is like to faint if she laughs or even breathes too hard. Perhaps you ought to give her to me, and I'll see that she is made more comfortable."

But at that moment, Alexandra began to awaken. She felt

time rushing back to her in a wave of urgency which took her breath away. She didn't know where she was nor what had happened to her. She had been lost in a place of childhood so sweet, so charming that only with the greatest of efforts was she able to force herself to return to the present.

"I was by the sea," she whispered. "Collecting shells."

"We're here, Alex," a man's voice murmured. "Are you all right?"

She heard Launceston's voice, she felt a cool hand patting her own. "A little tea," she murmured.

"I'll fetch it at once," the housekeeper said, scurrying quickly from the chamber, unwilling to wait for the maid.

Alexandra was still caught in a netherland between a glorious day of childhood and the present. She looked up at Launceston, her vision still blurred with bright sunlight and cool water on her toes. She reached up and touched his face with her hands. "I love you," she murmured. "There are roses everywhere."

Launceston looked down at Alexandra and didn't know what to make of her, or of what was happening to him. He realized she was not fully cognizant of where she was, or what she was saying, or that she was even held childlike on his lap. But having her so close to him, speaking so sweetly and lovingly, tore into his heart as nothing had ever done before. The radiance of her face, the gentleness of her words and her profession of love, was like a knife, slicing at his chest, his ribs, and laying exposed the hard flesh of his heart. He saw what the future could be with her and a longing so profound, of his lost childhood, of the deaths of his parents, of the lonely state of his existence even now, all to be redeemed in the acceptance of love, and it was all he could do to keep from taking her again in his arms and assaulting her as brutally as he had done a few minutes ago.

But that he mustn't do, in part because she wasn't fully conscious and also because he feared the violence of his kisses might cause her to faint again.

Looking down at her, he recalled her appearance just before

she had kissed him. Her face had appeared as though it had been lit from within. Love seemed to pour from her and when she walked toward him with affection and wonder on her face, he had done the only thing he could do. He had opened his arms to her and received her arms about his neck and her lips upon his.

Passion had simply overwhelmed him and he had kissed her hard, a kiss which he had believed she had shared with a like fervor. He had whirled her about, pressed her against the wall and let his body rest solidly upon hers. Then she had simply drifted away.

As he watched her now, her eyelids fluttering gently every now and again, her gaze sometimes fixed on him, sometimes hid within her drowsy state, he wondered what it would be like to be married to such a woman. After a few minutes, she seemed to awaken more fully though she was still confused about where she was.

The housekeeper returned and he helped Alexandra to take up the chair upon which he had been sitting. With every few seconds that passed she grew more lucid. He watched her take the strong, hot brew into her mouth and a little of her former color began to return to her cheeks. Her gaze became fixed to a coaching print hung on the wall next to the fireplace. What she was thinking, as he stared down at her, he couldn't know. Each time, she sipped, a furrow deepened on her brow.

"What happened?" she queried at last, looking up at him.

Alexandra could see that Launceston was deeply concerned, but it was Mrs. Morstow, standing next to her, who answered her question. The kind housekeeper drew up a chair beside her.

"You fainted, my dear," she said. "Drink a little more of the tea. In a few minutes, when you are feeling a trifle better, we can talk."

"Yes, thank you," Alexandra responded. One sip, two. A deep breath then another and suddenly the memories flooded back to her. She choked on the tea and spilled some of the tea on her gown of royal blue velvet. "Oh, my goodness. I do beg your pardon. Oh, Mrs. Morstow." She settled the cup on the saucer but found that her hands were trembling. She felt a blush begin burning her neck and covering her face in a deep embarrassment.

Mrs. Morstow kindly suggested to Lord Launceston that he leave her to tend to Lady Alexandra which request he acceded to instantly.

When he was gone, Alexandra breathed a sigh of relief. "I don't know what came over me. I am so ashamed. I threw myself at his head. Whatever must he think of me?"

Mrs. Morstow bid her take another sip of tea. When Alexandra obliged her, the housekeeper encouraged her with an understanding smile. "Tell me what happened," she commanded her gently.

Alexandra explained how one moment she was speaking and walking beside Launceston in a perfectly acceptable and modest manner when suddenly she threw herself into his arms. She could not bring herself to confess to the feel of oil on her lips and the redolence of roses which preceded her assault of Mrs. Morstow's employer. "It seems to be such a mystery," she finished lamely.

Mrs. Morstow lifted a brow. "I see no mystery at all—merely Cupid's hand at work." She then tilted her head and regarded Alexandra carefully for a long moment. "Why are you so afraid to love?" she asked at last.

"But I'm not!" Alexandra responded promptly. "That is, I never believed I was. Merely, that I have been waiting for the proper gentleman to happen along."

Mrs. Morstow nodded. "I see," she murmured. "I can't pretend to know your heart, Lady Alexandra, and though it may be impertinent of me to say so, I can only wonder if it is possible you have so romanticized your ideal that no man can meet the measure?"

"I'm sure that's not the case," Alexandra responded quietly, as she took another sip of tea. "At least, I have never believed I was overly strict in my requirements."

Mrs. Morstow chuckled. "If you are still thinking in terms
of *requirements,* my dear, then your ideals are probably too
high. Might I suggest, instead, that you begin to weigh the
good parts and bad parts of each of your suitors? We are all
such a mixture of the likeable and the undesirable, each with
strengths, each with flaws, that a good marriage is built on
the willingness of husband and wife to build up the strengths
of one another and discourage the flaws as gently as possible.
To believe that an unflawed spouse exists, is to believe fool-
ishness is wisdom."

Alexandra blinked, staring at the small pool of amber tea
which yet remained in the bottom of her white china cup. The
lesson was too hard to be absorbed easily. After she had finished
the tea, she thanked Mrs. Morstow for her kind attentions. As
she rose from her chair, she added, "And I shall think on what
you have told me."

When Mrs. Morstow was assured that she was steady on her
feet, she permitted Alexandra to leave her office.

Just as Alexandra reached the doorway, she turned back and
queried, "What does Lord Launceston think happened to me?"

Mrs. Morstow smiled sweetly. "I told him I thought your
stays were to blame."

Alexandra took a deep breath and murmured, "That explanation will do as well as any, I suppose," she said with a half
smile. She then pressed her hand to her stomach. "And you
may be right!"

When she reached the long dining room, she found Launceston
sitting in a chair near the doorway, his elbows on his knees, his
hands clasped between his legs as he stared down at the floor.
Whatever was she to say to him now? She decided to get over
rough ground lightly and put a cheerful smile on her face.

"I hope I have not overset you, my lord," she said, swallowing
hard.

He lifted his head with a jerk. "I didn't see you," he returned.
"I've been worried."

When he rose to his feet, she moved to step toward him.

"Mrs. Morstow thought my stays might be at fault and I must agree with her. I am mortified beyond words, you can have no idea." Her voice trailed off. He took one of her hands in his and brought her fingers to his lips.

"I blame myself. I was too hasty though I must say you did take me quite by surprise." He then pressed a kiss to the back of her hand.

She didn't know quite why it was that the feel of his lips upon her skin was one of the finest sensations she had ever known. He looked into her eyes. "I trust you are feeling much better."

She nodded. He still held her hand in his and because she was again feeling very drawn toward him, she drew her hand from his grasp. "We ought to be returning to my sisters and if you wouldn't mind, please don't say anything to them of my having fainted." She began to walk toward the door.

"Shall I tell them you kissed me?" he asked.

At that, Alexandra paused in her steps and turned to look up at him, astonished that he would ask such a thing. But when she saw the twinkle in his eye and the twitch of his lips, she knew he was teasing her and perhaps even trying to ease her embarrassment.

"Oh, you are just funning," she responded. "But indeed, I don't know what overcame me and I do apologize. I wish you will forget all about it."

He advanced toward her with a slight frown on his face. Searching her eyes, he said, "If that is what you wish."

She nodded, odd tears constricting her throat. "You are a very good man, Lord Launceston. I wish that I might explain my conduct to you, but I can't. I can only say that odd things have been happening to me since, well, over the past fortnight. And, and I don't seem to be enjoying my usual degree of composure."

"How fortunate for me," he said, smiling.

She gasped and would have remonstrated with him but there was just such a look of gentleness in his eye, that she felt to come the crab would have been hypocritical in the extreme.

"You are quite hopeless," she said at last. "Now do let us return to the ballroom."

"Before you lose your *composure* again?"

"You are being a rogue and I shan't listen to you anymore."

"Just as I thought—you intend to return to berating me."

"Only when you deserve it, my lord."

He chuckled softly and the moment slipped by as did the rest of the day.

Thirteen

On the following morning, Anteros awoke with a headache worse than any he had ever experienced before, even more piercing than those following one of Bacchus's more lively fêtes. He slid his legs over the edge of the straw bed and setting his elbows on his knees, sank his head into his hands. He moaned, not caring if the whole castle heard his complaint. Zeus take it, but his head hurt!

After a moment as he began unfurling his black wings and letting them reach out to either end of his bed, he glanced out the window and saw that the sky was a pure, deep blue. But that was impossible. The last he remembered, the weather was clouded and a storm was rising up from the Atlantic.

"Oh, no," he murmured. From what he could see, it appeared as though he had slept through Saturday. Which would mean today was Sunday, but only in the early morning hours if he was judging east from west properly. The truth was, he couldn't be sure of anything since his head felt swollen and dull from the sleeping potion.

He lifted a brow. Church. Alexandra and her family would be attending services and it was likely that Cupid would take the moment to be with his adored Psyche. Alexandra, therefore, would be unprotected. All he needed to do was to keep her from becoming betrothed to Launceston, so that Psyche would refuse to enter the portal at the appointed hour, and both his tasks would be accomplished. With Psyche trapped on earth he would fulfill his vow to his mother. Then he would fulfill his vow to himself by whisking Alexandra away to Olympus and taking her to wife.

Ignoring the throb of his head, he rose to his feet and again stretched out his wings. In truth, he wasn't overly concerned for he knew of Launceston's wager with Trenear. Even if Alexandra for some reason actually agreed to wed Launceston—though he thought it highly unlikely given how much she disliked the man—he knew he had but to inform her of the ruby brooch and she would undoubtedly fly into high dudgeon.

He chuckled at the thought, then laughed harder still at what fun he meant to have during the church service.

Later that morning, Alexandra sat with her family in the Marquis's box, listening to the good parson's sermon on the value of thriftiness and good management in a household, and found her mind wandering. Perhaps she couldn't keep her attention fixed properly on the subject at hand because of the dullness of the cleric pontificating before the good citizens of Stithwell, or perhaps because his left eye twitched every time his voice rose to emphasize a point which was far too frequently in her opinion. But whatever the case, time and again, most inappropriately, her thoughts turned to the memory of the day before, of the rose oil on her lips and of throwing herself into Launceston's arms. These were hardly proper reflections for a young lady during a church service, and her conscience did prickle her, but oh, the good reverend was so very boring.

What was worse for her comfort, however, was the fact that Launceston was in attendance and each time her gaze swept absently about the Church of St. Probus, somehow she could not keep from looking at him. She did so now, noting how elegantly he was dressed in a dark gray superfine coat, white shirt, a burgundy silk cravat and gray striped trousers. He was ever the gentleman in appearance. She felt her heart beating more strongly as she watched him, wondering what he was thinking about and what his opinion of her was after her odd conduct toward him yesterday—faith, had she truly kissed him so soundly, so passionately?

She wished she could forget all about it and perhaps for that reason, tore her gaze from his face. She glanced about the familiar faces of neighbors she had grown to love over the years and saw reflected there her own disinterest in the reverend's favorite subject. A yawn, a vacuous stare, a cough, and a downward glance, a twist of a ring beneath lace gloves, a longing glance through the arched windows of the stone church at a heavenly blue sky beyond.

She felt Victoria nudge her slightly and returning her gaze to the pulpit found the good reverend's critical eyes narrowed upon her. She sighed, clasped her hands lightly upon her lap, and feigned giving him her full attention. Really, she ought to be more devout. She would try. She would attempt yet again to glean some morsel of wisdom from the vicar's sermon.

But his left eye twitched again and his voice rose and she barely stifled a yawn.

Suddenly, behind the cleric, Anteros appeared. She barely suppressed a gasp as he searched the assemblage and after seeing her closeted in her family's box, began moving toward her, half-walking, half-lifting himself with slow beats of his wings. She felt wild with fright. Whatever did he mean to do—and that in a church service?

Her thoughts flew about madly. Could anyone else see him? What if he began to tease her or worse, try to kiss her again or steal her away to Olympus as he said he would? She was desperate with fear.

He was nearly upon her now. Movement caught her eye and turning she noted that Launceston's gaze was fully upon her and that he had risen from his seat opposite her family's box. She rose to her feet as well, placed her hand on her forehead and exclaimed loudly, "Papa, I am unwell!"

Lord Brandreth leaped to his feet, brushed quickly past his wife and Julia, and caught Alexandra as she pretended to faint. The congregation began whispering excitedly. Because she was now in her father's arms and was being carried from the church, she could no longer see Anteros. But she felt his black wings sweep over her face and she heard him whisper, "You will be mine. A minute past midnight, on All Hallow's Eve, you shall be mine!"

Fear took a strangling hold on her heart. She could hardly breathe as she slipped her arm about her father's neck and held him tightly. "Please, please take me home," she whispered into his shoulder.

"Of course, my pet," he said. "Evan, call for our carriage. No, no, she's fine. I heard her speak."

Launceston had seen the sudden alteration in Alexandra's face and a moment later, as he glanced the direction of her line of sight, he saw the black-winged man, the ghost of Castle Porth, appear behind the vicar. He had been deeply shocked that the spirit, or whatever it was, had actually invaded the church and even more disturbed to discover that he apparently held quite ignoble intentions toward Alexandra.

You will be mine—midnight—All Hallow's Eve.

Launceston had both seen and heard the ghost speak to Alexandra. He had watched dumbfounded as the being lifted one of his wings and touched her face with the tips of his feathers. The ghost had then drifted out of the path of the crowd of parishioners who had quickly followed after the marquis and his family, all anxious to be of assistance, if not with the purest of motives.

Launceston stayed in the shadows of his box, watching the black-winged man and occasionally glancing toward the other worshippers to see if anyone else was able to see the ghost as well. But not one member of the parish church gave the smallest indication the ghost, or whatever the deuce it was, was visible.

He shifted his gaze back to the man, noting that there was nothing ethereal about him. He was substantive, real, the color of his flesh vivid and alive. What was he then?

And why did he have designs on Alexandra. *Midnight—All Hallow's Eve.*

That would be the same night as the masquerade ball! Did this being's, this ghost's, intentions toward Alexandra have something to do with the masquerade for which she had wagered him? She certainly had seen him standing behind the vicar and there was no mistaking that she feared him.

The devil take it, he didn't know what to think.

He recalled her words of yesterday, that for the past fortnight strange things had been happening to her and for that reason she had not been able to account entirely for her conduct. Now that he considered the manner in which she had so suddenly assaulted him and kissed him yesterday—so at odds with her usual demeanor, just as she had said—a prickling of gooseflesh travelled down his spine. He was beginning to believe that something more than a simple haunting was taking place in the environs of Castle Porth and that somehow Alexandra had become the object of this bizarre happenstance.

His servants had said the black-winged man had appeared about a fortnight before his own arrival at Castle Porth—a timing which would match Alexandra's history. Was it possible, therefore, that this ghost had been haunting, even pursuing, Alexandra for that length of time? But to what purpose? To frighten her?

He could make no sense of it.

He recalled the moment as well when he and Alexandra had been searching through his home together, following the scraping noises, and how after mounting the short flight of stairs outside the chapel ruins, she had turned around and had been literally pushed into his arms. Had this being given her such a push? And what of the beautiful lady they had witnessed earlier in the direction of the long gallery, the same woman he had seen so many years ago in the chapel ruins? Did she have a role to play as well? But again, to what purpose?

He had no firm answers to the questions plaguing his mind, only growing doubts as to Alexandra's safety. He recalled how she had questioned him about his lack of fear of either the black-winged man or the ghost and until this point, he had truly not feared their presence in his home. Many ancient castles, great houses and manors throughout England had claims to resident spectres—all harmless, to his knowledge.

But having seen the look of fright on Alexandra's face and having heard the black-winged ghost tell her, *you shall be mine,* he was swiftly gaining a different perception. Fear now moved within him and the largest question of all loomed before him— who was this black-winged man?

Launceston decided to confront the ghost and moved to stand some eight feet away from the magnificent being who now turned toward him and met his gaze squarely. The man's lazy expression became a sneer. "I don't give a fig what the oracle says," he stated baldly, his teeth white and even, his skin flawless, his voice a rich sound in the now empty church. "I intend to take her back to Olympus. She shall be my wife and Plutus take your precious England." With that, he laughed and then simply disappeared.

Launceston was left in a state of shock. *I intend to take her back to Olympus.*

Olympus. Mount Olympus? But that was impossible!

Olympus did not exist, except in the traditions of a long dead religion which had been consigned to the dusty annals of mythology for centuries.

He stood blinking at the place where the black-winged man had vanished.

Olympus? God help him he didn't know what to think. His heart was racing in his chest.

Perhaps he was merely going mad. Perhaps he had only imagined seeing the black-winged man. But if so, then Alexandra was mad as well, along with many of his servants. Would a ghost, then, pretend to be from such a place merely to arouse alarm?

He couldn't think clearly. His thoughts raced about unevenly, circling around and around, keeping pace with the hard, quick beats of his heart.

Olympus. The creature meant to take Alexandra back to Olympus with him.

He considered this for a long moment. He considered Alexandra and all that he knew about her as well as her odd conduct over the past sennight, her request for a masquerade, her own admission that she couldn't always account for her conduct. If she was being pursued tenaciously by this resident of Olympus, then why wasn't she in an hysterical state? Surely a woman thus harried would be nearly beside herself with anxiety and fear.

None of it made sense to him.

Olympus! Creatures from mythology! Good God! What was happening in Stithwell?

He was now alone in the church, his mind feeling as though a lightning bolt had just been shot through it.

Mythology!

Easier to believe in ghosts than in mythological beings.

Yet he had seen the black-winged man, or god, or whatever he was. He had heard his voice. He had witnessed his assault on Alexandra's sensibilities. His servants had seen him, Ladies Alexandra, Julia, and Victoria had seen him, not to mention the beautiful woman.

Perhaps had he been alone in his sightings of strange creatures in his home, he would have simply sought out his physician. As it was, there had been too many witnesses to the presence of the black-winged man and to the beautiful woman to dismiss them as the imaginations of one addled mind.

He began trying to assimilate all that he had just come to understand. His thoughts were sluggish as he reviewed the several times he had seen the black-winged man—when he was thirteen, more than once of late moving about his home, and this morning assaulting Alexandra!

What did all of it mean?

And who precisely was the black-winged man and who was the beautiful woman?

The man's wings were quite mythological in nature, but he

could not recall to mind a black-winged man? He knew of Pegasus, a horse with wings, and of Cupid, a baby with wings. But was there a man with wings? According to his knowledge of mythology, Cupid had not remained a baby but had become a man once Aphrodite gave him a brother, a brother called Anteros.

He thought back to the time he was thirteen and to the hours spent in the chapel ruins late into the night. He recalled the night in which both the black-winged man and the beautiful woman had appeared. They had been plotting to get rid of a woman called Butterfly! The only butterfly he could recall was the mortal, Psyche, who became Cupid's wife—"Butterfly" was Cupid's nickname for her!

The pieces of the mystery suddenly fell together.

Psyche. Cupid's wife.

Then the black-winged man, in the image of a grown Cupid with wings, must be the younger brother, Anteros. Therefore the woman, extraordinary in her beauty, would most naturally be their jealous mother, Aphrodite, also known as Venus, goddess of love and beauty. Aphrodite had from the first opposed Cupid's marriage to Psyche.

He must be dreaming! This couldn't be happening! None of this could be real! Yet it was—all of it. As real as the hard gray granite of the church.

He took a deep breath and calmed the still rapid beatings of his heart. Slowly, he began to accept what was happening.

So, Anteros had designs on Alexandra. From his own admission, Anteros intended to take Alexandra back to Olympus with him, to take her to wife. Given his knowledge of mythology, this action was not without precedent—Cupid had done as much. Psyche had been a mortal when Cupid fell in love with her.

He shook his head, unable to credit that his home had become the focus of such extraordinary events. His wager with Trenear now seemed insignificant in the extreme and all but forgotten in the face of Anteros's intention of carrying Alexandra off to Olympus.

He wondered what the god of unrequited love had meant about not caring what the oracle had said with regard to Alexandra. Whatever the case, as he gradually came to accept the unbelievable truth of the situation, a strong conviction rose within his heart that he must now do all he could to keep Anteros from succeeding in his schemes. The thought of Alexandra belonging to Anteros sickened him to the depths of his heart. If a sentiment stronger than mere friendship attached to these feelings, he was unable to search it out. His mind was far too absorbed with the extraordinary circumstance of having spoken with an immortal from the kingdom of Zeus to do more than ponder what next he ought to do.

He wondered if he ought to speak with Alexandra about what she had been experiencing, but he wasn't certain he wanted her to know he was aware of what was going forward. For one thing, Anteros had said he would not act until midnight on All Hallow's Eve. For another, he didn't want to alert the vengeful god, and possibly incur his wrath. From his limited understanding of mythology he was conversant with the quixotic attitudes of the various deities—love and hate, jealousy and friendship, vengeance and justice were all relative notions depending upon the ever-changing whims of the gods and goddesses involved. For the immortals, vengeance for even the slightest insult was common form.

No, to be wise in this most incomprehensible and unbelievable of situations, he thought it best to be both silent and to wait.

Intending to leave the church, he turned toward the door only to hear a moaning coming from the direction of the pulpit. He wondered if Anteros was now up to more of his mischief. Steadying his nerves, he quickly sought out the origin of the moans and found, much to his amusement, that the good reverend was just now awakening from a swoon. Launceston helped him to his feet and kept him from falling by slipping his arm beneath his elbow. His wig was askew revealing a balding pate.

"Did you see him, my lord?" the vicar queried, pressing his hand to his chest. "He was a great, tall fellow, with black wings. Such palpitations, you've no idea. I am dizzy just thinking on it!"

"Whatever do you mean?" Launceston prevaricated.

"Oh, dear," the parson responded. "You did not see him then?" He groaned loudly when Launceston shook his head. "I should never have come to Cornwall. I am desperately unhappy living so near the sea and now a dark angel has come to torment me."

Launceston bit his lip. "Perhaps you ought to consider seeking out a living in one of the Home Counties. If you are of a mind, I have a great many connections and would not be adverse to recommending you for a more desirable position, let us say in Hertfordshire?"

At that, the parson's thin face took on a glowing aspect. "Would you do that, my lord? I would be ever so grateful. The truth is, I can't abide the natives hereabouts and—and I don't believe my pearls are received joyfully among the congregation."

"Not everyone has ears to hear," Launceston responded diplomatically.

"Just so. Oh, dear, now if you wouldn't mind, I think I ought to return to the parsonage. I am in need of a little brandy. Yes, yes, that will do to a nicety. A little brandy will set my nerves to rights."

"That would be just the thing, I'm sure."

"I think I shall be all right now," he added, permitting Launceston to remove his hand from beneath his elbow. But since he weaved alarmingly on his feet, Launceston quickly steadied him again then saw him safely delivered into his housekeeper's hands at the parsonage.

* * *

"Anteros was in the church and when he came toward me, I panicked," Alexandra exclaimed, sitting in the red velvet, button-tucked chair next to her bed and wringing her hands. "Why was he there? How could he be so unconscionable!"

"That family!" Psyche cried in return, a disgusted scowl on her face. She was lying on her side, her knee and ankle supported by pillows so that her back might know some relief from her prolonged bedridden state. "Imagine invading a church service! Of all the ill-mannered, inconsiderate, and unforgivable acts he has committed in the past several thousand years, this has to be the worst one yet!"

"I was never so frightened. I thought he meant to take me to Olympus then and there! But then he said, *one minute past midnight on All Hollow's Eve.* Psyche, that is just past the hour you are to depart through the portal. What could he mean by it?"

Psyche chewed nervously on her lip, but did not answer her.

"Why would he decide to wait? Not that I am ungrateful, merely, I don't understand what his purposes are?"

"He intends first to make certain I don't enter the portal. At midnight, the portal will vanish and if I have not passed through, well, you know the rest."

"So his first purpose is to keep you bound to earth. But why?"

"He wants to hurt his brother," Psyche said simply, all animation falling from her face as she sighed. "Anteros lives in the shadow of his brother. Even in the purpose of his birth, he is second to Cupid. When Aphrodite observed Cupid was not growing, she gave birth to a second son, Anteros, hoping that Cupid would grow up a little, which he did. So, I have come to believe that Anteros goes through life feeling extraordinarily jealous of Eros and unloved. Somewhere in his mind he has decided that since his purpose is to serve Cupid's growth and maturity, then he will make his life a misery in as many ways as possible."

"But what do I have to do with that?"

222 *Valerie King*

Psyche was silent apace then shifted her gaze to look directly at Alexandra. "He knows that I will not enter the portal until I know you will be safe."

"But I can never be truly safe," Alexandra said, trying to understand the situation and all of its implications clearly. "Once you are gone, there is no one to stop him from taking me whenever he wishes."

Psyche frowned. "I can't explain it all to you," she said cryptically. "I can't."

Alexandra searched her face carefully, in particular noting the manner in which Psyche had again shifted her gaze away from her. She sensed that either the young immortal was telling a whisker or she was not giving her the whole truth. Whatever the case, the subject was let drop when a scratching sounded on the door and the next moment, her father requested her permission to speak with her.

In a whisper, Alexandra said, "The worst part is having to lie to my father. He is now beginning to believe I truly am unwell, especially since Julia and Victoria were quick to tell him that I fainted yesterday as well."

At that, Psyche trilled her laughter which sent Alexandra's blue-devils scattering to the winds. "Come in, Papa," she called out.

When the door opened, Lord Brandreth stepped in, his complexion pale. "I heard the strangest sound just then!" he cried. "Of, of a woman's laughter, decidedly not yours!"

"Whatever do you mean, Papa?" Alexandra queried, startled that he had been able to hear Psyche's merriment.

"A beautiful trill of laughter. I have heard it before coming from your bedchamber."

"I have heard nothing, Papa," she said, hoping he would not notice how a nerve at the side of her mouth twitched at telling such an untruth.

He shook his head, scanning the chamber carefully and when his gaze shifted to her, she knew he was unable to see Psyche and she could breathe again. He shrugged his shoulders. "I'm beginning to wonder if we've a ghost like the one at Castle Porth." He advanced into the room, rounding the foot of the bed to approach her. "Well, enough of that, only tell me are you feeling better? Goodness, child, you gave me such a fright! Though I must say of the moment you look perfectly well. In fact your cheeks appear to be glowing with health. Do you have any notion why it was you swooned in church and is it indeed true that you fainted at Castle Porth yesterday?"

Alexandra nodded and took a deep breath as she looked up at him, meeting his concerned gaze squarely. "I have a confession to make, Papa, though I am utterly mortified to say as much to you."

His gray eyes opened wide. "And what might that be, my dear?"

Alexandra plunged on even though her heart was pounding in her ears. "Well, you know I am taller than both Victoria and Julia and because of that bigger, too. But I have always prided myself upon having as small a waist as either of them. The truth is, I have been eating so much of late, and, well, the fact of the matter is, I should have let out my stays a full sennight past, but I didn't. Mrs. Marstow, Launceston's housekeeper, told me my stays had, had caused my spell and I believe now she was right since it happened again in church! I should have heeded her, but I didn't. I am so very sorry!"

She could see that her father was both visibly relieved, yet embarrassed by the subject matter. "Your stays?" he asked, swallowing hard.

When she nodded, he began a hasty speech, the color on his face deepening with each word his spoke. "Your mother has complained unceasingly of the discomfort of, of her unmentionables. In her day, stays were not a requirement except," here he laughed a little too brightly, "except for the stout who wished to give a less curved line to their gowns. But, but the fashion of the day has altered so greatly, what with wasp-waists, that it is no wonder—that is, well, you know what to do then, so please see to it at once! I vow the entire village of Stithwell will be gossiping about your spell—though I don't see how I am to speak of, of—well, let us forget all about it then! Only, only pray loosen them at once!"

Alexandra rose and bowed her head. "I've been very foolish," she said. "I shall do as you bid me."

"Yes, yes, see that you do!" When she looked up at him, she could see that he was anxious to make his escape. He patted her on the shoulder, suggested she not eat quite so many meals if possible, and quickly quit the chamber.

Alexandra immediately turned toward Psyche and saw that her hand was clapped over her mouth and that tears were streaming down her eyes. Once the door was shut, the ladies laughed together.

"I—I thought I wouldn't be able to restrain myself," Psyche breathed, between gasps and chortles. "You tell your whiskers so convincingly."

"I've become a dreadful daughter," Alexandra said, also wiping her eyes and burying her laughs in her kerchief. "But did you ever see such red cheeks?"

"No—never!" Psyche cried, again letting out a long trill of laughter.

Lord Brandreth paused in the hallway outside his daughter's bedchamber and heard the familiar laughter again, only this time as though it was muffled somehow.

Ghosts, bah! He was just glad to be out of there!

Eros had listened to Alexandra's recounting of his brother's visit to the Church of St. Probus, and was appalled. He had been present in the bedchamber when Alexandra returned markedly early from church, her color high on her cheeks, her eyes wild with distress and knew instantly that his brother had awakened a full four and twenty hours before he was due to awaken and that he had already succeeded in causing a bit of mischief.

He had not waited to consult with Psyche upon what ought to be done next, but had quit the bedchamber after Alexandra's father had also left the chamber. He was angry and wanted words with his brother immediately. If he couldn't argue some sense into him, then perhaps a bout of fisticuffs might settle the matter.

He found Anteros asleep in his tower. "Wake up, you cur!" he cried. "You've a great deal to answer for! Where is my bow and my quiver?"

Anteros, who had returned to his tower after wreaking havoc at the Church of St. Probus, woke from his slumbers and blinked drowsily at his brother.

"Where is my quiver?" Eros again demanded.

Fully awake, Anteros responded. "I've hidden them in the woods to the south—you'll never find them in time, I can promise you that."

"You actually mean to follow through with this ridiculous scheme of yours and take a mortal to Olympus? What do you think Zeus will say about it! You can't have forgotten he's forbidden the taking of mortals!"

Anteros regarded him from half-closed lids and though Eros could not see his entire expression, he could feel his brother's enmity as though it had taken form and now surrounded him. "You have a wife of your choosing," he began evenly but with a hard edge to his voice. "She is a mortal, and I have no one. Had you even a mite of compassion you'd comprehend how unfair it is—how unfair it has always been. Lady Alexandra was part of a series of prophecies coming out of the oracle at Dodona and I grew intrigued by her. When I came to visit a few weeks ago, to see for myself if her beauty equaled Psyche's, I determined even then that I would take her to wife."

"Against Zeus's commands, you intend to bring her to Olympus?" he asked, shocked for Zeus was known to be extremely harsh in his judgments against those who would breach his laws.

"I find I care very little for his commandments or anything

else much of late and Mama has promised to protect me. Besides, I want Alexandra, and I shall have her."

"Even though you know that she must wed Launceston, or the future of the mortal world will be jeopardized?"

"As I said before, I don't give a fig for much of anything and certainly not for the world. After all, what are these mortals except vain, silly, incompetent creatures who, no matter how much love you give them, still behave as though they've only half a brain and half again as much sense."

"And you are aware that Psyche will not leave England until Alexandra is given to Launceston?"

Anteros turned on his side. "If she chooses not to leave, then let her suffer the consequences. No one will force her to stay."

"She will stay because she has a kind, loving heart. Would you fault her for that, would you condemn her to die because she is goodness itself?" He didn't answer his questions but closed his eyes as if to ignore Eros and return to his slumbers.

"Do go away, Eros. I am tired. I am finding that Mama's sleeping potion is still tugging at my mind."

"Why are you grown so bitter, Anteros? I had thought you had made your peace with Psyche and with me. I don't understand? Why do you wish to hurt my wife, to hurt me, for you know I can't bear the thought of living without her?"

At that, Anteros opened his eyes and stared piercingly at Cupid. "If you must even ask that question, then I've little hope you would even begin to comprehend my answer. Now do go away, little Cupid, for I am weary and need my rest. Very soon, after all, I shall be a bridegroom and shall need my strength. You however, will need to prepare for an entirely different future. In but a few decades I've little doubt you will be a widower."

At that, rage consumed Cupid. He had hoped to reason with his brother, or at least to come to understand him. But hearing his words and the terrible bitterness in his voice, he knew any further attempt to argue him out of his schemes would prove futile. He just couldn't understand why, regardless of Zeus's wrath, or the fate of the world, or Psyche's fate, Anteros meant to take Alexandra for himself or why he didn't care that the success of his plans meant Psyche's death. Well, it no longer mattered as to why Anteros wished for it. All that mattered now was that he didn't succeed.

Frustrated and furious, Cupid took a single step, a beat of his strong wings carrying him the remainder of the distance to the straw bed, and leapt on his brother. He planted Anteros a hard facer, catching his cheek with his fist once, then twice. The third effort however was blocked as Anteros's wing came around in a brisk sudden movement and flipped him upside down on the floor beside the bed. Anteros was now sitting on top of him, their hands locked together as his brother struggled to dominate him.

Anteros's wings beat at his face, and using one hand and a painful knee, he pinned his arms across his chest. Eros found he couldn't move. Even his wings were trapped beneath him.

He gasped as he felt Anteros slip his free hand beneath the long thin bone which composed the main span of his wings. "Don't do it!" he cried. He leaned his neck back and cried out again as he felt the pressure on the bone. He heard a snap and pain engulfed him. His brother had broken his wing.

There was no pain like this one. He couldn't see as darts of lightning flowed from the broken wing, traveled along his shoulder into his brain and crossed in front of his eyes. He felt consciousness drifting away from him as he was lifted high into the air.

The last words he heard from Anteros's mouth were an enigma, given how much hatred now ruled his brother's heart.

"Dear Zeus, what have I done?" the god of unrequited love said.

Fourteen

The following day, Alexandra worked alone at Castle Porth, making the final adjustments to the ballroom decor. Victoria had kept a previous engagement to visit friends in Falmouth and Julia had been requested by her mother to remain with her for the day, saying that she had begun to miss the company of her daughters. When Alexandra protested that to be alone again with Launceston at Castle Porth would hardly be seemly, Lady Brandreth had merely smiled and expressed her conviction that her eldest daughter would always show the greatest good sense.

Therefore, as she directed a footman to make a few final tucks in the gold, red, and orange silks, she found herself quite content. The whole of the project, from inviting the guests, to planning the decor, to choosing a theme for the costumes, had been very much to her liking. Though Victoria had frequently complained of fatigue and Julia of boredom, she had herself been invigorated by every aspect of the preparations for the ball, not less so than because for the past two or three days, Launceston had been both attentive and kind to her. So much so, that a great part of her contentment had its roots in a growing belief that they were actually becoming friends, and perhaps something more, a thought which caused butterflies to suddenly run riot in her stomach.

Was it possible she was experiencing feelings of true affection for Launceston?

She wasn't certain, all she knew was that his conduct toward her yesterday, in particular, had revealed such a tender side to his temperament, that her thoughts ever since had been decidedly warm toward him.

The sisters had spent Sunday afternoon at Castle Porth, arranging the silks and seeing to the final hanging of the yew garlands, dried flowers, ribbons, and laces. Mr. Trenear had teased Victoria away from her labors to play at a game of billiards with him which she did quite willingly. Julia had sat at one of the work-horse tables, twirling bits of ribbon about her fingers for hours on end, her disinterest in the proceedings disappearing only for those few moments when Lord Launceston would arrive to check the ladies' progress. A glow of relief would overtake her countenance and he would take up her many hints and entertain her for a few minutes each time, even going so far at one point to beg her to take a turn about the courtyard with him for he could see she was suffering from a want of exercise.

Alexandra had cast him a grateful glance since Julia's complaints were growing louder as each quarter hour moved the clock forward—when would they finally be done, she was sick to death of making lace bows and why did Alexandra insist on the garland travelling the entire circuit about the ballroom anyway!

Launceston had bowed to Alexandra, with just such a look of understanding in his eye, that she was for a moment overcome with wonder. That was the beginning, she thought.

Later, he had provided an exceptional dinner for them and had presided over it with a graciousness that she had never witnessed before. He had even seated each of the ladies himself and exclaimed his appreciation for all their hard work. After dinner, he had escorted the sisters home.

Once Launceston had handed each of them down from the carriage, Alexandra had remained behind to thank him for his kind attentions throughout the day.

"Especially with Julia. I daresay she will not look upon another such ball with equal enthusiasm, unless, of course, someone else agrees to do her share of the work."

Launceston had taken his hand in hers and given it a squeeze. "I could see how it was and that she was becoming a sore trial, especially to the servants. I could not myself keep from hearing her complaints each time I drew near the ballroom."

Alexandra chuckled. "She is made for much more livelier activities. The hunt suits her to perfection, and as you already know she is an accomplished dancer."

"That she is," he said, smiling down at her, the expression in his hazel eyes warmed by the light from the coach lamps. "Which brings me round to a point I have wished to address with you for some time. It would seem you and I have never danced before. Would you do me the honor of going down at least one set on Wednesday evening?"

"Of course," she responded, wondering how it had come about that in less than a sennight, her heart had so softened toward Launceston that few things promised a greater pleasure to her than dancing with him.

"Alexandra," he began quietly, holding her gaze steadily, her hand still clasped lightly in his.

"Yes?" she queried, when he did not immediately continue.

"I have been wanting to ask you—" he broke off, a slight frown between his brows.

Alexandra thought he seemed a little distressed. "Please, ask me anything," she prompted him.

"Well, I hope we might be friends," he stated at last. For the barest moment, she had the oddest sensation this was not what he had intended to say. He continued, smiling boyishly, "I know I have not always treated you with kindness, but I mean to do better. For one thing, I have made myself a promise not to set up your back so frequently as I have in the past."

"I would enjoy counting you among my friends," she had responded. "And in like manner, I will vow to do better by you as well."

He had then politely bid her good night and after seeing her safely within doors, had driven away.

Even now she wondered what it was he had truly meant to ask her. Perhaps she would never know.

"A bit to the right, my lady?" the footman queried, drawing her abruptly back to the present. "Is that what you've decided then?"

Alexandra gave herself a shake, releasing the skirts of her scarlet silk gown which she found she had been clutching while in the midst of her reverie. She had been so lost in thought that she had failed to attend to the poor footman who had been holding a length of gold silk high over his head for several minutes, awaiting her instructions.

She cleared her throat. "Yes, that will do to a nicety. Yes, that's it." She then glanced about the ballroom and could not keep from smiling. "It would seem we are finished," she announced.

Two maids were standing in readiness nearby for her orders and at her pronouncement each broke into smiles and clapped their hands together. She thanked them all, then directed the footman to descend the ladder. "And will you please first see that these last few remaining tables and tools are removed, then afterward inform Lord Launceston that he may now join me here." He had begged to view the ballroom earlier but she had forbidden him to see it again until it was completed to her satisfaction. His sincere interest in her efforts pleased her very much.

Within a scant five minutes the ballroom was empty of equipment and Alexandra moved to the doorway to survey the results of her and her sisters' efforts. She was infinitely pleased with what she saw. Several branches of candles, placed along each wall, illuminated the chamber in a soft glow of light. In addition, moonlight flooded the ballroom from the two long, glass-paned doors, which led onto the narrow ballroom terrace with a view of the south woods.

She closed her eyes and imagined what the chamber had looked like before when the walls were bare. She opened her eyes and felt a rush of pleasure at what she saw. Overlaying the dark green damask silk of the walls was first a draped swag of gold silk, then a shimmering orange and finally a red, all forming a veritable rainbow of rich autumn hues. To balance the colors, yew swags centered each red silk drape and had been laced with ribbons of gold. The deepest part of each swag bore long sprays of beautifully dried roses in the same colors as the silk and were bound with Brussels lace bows whose tails trailed several feet toward the floor. The effect was beautiful and festive.

Imagining the three chandeliers, which hung from the ceiling, lit with dozens of candles, she knew that the final effect would be all that she had hoped it would be and she sighed with immense satisfaction.

She thought she heard steps in the hall, but when she turned to greet Launceston she found she was mistaken—no one was there. Yet she had heard something.

She felt movement behind her and she turned again, but again no one was there.

Anteros, her mind warned her, and her heart began to beat rapidly.

Goodness, she had all but forgotten about him since she had not been accosted by him since early on the day prior. Was he here? Realizing that the presence of the servants may have been protecting her, she wished now she had not dismissed them all at once. But it was too late to think about that. *What would he do to her this time?* she wondered. If he made use of the rose oil again, she knew she would be enslaved by the potent fragrance. Would he decide against waiting until Wednesday and take her to Olympus now?

She thought she heard her name spoken behind her, but as she whirled around, just as before, no one was there!

This wouldn't do! She was dreadfully frightened now and began walking quickly toward the doors to the ballroom. She was about to break into a run when this time she definitely heard footsteps in the hallway beyond, familiar footsteps.

She breathed a deep sigh of relief, for Launceston was coming and she would be safe now. Calming herself, she stilled her racing heart and waited for a moment before she stepped into the hallway.

Before he could catch a glimpse of the decorations, she lifted a hand and stopped him with a smile, all the while taking another deep breath to further still her quickly beating heart.

"Wait!" she cried. "I wish to surprise you. If you will give me your hand and close your eyes I am persuaded you will more fully appreciate your first viewing of our labors if you see the ballroom all at once."

He obeyed promptly, extending his hand to her and squeezing his eyes shut. She took his hand and pressed it gently as she began to lead him forward.

Yes, Launceston was with her and now she could be easy.

"You won't believe what my sisters and I, along with your wonderful staff, have been able to achieve. I hope you are as pleased as I am."

"I have no doubt that I shall be," he responded genuinely.

She led him carefully the rest of the distance to the ballroom and placing him in the center of the doorway, finally released his hand. "You may open your eyes now," she said.

She watched his eyes open, she saw the quick lift of his brows, the parting then pursing of his lips, and she heard the soft whistle which followed. "I am astonished!" he cried. "I would never have thought you could have achieved so very much—"

"But *I* did not—"

He turned toward her and with a challenging expression in his eyes, exclaimed, "Do not pitch that gammon to me, Lady Alexandra. Yes, yes, I presume Julia was responsible for some of the artistic notions, as well as Victoria, but if you think for a moment I am not cognizant of the fact that you, and you alone, saw the task completed, you are greatly mistaken. My staff informed me of your part in the proceedings and my butler has praised you to the skies, which is no small accolade, I assure you. Mrs. Morstow has also assured me that there wasn't a servant who showed the smallest disinclination to enter into your schemes. You have very kind manners where they are concerned and yet a firmness of decision which leaves no one in doubt of your requirements. My compliments to you—and to you alone."

Alexandra was considerably taken aback and found herself speechless. He had never offered her such praise before—and that so sincerely. But because she failed to see herself or her skills in such a light, she found herself unwilling to accept his compliments so readily.

"You are too kind," she said, folding her hands in front of her. "But I promise you, I have done nothing so extraordinary as you seem to think."

His gaze dropped to her hands and in response he threw up his own, exasperated. "For once I am actually speaking properly to you, yet you still appear to be offended. Have I somehow offended you?"

"No, of course not," she assured him hastily, releasing her hands and gesturing widely. "But I am utterly confounded and I am finding it exceedingly difficult to agree with your quite handsome praise. I am flattered, but I feel your flattery is unwarranted. I have only done what Mama has taught me, what any well-trained miss would do."

She could see he now took a turn at being confounded. "What any well-trained lady would do," he murmured, then laughed in a manner that indicated he was more frustrated than amused.

"Why do you laugh?"

"Because I realize now how wrong I was about you—in every possible respect."

Alexandra smiled, her heart warming toward him. She had never found him so forthright, so willing to admit his mistakes. She then took a deep breath. "I was wrong about you, too," she said. "Even if you did bear an ill-opinion of ladies generally, I know that I drew every flaw I saw into an oversized portrait of the man you really are. If you laughed, it was too loudly. If you flirted, it was outrageously when in truth I know you pressed the ladies of your acquaintance no further than any other man I've ever known. If you snubbed me because I was on my high ropes, I set you down as unbearably high-handed. I am sorry, Launceston, for having been so mean-spirited toward you."

He took a step toward her. "And I'm sorry for not having sought you out last summer. I must have seemed like a Coxscomb to you, but in truth, I don't really know why I didn't. Perhaps I was afraid. At any rate, I wish you to know that I regret infinitely not having called upon you in Bath and that I deserved at least some measure of your ill-will this past season in London."

"I still shouldn't have let you kiss me," she said, holding his gaze steadily. "What an opinion you must have held of me! Perhaps in part, all these months, I have tried to prove to you that I was not the hoydenish young woman you had held in your arms and, and tumbled on the ground. Oh, Launceston, I am mortified when I think of how easily I fell into your arms."

He took another step and for some reason it seemed natural to extend her hand to him, and he took it gently within his own. "For myself," he said quietly and sincerely, "I was glad to have found such a passionate young woman among the *ton*. You gave me hope, for I had made up my mind to leave England that sennight and return to India."

"You had?"

He nodded. "The stultified drawing rooms, the growing air of constraint among the *beau monde* was becoming more than I thought I could bear. Having loved once, I couldn't bear the thought of taking into my home a woman who couldn't abide being touched, whose affections would be limited to a cold kiss upon the cheek in the morning, and one perhaps at night."

Alexandra felt her cheeks grow warm. "Well, I have certainly dispelled your fears on that score over these past several days, haven't I?" she queried, grateful that the moonlight could not possibly fully expose the embarrassment which she knew had overtaken her cheeks.

He laughed and as though he had meant to do so all along,

he drew her into his arms. She waited for him to kiss her, but instead he looked down at her, his hazel eyes full of affection. "Do you know it now occurs to me that I don't wish to wait until Wednesday evening to dance with you. I am a tolerable dancer, you know."

She nodded. "I know you are. When I knew you weren't looking, and I happened to be lacking a partner—"

"Which was never, if I recall—"

"Frequently, I assure you. At any rate, I used to watch you waltz and more than once wished I didn't hate you so very much so that I could be turned about the floor just as I saw you turning so many other ladies."

He chuckled, his features never more handsome as he watched her with welcoming warmth and tenderness in his eyes. He began to hum a familiar waltz and a moment later led her into the dance. She laughed aloud, thinking she had never enjoyed herself so much as in this moment. He moved beautifully and easily about the floor, his steps smooth and even, up and down, around, pause, turn again.

She began to feel dizzy and exhilarated in his arms, in the easy circle of his fluid, guiding steps. She closed her eyes, and let her ears hear the waltz in its fullness, the strains of the orchestra rising to touch the high ceiling and return to surround her with the magic of the music. Around and around he drew her, ever more deeply into a spiral of pleasure and intimacy. She felt she knew Launceston in this moment, understood him, trusted him. Her heart had never been more open to him, more welcoming.

When she opened her eyes, she saw that he was watching her with an expression that took the warmth of her heart and caused it to burst into a flame of hope and desire.

"Alexandra," he breathed. "Do you know how beautiful you are, how desirable?" His hand tightened on her waist as he drew her more nearly to him. His words were like honey to her soul. She wanted to hear more, to hear the resonance of his voice as he spoke, to hear the thoughts of his heart expressed fully.

He drew her slowly to a stop near the moonlight-flooded window and turned her so that the light was fully on her face. He touched her cheek with his hand. "Alexandra, I've fallen in love with you," he said. "I didn't know it until now. Until just now." His fingers touched her lips in a long, soft stroke and then his lips were on hers.

She received his kiss feeling as though she was sliding into a pool of warm water. She felt soothed, comforted, yet strangely alive. She couldn't believe he was actually kissing her again, nor that he had professed his love for her. Was she dreaming?

"I love you," he whispered over her lips, kissing her lightly, breathing, whispering his love again and again. His arm was still tightly about her waist as she sank deeper into the pool.

"I love you," she returned, echoing his affection as though she had always loved him and always would.

His lips were now anxious on hers and a profound desire grew in her until she was equally as anxious. She wanted him to kiss her fully, yet he didn't. He merely drifted his lips over hers, teasing her to a point of madness.

She moaned, slipping her hands over his shoulders and letting her fingers rake his blond hair.

"Alexandra, my darling," he murmured, drawing her closer still until she felt the press of his legs against hers even through her voluminous scarlet gown. Still he tormented her by drifting his lips over hers.

"Please," she whispered, tears starting to her eyes. "Please kiss me."

He groaned and obliged her, forcing his lips on hers in so painfully sweet a manner that she found herself clinging to him as though were she to release him he would disappear. She parted her lips, and as he had done before he possessed her until the tears rolled down her cheeks and she embraced him so tightly she could scarcely breathe.

Her heart was given, she realized as he continued to possess her mouth, her lips, her cheeks, her neck. She loved him as she had never believed she would ever love anyone.

Her heart was given, fully and completely.

"Were I to ask your father for your hand, would you want him to give it to me?" he asked between assaults.

"Yes, oh, yes," she murmured and had all the delight of again receiving his kisses. "Launceston, I love you so. I never thought, never dreamed—oh, my darling!"

Again, he kissed her hard on the mouth, his body strained against hers. Euphoria moved over her in light, whispery waves. Her mind seemed to disappear in the sweetness of loving and being loved.

But oddly enough, a strange sound began to dispel the enchantment which surrounded Alexandra in that moment, the sounds of hands clapping.

When she could no longer ignore the intrusion, she followed the direction of the clapping and saw that Anteros was standing in the doorway sardonically applauding the sight before him. Launceston turned as well and for a môment she thought he saw Anteros, but she wasn't sure.

"Ask him about his wager with Trenear," was all Anteros said, before he disappeared, the sound of fluttering wings a brief echo of his flight.

A wager with Trenear. Had she heard properly?

She looked at Launceston and saw that his eyes were wide with shock. Had he seen Anteros? Had he heard him?

From behind her, she heard Anteros's voice yet again, only this time but a faint whisper in her ear. "Ask him about his wager with Trenear. You will not be amused, but at least you will have your eyes opened."

At that, she looked levelly into Launceston's eyes and saw that fear reigned in them. "What is it?" she asked. "Why do you now appear as though you've seen a spectre, or have you?"

He shook his head. His complexion had paled, even in the moonlight she could see as much. "I didn't mean for you to learn of the wager," he said. "But there was a wager."

"You heard him then? You heard Anteros? You saw him?"

He nodded. "But I must tell you—"

"What does this mean?"

"I suppose now I will not get your horses!" a new voice called from the doorway. Mr. Trenear stood where Anteros once had, an amused smile on his lips.

Alexandra started, her heart now pounding with dread. Perhaps it was Anteros's sudden appearance and now Trenear's, or perhaps it was the mention of a wager or the fact that Launceston seemed to have heard Anteros's voice, but she couldn't seem to catch her breath. Fear now pounded in her temples and in her neck.

A wager.

"Your horses?" she queried, feeling sick in the pit of her stomach.

"My chestnuts," Launceston said. "Good God, this can't be happening. Alexandra, you must listen—you must try to understand. This can have no effect now. None. The wager was enacted, before—before any of this!"

"Here is my ruby brooch. You have won it when everyone else failed." Trenear tossed the brooch to Launceston who caught it in his right hand and held it to his chest. He looked down at it as though it was on fire. The redness of the stone appeared like dark blood in the blue moonlight.

Alexandra understood with a rush of clarity that was as painful as ice water on cold hands. "Oh, dear God, you wagered my love," she cried. "Was there never a greater fool born than a woman who could be seduced by a practiced man."

He tried to stop her, but she pushed past him and blindly sought the doorway. She ignored Trenear's protests that he had only been teasing the pair of them since even he could see that they were smelling of April and May, but she refused to hear him.

"I am a blundering nodcock," he said, the last words Alexandra heard before she picked up her skirts and ran to the entrance hall.

Launceston stared at his friend and shook his head. "I have never known your timing to be poorer, old chap. You will find much to be amused, however, in this situation, for that woman just took my heart with her."

"Dear God, I have made a mull of it. I heard enough to know that you had exchanged professions of love but I thought everything was settled. Did you not ask her to marry you?"

He shook his head, feeling dazed. "I stupidly asked what her wish would be should I ask her father for her hand."

"I'll go speak with her," Mr. Trenear said. "I'll set everything to rights, I promise you."

"No, please do not, for after this, I am sorry to say I sorely question your abilities on that head."

"Come then, at least follow after her," he said, urging Launceston toward the hallway. "Take her in your arms. Explain it was a stupid wager."

He shook his head. "No, I know her well. She tends to build her fortresses quickly and surely. Were I to make an assault now, she would likely repel my advances with a flurry of arrows which, given my current wretched state, would undoubtedly slay me upon the spot. No, I shall choose my next assault with greater care."

He glanced all around the ballroom but found no sign of Anteros. How easily the immortal had turned the situation against him. It would seem he now had an adversary of no mean ability. Leaving the ballroom with Trenear, he said, "No, I shan't speak with Alexandra just yet. In fact, tomorrow morning I will seek out Lord Brandreth and see what he thinks ought to be done."

Eros awoke to the feel of a cool cloth on his brow. He looked up and saw Artemis staring down at him. "What are you doing here?" he asked. "Good Jupiter, where in the name of Plutus am I?" He was lying on a bed in an unfamiliar chamber, a room decorated with the heads of rams, deer, and boar.

"In my palace. Merk sent for me when he found you on a grassy hill to the south of a rather forlorn-looking castle."

"Castle Porth," he murmured, his memories righting themselves.

"That sounds like the name he used."

"My wing—" Eros cried, trying to lift his wing but feeling another shaft of pain streak through his shoulder and into his head. "Oh, dear Zeus." He felt like retching the pain was so unbearable.

"You must rest. You may be immortal but your injuries will always require time to heal."

Cupid began taking deep breaths and forcing the pain to retreat and his mind to grow calm. "Does my mother know I am here?"

Artemis shook her head. "Neither Merk nor I believed she should be told. She—she is no longer pursuing her *beloved one.*"

At that Cupid could only smile as he recalled how adoringly she had regarded Zeus's centaur the night of his ball. "Mad as fire, eh?"

"A little worse than that, I fear. I would avoid her for the next century if possible."

"You need have no fears on that score. But have you seen Anteros?"

Again she shook her head. "No one has seen him for over a fortnight. Rumors have begun circulating that he is on earth trying to claim a mortal for himself but I don't know if Zeus has discovered it or not. Warnings from the oracle, however are arriving daily that there is a disturbance in a place called Well Corn."

He smiled, grateful that the pain was considerably diminished. "No, that's not accurate. Cornwall—a county in England. You would like England, Diana. Good hunting there."

"Yes, I know," she said narrowing her eyes. Dropping down beside the bed, she possessed herself of his hand. "I would be willing to help you, if you could find an appropriate way in which to show your gratitude. Merk says you mumbled constantly about needing to help your wife. The oracle says she is trapped in Cornwall and won't return unless your arrows can be found."

Cupid frowned and met Diana's gaze squarely. A different sort of pain now travelled through him. "I can't live without her. Does no one understand that? She is my heart, my soul. I will die without her."

At that Artemis leaned back on her heels. "You are serious, aren't you? For myself, I've never given a fig for romantical sentiments, but you! You certainly seem to take your avocation to heart, as it were." She smiled crookedly as she watched him.

"Yes," he said, nodding slowly. "It is no mean thing to be the god of love especially since the greatest irony of my existence is that I will lose my immortality if I lose the love which sustains me—*her* love."

Artemis looked away from him. "I've never cared for you very much, Eros, you know that. I enjoy my hunting and not much else. I've never really understood matters of the heart, but you disturb me by what you are saying. I am not entirely without compassion, but you must understand I have my own life, my own interests to command."

He understood her. "One arrow," he offered.

"Three," she countered, releasing his hand and rising to stare firmly down at him, her fists on her lean hips.

"Two, without potions."

"Done. Tomorrow morning I shall take my best dogs to England and begin the search for your quiver."

"One more thing," he said, catching her hand just as she turned away from him.

"Don't press your luck," she said, chuckling.

"I want only that you send the physician to me, as quickly as possible."

"He is on his way," Diana returned, the sternness of her features softening into another crooked smile. "Did you suppose I would not see your wounds tended to? I am not so bad as that, though I daresay many say I am!"

"Thank you," he said, letting go of her hand and closing his eyes with a smile. He couldn't believe his wing was broken. How was he to help his darling wife now?

That same evening Psyche cradled Alexandra in her arms and petted her soft black curls. "Men can be so wretched," she murmured soothingly, her heart breaking for the young woman. "I still cannot credit he could be so vulgar, so unchivalrous as to have wagered he could win your heart, like you were, were—"

"An object of derision and contempt!" Alexandra cried, tears again rolling down her cheeks. "He and his friends call me the Frost Queen, you know."

"How horrid!" Psyche responded, giving Alexandra's shoulders another sympathetic squeeze.

The unhappy mortal was lying on her side next to Psyche. Alexandra held a kerchief in her hand and blew her nose soundly. "And to think I actually believed he loved me. How stupid of me! How foolish beyond permission! And the worst part is, for a moment, just a moment, I actually believed myself in love with him. Oh, Psyche, we are such frail creatures when all is said and done. I knew his reputation. I watched him break a dozen hearts and more. I knew him and still I believed he loved me. What manner of pride do I possess that I could actually think I would be different from all the others? How could I have been so silly? You would think I was a chit of thirteen instead of a grown woman of three and twenty."

"Did he try to protest his innocence?" Psyche asked, again softly stroking Alexandra's hair, comforting her.

"Not precisely," she said, feeling tears again rise in a wave to her eyes and rush down her cheeks. "In fact, he admitted to the wager once Anteros broached the subject."

Psyche had listened to Alexandra's initial recounting of the incident and knew of Anteros's wretched role in exposing the stupid, thoughtless wager at the precise moment Launceston was taking possession of Alexandra's heart. The god of unrequited love was nothing if not clever and she knew that his timing had been purposeful. Alexandra had been so hurt by the knowledge that Launceston had actually wagered her heart— and that so confidently!—against his chestnuts that she would not easily be brought round again.

Whatever was she to do now to try to promote the match? Her ankle was still extremely tender whenever she moved it and walking on it was as yet an impossibility. Worse, however, was the fact that Cupid was missing. He had promised to come to her Sunday night and now a full turning of the sun had not seen his arrival. She knew, by the level of despair in her heart, that something was wrong, possibly even that her beloved Eros had met with mischief—mischief in the form of his dreadful younger brother.

Psyche was grateful Alexandra was now nestled in her shoulder for she didn't want her to know how distressed she was. *What was Anteros capable of?* she wondered, her fears now worrying the edges of her heart. She tried to shift her leg thinking she needed above all to see him, to speak with him, but the smallest movement caused a flash of pain to rush violently up her leg.

Biting the inside of her lip to keep from crying out, she looked down at Alexandra's head and for the first time realized that she had but two days in which to see Alexandra and Launceston at the very least betrothed.

Two days! And Cupid missing!

Her heart began to race suddenly in her chest. She had been so certain that she could see the task done, especially once Cupid arrived to assist her, that she truly had not feared she would be unable to accomplish her mission. But now! Now, her ankle still ached dreadfully and Eros had not come to her in more than four and twenty hours!

Panic seized her, not more so than when Anteros suddenly appeared by the window, wearing a gold velvet belt embroidered with green leaves and studded with diamonds.

"Well, ladies, how do you fare!" he cried, floating gently to the floor at the foot of the bed. "What is this? Tears, Lady Alexandra? This will not do, not by half."

Alexandra sat up and blinked at Anteros and immediately began to dry her eyes. She wasn't certain why, but there was just such a quality in Anteros's voice which she found especially warm and soothing. She looked into his eyes and drew in a quick breath. Oh, but he was so dreadfully handsome! She offered him a half-smile. "I want to thank you, Anteros, for revealing to me the truth of Launceston's motives toward me. If it weren't for you I would still be laboring under the most absurd illusion that he loved me."

Her heart was filling with the sweetest of sensations as she continued to gaze upon him.

"Anteros!" she heard Psyche cry out. "Take off your mother's Cestus! Oh, how can you! How wicked you are! Then it is true, you care nothing for me! You want only to see your brother hurt and the pair of us separated for eternity!"

Alexandra had listened to Psyche's complaints, but a fog had taken hold of her mind and she couldn't comprehend why her friend had taken to caterwauling, or why she had argued with Anteros about something called a Cestus. She didn't know what it was, though something Psyche was saying indicated the Cestus was the gold velvet band Anteros wore about his waist. How beautiful it was, she thought, glancing down at it, almost as beautiful as Anteros. She sighed deeply as she shifted her gaze back to his face. He was now standing near the edge of the bed. How could Psyche offer up even one word of complaint against a creature so beautiful, so charming, so intelligent as Anteros?

She felt drawn toward him and slid from the bed and moved toward him her arms outstretched. "Have you come to comfort me?" she asked, walking into his arms and feeling his wings gently enfold her.

"Of course I have. I love you, Alexandra. I intend to take you back to Olympus with me. You do want to go with me, don't you?"

"I have never wanted anything else."

"You love me, don't you?"

"I have never loved anyone else but you."

"Launceston means nothing to you."

Alexandra heard him speak, but the words didn't make sense to her. It was as though her mind refused to order the words.

"Launceston means nothing to you," he repeated.

"You mean everything to me," she said.

Psyche looked at her brother-in-law and felt tears of sheer frustration and fright burn her eyes. She didn't know what to do. If Alexandra confessed a dying love for Anteros, there was nothing she could do to prevent his taking her to Olympus with him.

Again he repeated, "Launceston means nothing to you."

"My love," Alexandra replied dreamily. "I don't understand what you are saying. Your words are jumbled together quite oddly. Help me to understand."

"You see!" Psyche cried. "She cannot deny her own heart. The Cestus will not prevail. For the moment yes, but not in a year or two when she has lived in your house, and the spells have worn themselves out, and your own bitter temperament rises up to destroy her. In the end, you will only know more bitterness and disappointment because it is you who are unlovable because you refuse to love. You cannot be loved if you do not love. Have you learned nothing from your brother these many years and more? Anteros, for the love of Zeus, let her go. Let her go!"

But Anteros ignored her, turning his back to her as he continued his gentle assault on Alexandra's sensibilities.

Psyche slid herself across the bed, toward Anteros. He was cooing words of love into Alexandra's ear, obviously enjoying immensely how thoroughly Alexandra was under the spell of the Cestus. She saw that he had tied the belt on with only a bow. She smiled to herself, reached up, grabbed the gold velvet string and gave a hard tug. The bow fell apart, the belt following quickly after, sweeping easily over Anteros's tunic of smooth black linen. She rolled it up and hid it underneath her.

"Alexandra!" she cried. "Leave the chamber immediately! Run!"

Alexandra felt her mind grow very clear suddenly. She heard Psyche's warning, and wrenched herself from Anteros's arms and wings.

"What the Zeus!" Anteros cried. He tried to stop her, but Psyche had taken hold of his black tunic and with every ounce of her strength held him back. He then turned and showered his curses over her head, but Psyche laughed at him and told him to take himself off, that he was done for the day trying to trick Alexandra into loving him.

Alexandra did not wait to hear more but sped from the chamber and returned to the drawing room to join her family who expressed their gratefulness she had decided not to retire to her bed so early after all.

Fifteen

"What do you mean, you wish to speak with my mother?" Alexandra queried, sitting up in bed, her mob cap draped awkwardly over her left eye. She pushed it back to better see the young immortal next to her as she blinked some of the sleep from her eyes.

Psyche was lying on her side, her hand tucked beneath her cheek as she looked up at Alexandra. "I have been awake for hours considering all our difficulties and because I greatly fear my ankle will not be healed well enough by tomorrow night for me to be concealed in a large wicker basket as you have suggested, I intend to ask your mother to help me."

Alexandra was surprised. "But will she be able to *see* you?" she asked.

"I—I think so. I don't know. Only, pray will you bring her to me? I must at least try."

"Of course," Alexandra responded. Psyche had several times expressed her sadness that neither Lord nor Lady Brandreth were able to see her on the several occasions they had visited Alexandra in her bedchamber over the past sennight. Once Psyche had even shed a few tears that her dear friend, who had once consoled her by the grotto at Flitwick Lodge, could neither see nor hear her. And even if she did, would she be able to remember anything of their shared adventures with Lady Elle, Annabelle, Mr. Shalford, and, of course, Lord Brandreth when they were all much younger?

She didn't know. All she knew at present was that Cupid had

not come back to her and she now needed help badly where Alexandra and Launceston were concerned.

Evanthea responded to her eldest daughter's request that she come to her bedchamber without the smallest ounce of surprise. She had seen Alexandra's unhappiness all through dinner of the night before and knew something untoward had occurred at Castle Porth.

She entered her daughter's scarlet and gold bedchamber, wearing her stays loose and her gown of burnished rose velvet set with new side panels. She was increasing rapidly and if memory served her right, far more quickly than a lady was supposed to in her early months but perhaps she was further along than the doctor had supposed. Whatever the case, she was happier than she could ever remember having been, except perhaps once when she was living with her dear Lady Elle at Flitwick Lodge, the month she became betrothed to Brandreth. That particular time had been a magical era for her just as carrying Brandreth's child so late in life now was another magical, incredible moment in the wide span of her years.

So it was with deep contentment that she was able to approach her daughter's difficulties, crossing the long chamber to place an affectionate kiss on Alexandra's cheek and afterward pushing her spectacles up to the bridge of her nose in order to scrutinize her face.

"Are you feeling better this morning, my dear?" she asked, searching each of her daughter's features carefully. What she found there, surprised her for small, anxious lines creased her brow, tightened her lips and caused her smile to seem forced and uneasy.

"I—I am perfectly well, I assure you, Mama, only—that is, there is someone here who wishes to see you again."

This was not at all what Evanthea had expected, neither Alexandra's anxiety nor her intention of introducing her to someone. She had not even been informed that Alexandra was entertaining a visitor in her room and so far as she could see, there was no one else present but the two of them. How very curious!

Alexandra drew in a deep, nervous breath, and continued, "She does not know if you will remember her for it has been many years since she last saw you and spoke with you." Her daughter then swallowed visibly and with a sweep of her hand, gestured to the right side of her empty bed as though someone was there.

Lady Brandreth glanced at the red counterpane which was untidy, and at the pillows which were propped in a jumbled heap against the headboard. She glanced back at Alexandra and felt her heart constrict. She remembered Lady Elle's illness of many years past and how Alexandra had been her favorite confidante in her mind's many ramblings and wanderings. "My dear," she began quietly.

"Evanthea." Her name came to her as though borne on a breeze and she blinked. Her spectacles had slipped down a trifle and she pushed them back up, turning her head once more toward the counterpane.

"Evanthea." She heard her name more clearly this time and could tell it was coming from the direction of the pile of pillows.

Her heart began to race. Fear poured through her and she clutched the collar of her rose velvet gown. Alexandra quickly slipped an arm about her waist to support her.

"It's all right, Mama," her daughter murmured.

Evanthea glanced sharply at Alexandra. "Have you some sort of spectre in your bedchamber?" she queried, frightened.

"No. No, not a spectre. A—a friend, a friend who once knew you quite well and who now needs your help." Alexandra turned toward the bed and said, "Do try again. I know she heard you. You can see how overset she is." She then guided Evanthea around the foot of the bed to the far wall and led her closer to the jumble of pillows.

"Evanthea, can you hear me?" the voice again called to her.

"I need you to hear me, to see me. Can you believe in me but a little?"

"I—I can hear you," Evanthea responded, searching the pillows. "But I can't—" Here she broke off and clapped a hand over her mouth as tears started to her eyes. Memories rushed through her like a powerful wave as Psyche, dressed in one of Alexandra's nightgowns, came sharply into view. She couldn't stop the memories, on they poured, of the past, of Lady Elle, of Flitwick Lodge, of the grotto, of seeing dear, little Psyche for the first time, of hearing her sobs, of trying to comfort her, of Brandreth, of feeling Cupid's arrow strike her neck, of seeing Cupid for the first time arguing with his wife, of falling in love with Brandreth because Psyche encouraged her to do so, of Annabelle and Shalford, of Psyche and Cupid reunited in their love at last, then lastly remembering how her memories had dimmed and faded quite suddenly as though a spell had fallen over her mind and erased every last one of them.

Only now, as she looked at lovely Psyche, did they come back to her and did she realize that her beloved Lady Elle had not been given to fits of insanity after all. Tears began to pour from her eyes and rush down her cheeks.

"Psyche!" she cried, dropping on her knees beside the bed, taking hold of Butterfly's hand and pressing her hand to her cheek. "And I had thought it all madness, but I remember now! I do, I do!"

By this time, tears were coursing down Psyche's cheeks as well. "You are still as pretty as ever and may I congratulate you on the little one to be born to you?"

"Thank you," she breathed all her fears dispelled. In their place was a profound love for Psyche, for life, for the memories she now possessed of once having shared a few weeks with the immortal wife of Cupid. "And you are as sweet and loving as ever I remember you. But how long have you been here? Why did you not summon me sooner? Oh!" she cried, glancing back at Alexandra and extending her hand to her. When Alexandra moved closer and took her mother's hand, Evanthea queried, "Is

this who you have been feeding with all the food you've requested from the kitchens?" She laughed aloud when her daughter nodded and wiped the tears from her cheeks. "And to think
your appetite was one of the reasons Papa thought you were
with child!" She laughed again, the amusement of the situation
delighting her, delighting them all, as their combined laughter
filled the bedchamber.

She then turned back to Psyche and for the first time noticed
that she was in an invalidish state. "Only what has happened?
Tell me all. You are ill, aren't you?"

At that Psyche very gently and politely begged Alexandra to
spare her a few moments alone with her old friend. Alexandra
did not hesitate to leave the room. The moment the door was
shut, Psyche began a long history beginning with the *forgetting*
potion Zeus had sprinkled over the inmates of Flitwick Lodge
and not ending her history until she revealed both the delicacy
of her mission with Alexandra as well as the horrid nature of
the wager between Trenear and Launceston which had nearly
broken Alexandra's heart.

"I see," Evanthea said quietly. She had long since drawn
forward the chair beside the bed and had listened attentively to
an explanation of Psyche's present trying predicament. "But
what can I do? How can I be of use to you in this situation?"

"You must find a way to encourage Alexandra's heart," she
said. "I do not know her as well as you."

Evanthea sighed deeply and nodded to herself. "I shall certainly do all I can," she said. "And don't worry, we shall contrive
something."

Later that morning, the marquis received a formal visit from
his new neighbor. Given his daughter's unhappiness of the evening before, following her return from Castle Porth, he was a
little surprised to see the viscount. Suspecting, however, that
Launceston's call was of a serious nature, he had had his butler
show him into his study on the ground floor.

"So, what you are telling me," Lord Brandreth said, trying to suppress a smile, "is that you bet Mr. Trenear you could break my daughter's heart and for your part in the wager you staked your chestnuts." He appeared to consider this as he moved to stand beside the now-seated viscount and repressed an urge to laugh. "Deuced fine horses. Tattersall's?"

"Yes," Lord Launceston returned, nodding uneasily. He was seated in one of the wool-plaid, winged chairs by the brick fireplace. The sky was patchy with clouds and a soft morning light lit the dark chamber in a welcome glow.

Lord Brandreth finally chuckled. "Bit of a coil, what?"

"The devil of a coil," Launceston returned.

"And you are certain you are in love with her?" he asked, peering down at the man who had just begged for his daughter's hand in marriage.

"Hopelessly so," he responded.

"Well, you certainly have all the hallmarks of having been stung by Cupid's arrow. You have behaved like a perfect nod-cock, you wear an expression as one who has had his heart ripped out of his breast, and you have kissed a female presumably you despised—and upon how many occasions did you actually assault my daughter—six? Good God! What a dreadful fellow you are—and perhaps not so wise in having confessed as much to your future father-in-law, for now I will never be able to look at you without thinking that for all your intelligence, your perseverance, and other fine qualities which escape me for the present, I will forever see you as nothing short of a moonling."

At that Launceston looked up at him, his eyes filling with hope. "Do you mean to tell me you will countenance the match should Lady Alexandra prove willing?"

"I wish you the very best in attempting to redeem yourself with her," he said. He was delightfully amused and in the most secret place of his heart thrilled that a man of Launceston's stamp had tumbled in love with his dearest Alexandra.

He would never tell the viscount as much, at least not yet,

but during the past few days since the moment he had learned his wife was with child and not his daughter, he had been making discreet enquiries in Falmouth where Launceston was known to have connections with men of Trade regarding his Indian exploits. The results were pleasing since the several men with whom he spoke, who bore reputations among the community as exemplary citizens, were one and all willing to expound on his lordship's many fine points.

Launceston, it would seem, was a man of honor, his word to be trusted, his dealings in Trade entirely above board and honest. He could uncover not a single breath of wrong-doing.

The unfortunate early deaths of his parents had left him and his siblings at sixes and sevens. Impoverished, orphaned, without connections of significance, he had worked diligently at Eton and could have gone on to university but chose instead to go to sea.

When prize money afforded him the opportunity to purchase a ship of his own, he began a commercial endeavor, trading in the Far East and in India—silks, tea, wines. Fortune had certainly smiled on him and his subsequent inheritance of a viscountancy, combined with his wealth, had been the final entree he had required to restore the place in society his uncle's improvidence and his family's disinterest had robbed from him.

Though many might disparage the source of Launceston's newly found wealth, Brandreth was not one of them. Not for him to despise a man for cutting his own path in life. Those who ignored the truths of the past eight hundred years—that nobility and wealth were won in a variety of ways, not least of which occasionally involved murder or the dispossession of one noble class by the conquering efforts of another—were men of small perception. He took his own inheritance with enormous seriousness and for that reason had already involved his distant cousin and heir in his affairs since the entail excluded the female line and he as yet had not produced a son who had survived beyond infancy. What the future would hold for the Staple family now that his dear Evanthea was increasing he couldn't know, but of one thing he was convinced, regardless of the nature of the century, only the very cunning, wise, or cruel would retain the inheritances passed on from generation to generation. Such was life. So it had always been and always would be.

In Launceston, he saw a man of wisdom and diligence who would not let his fortune slip from his hands. Therefore he felt confident in now believing that he could not have chosen better for Alexandra had he searched the far corners of the earth for his man.

"I feel it only right to warn you, however," he said, "that knowing Alexandra as I do, you ought to prepare yourself for a long siege."

Evanthea stood at the doorway of her lofty bedchamber, her heart heavy as she regarded her youngest daughters, Victoria with her arms stretched out and holding a fine, Merino wool yarn of a deep violet hue in a loop about her wrists and Julia slowly wrapping the yarn into a ball about her left hand. They were each of them quite solemn for the news of Launceston's arrival and of his having been closeted with their Papa for some time had just reached them. When they had informed her of the viscount's presence in her husband's study, she had given them the task of rolling her new yarn into a ball and had bid them not to leave until she could determine for herself what Launceston meant by paying a formal call upon their father.

Each had of course assured her that he was asking for the hand of one or the other. But she knew better. When she descended the stairs she found that her husband wished for her to give a little advice to a man who had just requested Alexandra's hand in marriage. She had not been surprised and had listened to Launceston's explanation of all that had occurred since his arrival in Stithwell some nine days prior. Because Psyche had already acquainted her with many of the essentials, especially to a large degree the state of Alexandra's heart, she felt confi-

dent she could advise the troubled viscount as to what he ought
next to do to speedily bring her proud daughter's heart round.

What she had to do next, was more difficult, as she took a
deep breath and entered her bedchamber of blue velvet and gilt.
Julia and Victoria were seated in a cozy *tête-à-tête* chair of
button-tuck blue velvet, the backs high, the legs low. Each wore
a solemn expression as each pair of large, luminous blue eyes
turned toward her.

Her heart went out to them and she knew the news she was
bringing would tear at their young sensibilities.

Evanthea took a deep breath. She loved her daughters but as
she looked at them she wondered if she had perhaps not spent
quite enough time with them for now each began to pout like
schoolgirls instead of grown women. Well, perhaps for some,
growing up came later, but if she could she meant to help her
young daughters gain some of that maturity now.

She drew a chair forward in front of the *tête-à-tête* chair and
seated herself. The window was behind them and a late morning
light flooded her face as she bid them continue to give shape
to the violet ball of yarn.

She began, "I will have no hysterics, tears, recriminations,
poutings, stamping of feet, or exclamations from either of you
or trust me, one word of complaint, one breath of ill-temper
and one, or the pair of you, will spend the remainder of the day
cleaning the scullery. Have I made my sentiments precisely
known to you?"

"Mama!" Victoria breathed, swallowing hard, fear entering
her eyes as well it should since Evanthea had never before spoken to her daughters in such a manner, nor had she ever promised such a vulgar, extreme punishment.

"The scullery?" Julia ventured as she blinked several times
in quick succession.

"You must promise me right now, before I tell you what is
going forward in your house. Not a single breath of unhappiness. Victoria?"

Victoria nodded solemnly, but quick tears had already filled her eyes.

"Julia?"

Her middle daughter nodded, but her chin was slightly set.

She leaned forward, outstretched her arms to them and took a chin in each hand. Gazing firmly into their eyes, first Julia, then Victoria, she began, "Launceston has requested your father's permission to marry Alexandra," then quickly, "Not a word, Jules! Not a whimper, Victoria!"

"But she doesn't love him!" Julia blurted out in spite of her mother's admonition, fear darting through her eyes.

"And you do, my pet? Is that what you are telling me?"

"You know I do!" Julia gushed.

"As do I!" Victoria exclaimed.

Evanthea released their chins and lifted a hand to silence what would surely be a storm of protests if she permitted full expression of their sentiments. "Remember, you promised. Not another word, now."

Her daughters fell silent. The ball of yarn and the loop over Victoria's wrists dropped to each respective lap. Evanthea then softened her expression. "Unfortunately, my dear ones, I don't believe either of you has yet known love. No, no, let me speak and search your own hearts to discover if what I am saying is true or not. When you think of Launceston, what is the first image which comes to your mind, of dancing with him at a ball? Of riding in an open landau with him at Hyde Park? Of having him lead you through a crush of people at a *soirée?*"

Both her daughters took on glowing faces, each caught up in the visions Evanthea described. "Just as I suspected," was her dampening response to their infatuated expressions. "When I first realized I might be falling in love with your father, he had just told me that I was stubborn and mulish. My opinions of him were no less unexalted. I thought him arrogant and caught up in his own conceit. So each of you tell me, what is Launceston's worst fault? What do you dislike most about him?"

Her daughters stared at her as though she had gone mad. "I don't know what you mean," Victoria said.

"He hasn't any," Julia responded flatly.

Evanthea laughed. "Have neither of you noticed that when he particularly wishes to make your sister angry, he begins to flirt with one or the other of you?"

"He does not!" Victoria cried hotly.

"No hysterics or arguments," Evanthea returned. "Now answer me truthfully, have you not even once noticed that he does as much?"

She saw that forcing her daughters to see the truth would be a feat of no mean order.

Victoria clamped her lips shut firmly, but Julia chewed the inside of her cheek and grimaced. "Yes," she said at last. "He has done so since the season last year only I never wanted to believe it."

"So tell me, Julia, was it right or wrong of Launceston to use you so ill?"

She began to see the statue of Launceston, worshipped so firmly in Julia's mind, begin to sway upon its pedestal. "Of—of all the wretched turns!" she cried. "Mylor, I mean Mr. Grampound was right. Launceston doesn't give a fig for me, he never has. I just never saw it before. Oh, Mother, he is flawed, terribly so."

Evanthea glanced at Victoria and saw that her expression had grown mulish. "When Launceston flirted with you, did he never once let his gaze drift to Alexandra's face? Did you never once have to drag his attention back to you? Did he never once, while looking at her, and reverting his attention, have to beg you to repeat your question or observation?"

Victoria's mouth dropped open. In a small voice she answered her mother's question. "A score of times—but, but I had always supposed it was because he disliked her so much. They were always brangling. Are you saying that a man only loves when he brangles?"

Evanthea laughed, "No, my darling. No, of course not. I believe in this case, in Alexandra's case, her pride has been so great that the more she was drawn toward Launceston, the more she feared the violence of her sentiments, and therefore the more she protected herself by setting up his back. I would venture that when Cupid directs your heart toward a man, there will be such a delightful flow of gentle words and sweet communion that you will not doubt that love has come to you. Only answer me this, was there ever such a communion between you and Lord Launceston?"

Victoria, whose sensibilities could not help but be wounded by her mother's revelations, began to weep. "No," she confessed between sniffles. "To own the truth, he always seemed a bit bored in my presence. And the more he seemed bored, the more lively I would attempt to become in order to more properly keep his affections—no, his attention—engaged."

Evanthea reached over and wiped her daughter's tears away with the tips of her fingers. "And aren't you fatigued from having to work so hard to be someone who you are not in order to please a man whose attention was so thoroughly caught by a different sort of female anyway?"

Victoria's tears subsided instantly and understanding entered her eyes. "I had never thought if it in those terms before. But you are right, I am sick to death of trying so hard to please him. But tell me, Mama, why have I done so?"

Evanthea said, "The same reason that when Lord Launceston walks into any room, every female, including myself, cannot keep her gaze from his manly bearing, his confident stride when he walks, the sound of his voice which is so resonant—my daughters, he is a devilishly handsome and charming man."

By now, both daughters were staring at her.

"Are you saying you have a *tendre* for Launceston?" Julia asked, shocked. The concept that their mother could hold any man in esteem except their father was evident in the repugnance visible on her face.

Evanthea laughed. "No, not in the least," she cried. "But I

can certainly value his attributes without believing that in order to be happy I must possess them."

"Is that what you are saying we have done?" Victoria queried.

"I think so. An honest mistake," she added. "And one that can be corrected even now, particularly when Alexandra is in great need of the support of her family if she is to overcome her most reprehensible pride." When she knew that her daughters were now fully attending to her, she explained about the wager and what she believed ought to be done next.

Both Julia and Victoria stared at her in disbelief. "I don't understand," Victoria said, giving her dark brown curls a shake. "You wish us to flirt with Launceston?"

"Precisely so," Evanthea returned.

The girls turned to stare at one another then burst out laughing.

"Oh, Mama!" Julia cried. "But you are incorrigible, though I cannot help but think that I shall enjoy very much seeing the expression on Alexandra's face when I take Launceston's arm and beg him to tell me yet again about climbing his ship's mast pole."

"She will roll her eyes as she always does!" Victoria exclaimed as Julia again lifted the ball of yarn and began turning. Victoria in turn lifted her arms and with just a few quick whips of Julia's wrist the ball was complete.

"I am beginning to see now that I have been little more than a silly schoolgirl about Launceston," Victoria said. "But are you certain he will make Alexandra a proper husband?"

"He will be a sore trial to her in a dozen different ways, as husbands always are to their good wives. But because she has no false beliefs about his character, she will know best how to encourage his proper conduct toward her and in turn how best to ensure his happiness."

Julia was considerably sobered by these words. "Mr. Grampound said something quite similar to me when we visited him a few days past. I thought he was merely being stuffy and overbearing as he always is—that is, as I always thought he was."

Evanthea lifted a brow and regarded her daughter intently. She had never thought of Mr. Grampound, whom she had always valued as a man of sense and excellent manners, as a potential son-in-law, but now she began to wonder. Realizing that whatever the future might hold for Julia, however, her thoughts for the present must be for Alexandra, she addressed the subject of Wednesday's final preparations. "What left remains to be done for the masquerade ball?" she asked. "Has Alexandra planned something in particular for this afternoon?"

"Only to bring some of Papa's clothes from our attics over to Castle Porth for Mr. Trenear and Lord Launceston to wear for the ball."

Evanthea clapped her hands together. "Most excellent," she pronounced. "But do you have your costumes readied?"

Julia said, "We had intended to search the attic trunks for some of your ancient gowns at the same time we looked for Papa's old clothes. That was when we heard Launceston had arrived."

"Why don't we begin now," she said. "I went through the trunks yesterday in order to select my own costume and there are several of my gowns from which to choose. I think any of a number would be suitable."

She then felt a strange sensation within her stomach. "Oh," she breathed, startled.

"What is it, Mama!" Victoria cried. "Are you all right?"

"Oh, Mama, are you ill? Are you in pain? Why are there tears in your eyes?"

"I just felt my baby kick, and so strongly. There! Again! And again! Goodness, such an active one."

Her daughters settled into warm smiles and shortly afterward, Evanthea led the way to the attics.

Sixteen

Later that afternoon, Alexandra rode silently in her father's town coach, sitting forward across from her sisters. She was greatly distressed that very soon she would have to confront Launceston. She knew that he had come to call on her Papa before nuncheon, perhaps to make a formal apology for his conduct toward her, but since her father had said nothing to her she supposed some manner of estate business had been transacted. Being such near neighbors, there would undoubtedly be many such occasions in which Launceston would have need of speaking with the marquis.

She sighed, as she looked out the window of the coach and again surveyed the gentle valley between Castle Porth and Roselands. The sky was clouded softly and the gray expanse made a lovely, contrasting background for the green, beech-studded hills and the verdant grasses all along the brook which separated the estates. At the mouth of the valley, a lone shepherd, his black and white dog and a small flock of perhaps fifteen sheep were trailing up a rise to another green valley beyond.

Roselands was such a pleasant place.

If only Launceston was not residing at the castle. How at peace she would be in this moment, content, diligently painting her next seascape, taking long walks through the hills and woodlands in the simple enjoyment of nature.

As it was, she sat stiffly in the coach, her hands folded deep within her fur muff, her bonnet tied too tightly beneath her chin and her choice of carriage dress—a burgundy velvet jacket over a plaid black, burgundy, and green skirt—far too formal for the frivolous nature of their call. How silly that they must now help the gentlemen choose their costumes from among the several found in her father's ancient trunks. Many of the coats, breeches, pantaloons, waistcoats, and long, white linen neckcloths were still in excellent condition. But how odd they appeared in contrast to the trousers of the day, the narrow silk cravats, and the longer coats.

As the carriage drew before the massive, arched front doors of Castle Porth, she could only take a deep breath and hope that the selection would be made quickly.

But in this, her hopes were soon dashed, for Launceston, as he led her sisters, each on one arm—so typical of the libertine!—into the great hall, made it known to her he hadn't the smallest intention of letting her or her sisters escape for at least two hours. She took up a seat by the window, therefore, and sat primly and silently, reading a copy of *The Times* while he teased Victoria and Julia, much to their delight, about everything—the silver combs in Julia's hair, the pretty lace about Victoria's wrists, the smallness of Julia's hands, the enchanting way Victoria moved about the chamber. Mr. Trenear joined in the warm flirtation with the ladies and it was all Alexandra could do to keep from giving them all a severe dressing down for behaving so stupidly.

How she despised Launceston, rogue that he was!

It seemed to her as well that the longer she sat, the more flirtatious the viscount's remarks became and the more her rage began to mount. The man had no conscience, none at all. She hated him, despised him! And as for her sisters, really she would have to speak with her mother about their outrageous conduct! It was almost as if the entire display was meant to set up her back.

Finally, when she heard Julia beg his lordship to tell her yet once more about the time he climbed the mastpole of his ship, she could bear no more and rising from her chair, she made a slow dignified progress from the great hall saying that she wished to take a little air in the long gallery.

As she passed through the antechamber then entered the hall which led either back to the entrance hall and the long gallery or to the ballroom and the chapel ruins, she decided instead to go to the ballroom in order to view her efforts one last time before the masquerade tomorrow evening. But before she had taken a dozen steps, she heard a scraping sound and stopped abruptly. She suddenly realized how reckless she had been to have left the great hall for Anteros could easily be about ready to take advantage of her solitary state.

Her heart began to beat rapidly as she listened intently, but no further sounds ensued, nor did she hear the telltale fluttering of wings which would indicate his presence. She was about to turn around and retrace her steps to the great hall when she heard quick steps behind her.

"Alexandra," Launceston called to her.

Relief flooded her, at least at first. But the moment she turned and saw the smirk on his face, her anger returned in full force.

"This is not the direction to the long gallery," he stated, drawing up next to her, challenging her.

She was irritated with him. How easily he spoke to her as though nothing was amiss, as though the wager had never existed.

"I changed my mind," was all she said to him as she continued down the hall.

"Fickle as ever," he said, provokingly.

She glanced at him, her anger rising hotly within her. "How dare you!" she whispered hoarsely. "A man who would wager a woman's love for a ruby brooch at the very least deserves fickleness, if thusly you intend to describe me."

She picked up her taffeta skirts and quickened her step.

"Are you running away from me?" he said, quickening his step to match hers. "How you tempt me."

"Leave me be, you scoundrel!" she returned and with the

she could not keep from breaking into a run. She was too angry to keep a lady's pace.

She was near the convergence of halls where the small ante-chamber leading to the chapel ruins intersected with the hallway. She moved quickly beyond the convergence and swept into the ballroom.

The sun was shining through the windows on the swags of orange, gold, and red silk and much to her chagrin she realized she had no real means of escape from this chamber. She turned around, thinking she might leave, but he had taken up his post at the doorway and she could see he was daring her to leave.

She met his gaze levelly and felt an angry blush begin to creep up her cheeks as he returned the strength of her gaze and added to it a devilish smile as he closed the doors behind him.

"I don't know what you imagine you hope to accomplish, my lord," she said, her nostrils flaring.

"I was hoping to speak to you alone for a few minutes today. How grateful I am you provided me just the opportunity I was seeking. So, tell me, Lady Alexandra, just how long do you mean to be angry with me?"

"Forever," she returned flatly, her fingertips gripping the sides of her skirts tightly.

"You will break my heart, then," he said, taking a step toward her.

She could see by the set of his features, the glint in his hazel eyes, the firmness of his jaw, that he meant to accost her. What a conceited fellow he was after all, believing her head could be turned by his flirtations as easily as the silliest of females. She took a step backward, then another as he moved toward her. "I cannot conceive of any female being able to break your heart. That would be an impossibility. One must first possess a heart to have it broken."

He paused in his advance on her. "Is this the way you are to be then, cold and unfeeling, unforgiving?"

Alexandra lifted her chin, her heart devoid of sympathy.

"That has always been your opinion of me and I don't see why I must prove it to be any different at this late hour."

He took another step toward her. "You told me you loved me yesterday," he said, his manner now altered. He held her gaze kindly and the tone of his voice was quite sincere.

She felt her composure slip slightly. She looked away from him before answering, "That was before I knew of the wager."

"And I had agreed to Trenear's wager before I knew what an extraordinary woman you were, before I had kissed you any number of times, before I had understood that I had tumbled in love with you. And I do love you, Alexandra, more than life itself. If I could undo the wager, I would, but I can't. I can only beg for your forgiveness."

Alexandra shifted her gaze back to him and found that there was this traitorous part of her that wanted desperately to believe him. She recalled how she had felt in his arms yesterday when she had given her heart so fully to him, how she had lost herself in his kisses, in the sweet strength of his arms about her, in his professions of love. Tears rushed unbidden to her eyes.

"Alex," he murmured again stepping toward her, reaching his hand out to her.

"No!" she cried, warding him off with one of her hands. The part of her which refused to believe he was capable of love asserted itself. "Don't come near me—don't touch me! You are a beast entirely beyond forgiveness."

He held out both hands to her. "Don't be a fool," he whispered. "I am in love with you, I want you to be my wife."

"So now I am a fool," she cried. "Why on earth, Launceston, do you wish to marry a fool? Oh, I see how it is with you—you think you have only to throw marriage at a lady's head and she will drop to her knees and bless the heavens for her great good fortune. Well, I can only say that you are the biggest sapskull that ever ranged Albion and I have quite had done with you, and your conceit and your stupid wagers. You may go to, to Hades, for all I care!"

She then brushed quickly past him and moved through the

doorway. She did not hear his footsteps behind her. When she reached the convergence of the hallways, however, she paused, wondering where she ought to go next. She had no desire to return to the great hall, perhaps she would go to the chapel ruins. The sun was undoubtedly shining within the ruins and she could spend the next hour or so in contemplation of the evils that was *man*.

She entered the antechamber and had just reached the gladiatorial table when she was startled by the sight of Anteros beckoning for her as he waited at the top of the short flight of stairs which led to the chapel ruins. Fortunately, she heard Launceston again approaching from behind. The next moment, Anteros disappeared.

She turned away from the hallway leading to the chapel and instead headed up the arched hallway which led to the entrance hall.

"Alex, wait," Launceston cried. "Perhaps I am a conceited, overbearing fellow, but won't you give me another chance to prove my character to you?"

She was a few feet from the two suits of armor which flanked the short stairwell walls and for a moment had an impression that one of the arms of the left armored man moved. Anteros, perhaps? "You needn't explain anything," she tossed coldly over her shoulder, her heart now beating rapidly. Where was Anteros? "I know perfectly well how a wager functions. I—"

"Alex, stop!" Launceston cried. She felt his hand about her waist as he pulled her backward and at the same moment, the arm of the suit of armor, bearing a heavy axe, fell forward, the axe striking the stone floor. The crashing of metal against stone made an enormous noise and before she knew what she was doing, she was spinning toward Launceston and casting herself into his arms.

"Our ghost has returned," he said, holding her close and petting her black curls. "You could have been killed! A step more and you would have felt the blade on your neck! Good God!"

"Launceston," she whispered, tears of fright now flowing freely. "I am frightened."

"There, there my darling, you're all right now." She felt his warm lips on her brow, her cheek, her neck. Her fears began to metamorphose and an answering tenderness rose from deep within her. He drew back from her slightly and looked into her eyes, searching them, hope appearing wildly in his own.

She felt vulnerable with him, extraordinarily so. Her heart, her resolve, began to slip. Her lips parted, a fact not lost on him, he leaned toward her, fully prepared to accept her invitation.

She felt his breath on her lips. A moment more . . .

"Alexandra!" she heard Julia call from the direction of the great hall.

"Launceston—where are you?" Victoria exclaimed. "What has happened? What was that terrible noise?"

When her sisters and Mr. Trenear arrived at the entrance hall, Alexandra had already pulled herself from Launceston's arms. "The armor," she murmured, gesturing to the knight on the floor.

"I don't quite know how it happened," Launceston explained, "but this deuced armor toppled straight over, nearly on Alexandra, but she is unhurt."

Alexandra withdrew a kerchief from the pocket of her skirts and dabbed at her eyes. "I was never more frightened. Th-thank you, Launceston." She then skirted the armor, now lying on the floor in several large, detached sections, and let her sisters take her hands and comfort her.

Later that day, Psyche looked wide-eyed at her husband, who was sitting in the chair by the bed, his healthy wing folded up tightly behind him and his injured wing partially unfurled and bandaged. He sat with one leg crossed over the other, his elbow on the arm of the chair and his chin in hand. He seemed per-
'exed.

"And there was nothing more you could do the rest of the afternoon?" Psyche queried.

Cupid shook his head. "I wasn't thinking! Had I realized that of course the crashing sound of the armor would bring the others from the great hall I would have arranged a silent mishap. The deuce take it, I am devilishly out-of-practice at this sort of thing and Lady Alexandra was so overset by what had happened that she turned to her sisters for comfort instead of to Launceston! I fear I was of little more use than a mere fledgling. How very much I wish I had my bow and arrows!"

Psyche took his hand and pressed it sympathetically. "Perhaps I ought to be distressed by your lack of progress with Launceston and Alexandra, but I don't seem for the present to care very much for anything save that you are here and you are well. Only tell me does your wing still hurt very much?"

"Not at all. The physician plied me with so many miracle herbs that after drinking a draught or two, I found I felt very little of pain afterward."

"But now tell me the truth—what did you have to promise Artemis to gain her support in hunting for your bow and arrows. And don't try to tell me she is helping you out of the generosity of her heart for I won't believe you. Artemis has never cared for anything but hunting and never will."

"Two arrows," he responded, glancing at his wife with a half smile.

Psyche returned his smile and giggled. "Well, she finally did it, but it took her several thousand years to wrest them from you."

He leaned back and smiled in satisfaction. "Yes, it did!"

"At least she has been faithful to her word. Only I can't credit that though she has searched all last night and all of today, and still she has not found your bow and quiver."

"Anteros has hid them well."

He seemed particularly downcast and Psyche again pressed his hand. "I'm sure we shall contrive something for tomorrow."

He frowned and shook his head, his gaze fixed beyond Psyche, looking into the near past. "I know if the others had not come running from the great hall, Alexandra would have permitted him to kiss her and then all would be as good as settled." He then gave himself a mental shake and returned his gaze to her. "So tell, me, my love, will you be able to walk tomorrow? I won't be able to fly to the chapel as I had hoped. My wing makes it impossible now. But I can support you with my arm." He then looked down at her ankle. "There doesn't seem to be as much swelling. Have you tried yet to walk?"

"No," Psyche said. "Will you help me to stand, Cupid? I should like to discover the truth now."

Slipping his arm about her shoulder, Eros helped her to her feet. Psyche gingerly placed her toes on the carpet and then the rest of her foot. "Let me stand for a moment."

She remained by the bed, wobbling slightly, her entire body feeling weak and useless from having been abed for so many consecutive days. "I feel lightheaded," she murmured, then carefully took a step, holding Cupid's arm for support.

She smiled and laughed as she took a second step. "Oh, it is vastly improved," she cried. "I am sure, with your help or Alexandra's I can manage it."

"I am so relieved," Cupid said, as she continued to walk tenderly on her weakened foot and ankle. "But do come back to bed now," he said gently turning her about. "It won't do to reinjure yourself at this late hour."

Psyche laughed. "Not by half."

Just as he was arranging her pillows for her, Alexandra entered the chamber bearing a tray of food.

"One more thing," Cupid whispered hurriedly, keeping himself invisible from Alexandra. "You must do all you can to encourage Alexandra's heart toward Launceston. I have seen females like her bolt at the church door."

Psyche nodded as Cupid faded backward into the wall and disappeared.

"How are you feeling?" Alexandra queried with a smile as she brought the tray round the foot of the bed and placed it on the table near Psyche. She took the linen napkin from the tray, unfurled it and tucked it gently into Psyche's nightgown.

"You are smiling," she said. "Tell me what has happened today? And thank you again for all your help and for this wonderful meal."

"You are most welcome," Alexandra said, arranging a bedtray over Psyche's lap, then placing a covered plate on the tray.

Psyche drew in a deep breath. "Yorkshire ham," she said, sighing with deep satisfaction.

"Potatoes and peas. A very plain repast, I'm 'fraid."

"And very much to my liking."

Psyche speared a bit of ham with her fork and addressed the subject nearest to her concern. "Was Launceston kind this afternoon?" she asked, slipping the ham between her teeth and chewing with great pleasure. There was nothing so pleasing as thin slices of Yorkshire ham.

Alexandra grimaced. "Yes, and no. At first he was horrid, flirting with my sisters in the most wretched fashion, then he had the audacity to call me foolish for not giving my heart to him as though any female with even the smallest particle of sense would after his wretched conduct." She huffed a sigh. "Then he, he saved my life."

"Indeed?" Psyche queried, hoping she appeared surprised. She poked her fork into another slice of ham then pressed a bit of potato and several peas onto it.

Alexandra proceeded to relate her version of Cupid's less than eloquent effort at bringing Launceston and Alexandra together. Her anecdote which included a frown when she explained the shock she had received when the armor fell over was identical to Cupid's except in one respect—Alexandra believed Anteros had caused the accident.

"Why do you say as much? Was he there?" she queried. "Did you see him?"

"Yes, but not near the armor. He was standing on the stairs leading to the chapel ruins, then he disappeared. I didn't think about it much until later but I am now convinced he passed through the wall, or whatever it is he does, and gave the armor a hard push."

"I suppose it is possible," she responded, again savoring a sliver of ham. Cupid had not wanted his presence known to Alexandra or to any of the mortals. He felt it was disgraceful that so many inmates of Castle Porth had frequently seen Anteros and at least on one occasion, his mother. He agreed wholeheartedly with Zeus that the mortals were far better left to their own devices. Artemis, too, had agreed to keep her presence in the environs of Stithwell a secret. Trying very hard to keep her hopes for a happy outcome between Launceston and Alexandra unknown to the latter, she queried indifferently, "But tell me, is your heart truly hardened toward Launceston?"

Alexandra looked at her with wide eyes. "Pray don't *you* begin to support his cause as well. I vow I am sick to death with everyone, *everyone,* including Papa who I would think shouldn't care above half for Launceston's suit, telling me that I ought to accept his proposals."

"His proposals?" Psyche asked, surprised. "You did not say he offered for you. Oh, Alexandra, tell me it is not true? Did Launceston beg for your hand in marriage?"

Alexandra sighed. "I suppose he did, but it was hardly romantical. He blurted out in a rather harsh manner, *I am in love with you. I want you to be my wife.* Can you believe he addressed such a serious subject in such an offhand, stupid manner? I was never more insulted."

Since Alexandra began to chew on her lip, and appeared much more like a schoolgirl unsure of herself than of a young lady fully grown, Psyche suspected her friend was suffering from a war between her pride and her heart. She watched her worried profile for a long moment and sought out precisely the words she needed to say to encourage Alexandra along the proper path without setting up her back so greatly that she would take the wrong path merely out of spite. "I'm sure it must be a grievous frustration to you that *everyone* is pushing you toward a match even I can see you dislike enormously. But

I begin to wonder since he is not adverse to marriage, and you have already admitted to having enjoyed his kisses, whether your heart is in conflict with the logical turn of your thoughts? You seem quite agitated as though you are unsure about what you ought to do."

Alexandra turned toward Psyche, the frown between her brows deepening. "Mama says I am just proud and I begin to wonder if she is right. It is just that I have no very great opinion of Launceston. I suppose for many reasons I do respect him and I admire what he has accomplished these many years and more, but he seems so unsteady, so given to flirtations and he is such a favorite with the ladies. I could forgive him the wager if I was truly certain he knew what love was and that he did indeed love me. Do I make any sense at all?"

Psyche thought back to the past thirty years and how she had doubted Cupid's love for her and how terrible her anxiety and loneliness had been for that period of time. "You make perfect sense. When a woman doesn't feel loved by the man who has chosen her to be his wife, she feels dreadfully insecure as though she has built her whole life on loose sand that begins to shift about with every step she takes."

Alexandra appeared more hopeful. "Then you at least understand why I must refuse him?"

At these words, Psyche began to cough. Dear Jupiter, what had she done! "N-no, I wasn't suggesting that you ought to—"

"Psyche, are you saying you want me to marry Launceston?"

"N-no—that is, I suppose in many ways I believe you are well-suited."

"Oh, not you, too!" Alexandra cried.

Psyche set her plate aside. She was no longer hungry. Her future was hanging in the balance and she was in the devil of a fix. She sensed that the wrong words at this juncture would ruin any chance of Alexandra accepting of Launceston's hand by tomorrow night. Deciding quickly that her first duty must be to show Alexandra her loyalty and friendship, she responded, "I don't want you to marry Lord Launceston if you have even the smallest doubt in your heart he is not the man for you. Marriage is the hardest road of all and no one should wed if those doubts appear insuperable."

Alexandra reached her hand out and overlaid Psyche's with her own. "I knew I could rely on you. I won't marry him, even if the whole world should come to my doorstep and beg me to do otherwise."

Psyche reached deep within her heart and drew out a morsel of courage with which to put a smile on her face. For at the same moment she was smiling, she was seeing in her mind's eye her own future, her own happiness slipping away from her. She could see the portal on the following night, shimmering its blue light, waiting for her, but knew she could no more pass through, and return to Olympus, with her most important task unfulfilled than she could dance a jig with her ankle still unhappily wounded.

"You must follow your heart, Alexandra," she said at last, for this much at least was true. "To do otherwise would be to court disaster."

Seventeen

During the day which followed, Alexandra found her thoughts turning frequently toward Launceston. Time and again she would attempt to busy herself with some project or other—the embroidering of a pillowslip, a perusal of her shell collection, a critiquing of the last painting she had executed of Falmouth harbor, even a paragraph or two of *Ivanhoe*—but invariably her thoughts would find themselves centered on the man who had stolen her heart.

Even now, in the late afternoon, as she dressed for the masquerade ball, her thoughts would turn and turn again to the viscount.

Yes, she admitted to herself, he had stolen her heart.

But she was not so missish that she believed simply because a man had somehow slipped stealthfully into a lady's dreams and hopes for the future that she must necessarily submit to her sensibilities. On the contrary, Alexandra believed the opposite was true—that for a woman to know profound happiness in marriage, she must choose her mate ever so wisely and not permit herself to be simply caught up in the passion of the moment.

As she reviewed, and reviewed again, the extraordinary circumstance of Launceston having somehow won her heart, she felt hers was precisely the case which ought to set an example for every young lady, in particular her sisters. For when she would consider each aspect of Launceston's character—and in particular the fact that he had been so vulgar as to have wagered his ability to break her heart—the viscount came up short in her estimation, regardless of his rank, his wealth, and his famous good looks.

No, Launceston was not for her. She didn't trust him and that was that!

Why was it then that no matter how frequently she reminded herself of his character, she had but to think of how sweet it was to be kissed by him, how safe she felt when she was held tightly in his arms and how comfortable she could be in his presence, and her resolve seemed to escape her like a morning fog when the sun rises and the mist just seems to magically disappear!

Thank goodness she had a strong mind. For regardless of the number of times the mist of her resolve vanished, she had but to bring her thoughts and sensibilities to order and her resolve would return.

As she sat before her dressing table, Lydia placed the last of several white satin ribbons into her hair and her toilette was complete. She held her gold, feathered mask up to her face, smiling as Lydia exclaimed how much Lady Brandreth's fashions suited her. As she regarded her reflection, the half mask covering her eyes and nose, she thought for her own sake that she ought to consider leaving Roselands once Psyche was safely returned to Olympus.

A great sadness suddenly came over her. Her thoughts became a blend of losses, of knowing that soon, midnight in fact, she would no longer have the sweet companionship of one of the gentlest and kindest ladies she had ever known and of knowing that if she left Roselands, she would probably not see Launceston again for months. She bit back her tears, grateful that Lydia could not see her unhappiness because of the mask.

"You do not like the coiffure?" Lydia asked, a question which drew Alexandra sharply from her reveries.

"Yes, oh yes, indeed I do," Alexandra murmured as she quickly set aside the mask and met her maid's gaze in the mirror.

"Everything is perfect and I am so grateful to have such a gifted abigail to attend to me."

Lydia beamed. "You will be the most beautiful lady present!" she cried.

How little Alexandra was able to enter into her maid's enthusiasm. "Thank you," she said. "And now would you please fetch Mama. She was wishful of seeing my costume before the ball."

Lydia dropped a quick curtsy and left the bedchamber.

Alexandra rose from her dressing table and fixing a smile to her face turned to face Psyche.

"Oh," Psyche breathed, a smile of delight on her pretty face. "How much your costume puts me in mind of helping your mama a score of years ago. But do let me look at you. Take a turn about the room then regard yourself in the looking glass. You will be very much surprised."

Alexandra did as she was bid, turning about the room as Psyche exclaimed again and again over her appearance, finally standing before the looking glass near the wardrobe. She blinked at her reflection. She could not credit her eyes and could not keep from smiling in honest fascination with what she saw. She resembled to perfection the large portrait of her mother which was hung in the music room—the gown being the very one her mother had worn for the portrait.

Her mother's gown, which fit her to perfection, was of an exquisite violet silk cut quite décolleté and caught up high beneath the waist. She turned to view the side and back of her gown and noted how prettily the many gathers at the center back of the high waist gave an elegant drape to the floor of the fine silk. She turned and scrutinized the bodice. A beautiful half-ruff of sheer tulle, rose like a standing collar from just in front of her shoulders up to the back of her neck. Her long black curls dangled over the ruff and the whole appearance was so magical, such a complete transformation, that she began to wonder if she had lived before.

Her black hair was swept in part high atop her head in a

chignon, with several loose curls gently trailing down her back. Her hair was parted in the middle on top—more the fashion of the day than during George IV's reign—but the delicate fringe of curls across her forehead was most definitely reflective of the time. She rather liked the effect of the curls. Somehow they softened her features, and set off to advantage her large blue eyes.

The truth was, she felt a trifle naked for she wasn't wearing her constricting stays. Her mother had told her that some ladies preferred to continue wearing stays during her time, but strong, young women frequently wore only their comfortable and modest shifts beneath the gauzy muslin, thin cambrics, calicos, and silks so greatly favored of the day.

She wore a necklet of amethysts and on each lobe an eardrop comprised of a small amethyst and a pearl. Her fan was painted with a tender scene—Cupid as a winged babe, flying above a flock of doves which pulled an exquisite chariot driven by Aphrodite. Silk stockings tied up by embroidered garters and slippers of a matching violet silk completed her toilet.

"Oh, my dear!" Lady Brandreth called to her from the doorway of her dressing room. "You appear like a ghost from the past—how lovely you are in one of my favorite ballgowns."

Lady Brandreth crossed the chamber and slipped her arm about Alexandra's waist. She hugged her as she gazed at her daughter's reflection in the looking glass. "Charming. Utterly so. Don't you think so, Psyche?" she queried.

"Indeed, yes, Evanthea, ever so charming!"

"Thank you, both of you," Alexandra responded, turning toward her mother and letting her gaze take in her costume. "De but look at you! So pretty in brown velvet and, and—"

"No, you needn't voice that thought aloud," Lady Brandreth said, turning to press the fabric of her Empire gown about the outlines of her swelling form. "Once released from my stays seem to have grown in only a matter of hours."

"Are you certain you are having only one child?" Alexandra queried, startled.

"Well, this one is certainly active enough for two," she said chuckling softly. "My only concern is that I am now so happy to be free of my stays that I have decided not to return to them and so may scandalize our neighbors."

"As though you give a fig for that," Alexandra murmured, giving her mother a quick hug. "You never were one to care much for the opinions of others."

"No, I was not, nor do I hope you are or your sisters. Who will see to your happiness when you have abided year after year by the wishes and beliefs of others? No one, I promise you. So, listen to your heart, Alex. Whatever decisions you make in the coming days and months, let them be your decisions alone. Yes, yes, I know I have been pressuring you to accept of Launceston's proposals but I was wrong to have done so." She held Alexandra next to her and kissed her cheek tenderly. "I have no worries for you, my dear. You have such a good heart and such strength of will that no matter what paths you choose, you will always make the best of whatever might come your way. I love you, my darling. I hope you know that."

"Indeed, yes, Mama," she whispered, overcome.

She then drew back from her daughter. "I must go," she said, glancing first at Alexandra then Psyche. "Brandreth is in the deuce of a temper." Here she smiled wickedly, "He still cannot credit that he can no longer wear his old buckskins. He's as mad as fire and when I left, he was complaining that the fabric must have shrunk while in the attics."

Alexandra laughed as her mother swept from the room. She thought Psyche would be amused as well, but instead she found to her surprise that Butterfly was weeping. "Why are you crying?" she asked, turning instantly away from the looking glass and moving to stand beside the bed.

Psyche lifted her head from her kerchief. "I am so unhappy."

Alexandra pulled the chair close to the bed and sank down in it, at the same time possessing herself of Psyche's hand. "Whatever is the matter? Why are you so sad? After all, in a

few hours you will be back in Olympus with Cupid. I will fetch
you at half past ten and—"

"But I shall not see you after tonight," she wailed. "And
seeing Evanthea, and enjoying her company—for she sat with
me for several hours this afternoon—is like losing a friend all
over again. If only there was some way to visit you. Oh, Alexandra, I shall miss you dreadfully."

Alexandra felt her eyes mist over with tears as well and her
throat constricted painfully. "I shall miss you too," she murmured, lifting Psyche's hand and holding it close to her cheek.
"I have enjoyed your companionship ever so much, particularly
at night when we would fall asleep giggling and telling secrets."

"Me, too," Psyche responded, wiping away Alexandra's tears
with her own kerchief. "But this will not do!" she exclaimed.
"You must stop crying at once! Tear-stained cheeks and red-
rimmed eyes do not flatter the purple of your gown in the least,
nor will Launc—that is, nor will any of the gentlemen present
find you remotely desirable as a partner."

Alexandra giggled. "You are right, of course. But I will miss
you. I will think of you every day for as long as I live."

"Dearest Alexandra."

"But how very touching!" a masculine voice called to them
sardonically. "Yet if the pair of you would but attend to me,
you wouldn't have to suffer in this manner."

At the sound of Anteros's voice, Alexandra rose quickly from
the chair and jerked about intending to ward off Cupid's wicked
brother. "Go away!" she cried.

Anteros merely curled his lip and began approaching her,
rose-colored vial in hand. "But you are not thinking sensibly,"
he said. "Do but consider! You and Psyche will be sisters for
eternity once you wed me and you will never have to say goodbye to her again, that is, of course, unless she refuses to enter
the portal tonight." His expression was taunting as he shifted
his gaze to his sister-in-law.

Psyche began to scoot down the bed, wincing only slightly
as she slid off the side of the bed and stood between Anteros

and Alexandra. "You know she can't go with you. She must stay here and keep her country safe."

"You refer in some oblique manner to Launceston? Don't be a goosecap, Psyche! Your concern for this land and for Alexandra are entirely unnecessary. These are a worthless people who will one day destroy themselves."

"If we are so worthless," Alexandra said, "then why do you wish to align yourself with me? Your logic falters."

Psyche turned around slightly toward Alexandra and murmured, "Go." Then just as quickly whipped back toward Anteros. Taking a halting step, then another, her demeanor changed. "Do you think I have been indifferent to you all these years, Anteros?" she queried, her expression soft and beckoning. "Do you think I don't know how you feel about me? Why is it do you think I bring you tea every Saturday morning?"

Alexandra was shocked by the sudden shift in Psyche's tone and manner, almost as if she meant to seduce Anteros. She did not therefore immediately obey Psyche's command to leave.

"I know what you are doing," he said, glaring at her and holding his ground as she approached him.

"Do you?" she murmured. "Are you certain? What if I told you that every time you draw near, each time the resonance of your wings comes within a breath of me, I tremble. And let me ask you this, are your dreams ever troubled for I call to you at night, silently, with every beat of my heart. Do you not hear my heart calling from the shadows? Why have you not come to me?"

Alexandra vaguely understood what Psyche was attempting to do, but now she was so stunned by Anteros's reaction to Psyche's ploy that still she remained frozen where she was. For the god of unrequited love, in all his strength of will and purpose, was staring at Psyche as though she was wearing the Cestus, which Alexandra could see she was not. Why was the dark-winged man so enthralled with Psyche of a sudden?

But it had not been of a sudden, she realized, recalling to mind how frequently Anteros would stare at Psyche whenever he was in her presence. She understood the sad truth at last of Cupid's brother, that he was in love with his brother's wife.

She watched Psyche place a hand against her forehead. "My ankle hurts dreadfully," she whispered, then crumpled against Anteros.

Anteros appeared to struggle within himself for a long, unblinking moment. Then slowly, he began to enfold her in his arms and a look of pain came over his face so excruciating that again, Alexandra's heart went out to the unhappy being. He closed his eyes and murmured her name as his lips touched her hair and his black wings covered her fully.

Psyche gestured for Alexandra to leave and she finally drew her thoughts to order. Whatever Anteros's unhappiness might be, there was little she, or anyone could do to help him. Picking up her violet silk skirts, she brushed quickly past him. When she reached the door she stole a final glance at him and realized that in this moment she did not exist—his eyes, his senses, his heart, were all for Psyche. Pulling the door open, she quickly crossed the threshold and left his suffering behind.

When Psyche heard the door shut, she began struggling against Anteros. "Let me go!" she cried.

"What the deuce!" he exclaimed, unfolding his arms and wings from about her. He glanced quickly about the chamber. "What have you done? Where is Alexandra? Of all the vile tricks—!" He glared down at Psyche. "You used my love for you to enable Alexandra to escape. How I despise you in this moment! You will never be anything more than a silly, wicked mortal!"

His face was twisted with hatred as he caught her hard by the elbow, then pushed her away from him. Just as she watched him fly quickly away through the window heading toward Castle Porth, the shove he had given her twisted her ankle again. She gave a cry, which became immediately silenced in the burst of

pain which followed the striking of her head against the hard
bedpost.

"Eros!" she whispered as she crumpled to the floor, the room
dimming in quick stages to a place of empty blackness.

Later that evening, at the masquerade ball, Alexandra stood
with Launceston near the alcove housing the orchestra. She
wished he didn't make her laugh. In the laughing, she felt her
resolve to remember precisely the sort of man Launceston truly
was begin to waver yet again.

"Yes, that is no," she responded, unsure how to answer his
query as to whether or not she thought he had a well-turned
leg. She lowered her gold mask to glance down at his limbs,
but could not bring herself to make a judgment. "Lady Elle
was used to tell me a gentleman was judged by the beauty of
his legs, but I find it hard to credit. But pray say no more, I
can feel that my cheeks are aflame." She again replaced her
mask.

Launceston, who wore no mask, merely chuckled at her dis-
comfiture.

"But do you like my breeches?" he murmured into her ear.
"And pray don't pretend you did not scrutinize my costume for
I saw you look me over from head to toe when you first arrived."

Alexandra bit her lip. "How unkind of you to have noticed
my indiscretion. It is just that it is so strange seeing you in
Papa's clothes."

"I see a smile playing at your mouth. There—there it is. Now
you must tell me, you must give me some judgment—how do
you like me in breeches?"

Alexandra knew it wouldn't do in the least to tell him the
truth, that she found him exceedingly attractive in the clothes
her father had once worn. He was wearing formal evening attire,
a tail-coat of black superfine, a black waistcoat, a white linen
shirt and a long, white linen neckcloth tied in neat folds about
his neck and supporting elegant shirtpoints, white satin knee

breeches, white silk stockings and black dancing slippers. The whole line of his costume, from the molded fit of his coat across his broad shoulders, to the tapering of his coat to his trim waist, to his firm, well-shaped thighs and calves revealed fully in the cut of his breeches and the snug fit of his stockings, all displayed his athletic figure to advantage. How could she tell him that she thought he appeared manly and attractive? Most assuredly she could not!

So instead, she moved past him, murmuring, "You are being most provoking, my lord. And though I don't like to mention it, I believe you ought to see to your guests."

He let her go and for a half hour she greeted her many friends and acquaintances. She found herself enjoying the masquerade more than she had anticipated primarily because the arrival of Launceston's guests and the sheer pleasure attendant in exclaiming over everyone's costumes helped to allay much of her fears about the approaching midnight hour. In addition, the press of so many people also helped her to feel relatively safe in Launceston's presence.

But after a half hour had passed, Launceston informed her that her mother had relinquished in favor of her eldest daughter, the right to be led out for the opening dance and would Alexandra please oblige them both by accepting the honor.

Because to have refused would have been entirely improper, Alexandra gave him her hand and he led her toward the alcove in which the orchestra had just completed tuning their instruments. A moment later, she was in his arms, a waltz was filling the ballroom, and her steps flowed into his.

He spoke to her throughout the dance on any number of harmless topics, knowing that all eyes were upon them both. He said nothing to embarrass her, nor did he bring forward the difficulties between them and for that reason when the dance was over, she thanked him warmly for behaving himself.

He laughed. "You will not thank me later," he whispered. "For I intend to waltz with you again and this time, I shan't be so well-mannered."

Since he moved away immediately, and sought out his next partner, Alexandra did not have the opportunity to admonish him for his improper speech. What a wretched man, he was, she thought as she watched him bow over the hand of the singularly platter-faced aunt of one of her friends from Stithwell. And what an odd combination of traits he was, both beast and gentleman. Why was it, she wondered, that this thought caused her heart to reach out toward him? She felt her senses come alive as she continued to watch him, devouring the way he moved, the way he spoke politely to her friend's aunt, the way he smiled warmly upon all his guests.

She liked him.

God help her, she liked him too much!

Several waltzes came and went and still he did not come to claim the dance with which he had taunted her. The hour was growing later and later and she had just begun to wonder whether she ought to return to Roselands to fetch Psyche when he found her, caught her by the arm, and insisted on his waltz.

A few minutes more and she was again whirling about the floor with him, his hand firmly placed at the small of her back, his other hand holding hers aloft in a gentle clasp. He was a wonderful dancer and of all the gentlemen with whom she had danced during the course of the evening, only Mylor Grampound approached his excellence. She smiled with delight, in part at the way he moved her so easily about the floor, but perhaps more so because her mama's gown made the steps of the dance so easy to manage.

"What is it?" he asked. "Why do you smile?"

"This gown," she responded in a low voice. "There is so little fabric I feel as though I am floating." She then giggled. "I suppose I ought not to have said such a thing to you."

"Are you afraid I will ask you again how many petticoats you are wearing?"

"Hardly," she responded. "Though I have little doubt you could properly guess the number tonight without much effort." She felt a blush creep up her cheeks as she realized just how

improper her remark was since it indicated how little she was
wearing after all—only a thin shift and a gossamer cloaking of
silk.

"You aren't wearing your stays either," he whispered, much
to her shock.

"Launceston!" she breathed. "You shouldn't say such a
thing."

"Well, I must confess I rather like these fashions and wish
that our more modern age had not ushered in so many yards of
fabric for every gown, not to mention the unmentionables. Although, now that I think on it, there is something to be said for
having to lift back one petticoat after the next in order to discover a beautifully turned ankle."

Alexandra swallowed hard and forced herself to take a deep
breath. What was it about this man that took her breath away
and made her feel things she knew she shouldn't?

He drew her more closely to him. "Alexandra, do put me out
of my misery and accept of my hand in marriage. I shan't let
you rest, you know, not for a moment, until you agree to it."

Alexandra did not respond at once. She was far too close to
him to be able to give him a rational answer particularly since
his words had been a burning whisper on her ear. She was momentarily lost in a sensation of desire so strong that she could
hardly catch her breath.

After a long moment, she was finally able to bring her mind
to order. "Launceston, you must understand. I cannot. It isn't
just the wager—"

"I know, you have a very poor opinion of me. Well, I suppose
that much is my own fault for I certainly did not enter tonnish
society with an intention of behaving at all times with perfect
propriety. Is there nothing I can say to change your opinions?"

Why was he being so forthright with her, and why did he
have to look at her as though the sun rose and set with her
smiles?

"Perhaps," she began softly. "Perhaps in time." Had she
opened a door she would one day wish had remained closed?

"Faith but you give me hope," he murmured. "The truth is, I fear losing you more than anything in the world which brings me round to something I think I ought to tell you."

She opened her eyes wide. Was he now about to make another confession? "Did you wager with another of your friends regarding your ability to steal my heart?"

At that he laughed aloud. "No. A thousand times no, I promise you."

She was relieved and at the same time thought it odd she could actually be joking with him about his wager with Trenear. "What is it then?" she asked.

"Do not be startled, but for the past half hour, Anteros has been standing in the doorway watching you."

Alexandra could not help but be startled, first by the fact that the immortal was present and then by the knowledge that Launceston not only could see him but knew who he was. "Oh," she breathed.

When the movements of the waltz permitted, she let her gaze drift for the barest moment toward the doorway. Anteros caught her gaze and nodded quite sardonically to her. She immediately looked away. Fear bolted through her and she looked into Launceston's eyes. "Do you know why he has come?"

"I saw him at church on Sunday last, I heard his threats to you and later he told me directly that he intended to take you back with him to Olympus. That is how I determined his identity, along with my recollections when I was thirteen of his conversation with a woman I believe to be his mother, Aphrodite."

"That would be her," she said.

"The same beautiful woman you saw at the end of the long gallery the other day?"

"Yes, precisely. But why did you say nothing to me?"

"I must say it took me some time to assimilate all that was happening, then I wasn't certain what I ought to do. Knowing the ferocity of the gods—faith, but I still can't believe they are real!—I thought it best to remain somewhat aloof. I had no interest in arousing Anteros's wrath toward me and he seemed so ready and willing to spar when he spoke to me on Sunday. I want to help, but I'm not certain in what way I can, though I suspect there is much more going forward than that of which I am presently aware."

Alexandra nodded.

"Will you tell me what is happening?"

"Yes," she responded. "But not here. Is there somewhere we could speak privately?" She glanced toward the doorway, wondering how they could pass by Anteros unnoticed, but she noted with intense relief that he was gone. She told Launceston as much.

"Good," he responded, also much relieved. "I shall take you to the Green Salon."

He glanced around the ballroom to gain his bearings and when in the progress of the waltz they arrived at a place near the doors, he moved out of the quickly swirling mass and led her from the chamber, into the hallways, and through a laughing, well-entertained maze of masked guests.

"What time is it?" she asked, as she walked briskly beside him toward the entrance hall.

He withdrew a watch from the pocket of his waistcoat and flipped open the engraved, brass lid. "Half past nine," he said, as they moved through the entrance hall and entered the long gallery.

When they were at last closeted within the Green Salon, with two branches of candles and a steady fire illuminating the chamber, she seated herself in one of the two chairs situated in front of the hearth. When he had seated himself as well, she told him everything, all of the past visions she had ever had, of Anteros's kisses, of Psyche's sudden and painful arrival when she passed through the portal, of her twisted ankle, of the terrible scheme contrived between mother and son to bereft Cupid of his beloved wife forever, of Anteros's intention of taking her back to Olympus with him, and of how it had come about she had decided her new neighbor must give a masquerade ball. "For then

I could bring Psyche to Castle Porth surreptitiously and also," here she could not continue without blushing, "Psyche thought that I might be safer from Anteros's advances if I flirted with you and, and pretended to be in love with you."

He opened his eyes wide, clearly dumbfounded. "I should be offended," he cried, teasing her. "Now I understand in full why you wished for the ball. So you are saying you purposefully kissed me as well?"

"Well, no, of course not!" Alexandra felt her cheeks grow warmer still. "I never intended once to kiss you. Oh, dear, now that I think on it, the whole of it was unconscionable!"

"As bad as my wager with Trenear?" he suggested.

"Certainly not!"

"I see no difference," he stated, folding his arms across his chest. "Are you telling me you were more justified in your motives than I in my wager with Trenear?"

When he saw she could not give him an answer, he smiled triumphantly.

She would not allow the circumstances to be the same. "There is a difference," she said at last, having gathered her thoughts. "I at least was acting on Psyche's behalf and not for my own amusement."

He grimaced. "Well, there is that! You've a nobler heart, but I still insist you were very wrong to have made use of me as you did."

"I was," she stated, "and I do apologize."

He sighed with feigned long-suffering. "When we are wed, I can see now that I shall have much work to do in reordering your character."

She didn't know which to address first, the fact that he spoke of their marriage as an eventuality or that she had need of his instruction or reproval. Realizing nothing could be gained from arguing with him, she said, "You are being nonsensical." She then brought forward Anteros's enigmatic conduct in having forced them together on several occasions.

Launceston considered this and shook his head. "But why

would he have overturned the suit of armor or pushed you down the stairs?"

"I don't know. I own it makes no sense, but what other explanation could there be?"

"But surely he would not have wanted you in my arms again. Although, now that I think on it, I ought to thank him for having driven you to me. How else would I have discovered what an extraordinary woman you are?"

Alexandra looked into loving hazel eyes and felt her resolve slip yet another notch. She tried to remind herself that he could not be trusted but still her heart leaned traitorously toward him. When he placed his hand over hers, she stared at his fingers for a moment feeling torn neatly into two parts—one part of her wanting his touch, the other knowing it could not be. Taking a deep breath, she withdrew her hand from beneath his.

He was silent apace then spoke in a quiet voice. "Yesterday you said you loved me. Is your affection lost so easily?"

At that she lifted her gaze to meet his and blinked at the anxious expression on his face. "You are being unfair in even your questions. I have refused you if for no other reason than that you refuse to acknowledge that your wager with Trenear was wrong—very, very wrong."

At that he rose suddenly from his seat and ran a hasty hand through his hair. "Of course it was wrong. Very wrong. Maddeningly wrong. But I was so piqued by your haughty self-consequence. If I was wrong, you were not less so than in always setting yourself above me as though I was some wretched being sent to earth to torment you."

He placed his hands on the back of his winged chair and stared down at her. "But I believe the truth of the matter is that from the first I have been afraid of you, of how I felt when I was around you, of how just looking at you would fill me with such nearly uncontrollable sensations of passion and desire. I still don't understand this power you have with me."

Alexandra was stunned. She had always supposed that the way he was with her was how he was with every woman. To learn that she affected him in much the way he affected her caused all of her thoughts to take a step to the right. "You? Afraid of me?"

"Now you are taunting me," he said, his expression almost hurt.

"No," she responded with a firm shake of her head. "I would never taunt you when the subject is as serious as this one. It is just that I had always supposed—"

Their conversation was interrupted suddenly by the sound of dogs barking. Alexandra rose from her chair and went to the window to look out over the valley. Moonlight flooded the dark expanse and through the shadowing landscape she was able to see a tall woman, dressed in buckskins, bearing a bow slung over her shoulder and dogs trailing at her heels.

"How very odd," she murmured, "But I do believe that woman is Artemis, for Psyche once described her to me and to my knowledge no such lady exists on earth that I have ever seen. But whatever is she doing here?"

Launceston moved to stand just behind her. "She is quite tall and athletic, isn't she?"

"You can see her then?"

"Yes."

The clock on the mantel struck ten and Alexandra's head jerked around toward the offending object, horrified at the lateness of the hour. "Is it so late then?" she cried.

"Yes, I should think it is," he said, again pulling his pocket watch from his waistcoat pocket and confirming the hour.

"I must fetch Psyche," she said, looking up at him. He was still standing close to her. "Launceston, will you help me?"

"Of course I will," he said.

"Thank you," she said. She had meant to immediately move toward the door, but he stayed her with a slight pressure on her arm.

"Wait," he said. "Just for a minute."

Only then did she notice the look in his eye, an expression of desire which caused her to place her hand on his chest.

"Launceston, no," she breathed, but it was too late. Already, his arms were about her and he was kissing her full on the lips.

Alexandra wanted to push him away, to reiterate her decision, but there was and always would be something so appealing about him that she let him assault her quite forcefully, though she kept her hand on his chest.

He held her closely to him. How different it was to be embraced in one of the gowns from her mother's youth. She could feel the strength of his legs, even his hips through the thin silk fabric of her ballgown. Sweet desire curled within her, warming her heart and causing a most improper moan to sound in her throat.

He drew her more tightly to him still and the hand that was on his chest somehow found its way to the back of his neck and she slipped her fingers through his blond hair. She parted her lips and his gentle search again forced a coo to rise in her throat and betray her.

He was too much for her, she realized. He seduced her so easily. In the future, she would have to take much greater care when she was in his company. She couldn't let this happen again.

With these thoughts she began pulling away from him.

"Tell me you will marry me," he breathed into her hair, refusing to let her go completely.

"I cannot," she returned, trying to draw away from him, yet not really wanting to.

"Kiss me again," he commanded.

She finally pushed him away, but he took a step forward and once again drew her firmly back to him and again his lips were upon hers and again she surrendered to him. Her caresses became anxious. He pressed harder against her still and she felt the wall of the castle against her back. She felt herself falling and falling as he kissed her over and over and again, professing his love for her, his need for her, his desire to hear her say she would be his wife.

When the clock struck the quarter hour, only then did Alexandra find the strength to disengage herself. Psyche's safety must come first! "We must go now!" she cried.

"Tell me you will marry me," he countered.

Tears sprang quickly to her eyes as she shook her head. "I admit you can seduce me and I greatly fear I shall always be in danger of falling into your arms whenever you are near, but I won't marry you, Launceston. I—I don't think you can make me happy."

Her words gave him pause. "I see," he responded slowly but afterward a smile broke over his lips. "Then you have just sealed my fate."

"What do you mean?"

"Well, it would seem that for the next fifty or sixty years I shall be busy proving to you that your happiness is my sole object."

Eighteen

At eleven o'clock, Cupid met Artemis in the chapel ruins as arranged. Her dogs jumped about him in wild affection. He began patting each on the head, then bidding them to heel, as he glanced anxiously at Diana. For a moment she forgot her purpose as she watched her dogs fondly. "They have always liked you, Eros, though I can't imagine why. They bark at Bacchus as though he was monster from Poseidon's realm and Merk as well. But you! I vow they would lick your face off if I permitted them to."

"I enjoy animals," he said, but immediately addressed the pressing matter at hand. "Only tell me, have you found the bow and the quiver?"

She shook her head, a perplexed frown between her brows. "Sorry, but no. I gave the dogs your scent, but they found nothing—and they're good hunters! I can't imagine why they've not been able to discover where Anteros hid your arrows."

"And you checked the tower, where he's been sleeping?"

"Yes, of course. The dogs seemed to be distressed while we were there, then I gave them your scent to follow and here we are—two days and nothing!"

"You checked all the woods?"

"Of course."

Cupid rubbed the ears of the nearest dog and was rewarded with a grateful whine. Where could his brother have hidden his arrows? "Thank you again, Artemis, for all your help. When I return to Olympus I shall see that Vulcan forges the arrows I promised you."

Diana moved toward him and placed her hand on his shoulder. "I wish I could have been of use. Damme, but I was so sure we would find your bow. But don't worry—Vulcan will make you a hundred more."

"You don't understand," he said quietly. "I don't give a fig for the arrows. I needed them to save my wife."

"Ah," she responded quietly. She had no interest in love or even in the companionship of another fellow immortal. He knew she had great difficulty comprehending his sadness. After a moment, she startled him. "Zeus take it!" she cried. "You don't suppose—dash it all, I am a perfect nodcock!"

Cupid looked up at her hopefully. "What?" he asked. "What is it?" He knew he was grasping at straws at this late hour, but he didn't care.

"Well, what if Anteros wrapped your bow and quiver in some garment of his own?"

"Then my scent—oh, was ever a more stupid fellow born than me! That must be it!" He rose and caught up the strong, lithe form of Olympus's most famous huntress in his arms. Taking care not to injure his broken wing, he swung her around in a circle which set the dogs to barking madly and nipping playfully at his heels and at the tips of his feathers.

"Return at once to the tower," he said, releasing her when she began to protest that he was crushing her ribs. "Perhaps that was why the dogs were restless when you were there. Take something of my brother's and let them at the hunt again."

"The deed is as good as done!" she cried, turning about abruptly and setting off on a dead run up the chapel stairs and beyond. The dogs followed in her wake in bounding strides.

Launceston had his racing gig harnessed to two of his chestnuts and drove the light equipage to Roselands in short order.

Just past eleven, Alexandra, with Launceston in tow, found Psyche crumpled in a heap beside her bed.

"Oh, no," she whispered, dropping quickly down beside her friend. "She must have tried to walk. Look at the bruise on the side of her forehead, near the temple?" Her complexion was a chalky white.

"Is she—?"

"No, she is breathing," she replied. She drew the beautiful young woman onto her lap and began gently petting her cheeks and her neck and calling to her.

After a moment, Psyche's eyes fluttered open. "Alex," she murmured. "Where—why am I on the floor? Oh, now I remember?"

"What happened?"

"We quarreled. After you left I said terrible things to Anteros. He didn't mean to hurt me but he released me angrily, I twisted my ankle and oh, I hit my head so hard." She was squeezing her eyes shut and moaning.

"Can you walk?"

Psyche placed her hand on the blue and black mark on her forehead near her right temple. Groaning again, she said, "I was supposed to help you and now look at me!"

"Hush," Alexandra returned. "Don't distress yourself. Launceston is come to help us and we've just enough time to get you back to the portal. It is only a little past eleven."

Psyche glanced past Alexandra's shoulder and smiled faintly at Launceston. She then quickly reverted her gaze, looking hopefully up into Alexandra's face. "Are you going to marry him?" she asked.

Alexandra frowned slightly. "No," she said, refusing to look at Launceston.

"Then you needn't bother taking me back to Castle Porth," she stated in what Alexandra thought was a strangely resigned manner.

Alexandra was quiet for a moment, as she watched Psyche's

eyes close and a tear seep from the corner of her eye. "There is something you haven't told me, isn't there," she said.

Psyche nodded slowly. "Your fate is entwined with Launceston. I do not know all, but for some reason, it is of the utmost importance that you wed him. That is why I was sent to you, to, to encourage your heart toward him. I can't leave until your heart and your mind are completely given."

Alexandra shook her head. "You are speaking nonsensically," she said, "as though you have powers no one has. If I choose to wed Launceston or anyone else it will be because I wish it so. And I know you well, Psyche. You would never insist on a marriage to which I was opposed. Therefore, of what use will your remaining here with me serve? I am the mistress of my own fate. But as for *your* fate, you are meant to return through the portal at midnight to continue enjoying your husband—and no arguments!"

Alexandra ignored her protests and looking up at Launceston, asked, "Can you lift her? She will have to be carried to your gig. I believe I can support her easily enough once we are both seated."

"Yes, of course," he said.

"It's no use," Psyche murmured, as the viscount reached down and gingerly gathered the beauty up into his arms. "I won't leave unless she will agree to marry you."

"Don't bother your head about that for the present," he said kindly. "Now, slip your arms about my neck if you can. Am I hurting your ankle?"

"Only a very little," she replied. "How strong you are, just like my dearest Cupid."

A few moments later, Alexandra was supporting Psyche, now covered up with a carriage blanket, in Launceston's glossy, black racing gig. The chestnuts, having been held by a footman, were restless to be moving. With a crack of his whip and the moonlight to illumine the gravel road, he immediately set his horses in motion.

By the time they were halfway to the castle, a faint blue glow could be seen hovering above the chapel ruins.

When Cupid had watched Diana leave the chapel ruins, he remained in the chapel ruins for several minutes, waiting, wondering what next he ought to do, if anything. He heard the revelers enjoying the ball in the distance and if he understood the order of events properly, a light supper, served at midnight would keep the guests occupied for the next hour or so.

Psyche was due to arrive shortly, but he wanted to know precisely what the hour was and also where his brother had been hiding himself so that he might effectively prevent his brother from fulfilling his purposes. He knew that Anteros intended to keep Psyche from returning to Olympus and also that he meant to take Alexandra back with him.

He left the chamber swiftly and entered the hall leading back to the entrance hall. He passed into the entrance hall, ran swiftly down the long gallery and climbed the stairs leading to his brother's bedchamber. When he reached the top landing, he pushed open the heavy, ancient oak door. A fall of moonlight through an open window revealed what Cupid could sense— Anteros was not in his chamber. A fresh, cold October breeze swirled through the window.

"Anteros," he murmured sadly. "What happened to you?"

"What happened to me?" his brother responded. "Why, whatever do you mean?"

Eros turned swiftly about as Anteros's dark figure stepped from the doorway into the room.

"I'm glad you're here. We must talk. Now."

"I have nothing to say to you. After so many centuries there is not a single syllable you could utter which might alter this evening's fate." His arms were folded across his chest and a grimness characterized his handsome features. Cupid, with a broken wing, was hardly a threat to him.

Eros looked his brother directly in the eye. "Are you aware of all that you are doing? Of how many lives you are affecting?"

"I am," he responded coldly.

"I don't think so," Eros said, eyeing him narrowly. "If you succeed tonight in keeping Psyche from returning to our homeland, she will no longer bring you tea every Saturday morning, nor fill the vases of your lonely bachelor's house with hyacinths, daffodils, and roses from her gardens, her laughter will not top the strains of your jokes, nor will you ever feel her embraces again."

Anteros, whose eyes glittered in the moonlit chamber, refused to respond to Cupid's remarks.

Eros continued, "Do you think I am unaware that you are in love with my wife?"

Anteros continued in his silence.

"So that is how it is to be. If you can't have her, no one can. You hate me so much then?"

"You don't know what it is like," Anteros said, each word strained and uneasy as it came forth from his aching heart. "She smells of lavender when she bends her head near mine. When she laughs, its like a string of bells all linked together—and she always laughs at my jokes, just as you've said. The truth is, I am sick to death of not being able to possess what I long for most. If she remains here, I shall no longer have to imagine her in your arms at night."

Cupid let out a deep breath. "So that's how it is."

"That's how it has always been."

"You don't love her, you know."

"I love her more than you ever will," he shot back, his eyes raging with decades of pain and hatred.

Eros took a step toward him. "You love her only because she's mine."

"I love her because she's sweet, kind, and beautiful."

"Yet you would punish her for not loving you in return? That is not love, Anteros, that is selfishness and hatred."

"How I despise you!" Anteros cried. "You stand there speaking so smugly—you have the best of everything, even Mother loves you more than me. And I—I was born to serve you, to help you grow up. Well grow up, Eros! Know what it is to feel pain, as others feel pain!"

As though feeling the impact of his brother's fist against the side of his head before Anteros even lifted his hand, Eros dipped right as the blow came toward him. His anticipation proved correct and Anteros's fist glanced off the side of his head near his ear. Instinctively, he tucked his wings close to his body, lifted his own fists and set his sandaled feet to dancing over the wood-planked floor. Back and forth, up and down, as Anteros taunted him.

Eros shot his right fist forward in a quick jab and watched with some satisfaction as Anteros's head bobbed backward. "You shan't prevent Psyche from returning to Olympus. I shall see to that!"

Eros again attempted to plant him a facer, but this time, his knuckles barely grazed his brother's chin and came up stinging.

"You won't be able to convince her to leave unless her mission is complete and it isn't. Only an hour or two past I heard Launceston again beg Alexandra to marry him—he even kissed her!—but again she refused him. Admit it, Eros, you've failed— you are nothing without your potent arrows."

"I never knew you until tonight," he cried. From far away, the sound of a clock chimed the three-quarter hour. It was nearly midnight! He gasped and for a precious moment forgot to keep his attention fixed on his brother. A split-second later, he felt a hammerlike blow pound into his jaw and a sparkling of lights rain down in a shower over his head.

Anteros stood over his brother, breathing hard, his hands on his hips. "Mother shouldn't have favored you," he said. He didn't know why precisely, but a deep and painful sadness swelled over him, at thoughts of his mother who he adored, at the sight of his beloved brother lying unconscious on the floor, but mostly at the thought that never again would he chance upon Psyche at a ball or a *fête,* he'd never see her smile, or enjoy the sparkle in her blue eyes as she greeted him so very warmly.

For several minutes he stood over his brother, his thoughts warring with one another. He was so close to achieving the revenge he sought that his blood ran hotly in his veins.

But then Psyche's image would steal into his mind, of her tender ways, of how she had bounced up and down when Eros had given her the pups, of how she always was able to cheer him out of the sullens, which was often, of how young and beautiful she was and always would be. If she remained on earth, she would wither, as all mortals did, then she would die.

But if she died, he would no longer be tormented by the fact that he could never possess her.

He lifted his chin, and again forced his thoughts toward his present purpose—to keep Psyche from the portal.

He stepped over his brother and left the turret, flying through the window and letting the cold night air further restore his mind to order. It was now time to guard the portal. Tonight, he would leave no stone unturned in preventing Psyche from slipping back to Olympus.

With but minutes to spare, Alexandra led the way to the chapel ruins. Launceston had quickly covered the ground from Roselands to Castle Porth but once inside the castle, their progress was marred for a moment by the circumstance of Launceston's bizarre appearance. Since Psyche was invisible to everyone else but them, he appeared to be walking with his arms outstretched to no purpose.

Several bucks milling about the entrance hall began teasing him and preventing his progress. But Alexandra took quick charge of the situation and explained to all that she had laid a wager with the unhappy viscount, he had lost and was now forced to play the idiot for her until midnight. Of the moment, she required he move about appearing as though he was carrying something quite large and awkward in his arms.

Since the several gentlemen, quite dashing in their assortment of Regency costumes, were half-foxed, her ruse worked and they were able after that to make a quick progress to the hallway leading to the ruins. A few steps more, up the short flight of stairs and they had arrived.

Alexandra opened the door to the chapel and paused in her steps. The blue funnel of light was now deep within the ruins and presented an awesome spectacle as it shimmered over every fallen, crumbling rock, every swag of moss, every leaf that had been blown in circles into the corners of the ancient chamber.

"Where is Eros?" Psyche murmured, her brow tight with pain.

"Eros?" Alexandra queried, a little surprised. She looked around the chapel ruins, but saw no one. "He is not here. Were you expecting him?"

"Yes," she responded. "Something must have happened to him. He must have failed to find his arrows."

Alexandra did not know what she was talking about. "It doesn't matter," she said. "All you have to do now is to pass through the portal."

"You don't understand," Psyche murmured, tears now trickling from her eyes.

Alexandra didn't understand but she knew what had to be done. She led the way down the steps, gesturing for Launceston to follow after her.

Once down the steps, Alexandra moved to stand to the right of the funnel and Launceston set Psyche carefully on her feet next to her but continued to support her with an arm about her waist.

"I shall miss you ever so much, Butterfly," she said. "I only wish you could return now and again to visit me."

"I'm not going," Psyche said. "You don't understand. I can't return. I am bound by all that is good and right to remain here until all is settled between you and Launceston, whether it is now or tomorrow or a year from now."

"There you see," Launceston said, peering over Psyche's

head. "The gods would have us marry. If they can overlook my crimes, surely you can."

"You are being absurd, Launceston," she retorted. "You know as much."

Psyche took Alexandra's hand and pressed it. "You are being too prideful and obstinate," she said, standing gingerly on her wounded leg. "Please reconsider. Lord Launceston is a fine man, a good man, a man of great abilities and determination—"

"There you see!" he cried again. "If Psyche believes me perfect in every respect—"

Psyche turned to look up at the viscount and smiled affectionately at him. "Of course he is full of every bad thing as well—he is arrogant and foolish, unkind at times, and undoubtedly selfish—"

Launceston placed a wounded hand at his chest. "You are not helping my cause," he complained.

She shook her head. "You don't understand. Women always love in full, in spite of a man's obvious flaws. I just don't think Alexandra comprehends the nature of love in this case."

"Perhaps I don't," Alexandra said, hoping to achieve a compromise. "What if I promised you that I would give great consideration to what you've said, that I would consider his suit? Would you then go?"

"I'm 'fraid the oracle was quite specific. You must be in love with him and prepared to wed him. Had I your assurance by the look in your eyes that you would let nothing part you in this life, then I could leave peaceably."

Alexandra wanted to relinquish her will to the situation and to Psyche's knowledge of the future, but she couldn't. She admired Launceston in many respects, and she was quite understandably drawn to him as to no other gentleman of her acquaintance, but she also believed there was a part of him that would throughout a marriage to him, be as a thorn in her side. She didn't think she could bear to live out her years with a man she did not trust to tend to her happiness.

Alexandra turned to Launceston. "You will have to force her

to go," she said. "She will never be permitted to return to Olympus if she fails to pass through the portal, she will remain here and die. Will you please see to it?"

He nodded. "Yes, of course."

He turned toward Psyche and before she knew what was happening he had picked her up. "No!" she shrieked. "Please don't. The entire world depends upon your union!"

"You have done your duty," Launceston said. "Now please us both by returning home. I promise you I shan't relent in my pursuit of her. Can you trust me in this?"

But Psyche did not have time to answer him for as he took one step toward the portal, a black figure moved with lightning speed, descended from above and placed himself firmly in front of the swirling blue light.

"I shan't permit her to leave," Anteros stated flatly.

"I don't want to leave," Psyche said, glancing triumphantly up at Launceston.

"She must return, Anteros," Launceston said, glaring at the haughty deity. "You know she must. She will die if she remains here."

"I suppose you intend to challenge me?" he suggested with a taunting laugh.

"If that is what is required," he retorted. Turning to set Psyche down next to Alexandra so that she might support her, he moved away from the portal intending to draw Anteros toward him.

Anteros merely laughed. "You will have to do better than that!" he cried.

"If only Cupid was here," Psyche moaned. "Where is he, Anteros? What have you done with him? He promised he would be here."

"Ever the concerned little wife. The truth is, we quarreled, over you, naturally. I believe he is still asleep in my chambers, high above the castle."

"You have hurt him again!" she cried.

She then began to ring a peal over his head, to complain about his conduct, to try to worry him into giving up his dreadful schemes. But Anteros only laughed at her, holding his place steadily in front of the funnel of light.

Alexandra listened for only a few seconds. A thought had struck her. Cupid was here, he had been here all along. She was sure of it.

Whenever she had questioned Psyche about Cupid and why he had not attended her during the past several days, she had been evasive in her answers, almost disinterested. Now, she appeared nearly frantic that her spouse had not come as he had apparently promised he would.

But when had he made such a promise to her?

There could be only one answer—Cupid had been here nearly from the first. He was the one who had been forcing her into Launceston's arms. Of course! When she had been pushed from the top of the shallow flight of stairs outside the chapel ruins, she had tumbled—as though by design—into Launceston's arms. And later, when the suit of armor had nearly toppled over on her, she had again found herself in Launceston's arms. She had previously attributed these acts to Anteros, though his motives remained obscure given his intention of taking her to Olympus with him.

But Cupid's motives were nearer to the point, now that she understood Psyche's obsession with seeing her attached to Launceston. Why he had kept his presence unknown to her she could only guess but for the moment she didn't care. Psyche needed him here, she needed him now. She sensed that he was the only one who could safely see his wife through the portal.

High above the castle. Whatever had Anteros meant by that?

Alexandra watched Anteros and Psyche, facing each other, locked in a centuries-old battle. She was still brangling with him, still trying to argue some sense into him, but he remained unmoved, disinterested in any of Psyche's pleas. Launceston tried to intervene, but Psyche warned him away, saying that even Hercules wouldn't dare to oppose a god of Olympus without another deity supporting his cause.

High above the castle.

Alexandra shifted her attention to determine where Eros might be. She turned around slowly and began an almost lethargic progress toward the staircase as she gave her mind over to Cupid's possible current location. Only minutes remained. Where could he be? Mentally, she reviewed every known chamber of the castle, those she had been in and those Launceston had described to her.

Suddenly, she knew where to go. The turret at the top of the narrow staircase near the Green Salon. No one went there. So many stairs were a discouragement in and of themselves.

Quickly, she mounted the chapel stairs, opened the door, stepped through, closed the door behind her and looked down the short staircase. She blinked several times, gaining her bearings, then began to run as though her very life depended on it. She picked up her violet silk skirts, ran to the front entrance hall where she ignored the same half-foxed gentlemen who now teased her by ogling her one and all through what were known as quizzing glasses, and stared down the long hallway which led to a winding staircase up to a turret.

High above the castle. Asleep. Anteros's chambers.

Again she picked up her skirts and raced down the hall, the soft thud of her slippers on the stone floor a counterpoint to the swish of her skirts. She mounted the narrow, winding staircase with the agility of her youth and the desperation of the moment. When she reached the door to the turret, she was gasping for breath for she had climbed four stories in but half a minute.

The ancient, oak door was ajar. One push and she saw what she had expected to see—Psyche's beautiful husband lying prone on the floor. She was struck with just how much hatred Anteros must have for his brother and his sister-in-law in order to have concocted a scheme which threatened their happiness so completely and quick tears started to her eyes. She moved to kneel beside the white-winged man and began shaking him gently by the shoulder. She was still gasping for breath.

"Eros!" she called to him. "You must awaken! We are in desperate straits!"

The room was cold and from the open, diamond-paned window she again heard dogs barking in the distance. Artemis perhaps? What was she doing at Castle Porth?

"Cupid, if you are to save your wife, you must awaken! You must!" She shook him harder this time. "Eros! Eros!"

He blinked, his eyes moved unsteadily about as though he was trying to focus and to remember. Then, as though he recalled everything all at once, he suddenly groaned loudly, sat up, winced and doubled forward placing his hands over his face.

"My wretched brother! I feel so ill! Only, only tell me what time it is and where is my wife?"

"It is nearly midnight. We've but a scant few minutes! She is being uncommonly stubborn and will not enter the portal and, and Anteros is blocking the way. You must come!"

He turned and looked toward the window. The barking of the dogs was louder now. "Artemis!" he cried. "Thank Zeus! Do help me up, Lady Alexandra. I'm 'fraid I will need to lean on you a bit. There! Excellent."

Alexandra was having great difficulty supporting the strong, athletic god of love, but after taking a few sliding steps toward the door she looked up at him and could see that he did not appear to be in quite so much pain. By the time they began their descent, though slowly, he wasn't putting quite so much pressure to bear on her shoulder. At the base of the stairs, he unfurled one of his wings and gently swept it through the air in long, slow, measured beats. The lift this movement caused began to ease them forward with each step as though they were being pushed by the wind.

When they reached the entrance hall, Alexandra heard the gasps of the bucks as they passed by and she realized they must have been able to see Eros.

"By Jove I've never seen anything like it!"

"A winged man!"

"I shan't touch another drop of Launceston's champagne!"

Cupid explained, "I can usually control who sees me and who does not. I think Anteros's facer has robbed me a little of my abilities."

"It doesn't matter," she returned. "They are in their altitudes and won't remember a thing in the morning." His laughter which followed, eased her heart a little.

Alexandra hurried Cupid ever forward toward the chapel ruins. Down the hall to the antechamber, turning right to run down the long hall, up the short flight of stairs, into the chapel ruins. As they descended the stairs, Alexandra saw the goddess Diana appear suddenly in the arch of the window.

"I found it!" she cried, smiling triumphantly at Eros as she held aloft a long, cylindrical object cloaked in linen.

"Well done!" Cupid cried.

"Eros, you've come!" Psyche exclaimed, adding her voice to the sounds of the barking dogs which were even now scrambling over the sill of the window. "You must help us! Alexandra is still proving stubborn."

"Psyche," he commanded firmly. "Go through the portal. I shall see to the rest. You must go."

"I shan't. Not until I know that all is settled."

Cupid released Alexandra and began to cross the room toward Diana. "Let me have the bow and quiver!" he cried.

Diana drew her arm back and threw the quiver toward him, but Anteros—uninjured as he was—gave a single, quick beat of his wings and crossed the few feet between his brother and Artemis. The quiver and bow landed easily in his hands.

"How unfortunate," he said, clucking his tongue in mock sadness. "Now you can do nothing and Psyche will remain here. She will grow old and she will die. And your broken wing will not permit you to vanquish me."

"But I am not injured!" Launceston cried, starting forward.

Cupid intervened immediately, holding the viscount back by grasping him strongly with scarcely the smallest touch of his hand. "I can't permit you," he said. "You would be killed. Let me deal with my brother."

"I don't care if I'm killed," Launceston retorted, trying to struggle out of Cupid's grasp. "He hasn't the right to hurt your wife, or the woman I love."

Cupid chuckled, "Easy, my lad. A fight won't settle anything at his late hour—you must trust me a little."

Launceston relented and when Cupid released him he bid the viscount support his wife for he could see that Psyche was still very much in pain. When Launceston was again holding Psyche about her waist, Cupid moved to take Alexandra's hands in his. He looked tenderly into her eyes. "Will you not open your heart to Launceston?" he asked. "Even if I could promise you that you would know great love with him?"

Alexandra stared at the god of love and gave her head a shake. "I can't," she whispered, tears brimming in her eyes. "I don't believe he can love me as I need to be loved." A tear rolled down her cheek.

He wiped the tear away with a touch of his fingers. "No, no, don't distress yourself. I understand and it is quite all right. You cannot be held to blame for this. If I had more time, I believe I could persuade you otherwise. But as it is, I commend you for following your heart."

He released her hands and stepped toward Psyche. He gently drew her into his arms. "My love," he whispered. "Will you not relent?"

"I can't, my darling. I know you don't understand, but these are my people. I will not leave until my task is done."

"Then I will kiss you goodbye," he said.

Cupid leaned down and placed his lips tenderly on hers.

Alexandra gasped, horrified at what she believed was a fare-well kiss. She turned toward Anteros and implored him. "She will die," she said. "I know how you love her. Anteros, do but think! You will spend eternity, thousands of centuries, without her and how then you will your brother remain your brother? Do you understand what you are doing?"

Alexandra watched Anteros's gaze shift to the sight of his

brother holding Psyche in his arms. Cupid was now saying goodbye to her.

Alexandra's attention was drawn back to the portal when it began to vibrate. Tears were now coursing down her cheeks. She turned toward Launceston and reached a hand out to him. His expression was grim as he drew close to her. She would promise to marry him, she would promise now for Psyche's sake.

She opened her mouth to speak but at the same time she heard the twang of a tightly drawn and released bowstring. A second later, a solid object struck her breast at her heart and robbed her of her chance to save Psyche. She looked down and saw that a beautiful golden arrow was sunk deeply into her chest.

"Oh!" she cried, surprised. She reached up to touch it wondering why there was no pain, but before her fingers passed through the arrow, the shaft and feathers simply vanished. The arrow was gone.

A warmth where it had ostensibly pierced her skin began to fill her heart and radiate throughout her whole body in waves of pleasure, longing and desire.

"I've been struck by Cupid's arrow," she murmured absently, her hand now pressed to the spot where the arrow had disappeared.

Nineteen

Alexandra felt very strange. She lifted her gaze and Launceston was before her. She was seeing him, but not seeing him. He was there, but not there. Her mind moved about magically, whirling around and around, then dipping deeply into her heart, then rising to draw her heart fully into her mind.

For the first time in her life she felt as though she was understanding love, not as a fractured being, but as a whole woman.

Before her was not the Launceston she had known for a year and more, but a new man—equally as handsome, equally as humorous and intelligent, but more deeply flawed than she had at first suspected or believed. His arrogance was more pride-filled than he permitted himself to exhibit in society, his treatment of women more disrespectful, even harsher than she supposed, and his temper more quick-silvered. She knew him as deeply human in this moment, with both his many attributes and his many flaws magnified by the work of Eros's potent arrow. She understood Launceston, she forgave him the past and for the future, she set her heart against every inappropriate gesture he would extend toward her or the world and received into her own every admonishment of her flaws which would undoubtedly pass his lips. Every particle of her being was now fixed exclusively on fitting into the deep crevices of his character and letting his attributes flood the deep crevices of her own flaws and failings.

"Can you love me now?" was the odd question he posed to her. "Or will you always see me as a god and not a man."

At that Alexandra laughed. "You are such a beast, Launceston!" she cried. She heard laughter all around her but it barely reached her mind. Her attention was still fixed exclusively on Launceston. She could see that he was dumbstruck by her strange remark, even chagrined, so she added, "But I do love you and I always shall." She then slipped her arms about his neck and kissed him hard on the lips. He responded passionately, holding her tightly to him as she gave her heart fully and finally to him.

"But will you wed him!" she heard Psyche cry out.

The urgency in Psyche's voice broke a little of the spell. Alexandra drew back slightly from Launceston and addressed the critical matter at hand. She turned instantly toward Cupid and his beloved wife, behind whom the portal was quivering and beginning to fade. "Yes, I shall marry him, my dearest of friends! Now, please go!"

With that, Psyche turned and with a gentle push from her beloved husband flew into the fading blue light. She was caught upward and even through the light, Alexandra watched as she turned back toward her and blew her a kiss. The smile on her face was euphoric. "Thank you, Alex," she called out. Then she was gone.

"I shall miss her," Alexandra breathed, her gaze still fixed to the light as it diminished steadily with each second that passed, then simply disappeared.

She felt Launceston's arm tighten about her waist, comforting her.

Cupid approached Alexandra. "My arrow was not at all what you expected, was it?"

"No," she said, laughing again. "I had expected to go blind with love, instead it is just the opposite."

"What do you mean?" Launceston queried.

"You don't want to know," she giggled, but turned into him and pressed her head against his shoulder.

Cupid addressed them both. "Everyone is surprised and that

is why love sent in such a manner prevails while rose-oil on the lips can only be a temporary excitement."

He then kissed her cheek, shook Launceston's hand and bid them enjoy a long and prosperous life.

Cupid turned and addressed Diana who was now sitting on the edge of the window sill, her five dogs grouped about her feet. She was rubbing their ears each in turn. "And now, Artemis, I want to thank you for wresting the bow from my brother—" his words faltered.

Alexandra stared at Artemis and realized she was not in possession of the bow and quiver. How then had it come about she had been shot with the arrow?

Diana shrugged her shoulders. "You do not have me to thank," she said. She then gestured to her right where Anteros was sitting in the shadows, on the cold stone floor, his head buried in his knees. The bow was beside him along with the quiver.

Only then did Alexandra realize what had happened, that he had shot her with the arrow himself. In the end, Anteros could not let Psyche die. Her heart again went out to the god of unrequited love. She pitied him exceedingly, for his was a hopeless case. Could she forgive him for nearly costing Psyche her happiness? She wasn't sure.

Cupid was about to address him, but Artemis leaped suddenly to stand on the sill of the partially ruined window. "I shall be leaving now!" she announced. "I've had enough of this nonsense and find I am longing to return home."

Cupid approached her and extended his hand to her. She took it in hers and gave it a hearty shake. "You have saved Psyche's life today, Artemis, and for that I am indebted to you forever. I am only sorry I have taken you away from your hunting for so many days."

Diana smiled broadly. "I didn't know playing Cupid could be so amusing," she said. "In fact, I'm of half a mind to forget you owe me anything."

"Indeed?" Cupid queried, a knowing smile on his lips.

"Half a mind!" Diana reiterated firmly, her hands on her hips. "I shall call at your door at eight o'clock sharp tomorrow morning to see to the collecting of this debt. Vulcan won't believe me if I go to his workshop and tell him you promised me three arrows."

"Two," Cupid contradicted firmly.

Artemis grunted. "Two, then. Now, I wish for a bath, my bed, and to see my hounds properly attended to."

With that, she called to her dogs and jumped lightly off the sill. The dogs followed suit, barking joyously all the while.

Alexandra could not keep from racing to the crumbled wall to watch the goddess of hunting run quickly down the hill, her dogs barking happily the entire way. As they entered the woods to the east, they began to fade and finally disappeared completely.

At that, Alexandra turned toward Anteros who was still sitting on the floor with his head pressed to his bent knees.

"Anteros," she called to him. "Whatever prompted you to do it?" She moved from the wall and dropped down beside him, the thin silk of her dress not much protection against the stone floor.

He looked at her smiling crookedly. "The deuce take it!" he murmured, his eyes filling with uncharacteristic tears. "I couldn't bear the thought of Psyche not bringing me tea on Saturday mornings. She always does, you know. The devil of it is, I am quite hopelessly in love with her."

"I know and my heart goes out to you."

"How can you be so kind when I have been a brute," he said, taking hold of her arm. "I'm sorry for all the trouble I've caused—"

He looked so much like a little boy in this moment that compassion for the errant deity filled her heart. "But your lot is not a pleasant one, is it?"

"I'm a spoiled child and well I know it."

"I only wish there was a woman for you," she said.

"Psyche is my Fate," he responded, laughing bitterly.

Cupid looked down on him and extended his hand to him. "Come," he said. "We ought to go home now before grandpapa has both our heads."

At that, some of Anteros's self-pity melted away and in its stead was the simple knowledge that Zeus's displeasure could be quite uncomfortable. "By jove you're right!" he exclaimed. "He'll be in the devil of a temper!"

He took Cupid's hand and rose to his feet to stand next to his brother. "Eros, will you ever forgive me? I've been such a sapskull and Mama does press me so at times. And though I have tried a thousand times to put Psyche out of my mind and heart, I never quite seem to succeed."

"Was it mother, then, who concocted this scheme?"

"Yes, two decades ago—here, in this very place."

"Well, I will have to have a word with her when we return."

"She won't be there, you know. If our plan failed she intended to pay a rather long visit to Poseidon—she knows how you hate the sea!"

"I rather think that was wise of her."

Anteros laughed. "So you made her fall in love with that ugly centaur who stands guard—and smells like Hades!—outside of Zeus's palace?"

Cupid nodded, then laughed. "She can't bear to be the brunt of a joke."

"No, she can't," Anteros returned. The brothers stared at each other for a long moment, then both burst out laughing.

When Anteros's laughter subsided, he again appeared contrite. "I'm sorry for everything. I don't know what I was thinking."

"I know what you were thinking. Bacchus's fêtes have grown a bit dull of late and you wished for some amusement."

Anteros smiled.

"Don't do it again," Cupid added.

"I won't," he promised.

"Now, give me a lift, would you?"

Anteros laughed and sibling equanimity had clearly been restored. The brothers walked to the ruined window and Anteros, holding Cupid about his waist, unfurled his enormous black wings and lifted them both into the air.

Alexandra watched them fly eastward and fade into the dark, starry night sky. She sighed, her heart growing sadder as each second passed by. "I will never see them again," she murmured. Launceston hugged her about the waist and she turned toward him looking up into loving eyes. The moonlight was on his brow as he lifted her chin with his fingers and placed a sweet kiss on her lips.

Alexandra embraced him fully, her heart warming to him in quick stages. She felt her future flowing through her and clung to him as he made a gentle search of her mouth. Her heart was fully given and she knew this time that no matter what happened, she would never again take it back.

He must have sensed as much, for his embrace tightened and his kisses became firm and demanding. She responded in kind letting the wonder of their union and the promise of their marriage fill her with every hope and delight.

Only after a long moment, did she hear her mother's voice calling her name. She drew back slightly from Launceston and found that both her parents were standing at the top of the flight of stairs, enrapt expressions on their face as they looked beyond her into the stars.

Lady Brandreth had tears in her eyes as she shifted her gaze to Alexandra. "I shall miss her, too," she said.

Brandreth frowned, shaking his head in disbelief. "I remember everything now as well. Why did we forget?"

Alexandra said, "Psyche told me that Zeus caused everyone to lose their memories of her and of Cupid. How it was Lady Elle continued to remember, I don't know."

Lady Brandreth glanced from her daughter to Launceston and back. "Were you struck by one of Cupid's arrows?" she asked.

Alexandra nodded. "Yes, but it wasn't anything as I might have supposed. I know him completely for who he is—"

"And yet you love him still?" she queried, an amused smile on her lips.

"I'm not afraid anymore," she said, leaning against Launceston as he slipped his arm about her shoulders.

Both Lady Brandreth and the marquis moved down the steps. They embraced their daughter and Launceston, welcoming him into their family. For several minutes, they talked about all the strange occurrences of the past fortnight and when the essentials of Psyche's strange visit to Roselands was marvelled over for about the third time, the subject shifted to the possibilities of a Christmas wedding.

Lady Brandreth was just reminding everyone that Annabelle would be with them during Yuletide when suddenly a strange man appeared, out of breath, on the sill of the ruined window.

"There you are!" he cried, his chest heaving. "Oh, good! You are all assembled. Thank Olympus. Now I won't have to scurry hither and yon to track all of you down."

He then sat down on the window sill. "Sometimes I truly hate my job as messenger. I go from one end of the kingdom to the other and back again. No one respects the difficulties of my job. I am in Hades one moment, then back to Zeus's palace, then in the woods hunting for Diana and then I must swim in the ocean in search of Poseidon which I really do hate because my hair has a natural curl to it and if you think the mist affects curly hair you can't imagine what the salt water of the sea will do to it!" He paused to take a deep breath.

"You must be Mercury," Alexandra said, stepping forward and offering him her hand the moment he broke his string of complaints.

He smiled broadly and accepted her hand, shaking it enthusiastically. *"A votre service!"* he said gallantly.

"But whatever are you doing here?" she asked. "All is settled."

"Yes, yes, of course. We know that. But the oracle would

insist that I tell your mother—yes, how do you do, Lady Brandreth—" Since he offered his hand, Lady Brandreth stepped forward and shook it, though her expression was quite puzzled. "The fact of the matter is you are to have twins," he stated. "Boys, very healthy, so you needn't worry."

Lady Brandreth gasped and took a step backward. "Twin boys," she breathed. "Oh, Brandreth did you hear that!"

"Yes my love," he whispered, coming to stand just behind her.

Alexandra looked up into his face and saw that her father's eyes were now filled with tears.

"Fine boys," Mercury reiterated. "But in two and a half decades they will be fighting over the same woman and you are warned to find the Bust of Zeus. Well, that is all. I must go now for once I return I've been informed that Vulcan must immediately forge a sword for Hercules."

"Hercules?" Alexandra and Lady Brandreth intoned as one.

Merk pulled a face. "Yes, yes, he is still about. I hate him, really I do. The mere mention of his name and all the ladies open their eyes wide, and sigh and carry on. Well I must go."

"Is that all?" Lady Brandreth cried. "Where will I find the bust? I thought Zeus had taken it."

"I know nothing more," he said. "And don't think you can press me for knowledge I don't have. I used to cast walnut shells about in order to discover the future, but I gave that up a few centuries ago. As for the message I just delivered to you, to own the truth I found it cryptic, even nonsensical but then that is the way things are in Olympus." He laughed as he turned about on the window sill, facing the woods. "Not unlike earth!" he cried, he leaped over the edge. His winged feet kept him in the air as he too headed east and faded from view.

Alexandra stared after him and sighed deeply. No one spoke for a long moment, and for that she was grateful. A cool October breeze blew over her and she shivered. She knew they ought to go back to the ballroom, but she didn't want to just yet. She didn't know how to let go of Psyche and of Cupid, or even Anteros.

Tears had constricted her throat and she could barely swallow.

After a time, noises from the hallway outside the chapel ruins grew louder and louder. When the door burst open, and several foxed gentlemen fairly tumbled down the stairs, Alexandra could not keep from laughing. At the same time, Brandreth and Launceston hurried to help them up and to make certain no one was hurt.

But because the gentlemen were in their altitudes, they were impervious to injury and rose to their staggering feet full of laughter. One man explained their purpose in a slurred voice, "We saw a man with wings on his feet. We've been looking for him but we can't find him? Wanted to ask if he'd fly each of us to the Stagshead for a bit of rum punch. Have you seen him?"

"No!" Launceston and Brandreth cried in unison.

"Ah," the inebriated gentleman responded. His eyes rolled back in his head and he promptly fell to the floor in a drunken swoon.

Lady Brandreth moved up behind her daughter. "Do you suppose this is what happens at one of Bacchus's fêtes?"

Alexandra giggled and some of her sadness drifted away.

"Do you think Zeus will cause us to forget again?" she asked her mother.

Lady Brandreth looked over her shoulder at the night sky. "I hope not. Somehow the knowledge of Psyche's existence is a comfort to me. But to think, I am to have twins!"

Alexandra embraced her mother. "And I shall have brothers!"

Brandreth and Launceston began herding the unsteady men back up the stairs and the ladies followed in their wake.

During supper, which was served shortly after their return to the ballroom, Lord Brandreth announced the betrothal of his daughter to Lord Launceston. The long dining hall resounded with whoops, exclamations, and applause which rang to the rafters for several minutes.

When the congratulations had quieted, Mylor Grampound

rose to his feet, his wine glass in hand. After giving Julia a very long, significant look, he lifted his glass and to the assembled guests, raised his toast. "To love," he said simply.

"To love!" the guests responded in one, full, enthusiastic voice.

Alexandra let the sweet thunder of their voices roll over her as she slipped her hand into Launceston's. He met her gaze, his eyes full of affection. She squeezed his hand in return.

"To love," she murmured.

Her heart was full and never in her life had she been so deeply satisfied and content as she was in this moment. Midnight had come and gone, her fears had vanished, and the future welcomed her with arms thrown wide.

"To love," he returned on a whisper, his smile a promise she knew he would keep.